ERIN'S DAUGHTERS

Michael Mannion

Haverhill House Publishing

DEDICATION

This novel is dedicated to
Artie, who helped me begin it.
Debra, who helped me continue it.
Trish, who helped me complete it.

This book is a work of fiction. All characters, events, dialog, and situations in this book are fictitious and any resemblance to real people or events is purely coincidental. All rights reserved. No part of this book may be used or reproduced in any manner without the written permission of the author.

ERIN'S DAUGHTERS
© 2018 Michael Mannion

ISBN-13: 978-1-949140-91-0 (Hardcover)
ISBN-13: 978-1-949140-92-7 (Trade Paperback)

"Part One" of this book appeared in different form in an earlier novel, *Colleen* (1978) by Michael Mannion

All rights reserved.

Graphic Design and setup by Dyer Wilk

Haverhill House Publishing
643 E Broadway
Haverhill MA 01830-2420

www.haverhillhouse.com

ERIN'S DAUGHTERS

PROLOGUE

1946

"Gray Granmar! Gray Granmar!" The young girl tugged at the sleeve of her great-grandmother's nightgown. The old woman was dreaming and could not be woken. The child was persistent. "Gray Granmar!" she whined but to no avail.

The child climbed onto the large, soft bed, nestled next to her great-grandmother, and spoke to the sleeping woman. "Mommy says it's your birthday...We have a party. Can I blow out the candles?" There was no answer. "Are you going to have a hundred candles?" the child asked breathlessly.

"Colleen!" her mother whispered-hissed. "Leave your great-grandma alone."

The child again tried to awaken the old woman. "Gray Granmar!"

Colleen's mother stamped her foot. "Come here, Colleen!" The child did not move and her mother went to her, picked her up, and carried her from the room. "I pray you won't prove a cross to your mother!" she chided her daughter.

The great-grandmother, the matriarch of the clan, continued to dream. To dream of Sligo so long ago. To dream of her parents and brothers and sisters. To dream of that day...that dreadful day ...a day of crucifixion not yet followed by any resurrection. She dreamed of sitting in her father's lap secure in his grasp, inhaling and enjoying the aroma of the tobacco from his pipe, entranced by his voice but not understanding his words.

"Ireland is a jewel...a jewel in the hands of a thieving murderer...a marauder who masquerades as a champion and protector of freedom and truth. A murdering marauder who comes in the night, who comes in the foggy dew of dawn, who lies and kills and explains it all with clever rhetorical skills...Yes, Ireland is a jewel that must be reclaimed!"

So the father spoke in Gray Granmar's dream as they sat in the cottage and the rain fell steadily outside. The old woman grew uneasy and turned in her sleep. Her father vanished and she was alone, not in the safety of her home, but naked on the hillside overlooking her birthplace.

They came up the road cocksure and violent. They spoke with foul mouths. Her father and brothers awoke and came outside. A row ensued and then violence erupted. In the dream, she relived what she had not seen but had only heard: the gunshots, the screams, the agonized cries, and the helpless pleas of her mother and sisters. Her brothers and father had died. They had been killed by the strangers who had traveled the seas and come over the hills like devils to take what was not theirs, to arrive unawares and to plunder and kill all the gentle.

As happens in dreams, Gray Granmar soon was in the church graveyard watching the bodies being lowered into the ground. A wagon awaited a wagon that had to be pulled not by mules but by relatives, a wagon laden with all the dearth of possessions that had once been home, a home now taken by those murderers who had come before dawn over the hills and taken her home. Who had taken her father and brothers and stolen their land. In the dream, she held her mother's hand as they walked along the rocky dirt road toward the unknown. *I will be strong as any man!* the young girl told herself. *No... I shall be stronger and cleverer than any man and I will teach my children the same!*

"Erin!" The dead dream-father's face appeared. "Avenge my name!"

The woman awoke from the dream with a heart-pained scream. She looked at the ceiling with eyes whose vision was blurred by cataracts. She felt her body expand and contract with each frightened dream breath.

She felt the fear of death. *I am one-hundred today...Oh, the dream...but father, I did avenge your name.* She wept. Then, mercifully, she slept.

Erin awoke and stared at the ceiling. She was not sure where she was. She heard the electric buzz of a fan. She placed her right hand over her left breast and thought, *I ought to be home, but I am not.*

Despite her impaired vision, it became clear to her where she was. Her mind roused itself from the terribly real dream world and adjusted itself to the mysterious real world. *I am still alive!* She tingled as the diminished energy in her body coursed through her, marvelously thrilling. *I am at my granddaughter's home.*

There was a knock of a tiny hand on the bedroom door, followed by the chastened, silent child voice that asked, "Gray Granmar...are you awake?"

The old woman felt a sweetness sweeter than the palate perceives upon biting a ripe, rich fruit. "Yes, sweetheart, come in!" She was seized with delight.

The young girl flew through the room like a water sprite and kissed her "gray granmar" with delight. "Gray Granmar...Gray Granmar! HAPPY BIRTHDAY!" The child threw her arms around the old woman and kissed her on the cheek. "Gray Granmar, do you know you have an old lady's smell?" the child asked ingenuously.

"Ah, darling, yes I do. But do you know what that smell may be? Do you know that it can only be smelled and admitted by one such as thee?" The old woman took the child to her and spoke, "It is the smell of eternity...Remember, Colleen, what I have said to thee...It is the smell of eternity." She looked into her great-granddaughter's eyes and saw the brilliant energy therein.

"Can I blow out the candles on the cake?" the child asked, but actually demanded as she pulled away from the old woman's embrace.

The old woman looked deeply into the child's face without a trace of jealousy, but with a longing for the graceful youthfulness and vigor that had once been hers. "Ah, darling, the world is yours!"

"Oh, Gray Granmar, I love you!" The child hugged her and became silent.

Silent with the silence of eternity, the old woman thought.

The whole family helped Gray Granmar blow out the candles on the birthday cake, and no one helped her more than little Colleen. The old woman tired easily, and after eating a sliver of cake, she asked to be helped to the bedroom.

"I'll help, Gray Granmar," Colleen volunteered. Erin had witnessed the murder of her father and brothers, outlived her mother and her sisters, all her aunts and uncles and cousins, and all of her own children, save one. But through the anger, sorrow, loneliness, and loss, she remained a loving woman. And she had a special love for Colleen.

"Yes, child, help me to my bed. I have a story to tell you." The old woman smiled as Colleen helped her parents assist her.

Settled comfortably in the soft bed, the room lit only by a small lamp on the night table, the old woman closed her eyes. "Come here, Colleen." The young child climbed into the bed and nestled her head on her great-grandmother's shoulder. "I'm going to tell the little one a story before we nap," the old woman said to her grandchildren. Colleen's parents smiled and left the bedroom, closing the door behind them.

"Do you dream, child?" The old woman asked.

"Yes, Gray Granmar...I dream a lot every night. I dream of flying. I dream of looking down on my house from the air. I dream of the little man who comes in the window. And mommy is there and she sees the little man, but she can't move. The little man talks to me, but mommy doesn't hear him and I don't remember what he tells me. And I dream of water. Big, big, big, BIG waves of water." Colleen snuggled closer to her great-grandmother.

"Do the dreams seem real, child?"

"Oh yes, Gray Granmar. They *are* real..."

"When you get very old, Colleen, what is real begins to seem like a dream. Sometimes I feel like my whole life has been a dream. That I am dreaming now...that now I know I am dreaming—and that I am just about to awaken." The old woman's voice was tranquil but strong.

"But Gray Granmar!" Colleen was alarmed. "What will happen to me if you wake up?"

"Oh sweet child!" She laughed and hugged Colleen. "Don't you worry! You have your own dream to live." After a moment of silence, the great-grandmother spoke with an earnestness that commanded Colleen's attention.

"Whenever I close my eyes, Colleen, I see colors. Close your eyes, darling. Do you see them?"

"Yes, Gray Granmar, I do see them!" Colleen was excited. "I play this game in bed at night! Do you play this game, too, Gray Granmar?"

"Yes, child...Yes, I do. Now, close your eyes and gently rub them. Do you see the colors change?"

"Yes! And they move too! Red and green and yellow. *Gold!*" Colleen sat up in bed. "Gray Granmar, I didn't know you played games, too!"

"Lie down beside me, Colleen. Let's play another game." She turned out the light. "Just lie quietly, child. And look into the corner of the room. Look into the darkest corner of the room and—"

"Gray Granmar!" Colleen sat up, excited. "You know this game, too!"

The old woman was pleased. "What game is that, child?"

"The stuff in the air! I didn't know you look at the stuff in the air, Gray Granmar!"

"Lie back down, Colleen. Lie quietly for a moment..." The old woman felt serene. "Did you know the stuff in the air is the same as the colors in your eyes?"

"Really, Gray Granmar?" Colleen grew serious.

"Did you know the stuff in the air, the color in your eyes, the blue in the sky, the tingle when you are happy and excited are all the same thing?"

"Noooo, Gray Granmar..." After a moment, Colleen asked "Are you *sure*, Gray Granmar? How do you know?"

"If you lie quietly beside me, I'll tell you a story. A secret story, just between you and me."

Colleen snuggled up as close to her great-grandmother as she could get. She was thrilled to be brought into the old woman's confidence. "Just our secret, Gray Granmar?"

"Yes, child. Just our secret. But," the old woman whispered into the child's ear, "you can tell this secret to your daughter one day when you become a mommy."

"Ohhh," Colleen uttered the sound with awe. "A secret I can tell *my* baby..." The child did not understand but was completely drawn in by the old woman.

"Lie on your back. Close your eyes. When you feel quiet, look at the darkest corner of the room."

They lay in silence. After some time, Colleen opened her eyes and looked into the far corner of the dark bedroom.

"Listen, Colleen. Listen to my story. Listen quietly to my story. Listen quietly to my story about a time long ago. Listen quietly to my story about a time long ago when I was your age. When I was your age and lived across the sea. Far across the sea."

The child was mesmerized.

The old woman spoke with the certainty of a natural storyteller. She spoke with the certainty of a storyteller telling a tale that was true to the teller because it had been lived by every nerve, muscle, and fiber of her being.

"You are flying, Colleen, flying fearlessly across the seas, through the great white clouds, the clouds as big as islands. You are happy and free as you fly across the sea. Below, on large white-capped waves sail boats large and small. Below, far below you, on the wandering winds, sail birds, large and small, airplanes, large and small. You are far away from home...but you feel you are close to home. As you fly, you feel you are closer than ever to home."

The old woman forgot herself, forgot the child, and forgot she was telling a story. She became immersed in the moment.

"You are moving through the clouds, flying lower and lower, the ocean is coming closer and closer, Colleen. The blue ocean is coming closer. *There*." With her eyes closed, the old woman raised her right hand and pointed. "There, Colleen! Look, it is so green in the sea of blue. A small patch of green. You are flying closer and closer to a small green island in the blue sea..."

"*I see it, Gray Granmar*," the child whispered, thrilled. "I see the green."

"You are very close now, child. The waves are smashing against the rocky shore...The green fields inland are separated by stone walls. Within the stone walls, much of the green field is filled with stones...There is only a thin layer of green growing over this age-old rock in the ocean...Look, Colleen, a small stream, blue and green...a stand of trees on an island in the stream...A valley into which the stream flows...Look, Colleen, homes in the valley...and green fields stretching out beyond the valley...You are coming back to earth, Colleen...You are getting closer to the ground...Can you see that white cottage, child?"

"Home?" the child's voice choked.

"Home," the old woman spoke. "Do you see the fields around the home?"

"Yes, Gray Granmar...One, two, three." Colleen paused. "No, *four*!"

"Yes, Colleen, we are going home...home to the fourth field. Oh, do you feel the earth beneath your feet now? Isn't it good to have both feet on the ground, child?" Erin was happy.

"Yes, Gray Granmar." Colleen was smiling.

"Look to the far corner of the field, child." Again, with eyes closed, Erin pointed with her right hand. "There is a mound there child. As big as this room. It feels very old, Colleen. It feels powerful. It feels *holy*. Do you know what is there, Colleen?"

"No, Gray Granmar. But it makes me feel like..." The child hesitated.

"Don't be frightened. The sun is shining. I am with you."

"Gray Granmar. It makes me feel like the stuff in the air."

"That's right child. It is a special place. It was on the land I once called home...when I was your age. And my mother told me the secret that I am going to whisper in your ear."

"A secret?" The child listened as the old woman whispered in her ear. The child was silent.

"Look at the corner of the room, child. Do not forget what I have told you."

The old woman snapped her fingers. "Gray Granmar..." Colleen spoke searchingly. "Gray Granmar, was I just dreaming?"

"What did you dream, child?"

"I...I feel funny, Gray Granmar. Tell me a story."

"Shall I tell you about when I was a little girl in Ireland?" The old woman smiled.

"Oh, yes, please...I love when you tell me about when you were a little girl."

"Maybe when you are older, you'll go to Ireland, Colleen."

The child was thoughtful. "I will...I just know it!" As the old woman told Colleen about life on the land in the west of Ireland, the young child fell asleep. The old woman fell asleep soon thereafter.

Colleen dreamed she was flying.

PART ONE

1959

When she awoke, Colleen felt sweet and peaceful. Wrapped in a soft dreaminess, she basked in the visions of her boyfriend holding her. It was not yet apparent to her that it had all been a dream. Her skin tingled and she felt something surging through her, a pleasurable feeling that moved wave-like from head to toe.

Suddenly her face froze. She was fully awake and the thought that somebody might be watching her came to the fore. The sweetness of the dream was overcome by fear. She looked about guiltily. She exhaled, though not completely, and changed her position under the covers.

She tried to recapture the lost feeling, tried to summon the dream incidents that had so pleased her, but they lacked emotional force. They fell flat and left her feeling empty. Colleen slipped her hand under her pajama top and rubbed her breasts the way her boyfriend did in the hallway or on the dark street near Ewen Park. She began to feel warm and excited again, but she no longer had the guiltless pleasure of the dream. She was afraid her mother would catch her.

Colleen thought about the party she was planning to attend that evening. She knew that Jim would be there and that they would be able to sneak off into the bedroom and kiss and...

She was afraid to pursue the thought.

She closed her eyes, knitting her brow, and forced fantasies of what she imagined it must be like to sleep with a boy. Nervously, she slipped her hands down her pajama bottoms, holding her breath as she did so.

Her attention was split between her fantasies and listening for the sound of a person approaching.

Colleen fell asleep, uneasy.

***

Elizabeth, the baby of the family, awoke excited and happy. She didn't mind that it was raining. She was just glad to have a day off from school and a party to look forward to in the evening. She looked at her sleeping sister and felt like waking her. She liked Colleen the best in the family but lately thought Colleen liked her less. She decided to let her sleep.

She took her favorite doll from its cradle and brought it back to bed with her. She pulled the covers up to its chin and tucked it in the way her mother tucked her into bed.

The child began to talk to the doll, whispering, confiding in it, and explaining everything that was going to happen during this busy day. "So don't get angry with me if I can't play with you today . . . I have a lot of things to do and it isn't because I don't like you." She hugged her doll. "It's just that your mommy has to do certain things," she mimicked her mother's words.

Elizabeth heard her stomach growl and she got up to go to the kitchen. Before she left the room, she gave the doll its bottle and kissed it on the cheek. "I'll be right back." She hurried out of the room, almost tripping on her nightgown which was just a bit too long for her.

"Lizzie, you're up awful early!" Mrs. Murphy was both pleased and disappointed. She liked the quiet of the early morning. It was her only time to be by herself, but the sight of her darling warmed her. "Come sit on Mommy's lap." She held her arms out to her daughter.

Delighted, the child ran over and jumped up on her mother's lap. "Daddy said he's taking me to the parade!"

"Did he now!" Mrs. Murphy decided to tease Elizabeth. "I don't know about that. You're getting to be a big girl now and I think it's time you helped your Mommy about the house." She hid her smile.

"Oh, I want to go to the parade!" she pouted...

"But it's lots of fun around the house—cooking, cleaning up, ironing, sewing..." She laughed and her daughter hugged her. "I'm just teasing, Lizzie. Of course, you can go to the parade. Your father wouldn't be without his pride and joy."

Elizabeth kissed her mother on the cheek. "Mommy, I'm hungry. Can I have pancakes for breakfast?"

"Sure you can...do you want to mix the batter?" Mrs. Murphy knew her daughter liked to do that.

"Uh-huh." The girl's eyes lit up.

"We'll make enough for Eddie. He'll be home from Mass soon."

"Mommy, can I be an altar boy when I grow up?"

Mrs. Murphy handed her daughter the pancake batter. "No sweetie. Little girls can't become altar boys. Only boys and men are allowed to serve at the holy sacrifice of the Mass."

"But . . ." she paused as she began to pour milk over the mix, "but that's not fair."

"You can serve God in other ways, Lizzie. You could become a nun or—"

"I don't want to serve God!" she interrupted her mother. "I just want to become an altar boy!"

Mrs. Murphy kissed her daughter on the head. "God love you!" She smiled and was warmed by her love for Elizabeth.

Grandfather Murphy sat up in bed. He stretched and let out a big yawn. He looked at his wife, sleeping so soundly next to him, and he couldn't resist waking her. "Get up, Grandma!" He slapped her playfully on the behind. "We're still alive! Don't be wasting this precious day; we don't have too many to throw away!"

He put on his favorite robe and went to the kitchen. "I'll put on the kettle," he said as he had nearly every morning for almost fifty years. He puttered about the kitchen cheerfully, setting the table, preparing the toast and poaching the eggs. He liked to make the breakfast because he liked to eat things the way he cooked them.

This morning was a special day and he was making sausages to go with the eggs. He always ate a big breakfast on St. Patrick's Day and topped it off with his own special Irish coffee. Brigid, his wife, didn't approve of his drinking. Of course, what she doesn't know won't hurt her. He reached into the back of the cabinet under the sink, behind the Clorox and soapsuds, behind the empty cans of roach spray and window cleaners, and took out his flask.

The water was boiling as he poured it into the cups over the tea bags. After the tea had steeped, he poured a shot of whiskey into his cup. He did not drink heavily. In fact, his morning drink was usually all he had. But it was a symbol to him, a symbol of his independence and he would not give it up.

He sipped his tea and smacked his lips. *Aaah! As I was saying, what she doesn't know won't hurt her!* He laughed to himself and hid his whiskey safely under the sink.

He heard his wife stirring in the bedroom. "Breakfast is nearly ready, Mother!" He sipped his tea.

"Just a moment!" she called out. "I'm making myself beautiful for you."

He smiled and shook his head. *That woman will keep me alive 'til I'm a hundred,* he thought.

Grandmother Murphy felt the dampness in her bones and a twinge of pain in her joints. She moved slowly across the room and looked at herself in the mirror. Her face had lost its youth but not its beauty. She let her hair down and it fell to her waist. Ever since she had been a child, she had been proud of her long blonde hair. It had changed color with age, from bright yellow to a kind of butterscotch, but it was as long and wavy as ever.

She looked at herself, full face, and then profile. "Ah, don't be so vain," she scoffed, "though I don't look half-bad. Better than most my age." She tied her hair back and went into the kitchen. *He must have had his whiskey by now,* she thought, smiling. For decades, she had waited until Tom had had his surreptitious drink before going to the table.

"Give us a kiss," he teased.

"Not until you put your teeth in!" She kissed him on the cheek and they both laughed.

"Morning, dear," Mrs. Murphy said as she kissed her husband on the cheek perfunctorily. Peter Murphy sat at the table in his pajamas and his wife put a cup of coffee before him. "What would you like for breakfast, dear? Pancakes or eggs?"

"Eggs, I think." He sat there, weariness making him look more gaunt than he actually was. He had thick, prematurely gray hair and a blank expression that would occasionally light up into contagious friendliness. "Is the rain supposed to stop?" He hoped it didn't ruin the parade.

"I don't know, Peter. I haven't heard the news yet. What time are you meeting the boys?" As did most of the women in her neighborhood, Mrs. Murphy called all women, no matter how old, "the girls," and the men she called "the boys."

"At ten-thirty." He would be marching in the parade with the members of the parish Holy Name Society. Most of the men were later attending a party at the Knights of Columbus, but the Murphys were having guests at their home. "Who's coming tonight?"

Irene Murphy put her husband's breakfast down on the table before him. "Your sister will be here. Jim and Maureen, of course. The O'Donnells, the Clancys, the Burkes. Your parents, I suppose, though they haven't said for sure. With the children, it should make for quite a number." She walked to the other side of the kitchen and took out her ironing board to press her husband's shirt. "Patrick, Maureen, and Johnny Burke have been practicing some tunes and they're going to play tonight."

"What kind of tunes? I hope not that be-bop or rock 'n roll or whatever they call that noise." He took a bite of his food. "That Elvis the Pelvis stuff won't be played in this house." His words were garbled as he spoke and chewed his food at the same time.

"I hate to tell you but it's played in your house all the time. Colleen and Tommy are always listening to it on the radio..." She paused and thought for a moment. "Instead of doing their homework..." She spoke more to herself than her husband. "But it's not so bad, dear."

"Well, I hope they play some nice traditional music, like Gary Owens or Kevin Barry." He looked up and saw his wife smiling at him. "What's so funny?"

"You—you are!" She laughed gently. "Such a stuffed shirt, yet when you were their age—"

"All right," he smiled, "that'll be enough of that." He shook his head. "The times we had..." He spoke a bit wistfully.

"You know, Peter," she spoke tentatively, "we're not ready to go out to pasture yet ourselves. We could still have ourselves some high old times."

"It's not that I feel old," his eyes went inward, "it's just that . . . well," he retreated from his thought, "well, it's just different, that's all. You know what I mean?"

"I do indeed...I do indeed..." She returned to her ironing, not wishing to pursue the topic. It was something she thought about often and it saddened her.

One evening they had had a fight over money and soon it all came pouring out. All the bitterness and recrimination, all the rage and sorrow, at their lost hopes and dreams.

> "We're saddled with a pack of kids that I can hardly feed! I can't even get my wife a new dress for Easter! Or a decent suit for myself! Why the hell did we have so many kids so early?" He stormed about the room and frightened his wife. Always a quiet, gentle man, she knew her husband must be suffering greatly to abuse her so. "Why don't you use something, woman? Or let me! For God's sakes, we can't just keep bringing children into the world, burdening them and us as well. You won't let me use anything so it's up to you!" He glared at her.
>
> "It's a sin, Peter!" Irene was aghast. "It's a mortal sin and you know it! I...I...couldn't..."
>
> "Won't, you mean. You won't." He grabbed her and shook her. "What's more of a sin? Going against some celibate priest who never had the courage to love a woman or try to raise a kid or to ruin your life by burdening yourself with worries and too much work and having to face little children who want to know why they can't have what their friends have?" His grasp tightened.
>
> "You're hurting me!"
>
> Shocked, he let her go, ashamed of himself.

Irene remembered the wild, pained look on her husband's face to this day. He stormed out of the house and did not come home until the early hours of the morning.

She remembered how mortified she had been, how frightened, when she had gone to Manhattan, seeking a gynecologist who did not know her or anyone that she knew. She tried to protect herself, but the guilt was too great. She could not bear up under the weight of it.

Irene never told her husband of the visit, or that for a while she had used a diaphragm and then stopped. She never told him what it had been like to violate her conscience. And it had come between them. *And now it's different*, she thought, resigned.

Peter got up from the table. "I'm going to wash up and shave. By the way, how is Tommy? He doesn't look too well."

"He's been at it again. Now, this is the third time this year and I think it's serious. Imagine, a boy his age drinking like that!" She gave her husband a stern look. "Remember what you told him the last time. Don't go back on your word. It's the worst thing you can do."

He turned and walked from the room. "I'll do what has to be done." As he left, Elizabeth called after him.

"Daddy, can I watch you shave?" She caught up with him and took his hand. "And can I help make the shaving cream?"

"Sure you can, sweetie; sure you can." He was thinking about his son.

"And can I put some on me and make-believe shave, like before?"

He didn't reply and she tugged his pajama sleeve. "Huh? Oh, yes, sure you can, honey," Mr. Murphy said absently.

After dinner, when the women had cleaned up, everyone retired to the living room to relax, chat, and have a smoke or a drink. The children were in the bedrooms, talking, playing games, or watching television. Cool air came through the windows which were opened just a crack for ventilation. The steam pipes hissed and heated the room until it was toasty, comfortable.

"Shall we have some music?" Johnny Burke asked.

A few of the guests applauded, others called out in agreement.

The three young people took out their instruments—a violin, an accordion, and a recorder—and began to warm up. They each loosened up, not playing together until they were ready.

"We're not too versed in traditional stuff," Johnny apologized, "so I hope you don't mind if we play some songs by the Clancy Brothers and things like that." He looked to the other players and they went into a rousing and spirited rendition of "Finnegan's Wake."

Most of the adults knew at least some of the words and sang along. It was a bit ragged but no one noticed. The trio next played a moving version of another classic, "Kevin Barry." By this time, lured from the television by the sound of live instruments and voices in song, the children had filled the room. They sat on the floor, in parents' or relatives' laps, anywhere they found room.

Although they were among friends, the performers were nervous at first. But after a few songs, they relaxed. The two men took off their jackets and ties. Mrs. Murphy brought them a couple of beers to "wet their whistles."

"Colleen," Maureen called out, "come sing with us!"

Colleen flushed and looked across the room at Jim. He smiled and nodded toward the crowd. She wanted to please him more than she felt embarrassed and she rose and joined the group. She laughed awkwardly and sat beside Maureen.

"We'd like to sing a sad song called 'The Butcher Boy,' and I think you'll be moved by Colleen's lovely voice."

Colleen cleared her throat. She looked about uncertainly and then began to sing:

In London city

> *where I did dwell*
> *a butcher boy*
> *I loved right well...*

Colleen faltered during the first verse but gained confidence as she proceeded. All her longing for her boyfriend, all her fears and dreams went into the melancholy song she sang. From the youngest to the oldest, there was rapt silence. Colleen was lost in the music and completely unaware of herself or the effect she was having. Mrs. Murphy was stunned by and proud of her daughter's obvious talent.

> *Oh dig my grave large, wide and deep*
> *Put a marble stone at my head and feet*
> *And in the middle, a turtle dove*
> *That the world may know, I died for love.*

When Colleen looked up, after a silence, her eyes were swollen and big tears rolled down her cheeks. She smiled through her tears as the room burst into spontaneous applause.

The band, manifesting signs of true showmanship, immediately followed the mournful tune with a rollicking Irish reel. A few of the women began to dance and they even coaxed some of the men to dance with them. Everyone congratulated Colleen, several guests asking her if she intended to study singing professionally.

"I'm very serious," one aunt told her, "you've a remarkable voice."

Colleen thanked everyone and made her way across the small, crowded living room. She finally reached Jim and she took his hand, hoping no one would see. She scratched his palm with her index finger—a secret signal between them—and the two of them felt a surge of excitement. "Let's go now!" Colleen whispered in his ear.

"Fine with me." Jim moved toward her, as if to kiss her, only half-joking, but she held him off.

While everyone was dancing and drinking and laughing, Colleen and her boyfriend left for a party at a friend's house. They walked down the stairs of the apartment building and, halfway between the lobby and the first floor, they stopped and began to kiss. They made no declarations of love or promises to love forever, as young people often do. They were too much in love to say anything at all.

Only when Jim reached under her jacket to fondle her breasts did Colleen suggest that they be on their way.

They stepped into the cold March night, warmed by one another.

The party grew in exuberance and in volume. The beer and whiskey flowed freely but not in the mythical proportions often ascribed to the Irish on St. Patrick's Day. There was good humor and a liveliness not often shown during the rest of the year. The first dance left everyone out of breath, but the second, third and fourth dances brought them more vigor and life than the older folks had felt in a long time.

The children were urged to join in the dancing and many of them did. Eddie stood on the side, wanting to dance, but afraid. Something held him back, even though at the same time, something was urging him forward. He looked with longing and envy at his cousins who were dancing with the older men and women, laughing and having a wonderful time. He kept a smile on his face so no one would know he was upset. He thought that if somebody asked him to dance, he would find the courage.

One of Eddie's cousins, a girl a year younger than himself, came over to his side. "Eddie, will you dance with me?"

He felt himself become tense. "I...I don't know how to."

She took his hand. "I can show you."

He had always liked her and knew that she liked him, but he felt that people would look at him and feared they would laugh and make jokes. "No, I can't . . . Please, Mary, I...I don't really want to."

"Well," she smiled at him as only a nine-year-old coquette can, "maybe later."

Tommy was dancing with another cousin, little Lizzie was jumping around, doing her own private dance, while Eddie watched from the side. He felt ashamed of himself for his shyness and went into the bedroom to be alone. He lay down on his bed, hidden behind a large pile of winter coats, and cried softly. He wished that he could act differently. Inside, he knew that he felt differently but outside, he was unable to show it.

The bedroom door opened and a dull yellow light fell across the walls and then vanished as the door closed. Eddie stifled his crying and tried to get rid of the sniffles in his running nose.

"Who might that be lying there among the coats?"

Eddie felt relaxed when he heard his grandfather's voice. "Me, Gramps." There was just a trace of tears in his voice.

"I have to get away from the noise myself sometimes." Grandfather Murphy let a judicious silence pass, enough to indicate that he wasn't there to pry. "What did you think of your sister's singing? Quite something, eh?"

"It was O.K.," Eddie granted.

"Just O.K.? Nothing more?"

"It was pretty good." Eddie sat up.

"Pretty good? I thought it was grand. A lovely voice she has." He reached into his pocket. "I brought you something. I was going to give it to you at the parade." He handed his grandson a small box.

"What is it, Gramps?" Eddie opened the box and tried to see the object in the dark.

"A bird call."

Eddie tried to blow on it. There was no sound. "How's it work?"

"You don't blow on it," he laughed heartily, "you turn it. Let me have it a moment." He took the Audubon birdcall and made it sound like a sparrow.

"Hey!" Eddie leaned forward, excited. "How'd you do that? Let me try." His grandfather handed it to his grandson. Eddie turned it and it made a sound.

"Well, it's a sound," Grandfather Murphy said kindly, "but not a bird sound. But you'll catch on. Just keep trying. Listen, I'll be going back outside. When you're ready, I've got a few stories to tell you."

"About when you were a soldier?" Eddie loved his grandfather's tales of his exploits fighting against the British in Ireland.

"And what else would it be about? About the time I was a nun?" He tickled the boy. "You come out when you're ready."

The old man left the room and Eddie nestled down among the coats, trying to make his birdcall sound like a bird.

"Your father is in the kitchen trying to give Tommy a drink!" Mrs. Murphy was outraged. "He won't listen to me."

"What's the boy doing?" Mr. Murphy sighed. *Here it comes*, he thought. *The party has been fine until now.* He realized the alcohol would start to affect the guests and that anything could happen.

"He's refusing him, of course. Not even a lad as brazen as he would drink whiskey before his own mother's eyes. You've got to get your father home. He's been drinking on the sly, I'm sure."

Peter found his father standing unsteadily in the middle of the kitchen, holding forth with tall tales of his exploits in the "auld sod."

"I was a lad, not much older than yourself, Edward, just a bit of a lad..." He thought for a moment and his two grandsons waited eagerly for his next words. "And I was in a pub with my father. We'd stopped in after a football game one Sunday and the Guinness was flowing.

"Well, one thing led to another and soon a bunch of the lads were talking politics. This particular pub was known for its republican sentiments and the British kept an eye on it, if you know what I mean." The old man sipped his beer. "As I was saying, they passed the day in drink and conversation, and then, a few at a time, the boys would head home.

"My father's friend, Daniel Ryan, long since passed on I'm sure, stumbled into the bar with an awful gash in his head. The fellows ran to him and just as they reached him, a bunch of Prods crashed in and an awful row ensued."

Peter had heard this particular tale, not to mention variations of it, hundreds of times. "Come on now, Pop. Don't be filling the boys with foolish notions." He tried to be light about it but his father took offense.

"And what's foolish about their heritage, may I ask?" He struck a pose.

"There's nothing foolish about their heritage, but I don't know if you've got it quite the way it was. You do exaggerate, Pop." He smiled falsely, hoping to avoid an argument.

The old man stared at his son, a long, cold stare that he turned on anyone who questioned or displeased him. "At any rate, as I was saying," he paused and looked at Peter.

"Just don't be offering the children drinks, Pop. I didn't notice you giving us drinks when we were kids. And what was good enough for us is good enough for them." He gave the boys a look of warning and left the room.

Grandfather Murphy resumed his tales. "The fighting was fierce and it was more than one lad that lost an eye or a handful of teeth. There must have been an informer in the pub. You know lads, the worst thing a man can be is a traitor to his own. The informer is the curse of Ireland... they've done more harm than the bloody British, if you ask me.

"Well, the next thing you know, just when the boys are getting the best of the fight, in come a bunch of British Regulars. I jumped behind the bar and heard the most awful sounds—bones cracking, grown men wailing. Then," he paused for dramatic effect, "a gunshot." He paused again.

"One of the Brits fell dead. I popped my head up at the wrong time and they saw me. The bastards had probably shot one of their own. None of us had weapons." He paused to sip his drink and when he had finished it, he did not resume his tale.

"Come on, Gramps," Eddie was impatient, "what happened?"

"Ah, boys, it grieves me even now. I can still see me own father lying on the floor, his face all swollen and bloody . . . there was never a finer man. . . ." A tear came to his eye, whether from drink or fine acting even he wasn't sure.

"When I popped up from behind the bar, wouldn't you know they tried to pin the shooting on me?" He became indignant. "The bloody cowards, and that's the British way, mind you, pinning their filthy crimes on the innocent victims. They came at me but I managed to elude them and run out the door.

"As I passed Daniel, he flipped a pistol to me. Why, I stood there frozen. Sure, I'd held a gun before and shot at cans or bottles but never this. I ran into the narrow lane and turned to my left." He turned brusquely to his left and looked frightened. "More of the British Regulars. I turned to my right. A regiment of the bloody Black and Tan. There seemed to be no way out.

"They were closing in on me and I had to think quick. I ran across the lane and dived through the window of a shop; getting up, all cut and covered with glass, a shot whizzed by my ear, so close I could feel it!" He paused to catch his breath. "I tell you boys, I was never as frightened as at that moment. I turned and fired blindly and saw a soldier fall.

"Somehow, I don't know how, but by the grace of God, I made my escape. I lived in the fields and the back alleys, a price on my head. I could never see my family again, my father or my own dear mother." Again tears came to the old man's eyes. "Never again did I lay eyes on my own mother.

"The Brotherhood found me, as they always did their own, and they whisked me away to America. I was the youngest man that ever had a price put on his head."

"Wow!" Eddie was flabbergasted. "I never knew you were a hero, Gramps. Tell us more!"

Even Tommy, experiencing the first waves of naive, teenage cynicism, was enthralled by his grandfather's tale. "Come on, Gramps, tell us more."

The old man sat at the table, worn out. "It's too difficult, lads. Too many lovely and painful memories to bear. Another time, I promise, another time."

He looked up and smiled wanly. "But there's one thing that I want you to remember. To be a man, you've got to be free. There's nothing worth having, not even life itself, God forgive me, if it isn't free. Without freedom, life dries up and dies, like a plant that gets no water or light. There can be no compromise in this matter." He took the two boys in his arms. "And remember to be loyal. Loyal to those deserving. If you try to keep those two things in your mind—freedom and loyalty—why, you won't go wrong. Now, be off with you and let your old grandfather recollect alone for a while."

The boys thanked him and went inside where the singing and dancing was still going strong. The old man sifted through the memories and tall tales, not sure which were which any longer, and thought fondly on his long and pleasing life.

At Victoria's party, all the kids were dancing to "Hound Dog" by Elvis Presley and their spirits were high. The music had been fast and loud all night—Jerry Lee Lewis, the Big Bopper, Chuck Berry—and now it was time for slow songs. Victoria took out a stack of 45s and placed them on the spindle of the record player. She went around the room, turning out most of the lights, leaving only one dim lamp on in the living room.

The couples held each other tight, the boys moving their hands slowly down their partner's back as the dance progressed, putting their hands on their girlfriend's bottom to pull them close. They danced in the darkness, kissing and feeling the warmth they craved, while some of the boys, the ones without dates, sneaked a few beers in the kitchen.

Colleen and Jim sat by the window in Victoria's room, silent, looking at the stars and the beautiful scene before them. The Harlem River coursed below, swirling with whirlpools. The Henry Hudson Bridge, its lights glimmering like stars, spanned the dark waters, casting shadows on its surface. Beyond the bridge lay the Palisades, monumental massive cliffs that seemed prehistoric, ageless.

They held hands and enjoyed the feelings that they brought to life in one another. Many of the girls that Jim knew were "fast" or "easy." Many of the boys that Colleen hung out with were more handsome or better athletes. But there was a tension about the others, a tension that seemed only to increase as they grew older, that was missing from Jim. When she was with him, she shared in his peace.

They both knew that many of their friends had gone to bed together and made love. Yet, curiously, none of them had been pleased by the experience. It was touted as the highest pleasure but it was also the greatest sin—and the greatest desire—of almost everyone.

Colleen felt that her friends had forced a situation that they did not really want. She knew, or rather, she sensed, that she and Jim would make love to one another when the time was right. There was no desperation in them that could drive them to try to take what, in time, would be freely given. She thought of how wonderful it had been in the few weeks that she had known Jim. "What are you thinking about?" he asked.

"Oh," she smiled coyly, "things. Just things."

"If it's nice on Saturday, would you like to go on a picnic? Just you and me?" He stroked her hair.

"I'd love to. Where would we go?" She sidled closer to Jim and put her arms around him.

"Well, there's this spot in Van Cortlandt, up past the flats, where there's a small pond and it's all surrounded by bushes and trees. Hardly anyone ever goes there." He imagined making love to Colleen there and became embarrassed. "What do you say?"

"I say...I love you." She kissed him.

As they kissed, another couple entered the room. They couldn't quite make out who it was. "I don't think they know we're here," Colleen whispered.

"Ssshh," Jim placed his finger over her lips.

The two people lay down on the bed and the boy got on top of the girl. He began to move his hand up her dress and she protested, moaning faintly, repeatedly, asking him to stop. But he persisted.

After a few minutes, another boy came in and then another. The three of them began to fondle the girl on the bed. One of them kissed her, the other opened her blouse, and the third lifted up her skirt.

The girl gradually stopped protesting and sadly yielded to the boys. As one by one they took her, Colleen didn't want to look but couldn't help herself. When they were finished, they left her lying there and returned to the party.

The girl began to cry, and lay there, alone, her clothes all awry. "It's Margaret," Colleen whispered. Margaret was known by all the boys because she would "go all the way." They joked about her, and, after a few beers, they had sex with her. And then they ignored her.

After a few minutes, she sat up in the bed and, with her back to

Colleen and Jim, began to fix her clothing. She sniffled, took a deep breath, and went back outside. Neither Jim nor Colleen spoke.

They returned to the party, danced for a while, and then Jim walked Colleen home.

The sounds from the party at the Murphys' drifted down the stairway as Colleen and Jim sat in the flickering light of a faulty fluorescent bulb. Colleen did not speak. She rested in her boyfriend's embrace and tried to reconcile her romantic concept of human love with the loveless, furtive, selfish sexual activity she had witnessed.

It frightened her to think about the incident. She wondered if this was all that lay ahead for her. Jim sensed her distress but was too uncertain to broach the subject himself. Many times, he had joked with his friends about "doing it" to this girl or that, with the false bravado of the frightened, and now that he had finally seen the reality of his fantasies, he was taken aback.

Colleen realized that she did not know very much at all about the most important things in life. She did not know why she acted certain ways at certain times; she did not understand what motivated other people, why they acted selfishly or self-destructively. She realized that she did not understand even the workings of her own body.

Colleen thought, not without some guilt, that while she knew the laws of the Church, she did not know the laws of her own life. She wanted to talk to Jim about the problems that were bothering her, but she didn't quite know how to go about it. Neither they nor any of her friends spoke about much other than events at school, the shows on television or the movies.

This upset her as well. *Why can't I even say what's on my mind?* She became uncomfortable sitting and stood up. She paced along the landing of the stairway, on the verge of speaking, but with something holding her back.

"Colleen, I...uh ...I just want you to know that ...well, I hope that you don't think that," Jim licked his lips nervously, "that I . . ." He couldn't finish his sentence.

"What's wrong?" She went and sat beside him.

"I ...well, you know, the thing with Margaret...I hope you don't think that that's what it's like, you know?" His face was red. "You know, that I..." He faltered again.

"Don't be silly." She felt very protective and hugged him. "It was just very upsetting...I don't know why Margaret would do that......She seemed so unhappy."

They kissed but stopped suddenly when they heard people coming down the stairs. Jim stood up and moved away from Colleen.

"Hello, Mr. O'Rourke, Mrs. O'Rourke." Colleen stood up and nervously brushed her hand through her hair.

"Why hello, dear," Mrs. O'Rourke was a bit tipsy. "You sang just lovely tonight, just lovely." Mr. O'Rourke was silent but friendly and they passed without further comment.

The young couple sat down again and began to kiss. Once more, they were interrupted as more guests left the party upstairs. Colleen politely greeted her parents's friends.

"I wish we had someplace to be alone...." She thought of all the nights kissing in the hallways or on the street. "I better go upstairs now. It's getting late."

"All right. Say, do you want to go to the movies tomorrow night?"

"Sure. Call me after school, O.K.?"

They kissed again and parted.

Colleen went to her room and lay down on her bed. Her little sister was asleep and the sound of the muted conversation from the living room formed a backdrop for her thoughts. She felt tired and not unhappy, exactly, but empty.

The guests gradually departed and Mrs. Murphy cleaned up after them. It had been a pleasant evening, with none of the scenes that occasionally darkened parties. She undressed and got into her nightgown. Before saying her evening prayers, she performed another ritual that was both more satisfying and more personal than even her prayers to her God.

Moving cautiously in the dark, she went into her daughters' bedroom to check on them. Little Lizzie lay snugly sleeping in her bed, the image of childhood innocence. Mrs. Murphy sensed that Colleen was awake and sat on the edge of the bed. "How was the party?"

"Oh," Colleen was still upset. "It was all right, Mom."

"Jim is a very nice boy. So clean-cut." Mrs. Murphy patted her daughter's hand and left the room. "Sleep tight, and don't forget your prayers!"

Next, she looked in on her boys. Thomas was sound asleep, snoring lightly, and she looked at him with fondness and concern. She didn't want to be harsh with him, but drinking was no laughing matter and had been the ruination of too many fine men and women. She was not about to stand by idly and watch her son ruin his life. Mrs. Murphy sensed that Eddie was not asleep. She didn't know why, perhaps it was his breathing, but she knew that he was wide-awake.

"Hey," she spoke softly. "Don't you think you should be getting some sleep, young man?" She lovingly brushed the boy's hair back from his forehead. "You'll need a haircut soon."

"Mom," he asked, his voice higher than usual, "am I Irish or American?"

"Why, what made you ask me that?"

"I don't know ...Gramps was telling us the things that he did when he was just my age," he sounded disappointed. "And he was a hero." Eddie propped himself up in bed. "He said we should always be loyal."

Mrs. Murphy smiled condescendingly. "Don't be paying so much attention to your grandfather. He...well, he has a way of exaggerating things." She kissed him on the forehead.

"But am I Irish or American?" He was adamant.

"Eddie, you are American of Irish extraction. Now, instead of worrying about these silly things, these stories of your Grampa, you should be worrying about your studies, getting a good education so you can raise a nice family of your own . . ." She kissed him on the forehead again. "And don't forget your prayers. Say a special prayer for your Uncle Billy. He's going to have an operation tomorrow."

Mrs. Murphy closed the door and there was silence and darkness. Eddie lay awake, long after he had said his prayers. He promised himself that he would go to the library the next day and see if his grandfather really was exaggerating things.

The whole neighborhood was asleep. In the distance, an occasional train could be heard as it wound its way through the Bronx toward Manhattan. There were loud explosions that Mrs. Murphy could not explain. The voices of people who had had too much to drink echoed in the empty streets.

She pressed up to her husband and wished that he would make love to her. He was deep in sleep but she knew that even were he awake, there would be nothing between them.

Mrs. Murphy began her prayers. "Dear God, bless my family, especially Peter. Bless his parents, bless...." And sometime during her litany of friends and loved ones she fell asleep.

March passed swiftly, with none of the cold, bitter weather that usually hits New York City at that time. The children looked forward to the end of Lent and the time they would be able to eat the various treats they had given up as a penance.

Eddie had decided that he would deny himself candy but he continued to eat cake and marshmallows and cookies. Tommy promised himself that he would give up drinking beer in the park with his friends. When asked what she was giving up for Lent, Colleen told everyone that she was giving up Coca-Cola. However, she drank Pepsi instead. Mrs. Murphy made it her duty to go to the six o'clock Mass daily. She tried to dragoon her children into it as well but with no success. Mr. Murphy was oblivious to the whole affair, concentrating on his work in the grocery store. Business was falling off slightly and as manager, he was being held responsible. He had more than enough to think about just trying to keep food on the family table.

When pressed by his wife one night to reveal what he was giving up for Lent, Mr. Murphy replied, "Buying Easter outfits for ourselves and all the children."

"You don't mean that, do you?" It was important to her that the children have their Easter outfits.

"Have you seen our bank book lately?" She obviously had. "We owe the butcher; not only is business falling off at the store but our bill there is rising; I don't know if I'll be able to make the payments on the insurance this month; the gas and electric and phone bills are due; the—" He was cut off.

"All right, all right. I understand. But you know what it will be like when all their friends are dressed up so nicely. You know how kids can get, Pete." Mrs. Murphy sighed and sat at the kitchen table.

"Well, what would you have me do? If I don't pay the butcher, then we'll have no credit to eat this month. I'm sure the children will understand. They don't care so much themselves. They can't wait to get out of their bloody Easter clothes anyway."

"That's not the point..." Her eyes turned inward.

"I know. The point is that you'll feel shamed if we can't provide nice new suits and dresses for the children." He took his wife's hand. "But we can't. I'm sorry, but we just can't afford it."

"I guess you're right, dear." She left the kitchen and went into the girls' room. Whenever she was not feeling well, Irene had the habit of sitting by the window and staring out. She would watch the traffic, the trains, the passers-by. Soon, her eyes would look but nothing would register. She would become lost in reflection or sometimes prayer. Her husband did not try to interrupt her at these times. He sensed that she needed to be alone and knew that there would be time for comforting later. Peter decided to have a beer. He rarely drank and when he did it was only one or two beers. They helped him relax. He went over all his calculations. There was only one possible conclusion. *I'll just have to take on another job.*

Years before, when they were just starting out, he had been forced to hold down two jobs. Although the money came in handy and made certain things easier, the strain and constant struggle to make ends meet took its toll. He would often come home late at nights, having worked all day in the store and then driven a cab during the evening, not having had a proper meal all day. His wife would be glad to see him but he would be dead to the world. All he wanted was sleep.

Peter Murphy winced as he thought of the number of times he had refused his wife's advances. It had gotten so bad that, at one point, she had convinced herself that he was seeing another woman. It wasn't long before she stopped trying to reach him, and they went through a trying period that caused lasting damage. He didn't want to dwell on such matters and went into the living room to watch television.

In much the same way as his wife stared out the window, Peter stared at the television screen. The images flashing across his retina made an impression there but no further. He was not conscious of what he was viewing and if asked would not have been able to say what was happening in the show. But the beaming images and the incessant chatter filled the emptiness or covered it up, and it was relief enough from his troubles.

Just before the evening news, Mr. Murphy went to his wife. He looked at her for a moment, silhouetted against the window, and felt a great sorrow and a great need to comfort and be comforted. She turned suddenly, having sensed his presence.

"Oh! You frightened me." She laughed. "Why so serious?"

Peter stood by the doorway, unspeaking.

"What's wrong, dear?" She went to him.

He suddenly realized how much he loved this woman. "Where are the children?" He put his arms around her.

"Colleen went out with Jim to a dance. Lizzie is staying over at the Moran's with her friend, Katie. The boys went to the school to watch a game of some kind." Mr. Murphy rubbed his hands down her spine.

"Then it's just us..." He spoke suggestively and his wife immediately caught his meaning.

"Peter," she spoke his name with grateful longing and together they moved to the bed.

When Eddie opened the door and ran through the house to his room, he heard his mother let out a loud, surprised sound. He stopped and listened, but there was no other noise. He went to the desk and got the book he was looking for.

He lay down on his bed and began to read when he heard his mother laughing. Then nothing. The boy's curiosity was roused and he put down *The Story of the Irish People* and listened intently. Unable to hear anything at all, he tiptoed into the living room. But he still heard nothing.

Eddie went to the kitchen to make himself a glass of chocolate milk. He wondered what was going on in his sisters' room but he sensed that he would be in trouble if he went in there.

As he drank his milk, Colleen came into the apartment out of breath. She looked at her brother, pausing to explain why she was back so soon. "I forgot my G.O. card!" She rushed toward the bedroom.

"Colleen! Wait!" He ran after her and stopped her. "Don't go in there!"

She looked at her brother, puzzled. "But my card's in there. I can't get into the dance without it!" She started to walk toward the room but then heard sounds and realized that someone was in there. Suddenly she blushed. "Come here," she pulled Eddie into his room. At first Colleen was shocked. She had never even thought about her parents making love, never mind been confronted by it.

"What is it? Why do you look so funny?" Eddie sensed that he didn't really want to know what was going on.

His sister stared at him and then burst out laughing. She fell to the bed and rolled over, doubled-up with laughter. Her brother was puzzled.

"Boy, you are acting crazy!" He walked from the room. As he passed the doorway he looked to see if he could see anything. He thought he saw an undressed figure and quickly averted his glance.

He tried to drive the image from his mind but it only became stronger. More than what he saw, what he felt upset the boy. He felt a feeling he had never experienced before. He had seen a naked woman and he liked it. He wanted to see more. But that woman had been his mother and he felt he was committing a sin.

Colleen came into the kitchen, her laughter had subsided but not yet vanished. Every few moments she would laugh once more. She couldn't wait to see the look on her parents' faces when they came out. "Maybe they don't know we're here. Do Mommy and Daddy know you're here?"

Eddie shook his head.

"What's wrong with you? You look so pale?"

"Nothing..." He wished the feelings would go away.

"Well, I better knock on the door. I have to get that card." Colleen walked inside, trying to make as much noise as she could without being too ridiculous, and knocked on the door.

"Hello?" Her mother called out, with embarrassment in her voice.

"It's me. I need my G.O. card!" Colleen felt embarrassed herself. "It's in my pocketbook on the vanity!" She didn't know why she was yelling but she was.

The door opened and her mother handed her the pocketbook, only her arm showing beyond the door.

"Thanks, Mom." As an afterthought she said, "Eddie's here... but I'll get him to go play . . ." She wondered if she should have said that but received no reply.

"Hey, listen, why don't you go out and play, Mommy and Daddy want to be by themselves awhile." She took his book and looked at it. "Why are you reading this?"

"There's nothing wrong with it!"

"I didn't say there was. Come on, you can read later." She motioned for her brother to come with her.

Eddie got up reluctantly. "But there's nobody out."

"Go out and play with your friends. Usually I can't get you to come home when you're out playing. Now I can't get you to go out and play!" They left and Colleen locked the door behind her.

Irene Murphy lay beside her husband, her head cradled on his shoulder and chest. "I love you, honey," He was silent but drew her closer to him. "I wish we had our own bedroom ...here we are, acting like two teenagers in our own home ...me the mother of four running about like I was fifteen . . . Oh, I wish we were rich ...I wish we'd win the Irish Sweepstakes or the Building Fund or anything, even just ten dollars!" She kissed her husband's cheek.

"Let's go out to eat. What do you say?" He rolled over to face her. "We'll splurge, all right. We could go to Donnelly's."

"Really?" It was her favorite restaurant. "Can we afford it?"

"Big time spenders like us? Why we're rolling in dough! Peter smiled as he embraced his wife and kissed her. "Why not? One dinner isn't going to break us."

Irene touched her husband's face lovingly. "You need a shave."

He rubbed his hand along her calf. "So do you." He moved his hand up her leg.

"Fresh!" She kissed him again. "I wish we could stay like this forever. If you won the sweepstakes, what would you do? If you had, say, a hundred thousand dollars?" She propped herself up on her side. "Come on, don't be a stick in the mud... *dream*!"

"Don't be silly." He reached over to his shirt and took out his cigarettes.

"You know what I'd do? First, I buy a house in the country. Then a nice new car. You know, one of those new Plymouths with the fins. I love those cars. Then I'd buy my dear sweet husband a wonderful wardrobe of Brooks Brothers suits."

"With a hundred grand you should be able to buy at least one, maybe two," he said dryly.

"What would you do with all that money, Mr. Wise Guy?" She tried to tickle him but there was no response. "Why aren't you ticklish? It's not fair that I should be the only-"

He began to tickle her. "Stop!" She shrieked out loud. "Oh stop it, please!" He continued to tickle her and she writhed on the bed, half-laughing and half-crying for him to stop. Just when she thought she would burst, her husband stopped tickling her.

He got up from the bed and started to put his pants on. "You beast!" Irene kicked him gently in the rear. Her husband turned and looked at her seriously.

"I've decided to start working another job again." He saw his wife's disapproval. "Now, now. It's my decision. I'm going to drive a cab for my cousin again and make some extra money. Once we get straightened out, then I'll stop."

"Do you have to?" Irene was upset. "Remember the last time?"

"I don't see any other way. Besides, it will just be for a month or two." He sat on the edge of the bed and kissed his wife again. "Do you want to know what I would do if I had a hundred thousand dollars?" She nodded yes, but still looked sad. "All right, the first thing that I would do, the absolutely, positively first thing that I would do..." He stopped.

"Yes, go ahead. What are you waiting for?"

"You don't look really interested." He teased.

"Oh I am, I am. I'm waiting on your every word."

"Good. The very first thing that I am going to do is to buy you and the children Easter outfits." He got up from the bed. "Now, hurry up and make yourself pretty. You have a date tonight."

Irene lay back on the bed and let out a deep, pleasurable sigh.

With the sleep still in her eyes, Colleen moved about the kitchen preparing a picnic lunch for Jim and herself. The night before, she had cooked Southern fried chicken for the first time, and now she was packing fruits, soda, and juice, which she kept cool with cans of dry ice. She also included pieces of homemade pie for dessert.

While she went about her tasks, Colleen felt bursts of excitement flash through her body. They were like pulses, beginning in her solar plexus, and spreading throughout her in sweet sweeping sensations.

She filled a large wicker basket and covered the contents with her mother's favorite tablecloth, which she was not supposed to take with her. Colleen yelled goodbye and hurried from the apartment. As she reached the second floor, Colleen heard her mother calling her.

"Where are you going, Colleen?" Mrs. Murphy felt she was somehow being deceived.

"Out with the kids! I'll be back at dinnertime!" Actually, she and Jim were going to be alone but Colleen didn't want her mother to know. She ran down the stairs and continued running out of the courtyard. On the sidewalk, Colleen paused. She took a deep breath and felt more excited than ever. She knew that this would be a special day.

When she reached the candy store she did not see Jim waiting outside. *Just like him,* she complained to herself, *always late.* She looked inside the store and saw him sitting at the counter, drinking a soda and reading the paper. For a moment she thought she might sneak in and sit beside him, waiting to see how long it took for him to notice. But she was too eager to be on her way.

"Don't say hello." She stood and smiled provocatively.

Jim didn't look up from the paper. "All right. I won't."

Exasperated, she pushed him lightly on the shoulder. "Oh, come on! Let's go."

"Just a minute." He continued reading a moment, slowly sipped his egg cream, draining every last drop, and only then, spun around on the counter stool and got up. He looked directly at Colleen and smiled. "Hello," he said as he took her hand.

"Hi." She spoke self-consciously, awed by her feelings for him.

They left the store and headed for Van Cortlandt Park. Another boy was sitting at the end of the counter reading a copy of *Mr. Blue* by Myles Connolly and drinking a black and white malted. Stella, the woman who owned and operated the store, came over to the boy.

"Mike, do you know those kids?" Not waiting for an answer, she continued. Stella never waited for an answer. "Very nice kids, I'm telling you, the nicest kids." She looked about the store and spoke confidentially. "Let me tell you," her accent grew thicker with each passing moment, "they're in love."

The boy looked up at her, bemused.

"Believe me, Mike. I know, I know. They're in love and they're too young." She looked at the boy's smile. "Aaach! I should be telling you...you haven't lived. You're too young." She shook her head and went off to help a customer. The boy continued reading.

The young couple crossed the highway cautiously, swiftly, and ran to safety on the grassy shoulder of the road. They laughed nervously, out of breath, and watched a car speed around the bend and whiz by them. Colleen held her breath as she thought of what would have happened had the automobile come by only seconds earlier.

She pushed the thought out of her mind and strolled along the roadside, arm in arm with her boyfriend, enjoying the warm sunlight falling across her face. She breathed deeply and closed her eyes. Across the dark danced splashes of red, yellow, and orange light. The land underfoot began to descend, and she opened her eyes.

The two followed a path down the incline toward a long row of hedges. There was an opening, an obviously well-worn opening, in the vegetation and they passed through it. When they broke through the shrubbery, they faced a small, grassy knoll at the bottom of which lay a tiny pond. The area was completely enclosed by the bushes. Colleen loved the sense of privacy she felt.

As Jim took off his shirt and rolled up the legs of his jeans, Colleen spread out the tablecloth upon the ground.

She turned from Jim and opened her pants, pulling out the tails of her shirt and tying them up underneath her breasts. She took a rubber band from her bag and put her hair up into a ponytail.

When Jim turned and saw her, he found himself facing a changing human being, no longer a girl, yet not a woman, a tender mixture of innocence and sensuality. His eyes said more than any words.

Embarrassed by Jim's gaze, Colleen became self-conscious and blushed. To cover up, she began to unpack the picnic basket and chatter aimlessly. The intensity of his feeling frightened her. "You know, Patty told me that she's going to break up with Billy. For real...this time, it's for real. Why at the last party he practically spent the whole night running after Marion," she gave a disapproving look, "And you know what she's like! Thinks she's God's gift to boys, acts so sophisticated!" She *humphed* and spread the food out on the cloth.

"Well, she is," Jim joked.

"What?"

"She is God's gift to boys," He whistled and moved his hands, outlining a shapely figure.

"Then why don't you fall all over her like the rest of you guys!" She stuck her chin out defiantly.

"Because," he came closer to her, "I," he knelt down beside her, "fall all over you!" Jim gently nudged her down and lay on top of her, kissing her.

They ran into the pond, still wearing sneakers to protect themselves from the broken glass and tin cans lodged in the muddy bottom. Jim dived in and began to splash Colleen, who was wading in slowly, gradually.

"Are you sure this water is clean?" She stepped carefully, cringing at the feel of the squishy, sticky mud.

"Stop doing that!" She was annoyed at the water hitting her face. Jim was on his way toward her, a malicious grin on his face, when Colleen, attempting to avoid him, tripped and fell into the water, letting out a piercing shriek.

When she emerged from the water, puffing and cranky, she was greeted with laughter. "Oh, so you think it's funny, do you?" She lunged at her boyfriend, hoping to knock him off balance, but he caught her and picked her up in his arms. "Put me down! Put me down you ...you . . ." She put her arms around his neck and kissed him.

The young couple made their way back to the blanket and lay down under the warm sun. Yet they felt a warmth that did not come from the sun overhead, but from within. It was gentle, pulsing and gradually growing more intense.

Colleen stretched in the sun and her movements, combined with sighs of pleasure, excited Jim. He embraced her and she did not resist. They yielded to their deepest feelings of love and desire.

Slowly, they explored one another. There was no concern other than to increase the flowing sensations of pleasure; to please and enjoy one another. Their love was part of the exhilaration of spring.

But they were different in the fact that they were human beings, members of a species that had made its God-given instincts to love forbidden. From the unconscious enjoyment of caressing, Colleen awoke with a start. Her heartbeat, once strong and full, now fluttered anxiously. Her face, flushed with pleasure, grew pale. Her hands, which gracefully massaged the nape of her boyfriend's neck, grew stiff and wet with perspiration.

She found herself at odds with herself. Colleen felt like somebody had just pulled an emergency break in her body. She moved away from Jim and felt that inside she was a shambles. Ashamed, she turned from him, hiding her face.

Jim lay on his back and sighed sadly. He stared at the sky and felt flat and listless. He also was in conflict. He desired Colleen but was filled with guilt. He felt his desires were both honest and furtive, natural and yet somehow wrong. He knew that he was not taking but giving, yet it was in his mind that he was "using" her.

"Colleen," Jim spoke tentatively, as if he thought she might not answer him.

"Yes?" Her voice quavered.

The young man sat up beside her and. put his arms around her. "I'm sorry, Colleen."

"I'm the one who should be sorry." She had barely finished speaking when she burst into tears. Her lower lip protruded as it does on a small child and her eyes became red and swollen. "I don't know what's wrong with me ...I...." She could no longer speak.

"Don't cry, Colleen. Please don't cry." She rested her head on his chest.

"Maybe......maybe we shouldn't...you know, uh, get each other too ... you know, too excited." She burst into another round of tears. "I'm so confused, I don't know what to do. I want to be with you but I can't stop thinking it's wrong." She looked at him directly, a longing, heart-rending expression on her face.

Before he began to cry himself, Jim buried his face in her hair and held on to her as if for dear life. They were not allowed their privacy for long and their sorrow turned to embarrassment as a group of teenagers entered the secluded area. Colleen searched for tissues in her handbag and went to the pond to throw cold water on her face.

One of the girls in the group was carrying a transistor radio and screeched when her favorite pop song came on. "Oh God, I love this song!"

The girl sang along with the chorus, flat and out of key. "Why must I be a teenager in love?" Colleen wished she could gag the girl and smash the radio. She hurried back to Jim, carefully hiding her face from the other teenagers, and packed the basket.

They walked home in silence, each wanting to speak to the other, to give and receive reassurance, each having confronted a crucial watershed of life—the awakening of sexuality and its discontents.

Colleen came into her room and found Eddie lying on her bed. "Would you get your dirty sneakers off my bed, please?" She was in a very bad mood.

"What's wrong with you?" Eddie sat up.

"Nothing that won't be gone once you leave my room! Now, get out!" She threw her bag on the vanity. "Just go into your own room."

"You think you're so big, don't you. All right, I'm going. But don't start yelling at me because you have problems." He walked slowly from the room and then slammed the door behind him.

Colleen felt like she was tied in knots. She sat on the edge of her bed, distraught.

She could see the sunset, and large cumulus clouds painted pastel colors by the fading light, but the beauty gave her no pleasure. Instead, she felt a growing rage inside.

She punched her pillow, weakly at first, but then with more and more strength. She hit it over and over again, her rage beginning to give way to sorrowful longing. Colleen clasped the pillow to her, burying her face in it to smother the sound of her crying.

She felt all alone in the world: adrift, confused and frightened. She felt that nobody knew her. Nobody understood her at all. She wanted to reach out, to get to know people, but no one else seemed to want to do the same.

Only half-spent, her tears ceased. Colleen sat up, breathing in starts, and felt a bit crazy. Objects in the room appeared foreign; she couldn't quite get in touch with her surroundings. All she could do was brood on the events of the afternoon and the stale feeling that was left inside.

She wanted to be with Jim.

She didn't know what to do.

Colleen closed the curtains in her room, and in the darkness, she sought the release and comfort of sleep.

A silvery haze, humid and enervating, hung over the city. Everyone moved slowly, tempers occasionally flaring over minor matters that would ordinarily have passed unnoticed.

It was the Labor Day weekend, the last chance for summer vacationers to get away, and even at six in the morning, the mass exodus was already underway. Millions of New Yorkers were abandoning the city for the mountains and the beaches. The Murphy family was no exception.

Mrs. Murphy cheerily roused her sleeping family. She was a trifle too cheerful, however, and met with cranky reactions. Undaunted, she continued packing for their picnic, singing along with the songs on the radio. It was a rare day that the whole family was able to spend some time together and Mrs. Murphy wanted to be certain that everything went perfectly. Her husband had borrowed a friend's station wagon and they were traveling to Blue Mountain in Westchester for the day.

"Good morning, Colleen." She kissed her sleepy daughter on the forehead.

"Mom, I'm going to go to the beach with my friends today, all right? We're all going out to Rockaway." Colleen sat listlessly at the table.

"But honey, don't you want to come along for the picnic? I was so hoping that the whole family would be together today." She stood behind her daughter and took her long hair in her hands, stroking it gently, admiringly. "I thought you loved Blue Mountain. Wouldn't you rather drive there with us instead of taking that horrible subway ride for hours?" She tried to coax her child.

"I'd love to come. But you know, there'd be nothing to do. There's no one my age coming. You know how it is, don't you?" She looked kindly at her mother.

Irene was unable to hide her disappointment. "Sure I do, sure I do." She tried to cover her feelings. "You go with your friends today." She went back to preparing sandwiches.

"Thanks, Mom." Colleen wanted to hug her mother but felt that she couldn't.

A deep sadness came over Mrs. Murphy, and she sought to shake it off. Nothing meant more to her than the family, the comfort of its togetherness. It was to the raising of her children and the building of a home that she had devoted her life. This morning she had seen the first indications of the dissolution of that way of life. Her first-born, her daughter, aside from showing the signs of increasing physical maturity, was beginning to manifest the desire to move away from the family, to go out on her own, to find her own life.

What's a mother without her children? Irene recognized the self-pity in her thought. *Ah,* she told herself, *they may move from the house but if you raise them proper, they don't move from your heart.*

When her family left, Colleen felt a new sense of freedom. The entire apartment was hers. She ran into her bedroom and took out her new bathing suit. It was hidden in the back corner of the bottom drawer of her bureau. She felt a wave of excitement shoot up her spine as she held it before her.

She had never worn a two-piece suit before. Colleen felt that her mother would not understand and was determined to keep it a secret.

She laughed aloud, twirled around, and fell on her bed. She couldn't wait to see Jim's face when he saw her in this suit.

Although it wasn't a bikini—she was not that daring—it was less than she had ever worn in public before. She tried it on and stood looking at herself in the mirror. Colleen thought she had an attractive figure and was particularly proud of her bust. She viewed herself from many angles before getting dressed.

While she was eating her cereal, Colleen's enthusiasm began to turn to anxiety. She wondered if she should wear the suit at all. She was afraid that her mother might find out. But more than that, she feared that Jim would become too excited.

They had been cool towards one another since the spring. It was not unfriendliness. They still went to parties, hung around with the same friends, held hands and kissed. Yet they avoided arousing any strong feelings. However, those same feelings were always breaking through to the surface.

This painful conflict had puzzled Colleen. In school, the nuns taught the girls that sex was holy in matrimony but profane outside. They were taught that sexual organs were made by God but were somehow bad. Sexuality was so pleasurable, they were told, only to ensure that people would bear children. Yet these feelings had come upon her long before she had either the desire or the ability to raise children. They were taught that God, in his infinite wisdom, had ordained things this way, but the situation seemed to be as troublesome and impractical as it could be.

"If I can't get married until I'm older, why didn't God work it so that I wouldn't have these feelings until I'm older?" Colleen felt she might have committed a sin even by asking such a question.

She had become so distraught and puzzled that she sought answers, not in religion, but in a field that she was afraid was considered the enemy of religion: psychology.

Colleen had heard many jokes about psychologists and psychology on television. It was always a man with a Viennese accent, sporting a funny gray beard, and he was always speaking incomprehensibly about "ze ego" or "ze id" or "ze trauma."

She didn't know why, but she had the impression that these jokes arose from fear. She thought that she might find answers to her problems in one of the books. She also felt that this knowledge was in some way sinful.

The other day, when she had bought a book by Freud, Colleen hid it the way one would hide a magazine with naked pictures. It was secreted in the bottom of her bureau, just underneath her new two-piece bathing suit.

Far from providing some insight into her difficulties, the book, *Civilization and Its Discontents,* confused Colleen even further. It had always been her understanding that psychology had something to do with sex. No one had ever told her that. It was just "in the air," as it were. To her, people's jokes about sex and their jokes about psychology had the same tone.

Colleen had assumed that these books would dare to say what she even feared to think: that sexual love was good, not bad. Yet, in glancing through Freud's book, she chanced upon a passage that bewildered her.

"A cultural community is perfectly justified," she read, "psychologically, in starting by proscribing manifestations of the sexual life of children, for there would be no prospect of curbing the sexual lust of adults if the ground had not been prepared for it in childhood."

This surprised her because it was basically what she was being taught in Catholic school. She wondered why we even had sexuality if all it did was cause trouble.

She went to her room and removed the book from its hiding place. She turned to another passage which seemed to contradict the first one she had read.

"I am, of course, speaking of the way of life which makes love the center of everything, which looks for all satisfaction in loving and being loved." Colleen paused. She knew that this was indeed her deepest, most powerful desire. It made her blush. She wished to love and be loved.

Cautiously, she read on. Freud wrote that sexual love had given people their most intense pleasurable experiences. Colleen did not know for sure if this were true, but she imagined it was. Yet, there was a dark side to this joy. "We are never so defenseless against suffering as when we love, never so helplessly unhappy as when we have lost our love object or its love."

Colleen heard the doorbell ring and guiltily put the book away. She pulled herself together and answered the door. She had the notion that her face would show her thoughts and tried to change her expression.

"Who is it?" She asked nervously.

"It's me, Jim. You're keeping everybody waiting!"

Colleen opened the door. "I'll be ready in a minute. Come on in."

The sun that broke its way through the grey, diaphanous cloud cover did not warm. Instead, it stung and burned. But Colleen lay on the blanket determined to deepen her tan as much as possible. Soon she would return to school, and there would be no more time for lazing in the sun.

Jim and the other boys were playing a game of touch football near the shore. Colleen thought they were funny when they became angry and argued over a fine point in the rules. She wished he would come lie beside her but knew that it was hopeless. He was a good athlete and enjoyed playing too much to be content to lie quietly in the sand.

With the approach of evening, a cool breeze came up. Many people began to leave for home, but Colleen and her friends were determined to stay until the last possible minute. She put on her navy-blue sweatshirt to keep warm and went down to the shore.

The ocean had always fascinated her. It never stopped moving and the sound of the waves washing the shore, so steady and constant, was relaxing to her. For some reason, being near the ocean made her think of things that usually did not come to mind. She remembered learning in her biology class that, just as life was formed in the sea, so we carried the sea still in our bodies, our blood cells floating in a salty solution as the first cells had floated in the ocean.

Colleen looked out to the horizon and up at the vast expanse of sky. She wondered what was out there, wondered what "out there" was at all. She felt very small, seeing her place in the vast scheme of things, and understood why people believed in a god. God was the infinite.

Suddenly, she was swooped up into the air. She shrieked and kicked as Jim spun her around. "Put me down! Put me down this instant!" She struggled in his arms but then relaxed as he kissed her gently.

"Come back to the blanket. Bobby went to the grocery store and brought back a surprise!" There was a twinkle in his eyes. Jim smacked her on the behind and Colleen chased him back to the blanket, Jim staying just beyond her reach.

Colleen was stunned to see a case of cold beer. "How did you...I mean, where did this come from?"

"I met this friend of my brother and he bought it for us. Great, eh? Here you go!" He handed them each a beer and they took it.

Jim drank occasionally and one beer was not going to affect him greatly. Colleen, on the other hand, never drank at all. She felt warm and giddy with the first flush of the beer and asked for another one.

"Don't drink so fast. It's not soda." Jim cautioned her gently.

"I didn't know beer tasted good. It has a terrible smell." She continued to gulp the liquid. Colleen felt light-headed and crazy. She started to tickle Jim and all her friends looked on with amused expressions. "I'm going swimming." She took off her sweatshirt impulsively and threw it aside. "Anybody else coming?" She ran off before anyone could reply.

"You better go with her, Jim. There's a strong undertow today." Bobby opened another can.

"I guess you're right." He ran after her.

"Come on in! It's great!" She began to splash water at him. "Come on in, chicken!"

Jim hesitated a moment but then ran and dived into the water. He swam under the surface, pulling Colleen's feet out from under her. They hugged each other and laughed.

The young couple stood in the waist-high water, nuzzling and kissing. For Colleen, the combination of cool water, a refreshing breeze, the warmth from the beer and the warmth of her boyfriend made her feel happier than she had ever felt. They stayed in the water until a large wave broke unexpectedly over them and sent them sprawling to the land.

Colleen still felt the effects of the beer as she entered her apartment. There were no lights on and it appeared as if nobody was home.

"Hello? Anybody here?" There was no reply. "I guess they're still at Blue Mountain."

She and Jim went into the living room. Jim put his things down and went to the bathroom. While he was there he heard the phone ring.

"Hello?" It was Mrs. Murphy. "Hi Mom. How was your day?" Colleen hoped she sounded all right.

"Just lovely. I called to tell you that we'll be home a little late tonight. We're all going out to dinner. There's plenty of food in the house. If you want something else, you can pick something up at Flynn's and charge it. I guess we'll be home around ten or eleven."

"Oh, okay. I hope you have a good time. I'll see you later." Colleen felt excited.

"See you later dear." Her mother hung up.

When she returned to the living room, Jim was sitting on the sofa reading the sports pages of the paper. "That was my mom. They won't be home until ten or eleven."

She sat down next to Jim and leaned her head on his shoulder.

The golden light of the late summer evening filled the room with a radiant, silent softness. In the silence of the fading light, the young lovers yielded to feelings which could no longer be denied. Without forethought or fear of consequences, they followed the instincts to love, guided by the flowing sensations that coursed through them as clear and refreshing as a mountain stream.

Although inexperienced in love, they did not feel hesitant as they had in the spring. They simply followed the path of mutual pleasure. However, when the two had finished their foreplay, exploring one another playfully as do two butterflies circling one another in a summer field, they lost their simple unity. Anxiety appeared. They feared to embrace one another fully; they longed to embrace one another fully. There could be no middle ground, no compromise. It was either love or not love.

Colleen faced a fear, a particular fear that had never crossed her mind before. She did not want to see Jim naked. She did not want to touch his genitals. But she wanted to as well.

And he foundered upon the same fear.

They lay beside one another unable to speak. All their training, all the anti-sexual teachings, all the fears of censure and punishment, came to the fore and combined with their own sense of guilt.

Desperate, feeling she could almost die from the tension she felt, Colleen spoke pleadingly. "I want to love you so much," she held him tightly, "but I ...I don't know how...I'm afraid...."

Jim felt released from the feeling that he was forcing her against her will and lovingly kissed her all over her face.

"I love you, Colleen." He said simply, quietly.

They felt connected again. Their fears subsided long enough for their love to re-emerge. They continued giving to one another, finally embracing fully.

The two were carried away by the intensity of the joy they felt, as they lost conscious control and at the height of the experience, lost consciousness as well.

They lay in one another's arms, enlivened and relaxed, life expressed and renewed in them.

The room had grown dark. The sky was purple. Outside, the wind rustled the leaves of the trees and a lone bird sang the last song of the day.

They did not think of the tired, resigned multitudes who sat flat and weary in their apartments, in whom the life force had either diminished or been transformed into something inimical to life. They did not think of the powerful social groups that would be allied against them. They did not think. They held one another, as grateful as two human beings can be toward one another.

Grandmother Murphy sat in her rocking chair and gazed at her family. Her children and her children's children had gathered for one more holiday season. She wondered how many more God would grant her.

It was the Sunday before Christmas and everyone had come to her home for dinner. She had prepared a large turkey, filled with her special stuffing—which even the children ate—and baked two delicious pumpkin pies. She relished the activity that was going on around her. The men were discussing politics, the women were discussing their families, and the brood of cousins was in the bedroom, watching television, playing games and occasionally bickering.

Grandfather Murphy, as he always did, tried to dominate the conversations, but his children had inherited his "gift of gab" and easily held their own. The old woman laughed to herself when she heard, more often than not, all of the men expounding their opinions and not a one listening at all. The conversation became a bit heated and Grandfather Murphy stormed off.

"Ah, you're all soft in the head, that's what I say. You don't understand politics at all. I say he'll be the next President and if you had any sense at all you'd do what you could to see that he gets elected!" He seemed to spit his words out. "He'll win even if he is Irish and Catholic. He'll win *because* he's Irish and Catholic!"

"Come sit by me, Tom." She eyed the old man as if he were being silly and it angered him.

"Don't be looking at me like that, Mrs. Brigid Murphy!" He sat across the room.

"And how would that be? You don't know what I'm thinking, Mr. Thomas Murphy!" She smiled at him, goading him.

"Unfortunately, I do. After fifty years I couldn't help but know what scatterbrained thoughts are flooding your mind, woman!" He spoke harshly, but his face softened into a smile. "Never discuss politics or religion. It's sure trouble." He walked over to his wife and kissed her forehead.

"You're a hard man, Tom—hard as asparagus tips."

"A bit of respect, wife of mine. That's all I ask." He headed for the kitchen.

"That and three squares a day, husband. Come, let's have a bit of tea together. And not your special mixture...just tea!" They walked off together.

Colleen left the other children and went into the bathroom. She locked the door behind her, nervously testing it to make sure it was locked. She looked at herself in the mirror but turned away. The color had gone from her cheeks and her face had become much thinner. There were dark circles under her eyes and the eyes themselves had lost their glimmer and become sad. Colleen sat on the edge of the tub and put her head in her hands.

She felt a knot in her stomach almost as big as her fist. It had been there for days and she couldn't get rid of it. The young girl awoke in the middle of the night, unable to sleep. She had lost her appetite and barely ate anything at all.

She thought she would soon fall to pieces.

Standing up, she looked at herself in the full-length mirror on the bathroom door. She studied her profile very carefully. Her figure seemed the same but there were changes that only she could recognize. She wondered if anyone else could tell.

She could hardly bear the weight of what she knew and wished to share her secret and her fear with someone else. She longed to be held and comforted like a child once again. But she did not know in whom she could confide.

She sat back down and listened to the sounds of the children in the next room and wished that she could turn time backwards, that it would suddenly, magically, be five years ago, two years ago, three months ago.

In her throat, she felt the impulse to cry but she was unable to and the feeling was replaced by a sensation of emptiness and hopelessness. Colleen tried to remember all the sad and hurting things that had ever happened to her, hoping that by doing so she could rouse herself to tears. However, it was to no avail. She felt nothing other than a despairing weariness. She felt trapped.

No matter how she tried, she was unable to reconcile her

conflicting feelings. Colleen knew that she was glad she had done what she had done but she also saw that it led her, inevitably, to where she now found herself.

Her thoughts were interrupted by a knock on the door.

"Just a minute!" She had to clear her throat before she spoke.

"Take your time, honey," Grandmother Murphy replied.

Colleen threw cold water on her face and tried to make herself look respectable. When she opened the door and saw her grandmother, her facade collapsed. A look of longing and fear came over her.

"Child!" her grandmother whispered, shaken. "What is it?" She put her arms around the young girl.

"Oh grandma..." Her voice trailed off in sorrow.

"Come with me, Colleen." The two went into the grandparents' bedroom and sat down. The old woman locked the door for privacy.

"You haven't been yourself lately, Colleen. What is troubling you?"

The kindness in her grandmother's voice and eyes touched something in Colleen and the flood of forbidden feelings that had been damned for months broke through. She threw her arms around the old woman and wept.

"That's it, darling. That's it. Yes, you get it all out now. Get it all out, honey." Grandmother Murphy knew what it was now. It was all too familiar to her. She recognized the expression, the depth of the fear in her granddaughter's eyes. She knew it well indeed.

It was sometime before the young girl could speak and she did so haltingly. She used a good number of tissues for her running nose while she spoke. "Oh Grandma, I've done something and I can't tell anybody. They'll be so ashamed."

"Are you ashamed of what you've done?" There was nothing accusatory in her tone.

"No," Colleen was a bit taken aback. "But I know...My parents won't...they won't understand." She fought tears again. "You see...I...Jim and I...." She caught her breath.

Grandmother Murphy felt her heart ache. She nodded her head and knew she had been right. She wished that she had been wrong.

"We've been...we've..." Colleen couldn't bring herself to say it at all.

"Do you love each other, Colleen?" She held the girl close, as much for her own comfort as for her granddaughter's.

The directness of the question startled Colleen. She knew that the woman understood, that something had been communicated on a much deeper level than words could ever reach. Colleen felt the knot in her stomach dissolve. It was as if in that moment that she felt understood, that she no longer felt the intense alienation and isolation that had plagued her.

For months, Colleen had felt unutterably alone. She felt cut off from contact with everyone around her and cut off from contact with herself as well. She had begun to think of herself as a kind of ghost, moving about the world but without any substance.

This simple, kind understanding had been like water to a plant that needed it desperately. Like such a plant, Colleen soaked it up gratefully.

"Yes, we do. We do love each other." She looked at her grandmother. "But I don't know what to do, grandma. I'm afraid my parents...They'll be so hurt...they might want to hurt me in return..."

"They'll be hurt, child. There's no escaping that. You must be prepared for that. But they'll take it to them; they'll come around soon enough and stand by you." She took the girl's hand. "Does anyone know?"

"Only you. I haven't even told Jim." Colleen clung to her grandmother.

The old woman smiled. She had seen the two of them together at family gatherings and had always had fond feelings for the boy. He appeared both kind and sensible. She was glad it was him.

"Why are you smiling, Grandma?" Colleen was confused.

"I think you two do love each other. Sometimes an old woman has eyes for things like this."

Colleen watched as her grandmother went to the closet and removed an old cardboard box, placing it on the bed. It was dusty with the dust of many years and when Grandmother Murphy blew on it, the dust filled the air.

"This box hasn't been opened for longer than you've been alive, child. It's where I keep my memories." She smiled sadly. "There are some things I'd like you to know, now that you've shared your secrets with me." The old woman searched through the box and removed a large maroon packet, bound by a frayed bow. It too had the dust of decades upon it.

"What is it, Grandma?" Colleen had almost forgotten her troubles.

"Patience, child." She inspected the contents briefly. "Yes, this is it." She sat close to her granddaughter. "I'd like you to look at some pictures, pictures from long, long ago." She carefully handed the packet to Colleen.

The first few photographs were landscapes in black and white, but without the clarity of the photographs with which Colleen was familiar. It often took her a few moments to decipher the shades of grey, recognizing a hillside here or a wooden bridge there.

"What's this house?" Colleen inspected the picture closely.

"That's where my family lived, where I grew up." She leaned over the young girl's shoulder and looked longingly at the image. Much faded with time, it showed a small cottage, a thatched roof, a gullied, eroded and rocky path and in the distance, full, tall trees. "We all lived in that little cottage—my parents and the six of us." Time had softened the memory and the feelings of fondness had endured while the painful feelings had long since faded.

Colleen looked at the next picture. Sepia toned, it showed a small brook, sun glinting from the rippling water and in the foreground, a stunning young girl of no more than fourteen or fifteen. "What a beautiful girl! Who is this, Grandma?" No sooner had Colleen asked than she looked at the old woman, then at the picture, and she knew who it was. "Is this you, Grandma? Is this really you?"

"You're very clever ...I would never have thought you'd guess. Let's look at the rest."

Dressed poorly, but obviously dressed as finely as possible, a young man smiled from the next photograph. Grandmother Murphy took it gently in her hands and looked at it with love. The expression in her eyes was more tender than anything Colleen had ever seen.

"And this, Colleen, was my young man when I was your age." The old woman's expression became dream-like and she seemed to drift away, across the ocean, across time, back to the loughs of Ireland, back to the simple, rugged days, to the heart-warming, heart-rending, contradictions of her adolescence. "And one day, one day in the beginning of September...hidden alone by the stream that ran at the edge of his father's land . . . we were joined to one another...in the bright sunlight, in the holiness of love...."

Tears fell from the old woman's eyes and she clasped the young girl in her arms. "And for our love, for our love which God ordains, we were punished, alone and afraid, and never saw one another again.

"I was sent away, to bear my child in disgrace, to give away in shame my own baby. He was sent by ship to Australia...a journey he never completed, his ship wrecked in a storm...my love and my baby gone as well . . . I learned early and hard how the world deals with love." For the first time, bitterness had crept into the woman's tone.

They continued looking at the photographs in stunned silence, the setting winter sun draping the room in sad evening shadows. The pictures showed Ireland as a harsh, barren land, immensely impoverished. Yet the faces of the young people beamed with life, though it was like seeing flowers blooming on a stony, forsaken field.

"What was his name, Grandma?"

"Kevin. Kevin Boyle."

For a long time, neither spoke to the other. The sounds from the other rooms drifted in. The two street lights outside cast conflicting shadows, while the two women sat in silence bound by their shared sorrows but more, bound by their vulnerability.

"You know, Colleen, I have often had a thought that I never dared tell a soul before. It seemed so blasphemous and profane that I don't know how I dared think it." The old woman's face was hidden in the shadows. "I've often thought of my first love and my first-born—no one knows of them but you; not even your grandfather—and I've thought of the Virgin Mary and Jesus."

Colleen was confused. She waited for her grandmother to continue. She felt flattered and proud to be part, so deep a part, of this person's life.

"And I wondered . . . perhaps she was like me. Perhaps Mary was a girl who loved, simply and purely, moved by God to love. And perhaps Joseph protected her and her baby, in a way that my poor Kevin was unable to do.

"And every Christmas, I celebrate the birth of Jesus, who also was born out of wedlock, whose parents were not bound by a license but by love. And I celebrate the birth of my lost baby, who was born on Easter Sunday." She took the young girl's hand. "But we'll keep these things to ourselves, all right child? I don't think anyone would understand."

"You can trust me, Grandma."

"And you can trust me, Colleen. If you want me to be with you when you tell your mom and dad, I'll be there. And you can count on me for anything you need." Grandmother Murphy stood up. "Now let's go outside." They walked to the door. When it was slightly open and the light from outside flooded into the dark room, Grandmother Murphy closed the door again.

"I just want you to know, Colleen. No matter what anybody tries to tell you-you weren't wrong. You weren't wrong to love. I know, child. Believe me, I know."

Elizabeth closed her eyes and looked at the colors. Blue, red, and green dots swam about before her, spinning, merging, bursting into splashes of colors. She pressed gently on her eyelids and the spinning lights changed direction, shape, and hue.

It was a game she played with herself many nights before drifting off to sleep. The tiny girl thought of the colors as her friends. She spoke to them—in thought not in speech—and told them of her joys and sorrows.

From the room outside, Elizabeth could hear her father speaking with her mother, the sound of the television set, her brother throwing his Spaulding rubber ball against the wall in the next room. All these sounds and the faint yellow light that came through the door left slightly ajar at her request, all these sensations eased her descent into darkness and sleep.

When she opened her eyes, Elizabeth saw something else in the air in the room. She saw points, grey-blue points, moving near the ceiling in the darkest corner of the room. She wondered what it was but never remembered to ask anyone the next morning. Whatever it was, it didn't frighten her at all. She rather liked seeing it.

Weary of watching the colors and *stuff in the air*, as she thought of it, sensing that she was about to slip off into sleep, Elizabeth clutched her dolly to her. She kissed it goodnight and closed her eyes.

Barely awake but not yet asleep, something began to trouble Elizabeth. She tossed in her bed and saw disturbing, amorphous visions. She wanted to fall into a deep sleep but something was preventing her. She awoke and, without opening her eyes, listened. She heard weeping.

The child listened more carefully. Frightened, not sure she wasn't dreaming, Elizabeth recognized her sister's voice. She held her breath. The crying was low and muffled. Elizabeth looked toward her sister's bed and saw Colleen lying there, curled up with the pillow over her head.

Elizabeth quietly left her bed and tiptoed across the room. She put her hand on Colleen's shoulder.

"Oh, Lizzie!" Her voice was deeply mournful.

In complete silence, the child sat beside her sister and held her hand.

As the Murphys slept that night, a gentle snow began to fall. It served to cover the harshness of life this Christmas, 1959, to soften the rough edges. But it did not ease Colleen's pain, as she wrestled with a nightmare that her child was born dead.

Nor did the snows, silently falling this silent night, change anything for Mr. Murphy, whose last conscious thoughts revolved around his desperate need for more money to keep his family in food and clothing.

This Christmas, 1959, found many millions uncomforted lost and hopeless. The snows fell, the earth spun tirelessly through what seemed a dark and forbidding universe. People everywhere felt cut off, anxious, fearful.

In the hearts of the young, while there was confusion and doubt, there was also stirring a new sense of hope. As they reached the first stages of independence, they were ready to shake off the dying decade, with its atomic terror, cold war, and prejudice. Like seeds bursting through the cold wet mud of early spring, the young were ready to take on the world.

PART TWO

1967

Lizzie got off the 100 Bus and walked over toward Music and Art, where she was a junior in high school, but instead of going to class, she decided to meet her boyfriend, a freshman at CCNY. She knew he had a painting class with Professor Bailey, a member of the art department who also happened to be a friend of her oldest brother.

When she entered the art studio, through the side entrance, she saw Craig, discussing his work with Professor Bailey.

"Now Craig, you're too tight in your movements." He smiled. "I'd like to loosen your movements up!" He said, imitating Mae West. "This is a monumental work…you're being much too circumscribed. Use the whole canvas. Feel the space." He stretched out his arms to the full length of the canvas. "You have a very interesting concept, don't cramp yourself in. And remember," he pointed to an area in shadows, "all shadows are blue. These are much too black. Painting comes from looking, not thinking about what you saw. Open your eyes and paint what you see, not what you think you should see."

He went on to the next student.

Lizzie thought there was something refreshing about him. She knew he had influenced her brother Tommy and could see that he was a fine art teacher. He didn't try to scold or humiliate. He attempted to educate, to lead out latent talent. She realized that he didn't impose his views on anyone but only wanted to help his students reach the technical capacity that would allow them to express their views.

"Craig!" She called to him, trying to reach him across the room without yelling. He turned and motioned for her to come over.

Professor Bailey looked their way and smiled. "Ah, it's Romeo and Juliet. Perhaps we can get the two of them to model for us someday."

Lizzie caught a glimpse in his eye that conveyed he was interested in them as more than models. What troubled her was that she wasn't quite sure which one of them interested him. "I decided to cut today. Can you meet me after class?"

"Of course. I don't have another class until this afternoon." He mock-leered at her. "But that doesn't give us enough time to go home and get back in time, does it?"

"Maybe you won't want to come back?" She pinched his rear end.

"Lolita!" He called out as she left the studio.

Lizzie found a place on the campus under a tree and lay down in the grass. She stared up at the blue sky and breathed deeply. Opening her bag, she took out a letter from her sister and re-read it:

> Dear Lizzie,
>
> I'm going down to Esalen at Big Sur to run a T-group. It was arranged by Prof. Nils and though I won't be paid, I'll be able to attend a week of sessions run by Maslow. By the way, you should pick up his book Toward a Psychology of Being.
>
> I would never have thought that things could turn out so well. When I look back to when I was pregnant, and how terribly the marriage turned out for both Jim and myself...
>
> There's something new and

> important in the country today. It's political, sexual, a new consciousness. You should really come out here.
>
> In our groups, we get into some very heavy trips (no, not acid), getting down to feelings we hide so well at such a cost. Our pain is covered up and prevents us from really sharing and loving. Anyway, what I want to say is that I love you very much.
>
> I was glad to hear that you like Dr. Walker. Also that you're taking the pill. Write me soon, okay?
>
> Love, Colleen
>
> P.S., Brigid got accepted into this really far-out free school. She loves it—it's so mellow, no authoritarian trips.

She folded the letter and carefully placed it in its original envelope. Lizzie lay down in the grass and sighed. She felt happy and wistful. It had been almost two years since she had seen her sister and she wished she could just appear, with the snap of a finger, in Colleen's apartment in San Francisco. She looked at her sister's handwriting on the envelope before putting it back in her bag.

Just as she was beginning to daydream, Lizzie remembered that she had an important phone call to make. An experimental college was opening in the Bronx and she had applied to it. It had a program which permitted a very few qualified high school juniors to skip senior year and go directly to college. She hadn't told anyone in her family that she had applied, except Colleen, in case it came to nothing.

She ran to the cafeteria to make the call to the faculty member who had interviewed her.

"Bensalem College ...may I help you?" Lizzie recognized the secretary's voice.

"Professor Bressan please." She held her breath. "Professor Bressan is in conference right now. May I take a message?"

"He asked me to call him this morning about my interview. He said he would tell me if I had been accepted."

"Your name?"

"Elizabeth Murphy." Her tension increased.

"Oh yes, Elizabeth," the secretary's voice changed from one of official distance to friendly camaraderie. "I just typed your acceptance letter this morning. You should receive it tomorrow or the next day."

"Oh that's great!" She spun around, beaming. "Thank you so much."

"If you want to call Professor Bressan later, he-" She was interrupted.

"That's all right. I'm so excited!" She laughed. "I guess everyone acts like this. Thank you so much."

"You're welcome. Just answer as soon as possible. Not many people are turning down their acceptances."

"Don't worry about that. Thank you so much."

"See you when school opens. Bye now."

Lizzie hung up the phone and was speechless. She had never felt so excited. She looked around the cafeteria, at the people cutting class, sitting glumly staring at a cup of coffee. She looked at what she was escaping and let out a loud, joyous whoop as she ran to tell Craig.

Lizzie sat at the dinner table, unable to broach the subject of her new school with her parents. She knew there would be trouble and wanted to delay it as long as possible. They would be curious when the letter arrived but she could not decide whether it was better to tell them now or later. It wasn't just the school that would bother them, she knew that. It was also the fact that she was only sixteen years old and would be living away from home—with all that that implied.

She decided to wait until after dinner. She knew she was only avoiding, not resolving, the issue, and that it would be unpleasant whenever it was faced.

Colleen drove along Route 1, still awed by the beauty of the Pacific and the rugged coastline. With the top down on her blue convertible 1957 Karmann Ghia, the radio playing loud and the salty air filling her lungs, she felt so glad to be alive.

She experienced a moment of concern for her daughter but realized that she was well taken care of. Colleen hoped that Mitch, the man she had been living with for three years, would get over his jealousy. *He's being so silly,* she told herself, denying her awareness that he did have some reason to feel that way.

At the seminar, Colleen knew she would meet Fritz Perls and that thrilled her. She hoped to meet Maslow as well. But most importantly, she longed to see Professor Nils again. He was so gentle, understanding, and intelligent. All the men she had known had been one or the other but none had combined all three qualities. She drew from his strength and he did not appear weaker but stronger.

She smiled to herself. *If he were a mystic and not a psychologist, I guess he'd be my guru.* Colleen did not think highly of gurus, although her reflection had more truth to it than she knew.

Her attention turned to the scenery and the feeling she shared with most of the people her age: anything was possible and the best dreams could not help but come true.

For hadn't everyone heard? The times were a-changin'. It was getting better all the time.

⁂

Mrs. Murphy hung up the phone. She was completely beside herself. She walked to the bedroom, had no idea why she had gone there, and returned to the kitchen. She peered out from behind the curtain. People passed below, shopping, chatting, and walking their babies. The normality of the scene, its perfect ordinariness, puzzled her. She turned from the window and hurried to the phone.

She dialed her husband's store once more. "Oh thank heavens you're there!" She was frantic, about to cry.

"What's wrong?" He turned from his customers and whispered.

"Your mother's been taken to the hospital. Your father just called. They think...." She choked. "It might be a stroke."

"Meet me in front of the store. We'll take a cab there. Is Dad with her?"

"Of course. He rode in the ambulance with her."

"We'll leave as soon as you get here." Mr. Murphy felt his heart racing.

⁂

Mrs. Murphy sat in silence beside her father-in-law. It had been some time since they had heard anything from the doctors and Mr. Murphy had gone off to see if he could get any information.

The initial shock had given way to a dull helplessness. They sat, staring ahead, lost in their own fears and reflections. "God have mercy on her. She's a good woman." Grandfather Murphy spoke through tears. Though she had never done so before, Mrs. Murphy put her arm around the old man and tried to comfort him.

Peter Murphy came down the hallway, walking quickly. He sat down beside his father. "She's going to be fine, Dad. She's going to be just fine. The doctors said she'll have to stay here for a week, maybe ten days. They'll have to keep an eye on her, to make sure she's completely out of danger, but she's going to be fine."

His father did not look up.

"She's asleep now. He says we should go. She won't wake up until the morning and you can see her then." Peter stood up and his wife did likewise, but the old man remained seated.

"I would just like to see her before I go." He rose and went down the hallway to find his wife. Mr. and Mrs. Murphy let him go alone.

When he found the room, he hesitated before entering. Opening the door, he peered in and saw his wife asleep. The faintest trace of light came through the window. There was absolute silence in the room. Grandfather Murphy sat on the edge of the bed and took his wife's hand.

He remembered a night near the beach. The sun had set and there was no moon. He and Brigid had been married only a few weeks and something was wrong. They were awkward together and neither knew how to make the other feel at ease. Grandfather Murphy let the feelings arise. It had been nearly half a century since the day recalled but it came back in full force: the cool sea wind, the salty air in his lungs, the lovely young woman curled in his arms, reading a poem.

And he saw how the reeds grew dark with the coming of nightide
And he dreamt of the long dim hair of Brigid his bride
Then he heard it
high up in the air
a piper piping away
And never was piping so sad

And never was piping so gay.

He heard his wife's voice as it was then, fresh and as sweet sounding as a mountain stream. She loved the poem not only because it had her name in it, but also because it reminded her of the first time she had heard it.

She had gone with her family to picnic at Windy Gap in Kerry. She stood by the roadside, stunned by the immense awesome majesty of the valley and the mountains. A storm was brewing and the large blue-black thunderclouds loomed ominous overhead while her cousin, who had been to college, read Yeats' poem to the family.

Grandfather Murphy gently kissed his wife's cheek and buried his face in Brigid's long dim hair.

"That's really beautiful, Stacy." Professor Nils took her hand in his and stared into her eyes, attempting to assume a penetrating mantic pose. "I think we should ask the group to comment on what you've just revealed. It's really beautiful that you were able to open up." He closed his eyes and shook his head gently. "Wow...just beautiful!"

Stacy's face glowed with delight and she basked in the approval of the T-group. Colleen looked at her with ill-disguised contempt but the woman did not notice it.

For the first time, Colleen was seeing Professor Nils as he really was. She noticed that his mellow tones were not mellow with human warmth. Rather, his manner of speech was affected and the voice was hollow and bland. She was taken aback by the way he acted toward the young woman. It was exactly the way he had acted toward her when she met him at Berkeley.

It's all a goddamn act! She thought, furious. *The gestures, the tones, the inflections, the goddamned guru look in the eyes.* She burned with embarrassment that she had been so easily taken in. The group was sitting in a circle on the floor, most with their legs crossed and arms folded in front. Colleen lay on her side, her head propped up on a pillow.

"Professor Nils, I think there's a member of the group giving off definitely negative vibes." A young man who had briefly flirted with Colleen, and been rejected, was speaking. "I think she thinks she's above telling us about herself. I think she has been condescending during the entire weekend." He glared at Colleen and the eyes of the group turned on her. "Even her body language shows it. Look how she's lying outside of the circle. It's a way of saying that she isn't part of the group ...that she's better than us."

Colleen was amused. "It's a way of saying that all of you are tedious and dreadfully boring." Colleen stood up. "And as for you, Professor Nils, I think that for the first time, instead of just `hearing' you, I'm finally seeing you. And you're full of shit!" She smiled at them. "Gee, I thought someone would at least say that it was beautiful that I could be so upfront." She laughed and left the room.

Colleen packed her belongings and just before she left Esalen, she called Mitch to let him know she would be home in a few hours.

"Colleen, for Christ's sake! Why didn't you call me back?" He was furious.

"What do you mean? I didn't know you called?" She was momentarily puzzled but then understood.

"Well, I hope you understand that son-of-a-bitch Nils a little better. He's about as sensitive as an old mountain goat and about as horny as one too. T-groups, my ass!"

"Well, what was it? Is Brigid okay?" Colleen was almost frantic.

"She's fine. It's your grandmother. She's had a stroke and is in the hospital."

"Will she live?" Colleen felt dizzy.

"They think so, but they aren't sure. Listen honey, I got the bread together and got you and Brigid tickets on the last flight tonight. I thought I would have heard from you yesterday. If you want, I'll cancel and make reservations for tomorrow."

"I think I should go tonight honey. Look, I better get started. I'll see you soon, Mitch." She paused a moment. "Mitch, I really love you, you know that?"

"I know that, Colleen. See you later."

"Yeah." She hung up.

As she started up her car, she stared into the sky and watched a cloud forming above. *That's how fragile we are,* she thought.

The old woman opened her eyes in the dark room and saw something moving in the air. Blue-grey vapors, cloud-like formations, points of light rising seemingly from nowhere and returning once again. At first, she felt apprehensive but gradually, the visions grew comforting.

A face appeared before her, smiling, tender, weary. "Grandfather!" she heard herself call, though she did not utter a sound. The face melted and she saw a cottage and two figures, eerie in the darkened doorway. She could barely make out the grim foreboding expression of the figure on the right. She heard the lonely sound of the wind in the mountains turn into a mournful desolate cry.

I don't want to die! Again she thought she had cried out but lay mute in her bed.

From the doorway an old man emerged, tapping a pipe against his leg. "Don't be afraid, Brigid." He spoke with a quiet strength. She looked at him with love. Long wisps of grey hair fell to his shoulders, framing a battered, worn face that for all its tribulations had not lost its softness and expressiveness.

The bedraggled figure, clothed in a tattered, threadbare wool coat, a stained, ratty jacket, pants too short and torn, this pathetic lovable figure beckoned to her. "Do not fear, Brigid. Come...come home..." He stood still and his features faded. The image vanished and the old woman closed her eyes.

Suddenly, she saw a young girl in a blue dress leaning against a yellow wall, a staff twice her height in her left hand. The girl stood barefoot in the wet morning grass and watched with longing as a young boy passed.

"That's me!" she exclaimed aloud. "Colm MacNeil..." A smile came to her face but the girl in the dream looked at the boy with forlorn longing. The young lad, astride a donkey, wearing his new cap, and Sunday best, with bare feet and lost expression, rode by without seeing young Brigid. "How I loved that boy!" the old woman whispered and cried.

A torrent of images from her earliest childhood came back to the old woman. She saw herself at Mass, frightened by the fierce sermon of the priest, unable to understand a word. She saw the body of her uncle laid out in his cottage. She remembered her first Fair Day and the thrill of the crowds and the bustle. She saw her brother standing before his home in the Liberties on the corner of New Row and Blackpitts one Sunday as they went off to St. Patrick's Cathedral. Countless images were retrieved from the past and seeing them once more filled the old woman with joy.

How good it is to live . . . to see and to feel. Tired and sedated, she drifted into sleep.

The plane landed shortly after six in the morning. Colleen decided to stop in the cafeteria, partly to eat breakfast, partly to avoid the morning rush hour traffic. Brigid was sleepy and cranky and Colleen wondered if it might have been a mistake to bring her. She wanted her Grandmother to see the baby once again. *In case . . . well, just in case.*

She felt increasingly happy to be back in New York. She looked forward to seeing her brothers and especially longed to see her sister. Colleen remembered how oppressive and unmanageable the city had seemed to her just before she left. She had been completely unable to cope with the collapse of her marriage, raising a child, the unspoken censure and sorrow from her parents, the sense of being adrift in the middle of an ocean, drifting directionless, no longer part of the world left behind and increasingly doubtful that anything lay ahead.

"Brigid!" Colleen was appalled to see the child pouring a mountain of sugar on her cereal. "How many times do I have to tell you not to do that? That stuff is very bad for you—it's poison!"

"But Mommy, if it's poison, why is it in the restaurant?" She continued pouring sugar until Colleen grabbed the jar from her hand.

"I don't want you to eat that!" She spoke sternly and took the bowl of cereal away. "Wait here and I'll get you another bowl." Colleen felt exasperated and could hardly wait to get to her parents' home. She knew Brigid would be kept busy night and day by her doting grandparents.

As she returned to the table, Colleen stopped in her tracks. "Dad! What are you doing here?" She rushed to him.

"Colleen!" He embraced his daughter but immediately felt self-conscious. "Colleen, you look wonderful!"

Although her father looked tired, as if he had been working much too hard, Colleen returned the compliment. "You look pretty good yourself." She patted his stomach. "Too much of mom's cooking?"

He laughed gently. "And how is my most favorite girl in the world?" He kissed Brigid on the forehead.

"Fine, Grampa." She continued eating as she spoke.

"Mitch called us last night and told us you would be in. So I took the delivery truck and drove out." He looked closely at his daughter. "Your mother is so looking forward to seeing you."

"I..." The memory of the years of pain and anger caused her to pause. "I'm looking forward to seeing Mom, too."

They stood silently, wistfully gazing at one another, both remembering how difficult things had been, both realizing that time and separation had nearly, but not completely, erased the bad feelings, both wishing they could look at one another without shame and regret.

Mr. Murphy nervously broke the silence. "Come now, don't waste your time here. Your mother is fixing breakfast for us now. It's your favorite, Colleen— Irish sausages from the delicatessen, French toast, coffee from the A&P...and powdered jelly donuts."

Colleen felt a great mix of feelings all at once. She felt separated, united, like a child, grown-up, forlorn, and grateful. Her mother was making her favorite breakfast...yet it was no longer her favorite breakfast. She knew it was her mother's way of saying her love for her daughter had assuaged her hurt.

Colleen wanted to hug her father but was unable to do so. Instead, she took her daughter by the hand. "Let's go. Brigid."

"Where are we going, Mommy?" She stood up and straightened her little dress.

"Home...home," she said fondly.

The Murphys were together as a family for the first time in many years but it was in quite a different way than Mrs. Murphy had wished. Colleen was back from California. Tommy paid one of his rare visits. Lizzie was home from school. Eddie sat beside his new girl. And little Brigid watched television in the bedroom.

The family, broken apart on the shoals of religion, politics, and lifestyles, was whole again...for a time.

Grandfather Murphy emerged from the bedroom. He seemed on the verge of tears. "Colleen, she's asking for you."

Colleen bit her lower lip and stood up unsteadily. "Brigid!" She called her child.

"Perhaps the child shouldn't witness this, honey." Mrs. Murphy put her hand on her daughter's shoulder.

"I think it will be all right, Mom." The child came into the room, smiling, but immediately sensed that all was not well.

"Is Grandma going to heaven now?" she asked.

No one spoke. Colleen took Brigid by the hand and went to the bedside of the dying woman.

"Colleen?" Her voice was thin but serene.

"Yes, it's me." She sat on the edge of the bed and took her grandmother's hand.

"I'm here too, Grandma!" The little girl climbed onto her mother's lap.

"I wanted to be here, Colleen. In my own home. In my own bed, not in some hospital." She could barely speak. Her face, partially paralyzed by the stroke, was distorted. But the stroke could not entirely destroy the beauty of the old woman's features.

"My time has come, Colleen, but it isn't as I thought it would be. There is no terror. I feel... peaceful..." She drifted away and it frightened Colleen.

"Grandma!" Brigid cried out.

"Don't be frightened, Brigid." The old woman's voice had lost more strength. "To be alive... to have seen so much... Colleen, I feel grateful...

to have lived and felt love...When you were in so much pain... in this room... do you remember? And now, your child, born from your pain, and your love, little Brigid, is with you... Colleen, loving is life... protect little Brigid...you and I, we suffered loving...so that she has a new world...where loving is not punished..." She closed her eyes.

Colleen was seized with sorrow and love. The infinite depth of the world opened up before her as it had never done before. She understood, not in words or ideas, how profoundly we have abused life, how we have demeaned and debased it, and that despite all our misguided efforts, how noble and enduring life is.

"I love you, Grandma!" She kissed the old woman on the lips.

"I love you too, Grandma." The child spoke thoughtfully, movingly. She also kissed the old woman.

"Would you call my husband, child?" She closed her eyes and Colleen stood up. She felt that all her strength had drained from her legs. Colleen made her way to the door.

"Grandpa?" She could barely make out the others in the room. Her eyes would not see.

Grandfather Murphy stopped before Colleen and kissed her on the forehead. He closed the door gently behind him. Sitting beside his wife, he ran his hands through her hair, brushing it behind her ear.

"Thomas... I..." She choked.

"Brigid...the love of my life..." Without forethought, he began to recite:

> *And he saw how the reeds grew dark with the coming of nightide*
> *And he dreamt of the long dim hair of Brigid his bride*
> *Then he heard it*
> *high up in the air*
> *a piper piping away*
> *And never was piping so sad*

And never was piping so gay.

He swallowed the last line, barely able to utter it. Tears streamed down his cheeks and his chest heaved as he wept. He held onto his wife's hand, though he knew that she no longer held his.

She was gone.

Some signal, some message moved from the bedroom and reached the other members of the family. They stood and walked to pay their last respects to their beloved mother and grandmother. Grandfather Murphy, staring at his wife as he spoke, stood tall.

"She has returned to her maker. Let us all pray for her soul."

It came as a shock to Colleen to find the sun shining when she stepped into the courtyard of the apartment building. She had expected to find a dismal, dreary rain soaking the streets. As she walked along, she felt off balance. Everything seemed much too small for her. As a child, she had played in the yard, often climbing the small guardrails to chase a ball into the gardens around the building.

Those spiked railings had once posed such a problem to her, had once been dangerous to climb. It surprised her to see how small they really were. She made her way along the streets and alleyways of her childhood, amazed that everything was both familiar and different.

Colleen was a bit guilty about leaving the apartment. She thought she should have stayed with the rest of the family but she couldn't bear to see her grandmother's death swamped by a sea of mundane events. Her parents were calling the funeral home to make arrangements for the wake. They were calling the parish rectory to arrange for the funeral Mass and announcements at Sunday services. Relatives had to be notified, friends contacted and worst of all—money had to be found to bury Grandmother Murphy "properly."

It was as if these events served to make the death bearable to the living. Attention to detail precluded, or rather, postponed, reflection upon the reality of death for us all. Colleen felt that she was suffocating and told everyone that she had to go for a walk. She found herself heading south and decided to wander through Inwood Park.

She walked along Broadway, the elevated trains passing noisily overhead, thinking about what the old woman had told her. She wondered how long her grandmother had had such ideas and how it felt to keep them in, to be unable to share them. She thought perhaps they had only been feelings and were formulated into words only under the pressure of imminent death. Colleen did not know.

The park was crowded with people playing softball, walking their pets, sitting reading in the shade or lying in couples on blankets. She knew that, once she walked into the hills, there would be few, if any, people. Colleen wanted to go to a favorite spot of hers, at the edge of the park, overlooking the Hudson River. On clear days, she could see upriver to the Tappan Zee Bridge and downriver out past the Statue of Liberty.

The path rose steeply, leveled off, ran downhill a few hundred yards, and then rose sharply once more. She met no one but saw unmistakable evidence that people came this way: broken bottles, beer cans, and even swastikas etched into the bark of trees.

Colleen observed the sky, the golden evening light falling upon the green leaves, inhaled the sweet smell of the flowers, spotted what she thought to be a pheasant as it disappeared in the underbrush. *You could almost forget where you are,* she thought. *Almost.*

When she reached her destination, Colleen was disappointed to see that a group of young men were already there. They were drinking and, as she came closer, she realized that they were also smoking marijuana.

She paused momentarily, uncertain as to what to do. An alternate spot did not immediately come to mind. She wanted to be alone, to lie in the setting sun, and let her mind go where it would. Colleen sensed something inside, something that wanted to express itself but needed solitude and silence.

Before she was able to decide, the young men began to walk away from the spot. She felt them look at her, sizing her up, the way men do when they are lonely and frustrated. She wished they would simply walk by without making any comments.

She turned away from them but as she did, a peculiar sensation took hold of her. Colleen spun about and found herself facing her ex-husband. He had put on a considerable amount of weight and had lost the glow his eyes once had. He didn't recognize her at first and when he did his face went from shock to joy.

"Col-Colleen!" He stood frozen.

"Jim . . . I..." She was embarrassed to see him drunk.

He stared at the woman who had once been his wife. His friends realized that something was going on and they excused themselves.

"How are you?" she asked with deep tenderness.

"Colleen, I..." He looked away. After an awkward moment, Jim cleared his throat and looked at Colleen. "I never thought I would see you again."

Colleen said nothing. She gazed at him, wondering what he had been through these last years that had caused him to become so different. She did not judge people by the way they looked, but she knew that appearance often mirrored a person's inner state.

She had left a young man, muscular, trim, and athletic. She now faced a man who had let himself deteriorate physically. He looked to her like one who had given up and settled for secondary pleasures in life. Colleen hoped he could not see how she felt.

"You look really great. That's some tan you've got." He looked at her with a sense of loss.

"I'm just one of those California girls," she tried to sound light and cheery but did not pull it off.

"What are you doing back in New York?" Before she could reply, he asked, "Is Brigid with you?"

"Yes, she is."

"I'd love to see her. Will you be here long?" He felt he was being pushy and tried to restrain himself.

"A week or so. I came in because my grandmother, well, she was ill and—"

"I hope she's okay," he interrupted.

"Well, Jim, she ...uh . . . she died today." Colleen tried to say it without making him feel uncomfortable but she did not really think that was possible.

"I'm so sorry to hear that. I really liked her ...I liked her very much." His face became blank.

"I was just going for a walk . . . to sort things out, if you know what I mean." She smiled at him.

"I'll let you go on your way...I didn't mean to interrupt you or anything." He was over-apologetic.

"Don't be silly..." Her words carried no force.

"I have to get to work anyway." He tried to conceal his desire to be with her. "But if you'd like, you could give me a call. Anytime. I'm off for the next few days. I'd really like to see Brigid."

"Sure, I'll call you. Probably tomorrow, if it's all right with you."

"Fine, that's fine."

They stood there, not knowing what to do. Jim reached out his hand after a brief pause and Colleen grasped it. She leaned toward him and kissed him on the cheek.

"I'll call you tomorrow evening. Perhaps we can have dinner."

"Great, that would be great. I'll see you then." He turned away, walked a few steps and then stopped and looked at her again. "I'm glad we bumped into each other."

"So am I."

He hurried off and vanished behind the overgrowth around the bend.

Colleen lay in the sun, warmed by its heat and the warmth from the rock she rested upon. For some time, she had been absorbed in watching the birth of a cloud in the clear sky. At first, there was only the slightest trace of anything—a vaporous white wisp—in the pulsating summer sky. It looped, like the tail of a puppy, and soon wrapped itself about another trace of a cloud also similarly shaped.

The two converging spirals grew, gradually, lengthening and broadening, until they had spun themselves into a circle. The small cloud expanded as it moved toward the east. Although it was drifting away, it remained approximately the same size, indicating that it was becoming even larger.

She wondered what forces formed clouds, what forces moved living creatures and planets. What was this cycle of birth, growth, decline, and death that all things participated in? She thought of a tiny seed, buried in the rich, wet earth, bursting with—with what? With *something*, something that pushed aside stones and earth, pushed through the surface of the planet, to grow, to synthesize light into life, to beautify, to reproduce, and to make way for the seeds born of itself.

Colleen let her thoughts flow and they took her to heaven and hell, to images of what life on earth could be like and what it was like.

She imagined her grandmother as a young girl meeting her first lover and knew that, if it had happened, Grandmother Murphy would have felt the same jumble of emotions that overtook Colleen when she first met Jim. Colleen had never pictured Jim as anything other than the young man she had left years before.

If we had lived in a saner world, she thought, *what unknown fates would have been in store for us. If we could have touched one another innocently. If we could have borne our children in joy instead of torment.* Colleen knew that this simple example mirrored the agony of humanity. *Heaven is in our hearts and hell is in our heads. And we tear ourselves apart trying to stop the resulting pain. And when we do, our hearts stop beating.*

She sat up and watched the boats sail up the Hudson. Speedboats whirred like wasps as they maneuvered between sailboats. Colleen had never been on the water but imagined that she would rather do it on a sailboat than any other type of craft. They moved so gracefully and silently, with much more class than the hot-rodding speedboats.

Colleen tried to remember something she had read in the newspaper recently. A survey of some kind, a Gallup or Harris poll, or a psychological study. *That's it, a study done at Harvard, I think.* She searched her mind. *We spend most of our time thinking about sex.* She paused for a moment. *And that other study showed that we only use five percent of our mental capabilities. Yet nobody makes any connections! If we weren't raised in such a repressive manner, if we let our love grow and not fester, distorted, who knows what we would be able to accomplish?*

Colleen thought of her child. She wondered if she were doing anything wrong, if she were raising Brigid properly. Her grandmother's last words came to mind. Colleen was uncertain that she was up to the task of bringing up another human being. It suddenly seemed a staggering responsibility. She was not sure she was equal to the task.

Growing restless, not wanting to continue her train of thought, Colleen stood up and, after one last glance at the river, turned and began to head toward home. Rather than walk back toward Broadway, she decided to head north to the end of the park, where she would take the pedestrian crosswalk over the Henry Hudson Bridge into Riverdale, and follow Riverdale Avenue as it wound its way down to Kingsbridge. The walk was not much longer but it was more beautiful by far.

Many times as a child, and later with her husband, Colleen had traversed this same path. Her favorite part was the middle of the bridge. Above her, the cars heading north, buzzed as they sped by. Below lay Spuyten Duyvil, where the meeting of the Harlem and Hudson Rivers formed dangerous whirlpools. Colleen remembered schoolmates who had perished when they foolishly attempted to swim in those seething waters. She would stand there, above even the seagulls circling in search of fish or refuse, and become mesmerized by the unceasing motion. She always was seized by an impulse to jump, an impulse she quickly denied.

When she reached the middle of the bridge, the sun was setting and though she was impatient to get home, Colleen paused. She recalled her honeymoon in Key West, where most of the town gathered every evening to watch the sun drop into the aquamarine Gulf waters. Colleen wondered why both sunsets and autumn unfailingly made her melancholy. Much more than dawn or spring, they touched the heart of her feeling about life.

Without warning, like a whale bursting through the ocean waves with wild force and speed, grief rose from the depths of Colleen's being. Her chest heaved, her throat was seized with spasms, and salty tears flowed from her eyes.

Oh Grandma, Grandma... I loved you so much. Alone, bereaved, on a bridge above wild waters, Colleen mourned the loss of a singular woman.

"But neither affirms life," the jerky motion of the bus interfered with her handwriting, "In sublimation."

Lizzie closed the book and looked out the window as the bus climbed the steep hill up to Kingsbridge Heights. She looked to the west, beyond the curve of the Harlem River, beyond the skeletal elevated train tracks, past the hills of Inwood Park and the Palisades, and for some unknown reason, the sight made her sad, forlorn.

She opened her textbook again and wrote another note. "N. says morality is a disease but reason at any price, life made cold, clear, and cautious: another disease." She lost her interest in the subject and thought about her grandmother. She hadn't known the woman very well and was surprised at how greatly affected she was. It was Lizzie's first experience of death in the family and it touched her.

Although she did not believe in an afterlife, much to the consternation of her parents, she wondered if possibly, just possibly something might exist after this life. She smiled to herself and dismissed the thought without further question.

Lizzie ceased paying attention to the progress of the bus and nearly missed her stop. She yanked frantically on the bell-cord just as the driver was beginning to pull out from the stop. Begrudgingly, he opened the back door and she hopped out, only to be drowned in a cloud of exhaust from the bus. She put her hand over her mouth and stepped backwards but was unable to avoid the fumes.

She was early for her tutorial so she decided to go to her apartment in the Bensalem College building to leave a few papers and unneeded books which she was carrying. When she was in the lobby, the pay phone rang and she answered it.

"Hello, Bensalem College." She sounded light and cheerful.

"Liz, it's me, Colleen."

"Oh wow, I was just thinking of you!" She was genuinely pleased.

"I didn't know if you had a class tonight. I wanted to spend some time with you, you know, to talk and stuff. Are you busy tonight?"

"Not at all, come on over. My tutorial will be over in an hour or so. This'll be fantastic! You can see my school and my apartment and everything. Do you know how to get here?"

"Not really. I know I take the twenty bus, but where do I get off?"

"Belmont Avenue and you walk one block north to 191st and then make a right to 558. I'm in apartment thirty-four. If the door's locked, buzz me and I'll come right down."

"Great. I'll see you in an hour and a half or so, okay?"

"Far out. See you then." Lizzie hung up the phone and ran up the stairs feeling full of life.

Colleen lay on the bed, holding her sides, the laughter threatening to become painful. "Stop, Lizzie! Stop! I can't stand it anymore!" She could hardly breathe any longer.

"And then," Lizzie continued, ignoring her sister's pleading, "and then..." she burst into laughter herself. She choked on her words and lay on the floor, unable to stop laughing herself at the memory of a childhood incident.

"I'm surprised," Colleen sat up, wiping the tears from her eyes as her laughter subsided, "that you could remember all that. How old were you then? Four, five?"

"Something like that." Lizzie sat up and her eyes met her sister's. "God, it's so good to see you again. You know, these things weren't so funny when they happened. But, it gives me hope, you know, that the bad things now won't seem so bad later on. They aren't what's really important. They're like...like thorns, you know? Thorns around the roses."

"You know, Liz, I had this thing happen this afternoon." Colleen looked thoughtful. She was not looking at her sister as she spoke. "I met Jim today." She paused a moment. "And I was shocked. I couldn't believe that after all I had gone through . . . being in Berkeley, the whole Free Speech thing, the antiwar stuff, trying to raise Brigid, living with Mitch . . . just everything that's happened the past six or seven years . . . I mean, it's like it hasn't affected him one bit." She was confused. "It was strange because . . . well, all the bad feeling was gone and I wanted to...I thought of being with him again ...and it just wasn't possible."

Liz was interested in her older sister's feelings and listened intently.

"In a way,' Colleen continued, "the whole neighborhood is like that. Last night, I passed the candy stores at about ten to nine and there everybody was, milling about like people out of *The Invasion of the Body Snatchers*. They were standing on the corners waiting for the Daily News. Whatever the News said was true, was true. That was it! No questions, no other ideas could possibly have any value." She shook her head. "When I saw Jim, I just wondered how he could have given up so easily." She looked up, apologetic. "I guess I'm getting maudlin—and judgmental."

"No, don't be silly. I didn't say anything because I really don't know Jim and I never see him at all." She tried to think of something to say, to change the subject and bring back their light-hearted spirits.

"Say, did you ever read the Maslow title I suggested?"

Lizzie was grateful her sister had changed the topic herself. "I started to read it but I couldn't get into it much. I was kind of busy and, maybe I'll get back to it, you know, when—"

"If you want; it's no big thing." Colleen thought of Professor Nils and grew angry. "I was really into Maslow for a while," Colleen felt she was not being honest and decided to tell her sister the truth. "Actually, I was *into this professor* who was into Maslow. And I thought he, Maslow, was pretty interesting, in a way, but I sort of got all enthused to be what this teacher wanted me to be. You know what I mean?"

"I sure do!" Lizzie laughed. "Oh boy do I know what you mean! I'm doing it right now. I don't really like philosophy but the guy I'm taking my tutorial with is really something!"

"Well, my little sister is not so little anymore." Colleen felt relaxed.

"Did you and this professor...uh ...I mean...well, you know, *did you*?" She felt very young all of a sudden.

"Liz!" Colleen's reaction was automatic. "Oh, don't worry," she laughed lightly. "Yes, *we did*. But I wish we hadn't. Mitch was very hurt and I don't know if—"

"You told him?" Lizzie was incredulous.

"No, but it wasn't hard to figure out. I think everything is all right but ...I think maybe I kind of ruined things in a way. Not completely. But I put something in the way or took away something special. I don't really know how to say it. But things are not as direct and uncomplicated as they were before." Colleen's eyes turned inward.

"Anyway, I finally picked up a book that Mitch had been trying to get me to read and it's incredible. I can't believe how heavy it is."

Lizzie got up from the floor and walked into the bedroom. "Do you mind if I put on some music."

"Not at all," Colleen replied. "Do you have Janis Joplin and Big Brother?"

"I sure do. That's just what I was going to play." Lizzie placed the needle on the record and sat on her bed, a mattress and box spring on the floor, covered with an Indian bedspread from Azuma, an inexpensive store favored by students and hippies. "Would you like to smoke?" She asked nonchalantly, holding out a joint.

"You really have gotten older," Colleen was surprised. "As a matter of fact, I wouldn't mind at all. But first, let me show you this book I mentioned. I've been trying to find others by the author but there aren't many in print for some reason." She reached into her bag and handed the paperback to Lizzie.

"*The Function of the Orgasm*?" She lit up a joint and inhaled.

"Well, that's what it's about." Colleen took the joint from her sister. "Look, I'm almost finished with it. I'll leave it for you before I go.

Promise you'll read it? It's far out, really."

"Okay, this one I'll read."

The two sisters concentrated on the task at hand—getting stoned to the sound of Big Brother and the Holding Company.

He had asked to be left alone but they had not acceded to his wishes. Grandfather Murphy was glad that they hadn't. He sat in his chair, his son across from him, in the living room he had grown up in, and they both knew the other's thoughts were on the woman, mother, and wife, who had given life to the son and maintained life in the father.

Grandfather Murphy, a voluble, expressive man, was perplexed by his feelings, or rather, the absence of feelings. Where were the grief, the sense of loss, the longing, the heart-breaking tender memories, the furious, futile rage, the childish pleading for her to come back, the desperate hope against all reason that she was not really dead at all, that this had not really happened and some act of will could recall his wife from death.

He remembered once standing on a flat Midwestern plain, strangely unnerved, wary, the sky growing green to the west, boding a terrible tumult. He now felt the same way he had on that afternoon when he had watched a tornado rise almost out of nowhere, tearing the neighboring house from its foundations, killing its inhabitants, leaving his friend's home safe, untouched.

The hand of fate had touched him. He knew he was awaiting the inner storm; that this time he would not be spared. Grandfather Murphy knew where the suffering lay—in the bedroom, at night, in the long morning hours where he had once held Brigid in his arms. It lay in the memory of her so human face. It lay ahead.

Irene Murphy joined the men, bringing them their tea, offering her father-in-law a shot of whiskey, which he refused. She wished there were something she could say to them, father and son, but she knew words would only act as irritants. When her own parents had died, so many years before, she had appreciated the sentiments spoken in earnest, but felt all words to be an intrusion, a distraction from the necessary introspection, the coming to grips with the permanence of the loss, and the anxiety brought about by the overwhelming reality of one's own mortality. She prayed quietly to herself.

"It's been a good life," Grandfather Murphy spoke with strained vigor, "made so by a remarkable woman." His voice trembled ever so slightly.

Without warning, he excused himself from the room. Mr. and Mrs. Murphy heard him close the bedroom door behind him. They came together, took one another in their arms, fully appreciating how precious life is.

They heard Grandfather Murphy cry out, calling his wife. And though they wished to go to him in his Gethsemane, they knew he had to drink this cup alone.

With the final prayers spoken and the coffin lowered into the earth, the mourners expressed their condolences to the immediate family, promised to keep in touch, offered their aid any time it was needed, and drove off in their cars to have lunch and take up their lives where they had left off.

Grandfather Murphy barely heard a word that was spoken to him. He watched great cumulus clouds cruise, like sailing ships of old, driven by the wind across the sky. He breathed in the crisp air and noticed that, though it was still summer, autumn had made its appearance. He could feel it in his bones.

Across the landscaped grounds of the cemetery, in the wild growth on either side of the superhighway that ran through the valley below, Grandfather Murphy spied the first red leaves of fall. He studied the landscape and found orange, yellow, and even blue leaves in the trees. He recalled a day many years before when he and his wife had gone to a wedding in Boston. The train, belching black smoke, carried them through the hills. The New England autumn was at its peak and he felt he was seeing a natural kaleidoscope. *Brigid loved the autumn,* he thought.

Mrs. Murphy took the old man by the arm. "Come, now, Pop. It's time to go home."

As he walked along the graveyard path, the word home took on a menacing tone. Grandfather Murphy realized that he did not want to go home; that home had been his wife, not merely a place. Wherever his wife was, that to him was home. *I have no home,* he heard his own voice in his mind. It was frightened. He kept these thoughts to himself.

During the ride home, Colleen sat next to her Grandfather and held his hand. Little Brigid sat in the old man's lap, asking him questions which he answered absently.

Mercifully, the ride was brief and they soon reached the Murphy's apartment. "Would you like to come upstairs for a bit, Pop?" Mr. Murphy asked.

"I think I'll go for a walk ...I'll stop by later. There are some things I've got to sort out." He stepped out of the car and stood by the driver's window, stooping a bit to talk to his son. "Don't look so worried. I just want to be alone for a while. I feel worn out, if you know what I mean...Drained."

"Sure... I understand, Pop. We'll see you later on." The old man walked away slowly, his head bent slightly, his hands in his pockets.

The rest of the family went upstairs to their apartment while Mr. Murphy drove off in search of a parking place. No one would ever admit they felt better now that the whole business was finally over.

Inside, however, they all felt relieved to be out from under the strain of the wake, the funeral services, and the burial. For Mr. and Mrs. Murphy the thought was not conscious, whereas for the children it was, with varying degrees of guilt felt by each for having such emotions.

As he walked along the streets, not looking where he was going, following a route he and his wife had taken countless times, Grandfather Murphy felt the icy numbness gradually melting away, yielding to an aching confusion.

He turned onto Broadway, just north of Gaelic Park and entered Van Cortlandt Park. The old man passed the children playing softball, barely hearing their screaming and yelling. He was oblivious to the track-runners as they circled round and round as he walked on toward the boathouse.

Grandfather Murphy was roused from his reverie when he heard someone called his name. He looked up frightened.

"How are you, old boy?" The man reached out his hand with a sad friendliness.

"Martin..." Grandfather Murphy grasped the outstretched hand with both of his and did not want to let go.

"I just heard about Brigid," he looked his old friend in the eyes. "I've been up in Boston with Patrick and his brood. Brigid was a fine woman." He shook his head sadly.

"That she was," Grandfather Murphy replied almost to himself. "It's funny going on without her......I'm kind of off balance now; adrift if you know what I mean . . ." He felt embarrassed.

"Are you busy now? Why don't you come and have a drink with me? It'll do you good to talk." Martin put his hand on his old friend's shoulder. "What do you say?" The old man nodded yes and they walked off silently.

The tavern was dark, lit by dim amber lights. The contrast with the brilliant sunny skies was so great, it took minutes before their eyes could fully adjust. Grandfather Murphy often found the darkness of bars, especially on a beautiful afternoon, depressing. This day, however, he found it matched his mood.

The two men shared a few beers, quietly discussing the wake, the funeral, and the burial. Martin listened to his friend, asking appropriate questions on occasion, but letting his companion speak his mind. He knew that soon he would speak his heart.

"You know, I'm almost afraid to go back to the apartment," he confessed. "When I'm there, it's like Brigid isn't dead at all. Everything's the same—her clothes are in the closet, her powders and perfumes are in the medicine cabinet." His voice choked slightly. "I half-expect...no, I fully expect that she'll just walk in ...I know I'm a damned fool but I can't get it through my thick skull that she's gone!" He pounded his fist to the bar in forlorn rage. "Goddammit, I don't want her gone!" Grandfather Murphy put his head in his hands to cover his tears. "I don't know what's to become of me, Martin..."

"I know I'm about as much use to you as a broken arm right now," Martin put his hand on his friend's shoulder. "What I say isn't worth a bit ...but you'll continue living, Tom." He was almost whispering but there was a gentle strength in his tone. It comforted Grandfather Murphy but it also made him weep more strongly. "Just let it out, however long it takes, and then, it will be gone. Like a great weight being lifted from your back. Your grief will slowly be gone ...and you'll find that deeper, much deeper than any loss, is the love Brigid gave you." He didn't know if his friend were listening or not but he continued. "It's there like the sun is there even when there's the most dreadful storm imaginable. The sun is still shining and it will still shine when the storm passes. Brigid's love is just like that sun. It will still warm you."

Grandfather Murphy began to cry uncontrollably and his friend waited for him, patiently.

No one knew what to say. They sat around the living room, reading or watching TV, every one of them trying to think of some way to relieve the pressure they felt. Grandfather Murphy sat by the window, watching the sun set, just as he always did. Mr. and Mrs. Murphy sat at the dining room table, their dessert and tea before them, just as they did each evening. The children sat in the living room as they had for years, but the only thought on their minds was how to make the most graceful exit possible.

Colleen stood up, excused herself, and went to the kitchen telephone. She dialed Jim's number let it ring for some time and was about to hang up when he finally answered. "Jim? It's me." She felt uneasy.

"Colleen, I'm so glad you called. I was beginning to think you wouldn't." He was overjoyed.

"Oh, you know how it is...the wake and all that." His excitement made her feel more uneasy. She wondered if she had made a mistake.

"Well," he seemed to have sensed it, "What's on your mind?"

"I don't know. Would you like to go for a walk or something?" Colleen did not sound particularly interested.

"Uh...If you want to..." He said, confused.

A silence ensued.

"Why don't I meet you on 231st and Broadway, in front of the bank? All right?"

"Great. What time?" Jim sounded pleased.

"Ten minutes? Or fifteen...better make it fifteen." Colleen was conflicted.

"Okay, sure. I'll see you later." Jim was happy he was going to meet with Colleen.

"Yeah... okay." Colleen hung up the phone absently, feeling out of touch with herself.

Colleen got her handbag, said goodbye to her relatives, and left the apartment. On her way downstairs, she paused and, for a moment, considered calling Jim and backing out. "I'm just being silly," she told herself. "It will be nice to see him again."

Colleen wondered if she were upset because Jim might want to be with her again, or more, that she might still be attracted to him. She decided not to think about it.

The local IRT subway train rattled overhead and pulled into the 231st Street station. She heard the voice of the conductor crackle over the intercom, comprehensible only if one already knew what he was saying. Colleen looked up the block at the clock outside the jeweler's shop. As usual, it was wrong. She found it amusing that the man who repaired your watch couldn't keep his clock working correctly.

Jim came up behind her and surprised Colleen. He tickled her ribs and kissed her on the nape of the neck. She was pleased and slightly annoyed simultaneously.

"Jim! Please..." She studied him. "Have you been drinking?"

"Just a couple of beers." He smiled at her. "Look, I brought my car. I thought you might like to go to City Island for dinner. I know this great restaurant there. What do you say?"

"Sounds terrific. Let's go." Colleen had expected to go to one of the local taverns, talk for a while, and fend off Jim's invitations to return to his place. "What kind of car do you have?" She asked as they walked up Broadway.

"A Chevy convertible. It's red ...a little beat up ...but it's in good shape. I work on it at the station whenever I get a free moment. It's got a brand-new engine." He was parked nearby and they reached the car shortly.

When she saw the automobile, Colleen almost laughed. It was so dilapidated, with paint rusting on the body and springs sticking out of the back seat, that if it weren't Jim's she would never get in.

"What a jalopy you've got . . . It's far out." She tried to open the door but it was stuck.

"You'll have to climb in. Door's broken." Jim went around to the driver's side. "Don't worry, Colleen. It's a very safe car."

"I doubt it but I'll get in anyway."

Jim revved the motor and a cloud of exhaust came from the back. The car smelled of gasoline. He pulled out of the space and they were on their way. Jim drove very well, maintaining a constant speed, making all the lights. He cruised along Bailey Avenue, turned left up "Suicide Hill" and along Kingsbridge Road. Colleen remembered nights as a teenager, rainy nights when she and her friends would congregate at the bottom of "Suicide Hill" and watch cars take the last sharp turn too fast, lose control, and smash into parked cars or the side of a building. She never saw anyone injured but she was now amazed that she had ever done such a thing.

They drove down Fordham Road, passed Jahn's Ice Cream Parlor, where she and Jim had gone on their first date. She remembered it so well. *I was wearing my white dress, and I was very tan...Jim couldn't keep his hands off my legs,* she thought and smiled to herself as she recalled their date.

"What are you thinking about?" Jim asked as he sped under the Third Avenue El, past Fordham University and Roosevelt High School.

"Just thinking," Colleen replied. She wanted to keep her thoughts to herself.

"Remember when we went to Jahn's?" Jim asked, glancing over at her but immediately turning his eye to the road.

"That's incredible—I was just thinking about that myself." Colleen shifted in her seat and turned to Jim. "It must be that I picked up your vibes...kind of like ESP, you know?"

"I think it's pretty logical that we would both think about that...it isn't really that," he paused as he turned into the fast lane on Pelham Parkway, sped up and beat a red light. "It isn't really that unusual."

Colleen leaned back in the seat. "I guess not . . . We had so much fun then, didn't we?"

"I guess we did... " He was focused on the road.

The air was cooler under the trees along the Parkway. Colleen watched the last rays of the sun glinting off the leaves. She saw the first few stars of the evening and the crescent moon shining in the sky. She was glad she had gone out with Jim.

Small sailboats came in from Long Island Sound to their slips on City Island. The larger craft, anchored off the island, listed and creaked in the night. Off in the west, Colleen could see the skyscrapers of Manhattan, the necklace-like bridges spanning the waters glowing blue-white, and an airplane taking off from LaGuardia airport, climbing lazily into the skies.

"You know," Jim spoke while opening another oyster. "There was a time when people thought that City Island might become a more important port than New York. They were actually rivals early in our history."

Colleen looked around at the quaint little island and could not imagine how such a thing would have been possible. "It's a bit more than wishful thinking. It's more like dementia!"

After they had finished their meal, Jim suggested that they go to another restaurant for dessert. "It's called the Black Whale and it's terrific. What do you say?"

"You're the expert," Colleen felt herself starting to desire Jim. She took his hand, squeezed it gently, and smiled. "Shall we be on our way?"

The Black Whale was a short drive down City Island Avenue. Colleen loved the place as soon as she entered. It was dark and intimate, with a lovely garden out back, tastefully designed with Tiffany lamps, and wrought-iron tables and chairs with marble tops and seats. "It's fantastic, Jim." She took his arm.

They were escorted into the garden by a waitress and seated in the corner, alone. "This is the best seat in the restaurant!"

"Only the best for us." Jim smiled broadly.

"Would you like a drink?" the waitress asked.

"I'll have a Heineken. What about you, Colleen?"

"Well, let's see . . ." She surveyed the menu. "I'll have a white wine cassis." She looked at the young man across from her and felt so comfortable in his company. "It's good to be with you again, Jim."

"And it's good to see you again, Colleen." The waitress placed their drinks on the table. They picked them up and toasted one another's health.

"Next on OR-FM," Colleen heard the radio disc jockey announce, "The Beatles with 'Yesterday.'"

"Jim, do you still see the people we grew up with?" Colleen asked, curious.

"Some of them . . . I still see Harry," they both smiled, "and he's still Harry. Most of the guys moved away...out to the island, upstate...some of them became cops. Lou—you remember Lou—he's with the F.B.I."

"What?" Colleen was shocked. "Wow...did he change. I can't imagine that they would even take him." She thought for a moment about her old friend's wild youth. "How is Billy, Billy Webster?" Colleen could see him, a fifteen-year-old splashing water at her in the local swimming pool on a summer day.

"He's dead...went to Vietnam...you know," Jim paused and thought for a moment. "He was drafted. He didn't know how to get out of it.

He wasn't in college or anything. He never even got to fight. A helicopter carrying him and a bunch of guys was shot down."

They looked at one another, Colleen saddened, Jim resigned. "A lot of guys from around here went. Some wanted to; some didn't but were afraid to try to get out. Sometimes I think that the guys who died are luckier than the ones who came back. Paralyzed; missing legs or arms; blind. Or worse, the guys whose bodies are sound but who are crazy. Quietly crazy, but someday going to explode."

"It's disgusting," Colleen said angrily. "Americans think they can inflict this violence on others without it affecting them. But like Malcolm X had said, the chickens will come home to roost. This war will ruin our country."

"Colleen, let's not talk about the war, all right?" Jim signaled the waitress. "I'd like another. You, Colleen'?" She nodded yes.

"But you do think it's insane?" She persisted in discussing the war. "It's madness! Taking lives, wasting resources, and throwing it all away bombing a country into oblivion; napalming babies; defoliating the land; propping up a corrupt, tyrannical dictatorship-"

"Colleen, please," Jim interrupted her, "it's all anyone ever talks about."

"People should talk about it!" She became angry. "People should scream and yell about it until everyone listens and stops the goddamn war."

"Colleen, listen to me." Jim motioned for her to lower her voice. "You're against the war. I'm against the war. But why do we have to discuss this now? I haven't seen you in years. I'd like to speak with you, not listen to speeches about the war. I can hear them anytime I want. But you'll be gone soon." He reached across the table and took her hand. "We were so close ...but I don't know you anymore. I'd like to get to know you again."

"I'm sorry, Jim. It's just that the whole thing is so...so frustrating." She sipped her wine, staring into the glass. "Would you like to go for a walk?"

"Sure... right now?" He called the waitress and asked for the check. "I know a place where we can be completely alone." He had a peculiar smile on his face.

"Why do you look like that?" They left the restaurant and Colleen followed Jim across City Island Avenue and down Fordham Street. The small wood-frame homes, tilting white picket fences, and the barely paved road made her feel as if she had stepped through a time warp and traveled back to the turn of the century.

"It's like Winesburg, Ohio here!" She joked.

"Like what?" Jim did not understand the reference.

"Oh, that's a novel about small-town America." She felt slightly bad, hoping she hadn't embarrassed Jim. "I can't believe something like this exists in New York." She took Jim by the arm and felt herself growing apprehensive. "Where are we going?"

"You'll see."

At the end of the road was an old dock and what appeared to be a ferry moored beside it. Across a small stretch of water lay another island and she could barely make out the outlines of a few buildings. Fog was drifting in across the sound and she heard the mournful moan of a foghorn far in the distance.

They turned onto a small street which ran parallel to the shore and traveled along it for a few minutes. Suddenly Colleen stopped, appalled. "I'm not stepping, one foot in there!" She took her arm away. "Don't be so childish. It's a lovely place." Jim held out his hand.

"You're crazy if you think I'm going into a cemetery in the dark!" She stopped and would not take another step.

"Oh, Colleen, come on. We'll just walk through down to the water. It's a lovely view. It's so quiet and nobody will be there to bother us."

"I don't know why," she spoke sarcastically. However, she relented and went with Jim into the cemetery.

Many of the tombstones tilted in the earth, their names and

messages worn smooth by the sea-wind and rain. Colleen felt reflective; she began to think about her grandmother's gravesite, about her own eventual death.

They sat in a secluded spot beneath a small tree and were silent. There were no stars to be seen. The sky sat above them was as flat and lusterless as a black cheesecloth stage scrim. "What are you thinking?" Jim asked.

"About my grandmother..." She replied thoughtfully.

Jim felt foolish. He realized that he should have known better than to go to a cemetery with her. "I'm sorry I took you here. I just...just wasn't thinking." He didn't know what to say. "I...I'm sorry Colleen...It didn't occur to me that—"

"Oh, don't worry, Jim. Everything reminds me of my grandmother right now. The neighborhood, Little Brigid, my grandfather...even you." She took his hand and gently stroked it. She felt close to him.

"Colleen." He cleared his throat. "Do you ever wish...you know...that it could have been different with us?" He cleared his throat. "Or that someday...do you ever imagine that we..." He couldn't bring himself to say it.

When she looked at him, it amazed Colleen that once more she felt her old love for him. A great tenderness arose in her, a powerful urge to comfort and be comforted in return. "I'm imagining right now." She kissed him. It was a new and familiar kiss.

Colleen lay in Jim's arms, eyes closed, thinking of nothing at all. Jim held her and the sweetness he felt almost pained. He thought of the years longing for her, of the dreams from which he awoke at four in the morning only to realize that he was not with Colleen, that she had not returned to him, of the energy spent thinking about her. He drew her closer to him, shivering with love and fear, knowing that shortly she would be gone.

As she turned her face toward his chest, Colleen brushed a piece of paper sticking out of Jim's pocket. "Oww, what is that?" She sat up.

"Are you all right?" Jim didn't want her to see the paper and he instinctively placed his hand over his pocket.

"I'm okay. It just startled me. What is it anyway,"

"Nothing ...just a paper with a note on it." He tried to remove it and place the paper in his back pocket but Colleen persisted.

"What is it? Some girl's phone number?" She tickled him and tried to get the paper from him. "Come on, let me see!"

"All right, all right. Now don't laugh...it's something I wrote after I met you in the park that night." He gave her the paper and turned from her.

"Jim, is this a poem?" Colleen was surprised.

"I don't know if it is . . . it's just my thoughts." He stood up and went down to the shore.

Colleen did not notice him stand up and walk away. She read and re-read the words written on the page.

It is a dream
of return
A dream revealing and concealing
a deep yearning

The image is of you
the act is
the embrace
The dreamer is in tears
at the sight
of your face

Suddenly all vanishes and his
eyes open
He knows he must

> *be silent for*
> *all deep emotions*
> *become clichés*
> *when spoken and the truth of the dream disappears*
> *like a scream in the night*
> *the moment you*
> *have woken*

Colleen could not collect her thoughts. She had never imagined that Jim would ever write his feelings down or that if he did it would be in such a manner.

"Jim," she called out, "let's go home." She went to him and put her arms around him from behind, kissing his neck as she did. "Let's go home together."

The morning light came through the cracks in the Venetian blinds. Colleen rubbed her hands on Jim's chest as he lay back, slowly smoking a cigarette. "You have a lot of hair on your chest now," she spoke sleepily, curling the hairs around her fingers.

"I'm older now..." He replied absently.

"I remember when you only had one."

"And I remember when you had none," he teased.

"None what?" Colleen looked up at him.

"Hair on your chest." Jim reached down and smacked her behind.

"Bully..." She lay her head in the crook of his arm.., "Jim, what's it been like for you? You know, these last few years...I wanted to call you or write you but something was there, in the way. It just didn't seem to be the right thing to do; it seemed selfish."

"It's been okay, I guess...sort of..." He took one last drag on the cigarette and crushed it in the ashtray. "Actually, Colleen, if you want to know the truth..." He hesitated.

"I do want to know the truth." She was sincere and serious.

"It's been pretty lousy...I...Well, as you can imagine, I pretty much fell apart when you left," Jim admitted. "It was like...it was wrenching...an agony that alternated with a dullness. Gradually, the pain lessened and was gone...but the dullness remained ...I went out with different people but it never worked out. Sometimes I liked them but they didn't like me; other times it was just the opposite. But even when it seemed to be working out it wasn't...

"I got lazy...wasted my time... didn't care about anything really." He looked into Colleen's eyes. "I don't think a day has gone by that I haven't thought of you...or a night when I didn't wish that we could be together again." He looked at her imploringly. "But, I know we can't."

"Jim," she kissed him softly. "I hope I haven't hurt you again...opened up old wounds."

"No, no! Not at all. You know, when I saw you the other day, I was ashamed..." He sat up in bed.

"What do you mean?"

"Well, in the years since we broke up, I let myself go to pot, really...and I don't just mean a pot belly, either." He smiled weakly. "And when I saw you I thought...I just wondered what you thought of me...I knew you could see how I'd changed and I felt really bad. But it turned out to be the best thing that could have happened. I had to face myself, look at myself, and realize that I was not acting in my own best interest. Things weren't terrible—I was making them not good."

"That's wonderful," Colleen held his hand. "I did see how different you were but didn't feel that I could say anything to you. I didn't want to hurt you."

"You used to tell me that I was the only person you knew who looked better without clothes than with them!" They both laughed at the memory. "Well, I want to be that person again."

Colleen laughed, surprised. "Did I say that? Oooh, what a forward wench I was!"

Jim lay back down beside Colleen. "Good night, wench."

Embracing, they fell to sleep.

Liz carried the last of her things into the apartment. She smiled to her lover and then, impulsively, ran to him and threw her arms around him. "I can't believe it—I'm now living with you. It feels so fabulous!"

"I love you, Lizzie . . . You aren't upset anymore?" He thought of her fears about telling her parents, which had disturbed her so greatly the night before, and wondered how she had resolved them so quickly, doubting that she had resolved them at all.

"Well, they'll just have to accept it," she spoke with false bravado, waving her hand in the air with self-conscious casualness as if to dismiss the problem lightly. "And anyway, I don't really have to tell them..." She looked at Lou. "Don't look at me like that ...I just mean right away, that's all. I'll tell them." She frowned.

"You're so funny sometimes..." He laughed lightly.

"Funny? What's so funny?" She sulked.

"Oh come on ...stop being silly." He reached for her but Liz left the room.

"So now I'm *silly*." She would not look at him.

"Don't be stupid, that's not what I-" He realized he now had both feet in his mouth.

"*Stupid!*" She yelled. "So now I'm stupid! Well, is that the kind of person you want to live with? A stupid girl? She looked at him and her pose failed. Liz began to cry. She hid her face in her hands. "I am stupid..." She spoke between sobs. "I'm afraid to stand up for what I want, for what will make me happy...I have all these conflicting feelings…I don't want to hurt my parents but I don't want to hurt myself." She sniffled and tried to stop her tears. "I want to live with you, Louis. I love you. But part of me thinks maybe I'm just doing this, you know, for some neurotic reason…But I know that what I'm doing is right."

"We all go through it, honey." He spoke lovingly. "If you don't, you remain a child your whole life. It's not neurotic to live your love life…just the opposite is true. It's neurotic to not have the strength to live your life, to sacrifice happiness in love and accept substitutes that can never cover the emptiness you feel all the time." He put his arms around her. "You'll do what you have to do in your own time …You know I'll be there to back you up."

Without warning, Louis lifted Liz off her feet. "What are you doing?" She yelled with delight.

"I'm just going to carry you across the threshold young lady, and into the boudoir."

"Oh my man, you're so strong. Hold me in your arms forever," she said in a feathery southern accent. Louis kicked the bedroom door closed behind him.

It puzzled Irene Murphy so deeply that she could not explain the feeling even to herself. Everyone was speaking so much lately about how things were changing but Mrs. Murphy resisted the very idea of change. She believed that things were declining morally rather than changing. Everywhere you looked, in the papers, in magazines, on the television—in your own home—there was revolution.

First it was the civil rights business, she mused, *then this antiwar and anti-America nonsense. And now they talk about a sexual revolution! All the traditional values are gone. Kids are taking all kinds of drugs, they don't get married, they live in these communes that you read about.* She was terribly discouraged.

It disturbed her greatly but she was now getting the first inklings of something much more disturbing. Mrs. Murphy felt that *she was changing*, being changed by the world events that were racing by. Even the Church is changing... Mass in the vernacular...and folk songs during Mass ...And now you can eat meat on Friday! She wanted to ask someone who understood to explain all of this to her, if only she knew someone who understood what was happening.

She spread some grape jelly on a Saltine cracker and looked up at her husband. She wanted to say something to him but didn't know what. Mrs. Murphy felt that soon she would have to say anything to him, just to start a conversation that might lead somewhere.

"You know dear," she began self-consciously, "I've been thinking about the children. It's all turning out so differently than I thought it would be when we were courting." She paused for a response but there was none.

He continued to read his paper. Realizing that she was probably speaking only to herself, Mrs. Murphy shrugged her shoulders and continued nonetheless. "I imagined a nice bunch of children, bright but not too bright; sometimes too much brains can cause trouble for you. I would picture them married, with children of their own, maybe a home in the suburbs...What went wrong? Was it us?"

"Certainly not," he replied quickly, proving he had been listening to his wife. "It's just that there's all this bloody nonsense going on and the young people are swallowing it all. They don't respect the old values. Mind you, I can see that some things were wrong . . . some things should have been changed ...but they've gone too far:" He never looked up as he spoke.

"But what about our children?" She asked plaintively. "We raised them properly, to be decent, honest, to be good Catholics. Poor Colleen had to get divorced and mixed up with all those California beatniks or hippies or whatever they are. And Eddie got his young head full of your father's tales of the old country and—"

"Don't go blaming Pop for the mess Eddie got himself into. The boy is old enough to know what he's doing and to know better." Peter Murphy still did not look up.

"And Tommy!" Her tone became harsh. "Living in sin the way he did..." She paused and reflected. "But now he's alone again...I thought I would feel so much better. The only thing I would have liked more would have been if he'd married her. He's alone again and I don't feel better at all. Now there's Lizzie... Lord knows what kind of education she'll get at that Bensalem School... and moving in with that young man."

Mrs. Murphy bit her tongue. She had completely forgotten that she had not told her husband of his daughter's new living situation.

"What?" Her husband sat up straight in his chair. "Did I hear you correctly? Elizabeth has moved in with a young man?" He put his paper down and took off his glasses. "How long have you known about this?"

"I only found out yesterday, Mrs. Murphy was flustered. I didn't know how to...She has moved in with one of the boys from school."

The anger vanished from Mr. Murphy's face, replaced by resignation. "What the hell could we expect ...Look at the example of her older sister and brother." He shook his head and picked up the newspaper. "I'm going inside to lie down for a bit."

In a way, I feel bad for the children, she thought, sitting alone. *I know they think they're being free ... but it seems so much harder for them than it was for us. We just did what one did, what one was expected to do. Today there are so many new things; so many things we didn't know anything about. All this assassination business, riots in the cities, crime everywhere, people protesting about this thing or that.*

Mrs. Murphy felt more tolerant than even a few years ago and wondered whether her tolerance arose from apathy or understanding. She decided it arose from her love for her children. *It's not like they have done anything terrible. They are honest; they are good. It's just this business of living together and all that ...Oh, I don't know.*

Time to get Father's dinner underway. Mrs. Murphy finished her tea and stopped her musings. She lost herself in the preparation of the food.

Lizzie sat in the kitchen reading by the warm amber light of an incandescent bulb in the wall lamp. There was a fluorescent ceiling light in the room but she never used it. She had finally gotten around to reading the book her sister had lent her, *The Function of the Orgasm* by Wilhelm Reich. Unlike most books, which she raced through, she could only read a few pages at a time. It was well written and interesting but it struck home extremely often, in specific and personal ways. Reading it proved very unsettling.

As she read, Lizzie began to feel all the things she was reading in her body. Her breathing *was* shallow, she felt her face to be taut, and she became aware of a tension in the pelvic region. She put the book down and walked into the living room. She thought for a moment. *This book is so well-written it almost makes me feel like I'm armored, like I've got the problems he's writing about... maybe I do.*

Lizzie began to feel anxious. She realized that it was what she was reading that was making her feel uneasy—because it was true. She decided to stop for the day. *I'll continue tomorrow.* She marked her place and put the book on her desk.

She tried to pass some time by paging through a few magazines but nothing caught her interest. For a few pages, she enjoyed a novel that was abridged in a woman's magazine but her thoughts strayed and she put it down. She could not stop thinking about what she had just read by Reich. Rather than attempt to avoid her thoughts any longer, Lizzie decided to give them free reign. She went to her desk and began to write in her diary.

> Colleen gave me a book to read: Reich's Function of the Orgasm. People react so peculiarly to the title and I must admit so do I. It disturbs me in many ways but it is fascinating. Most people build elaborate theories, based on a few facts. He uses many interconnected facts to construct the foundation of a simple but deep scientific theory. I feel that his thinking is both the completion of Western thought and yet stands outside of it. Reich says he is radical, meaning "going to the root of things." He doesn't mean it politically, or like any of the so-called radicals of today. I think this book, along with his others, will change me. That frightens me.

The apartment door opened and she stopped writing.

She heard Louis call out, "Margaret, I'm home!" He was imitating an old television show, "Father Knows Best."

"When are you going to stop making that corny joke?" She laughed and hugged him.

"Never...that's what makes it funny—repetition." He took an envelope from his jacket pocket. "And you and I are going to celebrate tonight. I got the fellowship!"

"Far out! I'm so happy for you!" She hugged him.

"Well, shall we dine in style at Rusty's? One of those great Rustyburgers?"

"Sounds divine, dah-ling," she said as she put her arms around his waist and placed her head against his chest. "You know, I used to be so pessimistic . . . which was silly for someone my age. But now I feel I'm just at the beginning of things ...really wonderful things."

She looked up at him, glowing.

"I think you are, Liz. I think you are." He kissed her, gently. "Come on, get your coat and let's celebrate."

Colleen sat at a table in the Japanese Tea Garden in Golden Gate Park writing letters to her family. She had finished the ones to her parents, her grandfather, and her brothers and was now writing to her sister. She had returned with her daughter to San Francisco following her grandmother's funeral. But she he had decided to move back to New York. Her relationship with Mitch was not working and there was nothing else to keep her on the West Coast.

> *Dear Liz,*
>
> *I was just re-reading your letter this morning. Glad to hear you're so happy. I have decided to move back to New York for a number of reasons which we can talk about in person. I should be in the city by the end of the month. I'm a bit ambivalent but know this is the right thing to do.*
>
> *This morning, in the aquarium, I saw a strange sight. One light seahorse was floating in a fish tank, being attacked by*

these ugly little fish shaped like boxes. They had sharp, pointed protuberances on their heads and they were tearing the poor seahorse apart. It was an awful thing. I began to think about people and how we attack one another. We do it out of a lack in ourselves; out of a malice that arises because we have lost the natural capacity to love. All too often, the victims are like the innocent seahorse. They just happen to be there.

Here we are injuring one another over the pettiest of problems. It's all a great noise to keep from realizing how lost and terrified we are. We don't know what the universe is; what the solar system is or how it got here; what electricity, gravity or magnetism are; why the earth turns; what is weather; where we came from; how life began.

Most of all we don't understand ourselves.

We don't know what life is at all. But we maim, kill, injure all those who differ from our view of life, which is sick life. If only we could turn our energies from fruitless pursuits, how much we could learn about Life as it really is, and not just life as we know it.

I don't want to sound melodramatic but I think that we—all of us on earth—have reached a turning point. We will have to choose Life over Death. Or perish. But how we will do that when no one knows what Life is, I don't know. Anyway, love to you and I will see you soon.

Yours,
Colleen

She read her letter over, folded it, and sealed it in the stamped envelope. Colleen finished her tea and left the garden. As she walked along, she thought of her daughter. *Maybe Brigid will know ...maybe the children will experience Life.*

She stopped and looked into the sky. Colleen thought she saw bright little particles dancing before her eyes. She wondered if they were just in her eyes. With a shrug of the shoulder, she started on her way home, wondering where the truth was to be found. She thought of a line from Goethe:

What is the hardest of all to see?
That which lies
right before your eyes.

PART THREE

1976

Colleen awoke moments before the birds began to sing. She was tense and trembling from the dream she had just had. Obscured by muted colors, faceless human forms with definite but unrecognized identities had engaged her in philosophic conversation. Some spoke of Heraclitus and Parmenides; some held exchanges on Plato and Augustine or Aristotle and Aquinas; one dream creature—now a medieval monk, now a 20th-century American nun—discoursed on the origin and continuance of Sin.

Colleen kept pace with them, attempting to join in. She spoke with conviction but was unheard. Frustrated, she tried ever more desperately to express her perceptions and thoughts but remained ignored.

Those discussing philosophy grew grey and vanished in an increasing mist but the androgynous mystic turned to Colleen and proclaimed with falsely humble malice, "There is no understanding possible of the origin or the continuance of Sin. There is no reason even to try...Accept...Yield to the divinely ordained human condition. Pray...pray and seek solace and wisdom in Him!"

As the figure vanished, Colleen found her voice and screamed, "I know the source of Original Sin and the origin of its continuance!" The figure was no more. Colleen stood alone, nowhere.

"We kill love in our children—that's the source of sin! It is their and our dead genitals that breed continued hatred and sin, sin no Satan could sow ...cruelty no Devil could devise."

Colleen awoke and lay in the bed feeling more alone than ever. She cried as the first birds sang in the moments before dawn. Then it dawned on her, *this is the day my Brigid was born...April 9...sweet sixteen.*

"Let's go watch the sun come up!" Brigid snuggled up to her boyfriend. "Come on, we'll walk up to the flagpole in the park and then go out for breakfast."

He moaned and pulled the blankets more tightly around him. "Five more minutes..." he pleaded.

Brigid poked him in the ribs. "That's what you always say...and then you never get up!" She yanked the blankets from him. "Get up!" She laughed as she threw the blankets to the floor.

He rolled over onto his back and turned and looked at Brigid. "Lie with me a moment..." He held out his hand.

Brigid lazily but excitedly gazed at his body and suddenly shivered, not from a chill, but from excitement. "No..." She spoke teasingly. "Because then we'll never see the sun rise." She mock pouted.

"Please?" He asked sincerely.

She lay beside him and both were thrilled by the soft warmth of their skin. They embraced, arms and legs entwined. "When will it be okay?" He asked longingly, not desperately.

Brigid, her head on his chest, her expression obscured from his view, replied with glowing blue eyes "Tonight..."

He put one arm around her, drawing her close to him, and stroked the nape of her neck as they both breathed lazy morning breaths.

After some time, without speaking, they arose, dressed in silence, and left the apartment to go watch the sunrise. In the open apartment doorway, he stopped, took Brigid by the hands, kissed her on the forehead and said, "Happy Birthday!"

Colleen and her dog crossed the meadow, wet and sparkling with grassy dew prisms, heading toward the hills of Inwood Park. They were alone together and Colleen observed her dog with a sad love. He was growing older and arthritis was limiting what he most loved — running, smelling, chasing fat slow crows. Sometimes Colleen almost believed that her dog was laughing as he watched the birds circle slowly, ever higher, crowing their raucous *caw*.

Colleen swallowed a proud happy sad swallow, admiring her setter, his red coat glistening in the early sun, nose to the ground and tail high, his rich color complemented so well by the new grass and cloudless sky. She wondered how much longer she would have her friend and companion.

"Billy!" She called to him, for he had headed off in the wrong direction. As he had done since he was a puppy, he made believe he didn't hear her. "He's such a nut," Colleen said aloud.

Colleen caught up with her setter at the base of the path that wound steeply up Inwood Hill alongside a cliff above the Harlem River Canal. Billy started to climb the hill, as he and Colleen had done for years, but his hind legs, pained from arthritis in his hips and spine, gave way. He fell as gracelessly as an old athlete who tries unsuccessfully one last time to perform a feat for which he was once known worldwide. Colleen turned away momentarily, peeked to see if Billy had gotten to his feet, saw that he couldn't, and went to help him.

He looked at her with eyes that, were they human, would seem to express embarrassment or fear of rejection for failure. Colleen sat down beside him on the path, set him in a more comfortable position, and placed his head on her lap, petting him. "I love you, Billy...Don't worry...we'll just rest here." She reached into her pocket. "Look what I've got!"

Colleen took a small plastic bag from her pocket. She removed a piece of chocolate and held it by her dog's nose. His eyes grew wide and he suddenly snapped it from her fingers. "Hey you! Watch it!" She gently chastised him. She held another piece of chocolate out and he slowly moved his head toward it, opened his mouth ever so slightly, and took the piece of candy in his front teeth. At that point, he jerked his head back and gobbled the candy furiously. Colleen laughed and gave him a big hug. "You really are a nut!"

She gently lifted his head and knelt beside him. "How are your legs now, baby?" She rubbed them. "Want to go home and eat? Want to glob some food? Food?" He understood and struggled to his feet on his own.

They walked back across the wide field. More birds were singing. The gulls had stirred and glided above the river. A subway train crossed the 225th Street Bridge. Colleen began to feel uneasy. She began to feel she *had to* get back into her apartment. *Something's going to happen,* she thought anxiously. *Nothing is going to happen,* she chided herself angrily. *All you have to do today is get things set for Brigid's birthday party.* She put her dog on the leash as they neared the street. *You can do at least that, can't you?* She thought disparagingly to herself. *Or has it gotten that bad, Colleen?*

The sun looked like a dirty orange in the east. The sky that appeared so blue straight above was brown along the horizons. Embracing, Brigid and Michael felt thrilled by their contact and by the beauty of even a sullied sunrise.

"Michael," Brigid spoke tentatively "I'm worried about something."

He nibbled her ear and said, "About what, honey?"

"About my Mom...she...well, she..." Brigid hesitated.

"She what?" He took a step back and held his girlfriend at arm's length. "Is she upset that we...that we're going to—" He was interrupted.

"No... Nothing like that! She just isn't herself." Brigid's eyes turned inward and lost their sparkle. "For a long time now...for months." She walked away from Michael and looked out toward the east. "See the red brick building with the clock in the tower?" She pointed across the river toward The Bronx. "I grew up right behind that building...We lived in an apartment there until I was twelve. My mother was so...so active then!" Brigid seemed almost angry. "Now she stays home mostly...rarely sees anyone...and..." Brigid began to cry. "She cries a lot late at night and very early in the morning..." She cleared her throat and continued. "When she thinks I'm asleep or can't hear her."

"Has anything happened to make her so sad lately?" Michael looked at Brigid who was staring at the sky.

"Colleen and I used to look at the sky a lot when I was a kid. She said that the sky was filled with energy...Life energy and deadly energy...and that you could see it if you would *just look*." She stared above. Without looking at Michael, Brigid reached out her hand. "Come...look at the sky...Do you see the spiraling points of light?"

He looked above and after a few moments said, "I don't know...I *think* I see something..." He felt embarrassed.

"Colleen says that you can see the life energy...and you can see energy that's turned deadly." She was quiet for some time. "I think the life energy in my mother is turning deadly and I don't know what to do!" Brigid hugged her boyfriend desperately.

"Brigid," Michael kissed her forehead, her eyes, and her mouth. "Brigid," he repeated "I don't really know what you mean. But...just let her know you love her...talk to her...tell her how you feel..."

"I'm afraid to...sometimes I think she wants to..." She could not say the words.

"Kill herself?" He said, scared.

"No... just... just die..."

Colleen fed her dog, gave him fresh water, and, as she had been doing for too long, lay in bed and stared. She no longer knew where she belonged or what she wished to do. She felt as if she were at a crossroads but she could not choose a direction. She who had once been so bold and confident was now afraid to lose...and so was now losing. It was if she had an unknown emotional infection that insidiously rendered her immobile, making her nearly incapable of doing even the simplest of chores—bathing, shopping, deciding upon anything.

She lay in bed for almost an hour, reliving and rewriting the past. *It's only the regrets I recall,* she thought forlornly. *The rest...the best...it appears I've forgotten it all.* Two small tears formed stillborn in her eyes as Colleen unzipped her pants, and slid her right hand between her thighs.

As she masturbated, she sought with all her strength to summon memories of the powerful pleasurable sensations she once enjoyed. Without enjoyment, she climaxed, but felt flat and frustrated.

She felt gritty within, as her skin often felt when the city air was still and dirty.

"I'm worried about Mom," Brigid said. She could not look directly at the others. "I feel funny...disloyal...but something's wrong with her and

I...I'm scared."

"Don't worry child," Colleen's grandfather said tenderly. "There is no disloyalty here. Only love."

"We are glad you had the courage to come to us," Colleen's mother, Irene, said sadly. "It was very brave of you." Irene Murphy was worried about her daughter as well.

The family sat in silence, concerned and confused, wanting to help but not knowing what to do.

"She just won't talk to me," Brigid said with sad anger.

"She doesn't have much regard for what I think...hasn't since —" Irene caught herself but all three knew she meant "since Colleen got pregnant at 16."

"Perhaps I can get her to open up," Grandfather Murphy mused aloud. "Perhaps...perhaps I can make it seem *that I need her help*. She's always there for others, God knows."

"But not for herself," Brigid said.

But not for her mother, Colleen's mother thought. "Perhaps that's the way, Pop," Irene said. "You have always had a way with her, ever since she was just a bit of a thing."

"Mom needs us...I'll help any way I can." Brigid began to cry but stopped herself. "Sometimes she is so down I'm afraid she might—"

"She wouldn't!" Irene cut Brigid off.

"Is she home now?" Colleen's grandfather asked.

"Yes...she's getting things ready for my birthday party. I wish nobody was coming tonight. Mom is so sad." Brigid now cried fully.

"That's all right, honey." Irene took the young girl in her arms. "We'll work things out...Everything will work out...You'll see." Colleen's mother was not as certain as her words.

"I think I'll pay our Colleen a visit—unannounced!" Colleen's grandfather picked up his walking stick, put on his hat, and strode to the front door. "Say a prayer," he said to the others, blessing himself with holy water from the font by the apartment door as he left.

Colleen sat in her living room, staring straight ahead. The late morning sun on the budding trees, the cool blue shadows on the Palisades, the great cumulus clouds coursing overhead, the songs of the birds in the hills of Inwood Park, the fierce currents of the Hudson and Harlem Rivers at Spuyten Duyvil, all made their impressions on her retina but not on her heart. She simply stared.

Although she had much to do to prepare for her daughter's birthday party, Colleen could not move. Tension immobilized her. Colleen did not want to feel as she did. Suddenly, as if impelled, she stood up and walked to the refrigerator, took out a bottle of cheap white wine, and poured herself a tumbler full. She thought for a moment, then reached into a cabinet above the refrigerator, took out a bottle of cassis, and poured some into the white wine. Colleen quickly drank half the glass. She filled the glass with wine and returned to her armchair. She hadn't wanted to drink, but...

As the alcohol took effect, her mood improved. Colleen sipped her white wine, leaned back in her chair, put her right leg over the arm of the chair, and thought of how happy her daughter was as she turned 16. Colleen recalled her own unhappy, turbulent teenage years. *Brigid is going to Bronx Science; I went to Catholic school. Brigid will soon have her own love life openly; I had mine in secrecy and fear. She can speak to me and her friends; I had no one to turn to.* Colleen sat up. She didn't want to become maudlin.

She walked to the window and finished her wine. *I'll just go out for a bit, get some fresh air...then I'll get things ready for tonight.* She enjoyed the view from her apartment. Colleen held the empty glass up to the light and watched it glint in the sun. *Well, the white wine has certainly improved my outlook on things.* She smiled to herself and sighed. *Things aren't so bad...*

Colleen paused in front of her apartment building. It was more beautiful out than she had imagined and she felt invigorated. She looked at her watch. Just after eleven. *I have the time.* She decided to buy herself a sandwich at the corner delicatessen and have lunch in the park at a favorite spot. She didn't admit it, but she was also going to buy herself some wine to go with lunch.

"And where might you be headed, young lady?" Colleen looked up to see her grandfather standing in front of her.

"Grandpa!" Colleen stepped back, surprised, and then leaned forward and hugged her grandfather. "What are you doing around here?"

"It was such a fine day, I thought I would go for a walk. On the way, I thought I might call on my favorite granddaughter!" He smiled as he studied her.

"I was just going to get something to eat and have a picnic in the park. Want to join me?" She knew he would say yes. Although she had looked forward to being alone, she loved her grandfather. He accepted her for herself and she felt at ease with him.

"I'd be delighted."

They each bought their favorite sandwiches—boiled ham and American cheese on white bread with mayonnaise for Grandfather Murphy; roast beef with Russian dressing and coleslaw on a roll for Colleen. After some hemming and hawing, Colleen told her grandfather she was going down the block to buy some wine while the sandwiches were being made. On returning, Colleen saw that her grandfather had purchased a Guinness stout for himself. It made her less self-conscious about having purchased wine.

Colleen knew her grandfather could not make the walk to the top of the hill where she usually went to relax, think—and sip her wine. Instead, she led him along a path to a single bench by the edge of the river where they could converse in privacy. They did not speak as they walked or as they set up their lunches.

Only after they both had their first bites of food and the first sips of their drinks did Grandfather Murphy speak. "I didn't just happen by, Colleen. There is something I want to speak to you about."

Colleen did not look at her grandfather. She was apprehensive. She feared he wanted to speak to her about *her* life. She feared he somehow knew her "secrets."

The old man cleared his throat. "Colleen, we've always been close. Not as close as you and your grandmother were, God rest her soul, but close."

His serious expression further worried Colleen.

"I've outlived my wife, most of my friends, all of my enemies," he smiled at Colleen. "Even some of my own children. In a bit, I'm going to be 90 years old, Colleen." The old man's eyes sparkled. "I still think of myself as a young man. But I know I'm not. Sometimes I think I'm like an old dog, resting on the porch. I hear a noise; I jump up and bark; then, all my energy is gone. I stand there and stare. Amazed that I even had it in me to jump up and bark. Grateful that I'm barking at all." He sipped his stout. "Colleen, for some reason, for quite some time now, I've wanted to go home...To go back to Sligo before...before I die."

Colleen took an extra-long sip of wine. She felt relieved that the conversation was not to be about her, but was saddened by her grandfather's words. "I think that's a great idea." She took his hand in hers. "How long has it been since you've been back to Ireland?"

"I've never been back, Colleen." He stood up from the bench and walked over to the railing by the shore of the river. "I came to New York City 75 years ago. Seventy-five years, Colleen. I spent 50 years with Brigid, 35 as an IRT engineer, nearly 10 years as a widower. But since I was 15...since 1901..." He turned to look at Colleen. His blue eyes were shining with a light Colleen had never seen before. "Since 1901, Colleen, I never wanted to set foot on that godforsaken soil *even once*!" He laughed, clear and light-hearted. "I never wanted to return to the bone-crushing, back-breaking, soul-killing toil that brought nothing but poverty, pain, and crumbs from the table. I never wanted to return to the bleak, barren, hard-hearted, mean-spirited, alcohol-sodden, broken, and discouraged town and townspeople I left behind. Not once, Colleen. Not once...until recently." He sat down beside Colleen and took her hands in his. "And now, I think of my home fondly..."

For the first time, Colleen noticed how old her grandfather was. She looked at his hands and saw that they truly were the hands of a very old man. It unsettled Colleen that his hands felt so light. *They look so rugged,* she thought. *These laborer's hands...but they don't feel strong.*

"When do you think you might go back to Ireland?" Colleen took her hands away, uncomfortably. She picked up her sandwich, although she did not want to do so, to draw attention away from the discomfort she felt holding her grandfather's hands.

"That's what I came to talk to you about." The old man smiled.

"I don't understand." Colleen was curious.

"Well, granddaughter, I'm too old to make the trip alone. And, even if that were not true, it would not be much fun to go on my own. I thought I would ask you to come along with me!" He looked directly at Colleen. "Not as a babysitter for some old fool. You could come and go as you please. But, as a friend...as a trusted friend."

Colleen was both flattered and wary.

"Now, I don't want you to say anything. I just want you to give it some thought. Money is no object. I'll take care of all the bills. Your mother will look after Brigid, I'm sure." He held up his hand to silence Colleen before she could speak. "I haven't mentioned this to anyone other than you. I just want you to give it some serious thought. See what may be in it for you."

Grandfather Murphy stood up. "I have to go now. There's a party I'll be attending tonight and I must get home in time for my afternoon nap or I won't be able to make the affair." He looked lovingly at Colleen. "You've never been to Ireland, have you?"

"No, never." Colleen was becoming suspicious. Of what, she was uncertain.

"This would mean a great deal to me." His serious expression gave way to a soft smile. "I'll see you at Brigid's party tonight."

"I'll think it over, Grandpa. It's quite an offer. It's not every day a handsome, mature man of means offers to take me abroad!" She smiled lovingly.

"That's the spirit!" He turned and headed briskly down the path toward home.

Colleen watched her grandfather as he walked away. When she was certain he could no longer see her, she eagerly drank the rest of her wine. "Ireland..." She spoke the word aloud, dreamily.

Exhausted, but happy, Colleen slumped into her favorite chair. She looked around her apartment proudly. "No one would believe how it looked this morning." Although guests were not due to begin arriving for two hours, Colleen was ready for them. The apartment was immaculate; the platters of cold cuts were ready; the baked dishes only needed to be heated; and the refrigerator was overstocked with beer, wine, mixers, and plenty of ice for those whose pleasure would be whiskey, vodka, or gin.

Unexpectedly, the front doorbell, not the lobby buzzer, sounded. A bit apprehensive, wondering who had gotten into the building without calling up first from the lobby, Colleen walked to the foyer and, without opening the door, asked nervously, "Who is it?"

"It's me!" An excited, familiar voice answered.

"Lizzie!" Colleen opened the three locks on her door rapidly. "Lizzie! You made it! When I didn't hear from you, I thought you wouldn't be here!" She hugged her sister.

"Colleen, I told you I was coming when we spoke last Sunday night!" Lizzie hurried past her sister, hung her coat on the coat rack in the hallway, and said, "Excuse me, but I just have *to go*," as she rushed to the bathroom.

Colleen was flustered. She didn't recall speaking with her sister on the phone about the birthday party. She tried, momentarily, to reconstruct Sunday evening, but could not. She felt panicky. *It doesn't matter. What matters is that Lizzie is here for Brigid's birthday,* Colleen told herself.

Lizzie emerged from the bathroom and joined her sister at the kitchen table. "Who's coming tonight?"

"The usual suspects," Colleen joked, "Mom, Grandpa, Tommy, Eddie, and Moira. Michael, the love of Brigid's life, some of Brigid's friends from school and the neighborhood. And, of course, I've invited 'Rent-a-Party' to liven things up."

"Colleen, you invited those guys to Brigid's sweet sixteen birthday party! God, I bet that Harry Knudson hits on every one of Brigid's friends!" Lizzie was only partly kidding.

"Oh, come on, Liz, they're a lot of fun. I need some other adults around, you know."

"I wouldn't say they counted as adult. They're okay at first, but then they —"

"I know you think they drink too much," Colleen smiled. "But, they're funny. I enjoy being with them. Besides, they're coming early. Just to give Brigid some presents, sing happy birthday, have some cake. Then they're off to a wild party down in Soho."

"Well, I'm on my own tonight. I'm glad you said I can stay over. That way I don't have to drive all the way home tonight."

Colleen turned from her sister. There was no problem but...she didn't remember that her sister was spending the night. "It'll give us a chance to talk," Colleen replied. "Say, can I get you anything? Wine, beer, vodka, gin and —"

"I'd love some juice. Any kind'll do. Orange, grapefruit, whatever."

"Coming up, sis." Colleen fixed herself a vodka and grapefruit and a glass of grapefruit juice for her sister. "Here you go," she handed Lizzie the wrong glass.

"Cheers," Liz toasted but then gagged as she swallowed the first sip. "Whoa, Colleen! This is some grapefruit juice!" She laughed lightly and handed the glass to her sister. "This must be yours. You sure don't kid around when you make a drink."

Colleen felt flattered. "I'm the bartender tonight, so watch out!" Colleen sipped her drink and then suggested that they sit in the living room. "It's more comfortable."

"I can't believe I have a 16-year old niece," Lizzie shook her head.

"Try having a 16-year old *daughter* on for size," Colleen sipped her drink. Her expression became sad, then worried. "I...I feel old, Lizzie. I feel..." She looked at her younger sister with envy. "I feel like I've made so many mistakes...wasted so much of my life...I feel like, like, if this is it, then..."

"Colleen, sis, I bet what you're really feeling," she said as she got up from the sofa and sat on the arm of her sister's chair, "is—"

"Like a failure," Colleen interrupted. "I'm feeling like a failure. I'm out of work, my unemployment is going to run out soon, I have no career, no idea of what to do to make a living...No *vision* for myself, Lizzie." Colleen leaned into her sister as Lizzie put her arm around her shoulder. "No hope of anything...Just memories, Lizzie...Memories of dreams that didn't become realities...No, that's not it. Of dreams that I couldn't make live."

Colleen began to cry. Lizzie held her silently. *So, this is what Brigid was talking about,* she thought.

"Colleen, it's a great party!" Harry Knudson said as he hugged his friend.

"You and Matthew and his brothers are very well-behaved tonight," Colleen teased.

"Colleen," Knudson feigned insult at her remark. "Colleen—it's early!" He laughed uproariously. "Give us time, Colleen!" He put his arms around her and whispered conspiratorially in her ear. "Say, those friends of Brigid, are they seeing anyone?"

Colleen pushed him away. "You dirty old man!" She laughed. "If you start bothering those young girls, you're out of here. Now," she turned him around, "go inside and mingle, make merry with the guests. That's why I invited you. You missed the pre-party but, if you're good, you can stay for the post-party."

"Ah, another first!" Knudson spoke as he walked away. "My first post-party!"

More of Brigid's classmates and friends came to the party than Colleen had anticipated. She saw that she was running low on ice, soda, cold cuts, and chips. "Those kids sure wolf things down," Colleen smiled. She was happy for her daughter. "Lizzie, I need your help."

Liz excused herself from a conversation with her mother. "What's up, sis?"

"I'm running out of things. There are more people than I thought. Will you come to the supermarket with me? Most of our family isn't here yet and I think even more of Brigid's friends will be showing up."

"No problem." Lizzie saw Colleen counting her money. "Let me pay for this, Colleen. I'm working and you're not. And you've spent enough already." Colleen started to resist but Lizzie insisted. "I won't go to the store with you unless you let me pay."

"Thanks, Liz, I can use the help. I'll just tell Knudson to keep an eye on things until I get back."

Lizzie laughed heartily. "He'll keep an eye on two things —Colleen's girlfriends and the beer in the fridge!"

The April evening sky was powder blue, streaked pink and purple in the west. The winter had been especially hard, making spring even more welcome. "God, it's beautiful tonight," Colleen said quietly, expecting no reply.

The supermarket was nearly empty and the sisters completed their shopping quickly. On the way home, Colleen surprised her sister. "Let's stop in the Donemay Pub a minute." The dark bar smelled of stale beer, sweet flat ginger ale, and cigarettes. "Jingles," Colleen called down the bar to the bartender, "has Louie been in tonight?"

"Haven't seen him in a few days," Jingles answered without looking up from *The Racing Form*.

"Let's have a quick one," Colleen did not wait for an answer. "Jingles, today's my daughter's sixteenth birthday. Two cognacs, straight."

The bartender free-poured two strong drinks and served them to the sisters. "It's on me, Colleen. Happy birthday to the little one!"

"Colleen, what about the party? Why buy a drink here when there's so much at home?"

Colleen sat on a barstool. "There's something about a bar, sis. Something about the darkness..." Colleen drank her cognac in one swallow. Her eyes were inward. "Saturdays, I come here alone to have a few drinks, to listen to the Irish music." She looked at her sister and smiled. "I come here alone, but I rarely leave alone." She smiled but there was no joy in her expression.

"Jingles," Colleen called.

"Another?" Liz was surprised.

"Can't leave on a buyback!" Colleen took her second drink and lifted it up for a toast. "To Brigid, born of love!"

"To Brigid," Lizzie clinked glasses with Colleen.

Brigid rushed to her mother when she entered the apartment. "Mom, where did you go? I was worried when I saw you weren't here!"

"Honey, sweetheart...I just went to the store. We were running out of things, sweetie." Colleen put her packages on the kitchen table, unnerved by her daughter's intense concern.

"Colleen, I think it's time for the cake," Mrs. Murphy suggested.

"So early?" Colleen resisted her mother's suggestion out of habit.

"Yes, mom," Brigid answered. "After our party, we're all going out."

Colleen felt slightly hurt that she was not among the "we" her daughter was speaking of. "Oh, I didn't know you had other plans."

"I told you, Mom! Don't you remember?" Brigid said, slightly annoyed.

Colleen did not remember. "Oh yes, that's right. It just slipped my mind, that's all."

"I'll light the candles, Mom," Colleen told her mother. "You and Brigid get everybody ready to sing happy birthday."

Colleen began to cry as she placed the candles on the cake. She took a deep breath, swallowed hard, and wiped the tears from her cheeks. "I love her so much!" She began to cry again. She took a moment to compose herself and then lit the candles. "Turn out the lights!"

As Colleen entered the dark living room, she saw her brother Eddie with his home movie camera filming the event; she saw her brother Tommy with his still camera poised for the moment Brigid would blow out the candles; she saw her mother put her arms around her granddaughter and guide her to the cake; and she heard herself lead all the guests in singing "Happy Birthday."

Brigid blew out the candles with one breath, cut the first piece of cake and gave it to Colleen, then settled down in the middle of the living room floor and began opening the dozens of presents that had been brought by her guests. The first one she chose was from her grandmother and great-grandfather.

"Grandma! It's so beautiful!" Brigid held up an off-white designer jacket and skirt for all to see. "Thank you, Grandma!"

"That's not all, Brigid. There are two more boxes for you!" Irene Murphy smiled shyly.

Brigid opened the next gift — a silk blouse to go with the outfit — and the second, a pair of fine shoes. "Grandma! You must have spent a fortune!" She gave Irene a hug and a kiss.

"I wanted to be sure you had something special for Mass on Easter, Brigid." Mrs. Murphy, unawares, shot a critical glance at Colleen. Colleen felt the sting.

Brigid flushed slightly. Her grandmother did not know that she no longer went to church.

"Now, I want you to open these, Brigid." Her great-grandfather handed her two presents, one quite large, the other quite small. "Your grandmother has seen that your body has been cared for," he smiled, "these presents are for your spirit!"

Brigid opened the small package first and let out a delighted squeal when she saw a tin whistle and spoons. "Great Grandpa, you are a character!" She picked up the large package. "This is heavy." Removing the wrapper, Brigid found a plain cardboard box. Opening the box, she was stunned. Her jaw dropped. "Oh my god! Oh my god!" Brigid held up a Martin guitar for everyone to see. She stood up and held the instrument out before her, one hand under the neck, the other under the body. She held it as if it were the most sacred, precious object she had ever touched. "This is so beautiful..." The young woman began to cry.

"It's from all of us, dear. Your mom, grandma, Lizzie, and of course, yours truly."

She threw her arms around the old man and buried her face in his chest.

"You *believe* in me! You *understand* me!" She turned, laughing and crying at the same time. "Look at this, guys!" Brigid handed the guitar to the friends with whom she played music.

Colleen felt ecstatic and melancholy. Her past—teenage pregnancy, the rage of her parents, the abandonment by all save her grandparents, the shame and loneliness, the grinding hardship of keeping the baby, her failed forced first marriage, the poverty of raising Brigid alone—it lived in her still. The emotions of those days came to the fore. But the words her daughter spoke washed the memories away. "You believe in me. You understand me!" The joy Colleen felt at hearing those words from her daughter caused her dizzying ecstasy. "I so wanted to be understood...to have someone believe in me..." Colleen felt, at that moment, that all the hardship had been worth it.

"What a birthday!" Brigid laughed aloud and began to open the rest of the presents. Colleen, unnoticed, stepped from the room into the kitchen. She poured herself a drink and drifted into a reverie. Images of her sixteenth birthday came to mind; vivid images of her grandmother dominated. She could smell her grandmother's scent. She could feel the woman's warmth as the frightened teenager, Colleen, was held in her arms and told, "No matter what anyone says to you, you were not wrong to love, Colleen. You were not wrong. I know."

Colleen drifted on the currents of memories, dimly aware of the "oohs," "aahs," and laughter that greeted the presents Brigid was opening. She was warm with drink and love for the woman who took her in when all others rejected her. Colleen remembered her grandmother sitting beside her during labor and holding her hands as Brigid was born. She recalled how proud her grandmother was when she heard Colleen call the infant "Brigid" — the grandmother's name.

Giving birth to her daughter in her grandmother's bed was a bright, pleasurable end to a grey and painful pregnancy. *Gradually...they all came around,* Colleen thought. But she still was angry. She still resented her mother. Her thoughts turned to her late father, but, Colleen was brought back to the present by a call of the wild from her living room.

"It's Ethnic Hour!" Harry Knudson bellowed. "It's time for song and dance!" He put an album of Irish music on the turntable, turned the volume up, and began to lead a singalong of "Finnegan's Wake."

Every year for the past decade, Knudson had led "ethnic hour" at Brigid's birthday party. Colleen loved the absurdity of her friend from the South playing commercialized Irish music for her family and friends, many of whom were from Ireland. Colleen waited in the kitchen for the recorded music to give way, as it always did after two or three songs by Tommy Makem and the Clancy Brothers, to a *seisún*, called for by her grandfather and led by her cousins and herself. Colleen knew her grandfather would call out "Tis Herself!" and that she would pick up her guitar and move to the living room to join in the singing.

On cue, after "Finnegan's Wake," "Wild Rover," and "Isn't It Grand, Boys," Colleen heard a voice call out for a *seisún*. This year, however, it was the birthday girl herself. Once again, Colleen was at her own sweet sixteen party. She remembered every moment of that evening. She remembered singing "The Butcher Boy," about a young girl, left alone and pregnant by her young man, who hangs herself. *And me soon to be pregnant.*

She filled her half-empty wine glass and sat at the table, staring. Colleen was unaware that she was staring; she was unaware of what she was thinking. Often, Colleen had seen her own mother sitting alone in the kitchen, simply staring straight ahead. She told herself that she would never become like that, so defeated by life that she sat alone, staring.

Lost in a sweet, dull melancholy, Colleen did not hear her daughter and her school friends begin to sing the *old* songs, songs that Brigid had learned from Colleen. She did not hear the loving words her daughter spoke as she introduced each song.

"My Mom often sang me to sleep," Brigid told her guests as she tuned the guitar between songs. "Sometimes, we would drive to the beach in San Francisco, just the two of us. Mom was one of the first single-mothers," Brigid said strongly, sadly, proudly.

"Usually, we'd go to the beach on a day she'd taken me to the zoo. We'd take a long walk and then, as the sun set, Mom would sing to me. We're going to sing one of those songs now, right guys?" Brigid indicated she was ready. "It's called 'Tiny Sparrow'."

Startled, Colleen caught her breath. She felt uncomfortable because she couldn't quite recall what she had been thinking. She inhaled, cleared her throat, and nervously smoothed back her hair. She heard Brigid finishing a song to applause from her guests.

"Those nights at the beach with Mom were special to me," Brigid said lovingly. "Not a day goes by that I don't find myself singing one of the songs she sang to me in my head." Brigid looked up. "Where is my Mom?"

"Colleen," Lizzie called out. "Come join us!"

Colleen drank half her glass, then filled it to the rim. "B'right there!" She called out from the kitchen. As Colleen entered the living room, her brother Tommy motioned for her to sit in the chair he had been in. Colleen did so and her brother sat on the arm of the chair. "She sings almost as well as you," he whispered in his sister's ear.

"Better!" Colleen said. *Almost as good,* she thought.

"Mom, do you remember, when I was little, how I used to ask you to sing this song every night?" Brigid was radiant, smiling at Colleen. "The bear went over the mountain," she was laughing too hard to continue singing. The whole family joined in on the family joke.

"The bear went over the mountain," Brigid's aunts and uncles, grandmother and great-grandfather all sang, "to see what he could see!"

"And all that he could see," Brigid and Colleen sang. "And all that he could see—"

"Was the other side of the mountain," the rest of the family sang in reply.

"The other side of the mountain," all sang together, "was all that he could see!"

Colleen felt part of the celebration. "Honey, sometimes I thought my head would explode when you would ask me to sing 'The Bear Went Over the Mountain' again! I could wring the neck of whoever taught you that song!" Colleen laughed.

"It was Daddy," Lizzie called out.

"No it wasn't," Tommy contradicted. "It was Jim. Jim taught Dad the song."

Colleen and Brigid looked at one another, each with her own feelings about Jim, former husband and absent father.

"Jim taught Dad the song," Eddie said with certainty. "But Dad was the first person to sing the song to Brigid."

"Well, whoever it was," Colleen held up her right hand, palm outward, "whoever it was, those days are finally over. Now, Brigid can sing herself to sleep—"

"Or Michael!" Brigid joked.

"Or Michael!" Colleen laughed, but noticed, as she was laughing, that her mother did not even smile. "Brigid can sing herself or her boyfriend to sleep with 'The Bear Went Over the Mountain' and I never have to sing it again!"

"That's the way I feel about *The Cat in the Hat*," Eddie's wife Jane said. "I can't wait until I don't have to read it to the kids ever again!"

"Mom," Brigid stood up, "we practiced this song specially for tonight, and I want to sing it for you. I also want to tell you and everyone here that I think nobody could ever have had a mother who was better than you. And that, except for Grandma," Brigid smiled at Colleen's mother, "I bet hardly anybody has had a mother as good as you!" Brigid crossed the room and kissed Colleen on the cheek. "When I was really upset and couldn't sleep or was sick late at night or scared, Mom would sing this song to me. Ready, guys? "

"Oh once I had a little dog, his color it was brown," Brigid became lost in the song. Colleen leaned back into the chair and closed her eyes, happy.

Brigid and her friends finished singing "Autumn to May," again to applause. "Now, here is one I know you'll love as much as I do," Brigid turned to her mother. "You may have hated 'The Bear Went Over the Mountain,' Mom, but I know you loved singing this song to me."

The phone rang and Colleen answered it as her daughter began singing "Puff the Magic Dragon."

"Pat! How good to hear your voice. We're having Brigid's Sweet 16 party. Are you in the neighborhood?" Colleen was overjoyed to hear from her old girlfriend. "Brigid's singing some of the old folk songs from our Village days."

"I'm with the *3 Westers*," Pat said, referring to mutual friends by their nickname, derived from their Manhattan address.

"Great! Why don't you hop in a cab and join us? My treat!" Colleen hoped Pat would take a cab to her neighborhood in upper Manhattan. "We could go for a few drinks after the party. I'd love to see you."

"Well, I'm actually—well, maybe I will—but I'm calling with some sad news."

"What?" Colleen became alarmed.

"Well, I just heard that Phil Ochs is dead." She let the news sink in. "He killed himself." Pat and Colleen had known him and many of the early Sixties village folk singers before their fame, when, as young girls, they were regulars in all the Greenwich Village folk clubs.

"My god...he killed himself?" Colleen was shocked.

"It hasn't been confirmed. But it seems he hung himself. Dave called and told me. It hasn't made the news yet. I...I don't know why he did it," Pat began to cry, "but I immediately thought of you and... I don't want to spoil Brigid's party...."

Colleen felt empty, as if part of herself had died. An image of Sheridan Square at Thanksgiving in 1961 came to mind. She had just turned 18 and had gone out with Pat and friends to celebrate. At a local bar, they met three Irish brothers and spent the night on a pub crawl, drinking and singing. They ended up in a club on Macdougal Street and had, for Colleen, the most exhilarating time of her life.

The club was filled with the just-about-to-be-famous and one or two of the just-famous folk singers of the day and Phil Ochs was one of them. Colleen was awestruck. The wheel was still in spin. To her surprise, the young Irishmen taking her on her whirlwind birthday tour of the Village were known to them all, and were even asked to sing.

They clambered to the stage, borrowed a banjo and guitar, took out a tin whistle of their own, and launched into a spontaneous concert of Irish folk songs. Colleen grabbed Pat's hand and squeezed it for nearly an hour.

"Colleen, can you hear me?" Pat was puzzled by her friend's silence.

"I'm sorry...I just drifted off for a moment." Colleen sighed. "I was thinking of my birthday party when—"

"So was I!" Pat needed Colleen. "So was I, Colleen. Listen, what's your address again? I'm going to get a cab and come up. Can I stay over?"

"Of course. Come right away...I'm sure Brigid would love to see you. She and her friends are going out on their own in about an hour."

"I'll be there as soon as I can. What's the address?"

"Right, sorry. I'm in the building on the corner of 218th Street and Indian Road. You'll remember when you see it. Just buzz and I'll let you in. See you soon, Pat. I'm glad you called."

Colleen hung up and sat on a stool by the kitchen phone.

"Puff, the Magic Dragon," everyone was singing in the living room, "lived by the sea. And frolicked in the autumn mist..."

Sorrow surged in Colleen. She tried to stifle a moaning, wailing cry, by burying her face in her hands and swallowing hard.

"One grey night it happened," Colleen drifted off into the past as they all sang.

"Without his lifelong friend, Puff could not be brave," Colleen could not control her deep crying when she heard her daughter singing.

No one heard her crying until the song was over. Then they came running to the kitchen. Lizzie and Brigid got to Colleen first. Mrs. Murphy was only a step behind. The males in the family stood awkwardly in the foyer outside the kitchen. Brigid's friends, apprehensive, remained in the living room.

Lizzie stood beside her sister, putting her right arm around Colleen's shoulder, taking both Colleen's hands with her left hand. Brigid, frightened, knelt before her mother, crying "Mommy, what is it? Did somebody die?"

"Yes, honey somebody died," Colleen managed to say between sobs.

"Is it family?" Mrs. Murphy asked.

Colleen shook her head no.

Mrs. Murphy was relieved.

Colleen continued to cry, her lower lip trembling like a baby's, her chest heaving. Gradually, her crying softened. She became self-conscious; she held her breath, exhaling shallowly. "I'll be okay..." She sniffled and looked for a tissue. "I'm sorry for spoiling your party, honey." She kissed Brigid on the forehead.

"You didn't spoil anything, Mom. But...who died?"

"Phil Ochs...the folk singer." Colleen lifted her head up and forced a smile. "I know it may seem silly to you all—"

Lizzie and Brigid protested that it wasn't silly. Mrs. Murphy didn't understand how the death of an entertainer could so upset her daughter but she remained silent.

"It just brought back a whole part of my life...from a long time ago...Dreams I'd had...hopes...things that didn't come true." She took a deep breath. "He killed himself. He was only 35 and...it just hit home." Colleen looked up and smiled sadly. "I can understand why ...When I was younger, I never could understand how someone could feel so hopeless. But..." She took a deep breath. "Oh, I feel so embarrassed." Colleen stood up.

"Come inside with us, Mom." Brigid took Colleen by the arm "Would you sing a song for me? For my birthday?" Colleen shook her head no but was pulled along into the living room by her daughter.

Knudson handed Colleen Brigid's new guitar and whispered into Colleen's ear.

"Okay, Harry." She looked around the room. "Most of you were too young or too old to know who Phil Ochs was," she sniffled and cleared her throat, "but when I was a teenager, I hung around Greenwich Village in the folk clubs. The famous were all there before they all became famous." Colleen strummed the guitar absently. "It was a wonderful time. It seemed that everything was possible. That, if you worked for it, good things would come about. And the music was so pure..." Colleen drifted off for a moment. "And Phil Ochs, to me, was one of the purest. He wasn't the most talented songwriter; he wasn't the best guitarist; he didn't have a great voice. But many of his songs were just so honest, so on target. They meant a lot to me."

"Sing your favorite, Mom." Brigid looked to her friends.

"We'd love to hear you sing," said Michael, Brigid's boyfriend.

"C'mon, Colleen. Like in the old days," Harry said. He went to Colleen and stood beside her. "It's a Sunday night, the place is closed, it's wintertime, only the regulars are left. You just pick up your guitar and sing." He put his arm around Colleen's shoulder. "No big deal. You just sing because it's in you."

"Okay," Colleen turned inward. "Okay, this song's called 'There But for Fortune'."

The room was quiet. The air was filled with love, anxious love, for the singer.

Colleen's voice was strong. It resonated with sad, soft anger. Her voice expressed belief in the lyrics, belief that was especially deep when she sang "Show me the whiskey stains on the floor, show me the drunkard as he stumbles out the door, and I'll show you a young man with so many reasons why...There but for fortune, go you or I."

Brigid's classmates and friends were enthralled. For many, raised on electronic images of performers, it was the first time they had ever been in a person's home and heard music performed as part of daily life. The intensity of their friend's mother entranced them.

Colleen segued immediately from "There But for Fortune" into another folk song she had sung as a teenager. "All my trials, Lord, soon be over," she sang, lost in herself.

From memory, from her days singing in a small cafe on Manhattan's East Side, Colleen followed "All My Trials" with a heart-rending performance of "Old Coat." "Take off your old coat and roll up your sleeves," she sang, "Life is a hard road to travel, I believe."

Colleen began to cry but continued singing. "I look to the east, I look to the west, a youth asking fate to be rewarding, but Fortune is a blind god, flying through the clouds, and forget me on this side of Jordan."

One of Brigid's girlfriends began to cry and took her boyfriend's hand.

"Silver spoons to some mouths, golden spoons to others," Colleen sang, now angry. "Though they smile and tell us, all of us are brothers, never was it true this side of Jordan."

The three women who cared most about Colleen—mother, sister, daughter—each feared for her. None knew what do for her. Colleen's grandfather prayed she would travel with him to Ireland. The young people, especially those who were musicians, were impressed with Colleen's voice and her sensitive guitar playing. They did not perceive the trouble the family sensed.

Colleen stopped playing and sat silent a moment. "I guess I'm being pretty morbid." She smiled weakly. "But there's just one more song I'd like to sing. Phil Ochs hung himself, my friend said. The thought of him choking to death, of the voice that sang out in love, anger, humor...choking that voice by his own hand...the thought of Phil doing to himself what his worst enemies could not do...Suicide stilling a big heart, a beautiful heart...No one knows why anyone kills himself. But many harshly judge people who take their lives."

Mrs. Murphy felt the last remark was directed at her.

"But...I want to sing a song by Buffy St. Marie, as my goodbye to Phil Ochs." Colleen tuned her guitar and then sang, "Be not too hard, for life is short, and nothing is given to man. Be not too hard when he's sold or bought, for he must manage as best he can." Colleen's voice and playing took on added power, almost majesty, as she sang, "Be not too hard, for soon he'll die, often no wiser than he began. Be not too hard for life is short, and nothing is given to man."

When Colleen finished singing, Brigid hugged her mother. "That was beautiful, mom. I know you won't believe me. But this is the best, most real birthday party I've ever had. I hope you don't mind...But we've got to go now. I'm being taken out dancing and we're meeting some friends downtown."

"No, you go enjoy yourself, sweetheart. Have a wonderful time." Colleen hugged her daughter. "Happy birthday, baby. Bring your keys...I may be out." The buzzer rang. "That's Pat —I'll definitely be out," Colleen laughed.

"I didn't know Pat was in the city!" Brigid loved her mother's exuberant, wild friend.

"Pat?" Colleen asked at the intercom in the hallway of her apartment. When she heard her friend's voice answer, she replied, "Go left when you get out of the elevator. All the way to the end of the hall." She buzzed to allow Pat into the building.

"Hey guys, can we hang out for a little bit? I haven't seen Pat in years and she is so cool!"

"It's your birthday, Brigid," Michael assured her and her friends agreed.

"And you have until dawn to be a dancin' fool, Brigid," Harry Knudson volunteered, only partly teasing.

"Harry," Colleen whispered, poking him with her elbow. "Don't embarrass yourself."

The apartment doorbell rang and Brigid rushed to answer it. "Pat!" She squealed and threw her arms around her. "Pat! What a surprise!"

"Happy Birthday, baby!" Pat picked a shopping bag up from the floor and took out a small gift-wrapped package for Brigid. "It's not much—but I didn't know it was your birthday until an hour ago."

"You didn't have to bring anything, Pat." Brigid took Pat by the hand and led her into the living room. "Seeing you is my birthday present."

Colleen looked at her old friend and smiled sadly. Pat reached out her arms and Colleen walked toward her silently. They hugged one another with a weariness only they understood.

Pat, at five feet, ten inches, stood nearly a half-foot taller than Colleen. Her long, honey-blond hair contrasted strikingly with Colleen's pitch-black hair. After a moment, they stood back from one another, at arms' length, holding hands. Pat noticed that Colleen's hair was showing its first signs of gray. Colleen saw that there were a few new wrinkles around her friend's eyes and at the corners of her mouth.

"Brigid, introduce Pat to your friends." Colleen ushered Pat into her daughter's care. "Can I get you a drink?"

"God, yes!" Pat laughed. "Irish whiskey?"

"Bushmill's good enough?" Colleen smiled; it was her friend's regular drink.

"Pat, this is Michael." Brigid blushed slightly. Pat sensed why. "And these are my friends from school and the neighborhood." Brigid went clockwise around the living room, rattling off the names of her guests.

"Of course, you know Grandma and Pop."

"And I see you've rounded up the usual suspects," Pat laughed and waved her left hand to indicate Colleen's brothers and sister. "I haven't seen any of you since you were about Brigid's age. Lizzie...why you're a *natural* woman!" Pat teased, referring to Liz's appearance and a popular song.

"And you look like you're still into—"

"Sex, drugs, and rock 'n roll!" Pat said with enthusiasm.

"All right!" Harry Knudson seconded her.

"Oh, excuse me," Pat apologized, sincerely but lightheartedly, directing her apology to Colleen's mother and grandfather.

"It's the children I am thinking of," Mrs. Murphy said icily.

"In my day, Pat," Grandfather Murphy spoke with the kindness of one who has learned from experience, "you would have been a Bohemian in Greenwich Village. Or one of the wild `free love' crowd after the Great War." He smiled, and looked, at the young people. "There's nothing new to all this. It just goes round and round."

"We've been singing some of the songs you and Mom used to sing in the Village, Pat," Brigid said, to change the subject.

"Ah, but I bet Colleen has had you all singing or listening to the sad old morbid songs that she loves." Pat took her drink from Colleen and sipped it, sighing with relief. "Am I right? Songs like 'There But for Fortune,' or 'Old Coat' or 'Be Not Too Hard.' Am I right?" Pat took a longer sip of her whiskey.

"Colleen sang every one of those! How did you know?" Brigid was amazed.

"I'm not your mother's oldest and dearest friend for nothing. I had to listen to all those songs for years. Those were your mother's signature songs when we were young. In the coffee houses, at `hootenannies', in the Village folk clubs, Colleen's voice caught the ear of all. When your mom sang, there was silence in the noisiest, most boisterous room!" She finished her whiskey. "I'll have another,

Colleen."

"I'll get it." Knudson took her glass.

"Thank you," Pat said graciously. "Now, Colleen why don't we do some of the fun songs for the kids before they head out for the night?"

"Well, Pat, they may want to be on their way now. They're meeting friends downtown." Colleen looked about the room. Partly, she didn't want to interfere with her daughter's plans; partly, she wanted all the guest to be on their way.

"Let's sing one before we go," Brigid suggested. "Okay, guys?" She didn't look to see who agreed with her. "Why not one by Phil Ochs. Your choice, Pat."

"Okay..." She thought for a moment. "Let's see...`Here's to the State of Richard Nixon'... No... `Draft Dodger Rag'... No..." Her eyes brightened and Pat snapped her fingers. "I've got it! Let's sing `Small Circle of Friends'."

"Oh, Pat!" Colleen was embarrassed.

"Here's your drink, Pat." Knudson handed her an eight-ounce tumbler of whiskey on the rocks.

"We can teach the kids the chorus, Colleen! C'mon, where's your spirit?" Pat's enthusiasm excited the teenagers.

"We know some of the lyrics," Michael said.

"That's right, we do," Brigid joined in. "You guys can sing along too," she looked at her friends. "It's easy to get the chorus."

"Oh, all right," Colleen agreed. "Pat, you sing lead. I'll play and do the chorus."

"Great!" Pat took a long drink and smacked her lips. "Now this is a drink, Harry!"

Knudson smiled proudly. "Anytime, Pat."

Pat and Colleen led the teenagers in a rollicking, enthusiastic rendition of Phil Ochs's cynical but sincere satire of America. By the second chorus, all of Brigid's friends, Colleen's brothers and sister, and even Colleen's grandfather were singing along with the chorus.

"Look outside your window, there's a woman being grabbed," they all sang one last time, "they've dragged her to the bushes and now she's being stabbed. Maybe we should call someone to try to stop the pain. But Monopoly is so much fun and I'd hate to blow the game. And I'm sure it wouldn't interest anybody...outside of a small circle of friends!"

Brigid and her friends clapped for Pat and Colleen and, all in a great mood, got ready to leave for a night of dancing.

"You have your key, Brigid?" Colleen whispered in her daughter's ear. "Pat and I are going out and I'm not sure what time I'll be home."

"Don't worry, Mom. I've got my keys. Michael will bring me home." Brigid looked searchingly at her mother. Colleen averted her eyes. "Are you feeling better, Mom?"

"Yes, baby. I'm very glad Pat is here. You go out and enjoy yourself." She kissed her daughter on the cheek. "Take a cab home, you hear me?" Colleen was firm. "No subways late at night. You have the money I gave you?"

"Yes, Mom, don't worry." Brigid wanted to tell her mother that her boyfriend was going to spend the night with her—for the first time—and that they were going to make love—for the first time—but there were too many people saying goodbyes, getting their coats, hugging and kissing and soon Brigid was swept out of the doorway with her small circle of friends.

Suddenly, the apartment was quiet. Colleen locked the front door and went into her living room. Her mother and grandfather were seated on the sofa. Pat and Harry Knudson were across from them, relaxing with their drinks in two comfortable armchairs.

"She had a grand time," Grandfather Murphy said. "I'm glad you suggested that we all go in together on the guitar, Colleen. Brigid loved it!"

"I'll help you clean up, Colleen." Mrs. Murphy said as she stood up.

"No, that's not necessary, Mom. Pat and I will take care of that."

Lizzie came from the bathroom into the living room. "Oh, Liz! I thought you had left with the crowd."

"Did you forget me again? I'm staying over, Sis, remember?"

"Right..." Colleen was embarrassed. "I did forget. Pat and I are going to go out for a while. Do you want to join us?"

"No thanks, Colleen," Liz knew she would be in the way, that the two friends wanted to be alone together. "I'll just watch some TV, read."

"You sure?" Pat said. "You're welcome to join us."

"I'm sure. You guys go out. I'll be here to let Brigid in... And take care of her if she imbibes anything too strong tonight!"

"Well," Knudson finished his drink. "I'm taking a cab downtown. Where are you guys headed?"

"Want to go to the Village? For old times' sake?" Colleen clearly wanted to go there.

"Sure," Pat said. "We'll have a hell of a time!"

It was an especially balmy spring night in New York, after an invigorating day, and Christopher Street, in the heart of gay Greenwich Village, was barely passable. Small groups gathered at corners and midblock, cruising, talking, and laughing. In front of every gay bar, crowds milled about on the sidewalk as people spilled out from the bar, drinks in hand, or waited to get into the bar. In 1969, the gay revolution began with resistance to a police raid on the Stonewall, a bar in Sheridan Square. What had then taken place furtively, behind the heavily-curtained windows of gay bars, far from the eyes of family, friends, employers, neighbors, and police, now was occurring quite light-heartedly and openly on the streets of the Village—men holding hands with other men; women walking down the streets, alleyways, and avenues arm in arm; passionate and playful camaraderie, kissing and hugging in the open by gay men and women.

Colleen and Pat still thought of the Village as it had been when they were in their late teens and early twenties. They had been intimately involved in the vibrant musical, cultural, and political scene of the early 1960's. Yet, all that had passed, to remain in photographs and memories alone. As they walked along Christopher Street, judged by many who noticed them to be a striking gay couple—light and dark, short and tall, shy and outgoing—the two women felt only a vicarious pleasure in the excitement that was evident everywhere. They were not a part of it. They were not participants in, but only witnesses to, another development in the sexual evolution of America.

"What a wild scene!" Colleen felt a shiver run up her back. "Makes us seem tame by comparison."

"Not really," Pat looked about as she spoke, taking in the flamboyant colors, styles of dress, language, and behavior all around her. "Our appearance seemed just as outlandish 15 years ago. It's what's *really going on* that gets people angry. You know that, Colleen."

"People living their own lives," Colleen replied quietly.

"People living their own *sexual* lives," Pat emphasized.

When they turned onto Hudson Street, Colleen saw a sight she hadn't seen in years. "The White Horse Tavern! God, the bar *you* couldn't leave!" Colleen laughed.

"The bar *we* couldn't leave!" Pat corrected her friend. "And that we never left alone—unless we wanted to!"

Both women had memories of love affairs and one-night stands that had begun and ended in the old bar. Of heated arguments that raged only to be waged, with no thought of a solution to the issues raised. Of laughing, of dancing, of drinking until dawn. Of a thousand faces from a thousand places telling their stories, true and false, tragic and comic, enthralling and boring. Of tourists traipsing in, hoping to see another Behan die from drinking.

"It's like I never left," Colleen mused, sadness sounding in her voice. "Or like it never happened."

"Colleen!" Pat commanded her friend's attention by stopping in her tracks. She spoke her friend's name almost harshly. "There will be no maudlin self-pity tonight!" She looked at Colleen kindly. "Come on, let's enjoy ourselves. We'll toast our departed acquaintance and then toast ourselves—E Viva!" Pat raised her hand as if lifting a glass. "E Viva! To us—the living!" Pat took Colleen's hand and raised it with hers.

"All right, all right," Colleen smiled. "I'll try."

"There'll be none of this *trying*, Colleen," Pat teased.

"You *vill* enjoy yourself," Pat said, imitating a German accent while clicking her heels like a Nazi.

"I *will* enjoy myself," Colleen countered, imitating Bert Lahr as the Cowardly Lion in *The Wizard of Oz*. "I *will* enjoy myself, I will, I will, I will."

The bar was crowded when Colleen and Pat entered. They considered sitting at a table in the back but noticed that two men were leaving their seats at the far end of the bar and the women headed in that direction. Offers of drinks were made by men the length of the bar. Pat ignored them; Colleen replied with a barely audible "no thanks."

"Do you believe we started to come here 15 years ago? Underage!" Colleen saw the bartender coming toward them. "What are you having, Pat?"

"Bushmills, on the rocks." Pat looked carefully around the bar.

"Good evening ladies. What'll be your pleasure tonight?" The bartender asked, smiling.

"It's too early to answer that. Why don't you start with our drinks?" Pat said, flirting with the handsome young man.

Colleen looked at the bartender and shook her head, a small smile on her face. "She can't help it. She likes all the boys."

"And you?" The bartender flirted with Colleen.

"A Manhattan." Colleen liked him. "Dry...and no cherry."

The bartender laughed lightly.

"And one Bushmills Irish Whiskey," Colleen announced with a flourish, "on the rocks for my friend. She's top-shelf all the way." Colleen whispered conspiratorially to the bartender, but loud enough for Pat to hear. "They say that's because she's been to the well once too often."

"Bitch!" Pat exclaimed, laughing. "Colleen, I didn't know you had it in you!"

The bartender repeated their order and then left to make their drinks. "He's cute," Pat said, nudging Colleen.

"Too young," Colleen looked around the bar. No one caught her eye.

"Not for me." Pat studied the bartender carefully. "If nothing better shows up, I may make a play for him."

Colleen laughed softly. "You do that."

The night passed both slowly and quickly. Neither friend had been able to make real contact with the other. Though they had much to share with each other, they were unable to open up. And throughout the night, men came over to Pat and Colleen, awkwardly introducing themselves, starting conversations revolving around themselves and their work, hoping to pick up one—or both—of the women. Neither was interested, however, in any of the dozen or so men who had approached them. The conversations, and the pauses between them, passed slowly. Yet, both Pat and Colleen were surprised to see it had become one in the morning.

"Are we losing our touch?" Pat asked. "Or is there not much worth touching out there?" Pat signaled for another drink.

"I don't know about you," Colleen stared at the bottles behind the bar, "but I'm just not interested tonight."

"That's because nothing interesting came up to us, dear. I know a place we should go. Nearby. After this drink."

The bartender put down a drink for each of the women. "This is on me," he smiled, lingering briefly, looking at Colleen.

When the bartender was out of earshot, Pat said, "He's all yours, Colleen. Go for it!"

"I'm too old for him, Pat. Besides, I...I just don't feel up to it right now." The alcohol was changing Colleen's mood. Pat had seen her become melancholy and withdrawn frequently near the end of a night of drinking.

"You know, Colleen, maybe you shouldn't have that drink." Pat knew she was on dangerous ground. "Let's just get some fresh air, walk back over to Sheridan Square, have a nightcap at the 55 Bar. What do you say?"

"Who are you," Colleen answered hostilely, "to tell me not to have that drink?"

"Whoa, back off, Colleen." Pat felt herself becoming angry. "Listen, you just seem to be getting down, that's all." She softened her tone. "Come on, this place is dead. We came out to have fun, right?" Pat saw Colleen relax. "Let's just finish our drinks and head over to the 55, okay?"

"Pat," Colleen's mood improved as she sipped her Manhattan, "you know you can't leave on a buyback. Bad bar etiquette." Colleen smiled apologetically. "One for the road and then we'll go over to the 55 Bar."

"Great...I know the bartender, the crowd. Some terrific musicians hang out there." Pat leaned over and whispered, "You ever done any coke?"

Colleen shook her head no. It was almost as if she hadn't heard her friend. She had her cocktail in her hand and was watching the light reflect off the reddish brown liquid in her glass.

"Well, tonight's the night." Pat drank her whole drink and signaled for another. "Wait 'til you do a few lines, Colleen. No more Irish maudlin self-pity for you!"

"God I feel *incredible!*" Colleen stood up from the barstool and took a deep breath. Jesus Christ, Pat! If I could feel like this, I'd do this all the time!" Colleen laughed recklessly. "Pat," she whispered conspiratorially, "how much does this stuff cost?"

Pat whispered the price into Colleen's ear.

"*What?*" Colleen took two steps backward. "Are you kidding? How the hell can you afford—"

Pat gestured for Colleen to be quiet. "Colleen, be cool. Sit down...Listen to me. There are other ways to pay for it besides money. See that guy over there—the tough-looking Italian-stallion-type?"

"He's kinda cute," Colleen wanted to walk over to him and kiss him.

"Well, I *know what he likes,*" Pat laughed derisively, "so I give it to him. And he knows what I like," she mimed snorting cocaine, "and he gives it to me."

"Really..." Colleen stared across the room, titillated by her friend's talk. "What does he like?"

Pat whispered to her friend and both women laughed, a little too loudly at first. They stifled their laughter momentarily and then burst out laughing again. "That seems like a very small price to pay," Colleen said. "And, anyway, I kinda like that too!"

"Let me introduce you to him," Pat stood up, experiencing a vicarious thrill. "You're his type...He hits on a lot of women who look like you." She pulled Colleen along with her across the bar.

"Hey Tony! Tony!" Pat weaved across the room.

"Pat! Good to see you, babe," he looked at Colleen as he spoke. "Who's your friend?"

"Tony, this is Colleen." Colleen felt herself blush. "Colleen is my oldest and dearest friend."

"Sit down, sit down," he stood up from his seat, pulled an extra chair over to his table, and politely moved the chairs to make it easy for the women to sit. "What'll you have?"

The women accepted his offer and ordered their drinks.

"Nice to meet you, Colleen. What brings you into this den of iniquity?" Tony laughed gently.

"Pat and I are out on the town. You know, have a few drinks, see who's available. You know what I mean. Pretty slim pickings so far." The waitress put their drinks on the table. "But I think my luck might be about to change!" Colleen looked Tony directly in the eye as she held up her drink. "A toast—to Tony, a guaranteed good time!"

"Hey, Pat!" Tony laughed. "I like this Colleen friend of yours!" He reached across the table and took Colleen's hand in his. "A lot..."

"Well, that takes care of you, Colleen." Pat downed her drink and stood up. "Let's see what I can scrounge up." Pat noticed a new patron enter the bar. She turned to Colleen and smiled. "Watch, Colleen. That one's mine. In 10 minutes, we'll leave together. Just you wait and see." Pat went to the ladies' room to fix her make-up.

"Pat's something, eh?" Tony moved his chair closer to Colleen.

"So, Tony," Colleen moved her chair closer to Tony. "What do you do? What business are you in? Construction, restaurant, garbage, Mafia?"

"And you, Colleen? IRA? Barmaid? Nanny? Cleaning lady? Frigid Bronx Irish Catholic bitch?" Tony leaned back in his chair and sipped his drink.

"Touché, Tony, touché!" Colleen felt slightly insecure.

"Let's cut the crap, Colleen," he smiled as he looked directly at her. "I'm a printer's rep. I'm a salesman. I got a nice job, make good money. I'm single and like it that way. And I'm a pretty nice guy. I don't hassle you; you don't hassle me. Know what I mean? Maybe we go out for dinner. Maybe we hit it off, maybe we don't. Either way—next time we meet, no hassles. No bullshit. Know what I mean?"

Chastened, Colleen smiled sheepishly. "Sorry, Tony." The cocaine was wearing off. "You know, I did something for the first time before and—"

"I know. I saw you and Pat head for the back room with Louie. That means only one thing. One pretty expensive thing. What do you do for a living, Colleen?"

"Oh, me...N.Y.U." Colleen smiled.

"Really, N.Y.U. You a professor? What do you teach? I went there for a year but I dropped out."

"N.Y.U.—New York Unemployment, not New York University!" Colleen laughed and Tony laughed with her.

"I like that, Colleen. I like a woman with a sense of humor." He shook his head. "NYU...I gotta remember that one. Say, listen," he motioned for Colleen to lean across the table. "Did you like it?"

"Loved it!" Colleen looked at him coquettishly. "But I don't know how I can afford any. One tiny bit costs more than a whole unemployment check."

"I like you, Colleen." Tony looked at her lips.

"I like you, too, Tony." Colleen puckered her lips ever so slightly, forming little kisses, one after the other.

"Maybe we can work something out." Tony moved his chair away from the table.

"I'm sure we can, Tony. I *know* we can." Colleen moved her chair away from the table and stood up behind Tony. She massaged his neck and shoulders firmly. "I liked you from the minute I saw you." Colleen moved her hands from his shoulders to his chest, opening a shirt button and rubbing one hand on his chest.

"Let's step into my office," Tony stood up and took Colleen by the hand.

The back of the bar was barely lit and no one noticed as Tony led Colleen into the men's room and locked the door behind them.

Colleen returned just in time to see Pat leave with the man she had picked up at the bar. Ordinarily, Colleen would have felt frightened at being left alone in a seedy bar late at night, a seedy bar where she was not a regular, that is. However, this was not an ordinary night for Colleen. She felt emboldened and emblazoned by the cocaine. She felt more expansive than ever in her life.

Colleen looked at Tony as he ordered their drinks at the bar. *God, he got so hot I got turned on! I want more,* she thought excitedly. More cocaine, that is.

"To Colleen!" Tony raised his drink and Colleen did the same.

"I'll let you do anything you want!" Colleen heard herself softly say as they clinked their glasses. She saw how excited Tony became at her words. "*Anything,*" she whispered.

Tony quickly finished his drink. "I gotta head out, Colleen."

"No, stay." She slid her chair close to his and rubbed her hand up and down the inside of his thighs. "That was just the appetizer."

"You're great, Colleen. I owe Pat for bringing you around." Tony kissed Colleen on the cheek. "But I gotta go. I got a noon plane to catch and it's after four." He stood up. "Listen, I'll be back Wednesday. Call me." He gave her his business card. "My home number is on it. Call me at home or work ...if you want."

Colleen felt angry and too proud to feel rejected. "One for the road?" She smiled coquettishly. "One for the road and a quickie?"

Tony reached out his hand. Colleen let him help her up. She began to walk toward the back of the bar. "Not in here," Tony turned her around and led her to the front door. "My car is just around the corner on Waverly Place."

"I never did it in a car before!" Colleen spoke loudly and her words echoed in the empty early morning streets of Sheridan Square.

"Never? Really?" Tony took Colleen by the arm and she leaned her head on his shoulder as they walked.

"I'm a city girl," Colleen said in baby talk. "I use the subways, not cars."

Tony opened the front passenger door of the car. Colleen closed the door. "Open the back for me, will you?" He did as she asked. "You get in first." Tony got into the car and Colleen followed him. "Anything," she whispered fiercely as she locked the car door.

The sky turned deep purple at the horizon and the cirrus clouds high above at the zenith became pale pink. "I better take you home," Tony said as Colleen fixed her clothing.

"You don't have to. You must be *so* tired. And I live way uptown. Let's do one more line. Then, you can drive me home if you really want to or you can treat me to a taxi. I spent most of my money drinking with Pat." Colleen kissed him lightly.

"It's almost five. There won't be any traffic. Where do you live?" Tony stepped from the car and stretched. "I've got my second wind."

"Up by The Cloisters," Colleen said hesitantly.

"Piece of cake," Tony smiled. "You can stay back there if you like." He got into the driver's seat and started the engine. "You could do kinky things in the back while I watch through the rearview mirror."

"The rearview mirror...That's fitting!" Colleen laughed roughly. "God, I feel great! I feel I want more than I ever wanted and that too much couldn't begin to be enough! No wonder people love coke!"

"It's the real thing," Tony quoted a popular soda commercial.

"It sure is." Colleen lay out in the seat, her back propped up in the corner against the door and the back cushion. She lay her right leg across the seat, with her foot on the floor. She put her left foot up on the seat. Her dress fell to the seat, revealing her navel, her panties, and her thighs. "I want more, Tony. I want more right now." Colleen slid her hand down the front of her panties.

"Well, you're on your own right now," Tony's concentration was entirely on the road. "They should tear this part of the highway down. Guy I knew got killed here." The damp, smooth old cobblestones were slippery and treacherous. The danger was heightened because the old roadway, too narrow for modern automobiles, twisted sharply in two nearly 90-degree turns. "I hate that turn," Tony was genuinely relieved. He glanced in the rearview mirror. "What! What are you doing back there?"

"You like it?" Colleen felt wild and uninhibited. She felt as if she were another person.

"I better get you home!" Tony liked watching Colleen in the mirror.

"There's a place we can park near the Cloisters," Colleen said huskily, her voice deepened from whiskey and the smoke-filled bars.

"Baby, if I didn't have that plane to catch I don't think I'd ever leave you. But I gotta be there clean and sober and ready for work at 7 a.m. tomorrow morning," he focused on the road as he spoke. "I love to party, Colleen, but I keep my partying to the weekend. Sundays I chill out and Monday I'm back in the game. They get Monday through Friday. I get Friday night through Sunday." There was pride in Tony's voice.

He was silent a moment and then continued. "I didn't finish college, Colleen. But I got a good career. I own two houses on Fire Island. One I rent summers. It pays for itself and the other one. I got a powerboat at the 23rd Street Marina for business and pleasure. I own some nice lakefront properties in Maine. I even bought some land on the Oregon coast as a long-term investment. It's in a sleepy little town even people in Oregon never heard of!"

"I'll give you the directions to a nice place we can park and no one will even know we're there." Colleen sat up and kissed the back of

Tony's neck.

"You didn't listen to a word I said," he was slightly offended.

"Yes I did. You said you got plenty. I say I got plenty of nothing...So..." She nibbled his right ear. "We're even."

Colleen sat back in the seat and dreamily watched the waters of the Hudson River race out to sea. A lone tugboat made its way upriver against the tide, one red light on its bow, an amber glow coming from its cabin. Since childhood, Colleen had longed for the life she imagined was lived by tugboat captains and crew. *Rugged, romantic, solitary, satisfying. And predictable...predictable...* Colleen ached inside.

"Sometimes I feel like a spectator at my own life," Colleen said aloud. "You ever feel like that, Tony?"

"No, can't say as I have. Don't know what you mean, really." He increased speed along a long straightaway on the road.

"It's like...like there's all this great *drama*," Colleen spoke the last word with contempt. "All this emotional upheaval and *drama*," she continued, "and you're in it. You're even the *center* of it for Chrissakes. The goddamned center of the drama...teenage mother, hippie lovechild with child, California commune free lover, open marriage without guilt trips, timeless tripping along the edge of America engaged in an effortless struggle for change...And all the time, standing on the sidelines of my own life...looking, observing, judging...not *really* feeling...feeling like an actress feels, not like a living person feels...like an actress feels love or sorrow or death or birth...not like a living person..." Colleen leaned forward in the seat. "You know, yesterday was my daughter's sixteenth birthday. We had a beautiful party. Our whole family was there...Brigid's friends were there...Since she was a baby...I had this idea..." Colleen sat back in her seat.

"What idea?" Tony asked, genuinely interested.

"You really want to know?" Colleen was embarrassed. "You might think it's silly."

"Try me." He smiled and looked at Colleen in the rearview mirror.

"Okay...but...just don't laugh at me. Even if you feel like laughing at me...just don't." Colleen sighed. "I never told anyone this and it's important to me...real important to me..."

There was silence as they drove along the West Side Highway. The George Washington Bridge spanned the Hudson, its lights necklace-like against the powder blue morning sky. The road dipped and curved under the bridge and rose to meet the walls of an old castle that once sat on the edge of the Hudson. Ahead, the tower of the Cloisters stood out clearly amidst the budding but bare branches of the trees in Fort Tryon Park.

"Get over into the far right lane," Colleen guided Tony. "Slow down...the exit comes up quickly. It's a sharp right turn so slow down...slow down to about twenty..."

"Colleen, I'm taking you home, not to park in the Cloisters."

"I know...I live right near there. I just want to show you something. And I want to tell you something in a special place. Then you can get right back on the highway home."

They turned off the highway and drove uphill under a massive stone archway that spanned the roadway nearly 100 feet above them. They followed the road as it curved uphill, looped around the Cloisters Museum, crossed over the stone archway they had just passed under, and led them to an old greystone building with a green tile roof. "Park here," Colleen said, "and we'll walk up that path to the lookout point."

"It's colder up here," Tony shivered slightly and rubbed his hands together as they walked.

"Did you know this is the highest natural point in New York City?" Colleen asked. Without waiting for an answer, she continued. "And did you further know that the Rockefellers donated this land and the Cloisters to the people of the City of New York? Partly because they are a great philanthropic family and partly to keep the murders of union mine workers by Rockefeller Pinkerton goons out west out of the New York papers. Philanthropic munificence overshadows robber baron brutality any day in the newspaper that prints what it deems fit and even in New York's picture newspaper."

Tony was impressed when they reached the lookout. "God, look at that river! What's that bridge way up north?"

"The Tappan Zee," Colleen answered, proudly. This was her favorite spot in her favorite park and dawn was her favorite time of day to be there. "It's about 30 miles away. Looks so close though, doesn't it? And look at the Palisades...formed by glaciers...and the Hudson...My father always said that no river in America could compare with the Hudson. Tony, see those high-rises south of the George Washington Bridge?" Tony answered yes. 'Then, north of the bridge, nothing. No buildings, except that monastery across the river. Can you see it there? There will never be any buildings there no matter how crowded this area gets or how valuable the land becomes. Do you know why?"

Tony smiled at Colleen because of her enthusiasm. "No, why?"

"Because it's in the deed of the gift to New York City from the Rockefellers. They can look south down the river from their estate in Westchester and see all of this. And they want it to be kept just like this...undeveloped...or..." Colleen stared across the river.

"Or?" Tony asked.

"Or the deal is off!" Colleen laughed lightly. "Come with me..." She pulled him by the hand up a few steps and past the wooden benches under the tall shade trees to the eastern side of the lookout. The sun, a fat orange oval, was just above the buildings in The Bronx. "Now, look back to where we were!" Colleen pulled Tony along with her, laughing inexplicably. When they reached the western side of the lookout, she pointed and said. "Look! Just on the edge of the Palisades. You can barely see it! Look!"

Tony searched and at first saw nothing. Then he exclaimed. "The moon! The full moon is sitting on the edge of the horizon! Wow! You can barely see it! If you didn't know it was there, you'd never see it."

"Isn't it great?" Colleen was terribly excited. "Today, the sun rises and the moon sets at the exact same time. And isn't this just the best place to see it from? Don't you just love it here? I come here all the time."

Tony stared at the barely visible moon as it disappeared below the Palisades. "I've never seen anything like this. You're something, Colleen. I'll say that."

"Say it," Colleen snuggled up to him.

"You're really something." He put his arm around her shoulder and Colleen pressed her cheek into his chest. They stood in silence for some time. When Tony looked up, the moon was gone. "I better get you home." They started to walk back to the car. "But you never told me your idea?"

"Oh..." Colleen was embarrassed. She sat down on one of the park benches. "Well, ever since Brigid, my daughter, was young..." Colleen cleared her throat nervously. "I knew that I would have to talk to her about sex, you know, or *Es-Eee-Ex*, as my mother calls it." She laughed self-consciously. "And I always thought I'd do it on her sixteenth birthday. I guess because I was 16 when I got pregnant." Colleen turned inward. "I didn't want her to go through what I went through. I want her to know that sex is good and natural and fun and pleasurable and that I'm on her side. That I'm there for her. And that she can bring her boyfriend home. They can stay in her room and that they don't have to hide and be scared." Colleen began to cry. Tony sat beside her and put his arm around her shoulder.

Colleen forced herself to stop crying. She caught her breath and swallowed hard. She smiled weakly. "And now...well, now she's 16. Later today, after I get some sleep, I going to have that talk with her. She has a boyfriend. He's so nice and very cute—"

"Don't get any ideas, Colleen!" Tony teased.

"Oh, don't be silly." She sniffled. "I want them to be able to make love without all the anxiety that I had. Without all the sneaking around. Afraid of getting caught. I want to make sure she knows what she needs to know about contraception. I don't want her to be like I was at her age—ignorant, with no one to ask for advice, winding up pregnant in high school."

Colleen stood up. "I'm not being fair to you. Keeping you up like this."

"Well, as long as you've kept me up," Tony whispered in her ear, "how'd you like to get me up one more time?"

"You're wicked," Colleen smiled. "And I was getting worried."

"Worried?"

"I was worried you'd never ask." She laughed and kissed him.

"Mom!" Brigid called out, shocked. "Mom! I can't believe you sometimes!" She was happy but concerned to see her mother.

Flustered, Colleen turned toward her daughter. Nervously, she began to straighten her hair and close the top button on the front of her dress. "Brigid..." Colleen laughed a high, self-conscious, unnatural laugh. She was worried that her daughter and her boyfriend would notice that she had been doing drugs. "Whatever are you two doing here at this hour? Have you been home yet?"

"Mom, we've been home *and* had a good night's sleep. Which is more than you can say, Mom," Brigid laughed tenderly, "you look *wild!*

"Oh, Brigid!" Colleen blushed. "Tony, this is my daughter, Brigid. And this is her..." Colleen hesitated, "friend...boyfriend ...Michael."

"Nice to meet you both," Tony smiled, at ease. "Even under such unusual circumstances. But then, Brigid, I'm sure you know better than Michael or me, that your mother is a very unusual woman!" He laughed and the teenagers laughed with him.

"Well, I'm glad you all think I'm so funny!" Colleen said with mock indignation.

"Oh Mom!" Brigid said with exasperation. "Did you guys see the sun come up? We were too late."

"I had a hard time getting Michael up this morning," Brigid said innocently.

Tony smiled and started to speak.

"Tony! No jokes from the jaded." Colleen was serious. "Honey, I don't want to pry but did you say—"

"Mom, can I talk to you a minute...*in private*?" She looked at Michael and Tony.

"Sure, baby. You understand, don't you?" Colleen looked seriously at Tony.

"Maybe I should take this opportunity to head on home. I'll get your things from the car." He turned to Michael. "Come on, walk me to the car and let the women talk."

Michael gladly left Brigid with her mother.

"You stayed over last night?" Tony asked nonchalantly.

"Yeah, we were out dancing...got home late..." Michael was slightly embarrassed.

"Hey, I think it's great." Tony punched him lightly on the shoulder "Let you in on a little secret. Colleen thinks it's great too!"

"What?" Michael stopped in his tracks. "How could she know?"

"Hey, Mike. We've been around the block a few times, you know what I mean? We were talking about you guys just before you showed up." They reached the car and Tony got Colleen's belongings. "Colleen thinks you're terrific. It's not like she knew that tonight was the night. It was, wasn't it?"

Michael smiled. "It sure was!" He paused, then asked, "How did she know?"

"She could just see what was happening. Let me clue you in on something...on the off chance that you don't already know." He spoke with a kind sincerity. "Your girlfriend's mother is special. And she cares a lot about you two kids. You can be honest with her. You can tell her anything. Don't forget that. It's rare, Michael. It's very rare."

When they returned, Colleen and Brigid were hugging and crying. Tony and Michael looked at one another and shook their heads. "I hope those are happy tears," Michael said.

"Colleen, I really gotta go now," Tony gave her a hug. "I'll be home Wednesday. I'll call you or you call me, okay? Nice to meet you, Brigid. You too, Michael."

Colleen watched Tony disappear around a turn in the path. "Say, I'm exhausted. I'm heading home now." Colleen looked at Michael lovingly, silently. She held out her arms. "Come here...both of you." She embraced her daughter and her daughter's lover. "Happy birthday, Brigid. I'm going to take the elevator down to Broadway and I'll get a cab home."

As she rode in the cab up Broadway, Colleen saw an old friend in the doorway of the Donemay Pub. "Stop at the corner!" She yelled at the cab driver. She rolled down her window. "Tommy!" Colleen caught his attention. "Wait there!" She fumbled opening her purse. "I'll get out here, driver." Colleen was stunned to see two $50 bills in her purse. She paid the driver and gave him a generous tip. Colleen hoped Tony gave her the money in the spirit in which she was accepting it.

"Tommy!" Colleen hoped she could stop off at the bar before going home. "Good to see you!"

"Noon seems so far away in the wee hours of a Sunday morning," Tommy teased, affecting a brogue. "Terrible to wake up in New York City and know that not a drop can be had until the clock strikes twelve!"

"Join me for a quiet one?" Colleen asked. "Then breakfast at Arthur's Diner—on me!"

Tommy paused a moment. "A few of the regulars are still inside. Big poker game going on." Tommy rubbed his chin with his thumb and forefinger. "I don't suppose anyone will notice if we pop in and have a few." He held the door open for Colleen. "But, we've got to sit at one of the tables in the back. The parishioners are heading to and from

Good Shepherd for Sunday Mass. It would reflect poorly on the management were we to be seen drinking away, plunking our money down on the bar instead of in the collection plate."

"Tommy, I have had the wildest night of my life! You won't believe what I'm about to tell you!"

Tommy poured them both a triple of Irish whiskey. "I always believe you, Colleen. And I'm always amazed that you lived to tell your tales! Now—who's the guy?"

"Well, I don't know him that well. But he seems so sweet. And we had the hottest—" Colleen paused as Tommy held up his hand for her to stop. "What?"

"You know, Colleen, you know that I have certain feelings for you...feelings that aren't reciprocal." He was gentle but serious. "So...I get the overall picture. Spare me the enthusiastic recounting...the blow-by-blow details. And the pun is completely intended." He sipped his drink.

"But Tommy...it wasn't just the sex...Tonight, why the whole night was like a roller-coaster ride. So many emotions...so many ups and downs. Love and friendship and family and friends and such hot, hot—" Again, Colleen saw Tommy raise his hand for her to stop. "No, I'm going to say it. *Sex! Wild, hot sex!*" Colleen's loud laughter brought the owner out from the backroom.

"I didn't know you two were here." He was annoyed that he had gotten up for nothing.

Colleen leaned toward Tommy and whispered, "And... I did coke for the first time!"

"Oh, be careful, Colleen!" Tommy was in earnest. "Stick with the booze, Colleen. The booze can be bad enough. But it's legal. And it's cheap. Get caught up in that nasty white powder, Colleen, and it's all downhill."

"But it makes you feel *fantastic!*" Colleen's eyes glowed. "It makes you feel like nothing can get in your way. Like I can do anything!"

"Ah, but Colleen, you know that isn't true. And just as every toot, every spree, comes to an end, Colleen, you come to the end with the little white powder," he spoke earnestly. "It's a hard one, Colleen. I've seen 'em crash. Most are quite mad at the end. It brings 'em down hard, Colleen, hard and fast. Their money's all gone, their brains are either fried or coming out their ears, and they all wind up doing things they'd never do—all for that little white powder." Tommy took Colleen's hands. "Stick to drinking, Colleen. That's bad enough!" Tommy finished his drink. "Let's get some breakfast."

By the time the waitress brought their meals, Colleen had begun to feel agitated and restless. By the middle of breakfast, a fierce dread came over her. Before she could finish her food, Colleen had to get up from the table. "I need some air," she said, her voice choked.

"Are you all right?" Tommy started to get up.

"Stay!" Colleen said, frightened. "I just need to get outside a minute." She rushed from the restaurant. She exhaled deeply and looked searchingly to the sky. The blueness brought her to tears. She didn't understand why, but the blueness of the sky softened something in her, something that held back deep sorrow. Colleen walked to the curb and grasped a parking meter for support. Her whole body shook, pulsating wave after wave, with her weeping. Although she tried to suppress her crying, the energy of her emotions was too powerful. Colleen's sobbing and heart-rending cries were heard by passers-by who turned from her and quickened their pace.

Tommy paid the bill and came to Colleen. He was frightened by what he saw. She was slumped over the parking meter, pale and sweating, seized by uncontrollable crying, her lips pursed, and her mouth pushed to the side and up to the right with such force that her right eye was closed. Her lips looked like those of an infant desiring and despairing of ever receiving the nipple. Her right eye fluttered with a tick. Her throat was seized with choking spasms. Tommy tried to touch Colleen but she shrank from him. She seemed to him to be collapsing from within. As if she were empty inside, like a TV vacuum tube, and now was imploding. He hailed a cab and gently, but forcibly, got Colleen into the back seat.

Fortunately, Brigid was at home and let Tommy into the building. She came to the lobby, where her mother had seated herself and refused to move, crying less violently, but with more heartbreak. Brigid silently coaxed her mother to stand and, with great effort, led her to the elevator. Tommy came with her to the apartment door.

"Can I help?" He asked, frightened.

"I can take care of her now, Tommy. I can't begin to thank you for getting my mom home. It must have been so embarrassing." Colleen hung on her daughter's shoulders, muttering "my baby, my baby."

"I'll call you in a bit when I get home. You have my number if you need me. And Brigid, if you think she needs to see a doctor, I'll take you to the emergency room at Presbyterian." He was worried. "Don't wait for an ambulance, honey. But she's probably just had too much to drink, Brigid. She might have the shakes in an hour or two. Let her have a bit of the hair of the dog—"

"Let her?" Brigid said angrily. "How could I ever hope to stop her?"

Tommy stepped backward away from the young girl. "I know, Brigid. We'll talk..." He turned and went on his way home.

The morning passed slowly. Brigid grew angrier by the hour. She refused to talk to her aunt when Lis tried to get the young girl to open up. "How can she do this to herself?" Brigid repeated that question again and again at irregular intervals.

"We don't know *why*, honey. We know *what's* wrong but we don't know *why*," Lis looked out the window at two young girls playing in the park across the street. It reminded her of herself and Colleen when they were children. "And worse...we don't know what to do about it."

"You know, there she was up in Fort Tryon Park at five-thirty in the morning, *drunk*, with some guy she picked up in some bar—" Brigid was cut off by her aunt.

"Honey, you said he was a nice man. Michael said he was a *very nice* guy." Lis defended her sister, partly because she saw nothing wrong with Colleen meeting a man in a bar—the drinking aside—and partly because she had done similar things herself. "Don't judge so harshly, Brigid. It's *the drinking* that's the problem."

"It just makes me so angry!" Brigid turned red. "You don't know, you can't know; you don't live here and see it day after day!" Suddenly, all the young girl's energy was gone. She sat down on the sofa, sighed, closed her eyes, and leaned back.

No sooner had the two women begun to relax than they heard Colleen moving about in the bedroom. Both hurried inside. They saw Colleen sitting on the edge of the bed, eyes open but unseeing, trying unsuccessfully to light a match. A cigarette dangled from her lips, the filter end outward. Colleen dropped the match and unsteadily leaned over to pick it up. When she retrieved the match, she dropped the book of matches. When she retrieved the book of matches, she could not light the match. She cursed and, when she cursed, the cigarette fell from her lips to her lap. She picked up the cigarette and put the wrong end in her mouth again. She finally struck a match and it lit. When she put it to the filter end of the cigarette and puffed and puffed, the cigarette, of course, would not light. The match burned down to her finger and she shook it from her hand onto the rug.

"I can't watch this!" Brigid left the room.

Colleen began the process all over again. Her sister took the matches and the cigarette from her and eased her back into bed. "You need sleep, Sis. You need sleep now, Colleen." Colleen turned over on her side and Lis pulled the quilt up over her sister. In a few moments, Colleen was sound asleep.

"Last night she gets all weepy and teary over some singer! And look how she treats us! Look how she treats herself!" Brigid felt guilty about her anger.

"We'll work this out, Brigid. You'll see, I mean it. Colleen will get through this." Brigid had her back to her aunt. "Look at me, Brigid. You know very well that your mom was crying over her life last night. You're smart enough to know that. She feels she's failed. Failed herself, failed you. Colleen is down, Brigid. Down on herself. And she's being harder on herself than anyone would be to her. She'd never do to another person what she's doing to herself. When I was your age, I turned to Colleen for help, advice, support. Now, I have to be there for her."

"I know," Brigid said softly, "it just wears me down, you know? I love mom and she's so great, you know? I mean, she understands me, and she's on my side. But I feel so helpless and angry and guilty all the time lately. I want to run away somewhere. Not even with Michael. I just want to run away where I can have a normal life, Aunt Lis! Just a normal life. The way it is with mom is...is...it can be great, really great..., or really scary! And I never know which it will be or when things will turn. Colleen can start out happy and then get...get kind of crazy." Brigid put her head in her hands.

Lis sat on the sofa beside her niece. "What do you mean by crazy, honey?"

"Well, sometimes..." Brigid looked directly at her aunt. "Sometimes she doesn't know who I am! She walks around the apartment as if she were somewhere else...as if she were someone else. It scares me, Aunt Lis!" Brigid began to tremble. "Once when she was coming home, and I was going out, we met by accident in the lobby. I said 'Hi, Mom. I'm going to the supermarket. Need anything?' And she said, 'Excuse me, young lady, do I know you?' Imagine...I've never told this to anyone, Aunt Lis."

"When was this, Brigid?" Lis was even more concerned.

"This year...February. I was home during the winter break from school. I was afraid to tell anyone. Afraid no one would believe me."

"I believe you, honey," she hugged her niece. "Don't worry, I believe you." They sat silently for a moment. "I think we need to get Colleen to a doctor, a psychologist. I don't think we should try to do this on our own."

"She's so stubborn," Brigid said, her anger returning.

"I know...Don't worry. It's not your job to be a parent to your mother. Are you meeting Michael today? It's a beautiful spring day!"

"I was going to but I don't think I should leave Mom—"

"Brigid, I'll be with her." Her aunt was reassuring and protective. "You get on the phone and call Michael right now. It's important that you be together today. Can I share a secret with you? About love and sex?"

Brigid smiled. "Yes!" She replied eagerly.

"Well, after I made love for the first time," Lis smiled at the memory, "when I was your age and living at school, the next day, we had to be apart. And during those hours we both began to feel funny. And we didn't call each other. And then the night went by and we both felt more uncomfortable. And so we didn't call."

"What happened?" Brigid needed to know.

"Well, I was studying psychology then and I came across a story about a note that the physician Dr. Charcot wrote to Sigmund Freud regarding a female patient Freud had referred to him. She was suffering from severe anxiety...Charcot told Freud that his prescription for the woman was *'Penis Normalis. Repetatur.'* You know Latin, Brigid?"

Brigid was laughing. "Give me a break, Aunt Lis! I don't have to know very much Latin to know that that doctor was right!"

"So, I went to the student clinic and got a friend to get me a page from a prescription pad. I wrote out Charcot's prescription, signing Dr. Charcot's name on the bottom," Lis was enjoying her memory and the recounting of it. "Then I called my guy and told him I had been to the clinic and gotten a prescription and asked if he would come with me to get the prescription filled."

"What did he say?" Brigid leaned forward in the chair.

"Well, I could tell right away that *he thought* he had given me something!" Both young women laughed. "For me, it was the first time. But for him it was only the first time with me!" She paused briefly. "Maybe for him it was only the first time that day!"

"Aunt Lis!" Brigid was shocked.

"So, he came over to my apartment at Bensalem and sat down in my bedroom on the edge of the bed. He was nervous as hell. I sat next to him and said, 'Sweetie, I went to the doctor because I had this funny *sensation*,' and his mouth got dry. I could see him nervously moving his tongue around and hear that dry sound, you know? I told him the doctor gave me a prescription and that I should show it to him."

"What'd he do when he read it?"

"Well, he let out an explosive laugh! God was he relieved! But then, he got this look in his eyes. I'll tell you, Brigid, he had killer eyes! That's how he got every girl at school to go to bed with him. Every single one of us! And then I noticed," Lis blushed.

"He was hard?" She squealed.

"Like a rock!" Lis laughed and hugged her niece.

"I'm calling Michael right now!" Brigid ran to the phone in the kitchen.

Lis sat back on the sofa and thought of her years at the experimental college. She thought of her lovers, of the man she lived with, of her friends from those days. Her feelings for them all were as real and strong to her at that moment as they had been long ago.

"I'm going to meet Michael in ten minutes, okay?" Brigid went to her room to get ready.

"More than okay, honey. Much more than okay." Lis went to look in on her sister. Colleen was sleeping in the same position as before. Lis hoped she slept for hours and hours. And she hoped that when

Colleen awoke they would be able to talk to one another, honestly.

It was evening when Colleen awoke. At first, she didn't know where she was. She did not know what time of day it was. Colleen wondered whether it was Sunday evening or Monday morning. She looked at her clock and it said 6:30. But that was of no help to her. She did not know if it was a.m. or p.m. She felt an oppressive dread. It was as if just outside her room some unfathomable horror awaited her. She closed her eyes.

After a few moments Colleen began to come to her senses. And what she sensed was distasteful—her dry mouth tasted of whiskey, beer, and cigarettes. What she sensed was unpleasant—her stomach ached and felt sour. What she sensed was painful—her eyes could not bear even the waning light and her head throbbed. She tried to sit up but couldn't.

Without looking, Colleen reached out and opened the top drawer of the bedside table. She felt around inside and found her pint bottle of vodka. She moved her hand about the tabletop, searching for a glass of water. She realized she had forgotten to place a glass of water at her bedside before going to sleep. Bracing herself, Colleen opened the pint bottle, tilted her head upward slightly, and drank the vodka straight.

She collapsed back down, holding the bottle firmly upright with both hands, resting it on her stomach. A few moments later, Colleen took two long swigs of vodka. The alcohol began to take effect and Colleen sat up. She began to try to piece together the night before. Images, like shards of a shattered stained glass mural, flashed before her. Brigid opening presents; a cab racing down the West Side Highway along the shimmering river; Pat laughing outside the White Horse Tavern. Colleen shivered, startled. She recalled the cold tiled floor of the men's room digging into her knees; she saw herself slowly unzipping a man's zipper.

Colleen stood up. "Oh God!" She had stark, vivid memories of snorting coke and performing oral sex in the bathroom of the bar. *Oh God, oh God, oh God ...What was I doing?* Colleen opened her closet door and looked at herself in the full-length mirror. She quickly averted her eyes.

Sitting at her bedside, Colleen sipped more vodka. *This'll get me back on an even keel. Then I'll see who's outside.* Colleen heard the radio playing in the living room. Suddenly, she felt sick to her stomach, so sick she wasn't sure she could make it to the bathroom. Colleen picked up the wastepaper basket beside her bed, dumped all the tissues onto the floor, and pulled out the plastic garbage bag that was lining the wicker basket. She vomited the vodka and bits of breakfast into the plastic bag. Her heart raced and she broke out into a greasy sweat. Colleen continued to vomit. Blood came, and bile, and more blood, followed by the dry heaves. She began to cry and moan from the pain of the retching. She knew that whoever was in her apartment heard her, and she felt humiliated.

Colleen knelt down beside her bed until she was sure that she would not throw up again. She began, slowly, to breathe more regularly. Her complexion turned from grey to a healthy rosy color. She felt less tense than before and drank some more vodka. Colleen went to the mirror once more and, without really looking at herself, fixed her hair, wiped her mouth clean with a tissue, blew her nose, and changed from yesterday's clothes into a sweatshirt and old jeans.

She paused before the bedroom door, took a deep breath, and stepped quickly into the hallway, almost running the four steps to the bathroom. She swiftly closed the door behind her and turned the shower on full blast. The room rapidly filled with steam. Colleen stripped and sat slumped over, naked on the toilet, hoping the alcohol would ooze out her pores in the hot steamy room.

When she felt she was perspiring enough, Colleen reached behind the shower curtain and adjusted the hot and cold water to a comfortable temperature. She took a long shower, turning round and round, lathering up and rinsing off repeatedly, shampooing and conditioning her hair. Under the soothing waters, she shaved her legs and underarms. After toweling dry, Colleen liberally applied a skin softener and moisturizer to her whole body, gently massaging her body as she did.

I almost feel human again, she smiled to herself, already beginning to forget the night before and the morning after.

Colleen took her favorite terrycloth bathrobe, thick and deep blue, from the back of the door and wrapped it around her. She dried her hair with a towel and used her blow dryer for a few minutes, stopping before her hair was completely dry. *It's funny—but I feel great!* She looked at her face in the mirror. *I guess I can still bounce back quickly!* She thought with pride.

Colleen left the bathroom and quietly walked down the hallway to the kitchen. She heard her daughter and sister talking. They were preparing dinner. "Hi," Colleen said sheepishly. Both looked at her but said nothing. "That bad, huh?"

Before either woman could speak, Colleen returned to her bedroom. She lay down on the bed, her feet still on the floor, her hands behind her head. She wished she were alone. Colleen wanted to have a few drinks to *take the edge off,* she thought. Instead, she drank more vodka in her room, stopping only when there was an ounce or so left in the bottle. Colleen never liked to finish a bottle.

At dinner, both Brigid and Lis were astonished by Colleen's ravenous appetite. She ate half of the roast chicken herself, one and one-half roast potatoes, a generous helping of spinach, all followed by a large salad. Colleen's dehydration was evident—she drank one whole quart of orange juice with her meal.

"You were pretty sick before," Lis said.

"Comes with the territory," Colleen replied as she rose from the table.

"We have to talk, Colleen." Lis remained seated.

"Not now, Lis." Colleen left the room.

"Mom! You're going to listen to what we have to say!" Brigid stormed after her mother. "You may not want to talk to us but we have something to say to you—whether you want to hear it or not!"

"Listen, I know I had too much to drink last night—"

"And every night for months now," Brigid shouted. "You're turning into an old drunk, Mom! An old drunk!"

"Brigid!" Colleen was furious. "Is that the kind of *talk* you want to have," Colleen spit the word talk out at her daughter.

"I think you both better calm down," Lis tried unsuccessfully to intervene.

"Keep out of this, Lis!" Colleen yelled. "What are you doing here anyway?"

"*You invited me, Colleen!"* Lis lost her temper. "But I'm sure you don't remember inviting me, do you?"

"I bet she doesn't even remember how she got home this morning!" Brigid stared at her mother while talking to her aunt. "Do you, Mom? How did you get home?"

Colleen felt panicky. She didn't remember how she got home. She remembered the White Horse, the 55 Pub. "What's his name... Tony...and Tommy?" Colleen remembered the Donemay with Tommy. Desperate, she guessed. "Tommy..."

"Good guess, Mom. Tommy *what*? Huh, Mom? Tommy what?" Brigid was frightened by her anger. "Kind of a blur, Mom?"

"Brigid, this won't get us anywhere." Lis put her hand on Brigid's shoulder. "Colleen, it's not us against you."

"Oh, I get it!" Colleen went to her room. "I get it!" She yelled as she got dressed to go out. "Good cop-bad cop! You two need a better act than that! Lis, I'm asking you to go home now. We can talk another time. Brigid, I'm sure you have homework to do."

"And you, Mom? More drinking to do? Going out to hang out with those losers at the bar?" Her anger was mixed with grief and fear.

"Don't you call my friends losers, Brigid." Colleen stepped into the living room, livid. "Don't you dare call my friends losers."

"I don't even know how you call them friends! What do you do together? Drink! That's all you do—drink! You don't see your real friends anymore, Mom. You don't do anything anymore. Remember you used to take me to the theater? Off-Broadway, Off-Off-Broadway? Remember you used to take me with you and your real friends to plays, movies, political rallies, concerts? Remember? And we used to go to the country, the beach, the museums, galleries, and shows? Have you forgotten all that?"

Colleen knew her daughter was speaking the truth. However, these truths made her think of only one thing—a drink, a drink in a dark bar, alone with others.

"I'm sorry..." Colleen could not look at her either her sister or her daughter. "I owe both of you an apology. I know that I...uh...I know that I've been under a lot of pressure lately and that I...uh...my drinking...uh...that I've let things get out of hand. But..." Colleen walked to the front door and opened it. "I just can't talk about it now. I'm sorry, Brigid. I'm sorry, Lis. I'm going for a walk. I'll see you in an hour or so."

The streets of Inwood looked particularly dreary to Colleen but she knew that was simply a projection of her own feelings. She knew she was seeing the world with eyes altered by alcohol, sensing the world with nerves deadened by alcohol. "I don't know what's come over me these past few months," Colleen struggled to be honest with herself.

"Brigid's right...I don't do any of the things I used to enjoy...I avoid my friends..."

Colleen stopped for a red light along Broadway. Across the street, on the corner, amber lights glowed in the windows of a neighborhood bar. The brisk evening winds were bracing and Colleen felt the lure of memories of cognac on a cold night, of the harshness of the drink going down and the warmth from the drink spreading throughout her body. She felt the lure of the memory of the easy glow of the first drink, the easy camaraderie that comes with idle bar chatter, of the easy painless passage of time. *Reality's on hold when I'm in there,* Colleen thought.

The light turned green but Colleen did not cross the street. Instead, she walked further north along Broadway. As she passed another bar Colleen quickened her pace. However, only one hundred feet or so from the tavern, she stopped. Agitated, Colleen turned her head from right to left as she shrugged her shoulders, attempting to shake off the stiffness she felt. Colleen stared down the driveway of an auto repair shop that she had passed thousands of times, startled by what she saw. Spanning the one-story garage and workshop, at the end of an alley covered with oil, grease, and discarded automobile parts, stood an elegant, old stone archway, weather-worn and obscured by the mechanical mess at its feet.

Colleen could see that it had once been the gateway to something grand. But what could have been here? Colleen had lived much of her life in Inwood and its environs yet hadn't a clue as to either the existence or the origin of the arch. *I'll go to the library tomorrow and see what I can find out.*

Colleen turned slowly around and looked at the scene before her. The old IRT elevated subway tracks stretched from the 225th Street Bridge, passed the turn-of-the-century bus depot and the rundown warehouses that stretched from Broadway to the Harlem River, and disappeared behind the tenements that stood only 20 feet from the train tracks, shaking every 10 minutes with each passing train.

To the west, the street rose sharply upward, like an escarpment, to the bare brick walls of the apartment buildings above. The rear of the buildings, dimly lit by light from the kitchens and living rooms, ran together and seemed to form a massive castle wall, a defense against the urban industrial ugliness below. On the other side of the buildings, Baker Field stretched to the hills of Inwood Park; the Henry Hudson Bridge spanned Spuyten Duyvil, and the Palisades stood tall on the west bank of the Hudson River. The natural beauty had made a powerful impression on Colleen as a child, an impression that deepened with time.

Colleen decided not to stop off at any of the neighborhood bars. *Not tonight...I'm going to go home...Maybe I'll sit down with Brigid and share with her all these feelings I've waited so long to express. She's old enough now.*

With determination, Colleen turned toward home. In her mind, she was engaged in conversation with her daughter. She was practicing what she would say to Brigid about love, about sex, about pleasure. She was imagining her daughter's responses. In her fantasy, she was thrilled by her daughter's admiration for her mother.

As she passed Good Shepherd Church, Colleen heard her name called. She turned to see Tommy walking down the stairs of the church toward her. "Colleen! Who says the dead don't come back to life! God, when I left you this morning it seemed 50-50 that the undertaker would see you before I did! It's a miracle, Colleen. A bloody miracle! I was just inside lighting a candle for you, saying a prayer for your immortal soul."

"How about a prayer for my mortal body?" Colleen smiled at her friend.

"Oh, I've prayed for your body, all right, Colleen. Prayed hard and long!" Tommy's eyes twinkled.

"Hard and long, eh? What kind of prayers, Tommy?" Colleen continued before her friend could reply. "Ejaculations?"

"Ah, bawdy wench!" He laughed heartily, blushing noticeably.

"Look at you! You're turning so red!" Colleen laughed good-naturedly. "Was I on target? Did I hit a bullseye?"

"That's for me to know and you to find out, Colleen," Tommy sought to compose himself. He could feel the heat from his blushing. "But...I always said you're the stuff that dreams are made on, love."

Colleen knew that Tommy had long desired her, or his image of her, and on occasion, especially just before closing time, she had nearly invited him home with her or gone home with him. *We're just good buddies,* Colleen thought. *Good drinking buddies. Why ruin it?*

"Where you headed?" Tommy had drinking on his mind.

"Oh, just home, I guess."

"How about a quiet one? Just the two of us?"

Colleen hesitated. She wanted to say no; she wanted to go home and be with her daughter. She looked at her wristwatch. "Well...just one, though, Tommy. I've got to get things under control a bit. I've been out partying too much lately."

"Just one, Colleen." Tommy was happy Colleen was joining him. "Just one to keep you mellow."

As they walked toward their favorite bar, Colleen asked, "Say, what were you doing in church anyway?"

"Lighting a candle for you," Tommy answered. Seriously.

Colleen shook her head but did not pursue the subject further.

Hours later, just before eleven, Colleen left her friend at the bar. "I gotta get to the deli before it closes. Really, Tommy, I shoulda been outta here hours ago. Hours ago." Colleen stepped back from the bar.

"One more, Colleen. Then we'll both go. I'll walk you home." Tommy signaled for the bartender.

"You said that an hour ago." She kissed her friend on the cheek. "Gotta go." Colleen started for the door, unsteadily. *I hope Brigid's asleep,* she thought, ashamed that she had not gone directly home.

Colleen bought two six-packs of beer moments before the

delicatessen closed. *That was close,* she thought. She didn't intend to drink all of them. But better safe than sorry.

She slipped the key into the top lock and turned it as quietly as she could. Next, she turned the cylinder of the bottom lock and gently leaned on the door, hoping to nudge it noiselessly open. But the door did not move. Anxiously, Colleen turned the key in the top lock in the opposite direction and did the same with the bottom lock. She pushed the door but it still would not open. "Shit, one of the locks wasn't locked!" Colleen whispered aloud.

"Is that you, Mom?" Brigid called as she walked down the hallway to the door. She sounded as if she had been awakened by the sound of her mother trying to open the door.

"Yes, honey," Colleen hoped she wasn't slurring her words. She put her grocery bag down on the hallway floor, around the corner where Brigid could not see it.

Brigid did not look at her mother when she opened the door. "I fell asleep on the sofa," she said as she walked to the bathroom.

Colleen did not let the front door close behind her. When Brigid went into the bathroom, she quickly retrieved the beer from the hallway. Colleen put one six-pack in the refrigerator vegetable bin and the other in the back on the bottom shelf.

Colleen sat in "her chair" in the living room and watched the late news on TV. It was a slow news night. Stories about President Ford's plans to fight inflation and the Democratic Presidential primary in New York were followed by local pieces about a health clinic that was closing, a school that was laying off teachers and cutting out afterschool programs, cutbacks in subway and bus service, college students approaching graduation with dim job prospects, and an increase in the number of people applying for unemployment for the week just ending.

Colleen was an avid TV news *junkie*. She loved the late Sunday night news on her favorite local station because the show always ended with a sad but beautiful song as the soundtrack accompanying sad but beautiful images of New York City from dawn to dusk that day. To her surprise, the last segment of the show began with a live report from Bleecker and Macdougal Streets in Greenwich Village. "It was in the clubs of Greenwich Village in the early 1960s that the folk music revival began and that, in the mid-60s, folk rock was born. One of the most influential—though not one of the most financially successful—performers of that time died this weekend. Phil Ochs took his own life on April 9th, at the age of 35."

"Brigid, come here, honey. There's something I want you to see." Brigid sat down by her mother's feet and Colleen gently stroked her daughter's hair.

"The times they have 'a-changed," the reporter continued. "But not necessarily for the better, in our nation and our city." Behind the reporter, a few teenagers mugged for the camera but most New Yorkers walked on by, oblivious to the TV crew. "A few close friends have told us that Phil Ochs was depressed and emotionally troubled recently. The Sixties were angry times and Phil Ochs' anger found its outlet in such songs as *'I Ain't Marchin' Anymore,'* and "*Outside of a Small Circle of Friends,*' and his songs were meant to move people to change things for the better. The great Civil Rights battles are over; the Vietnam War is over. Some say that depression is anger turned inward. Whether Phil Ochs' anger turned inward and contributed to his death, we do not know. But, with the death of Phil Ochs, another part of a painful era in American history has passed from the scene. In memory of Phil Ochs, we close tonight's broadcast with a look at his Greenwich Village and ours."

The usual Sunday night images consisted of the sun rising behind the Statue of Liberty; people playing with Frisbees, row boating, and strolling in Central Park; tourists window shopping on Fifth Avenue or riding hansom cabs on Central Park South; the George Washington, Triboro, Queensboro, and Brooklyn Bridges shining over dark waters;

all ending with a single yellow cab cruising for a passenger along deserted Sixth Avenue, passing the dark corporate headquarters of the oil, publishing, and television empires. A Muzak version of a classic song about New York generally provided the soundtrack for the pictures and the credits for the show.

Instead, Colleen and Brigid listened to a live version of a Phil Ochs' song and watched nostalgic video images of Greenwich Village, from about 1962 through 1968, intercut with the same street corners, cafes, and clubs as they looked at present. Colleen recognized the song from the first note on the guitar. "Changes," she spoke the title of the song aloud, sad and excited.

"Sit by my side, come as close as the air," Colleen silently mouthed the words along with the singer. "Share in a memory of grey, and wander in my words, dream about the pictures that I play," Colleen cleared her throat and sang softly out loud, "of changes."

Brigid was mesmerized by the tender sorrow of the music and by the change in the people in the stock footage of the Village. The clean-cut, smart look of the early Kennedy years—all in black and white—suddenly exploded into the colorful psychedelic Sixties. Serious, studious college students and slightly older Peace Corps types sitting at folk concerts and teach-ins gave way to hippies and flower children, smoking pot at a free Grateful Dead concert in Tompkins Square Park and at a Be-In in Washington Square Park.

"Wow, that was fast!" Brigid said.

"God, Brigid, it didn't seem so at the time! It seemed we had all the time in the world." Colleen saw a young woman walk into Gerde's Folk City with a young man. "That's just how I used to wear my hair and dress, honey!"

"Moments of magic will glow in the night, all fears of the forest are gone," Phil Ochs sang a verse Colleen did not remember.

"Mom, I'm sorry I was so angry before." Brigid did not turn from the TV when she apologized.

"I'm the one who should apologize to you, honey. I'm the one who's been screwing up." Colleen pulled her daughter's long hair behind her ears and began to braid it.

"Scenes of my young years were warm in my mind," the singer sang over images of hippie boys and girls kissing, "visions of shadows that shine." The images changed to antiwar rallies and battles between police and demonstrators. "'Til one day I returned and found they were victims of the vines of changes."

"Mom, were you happy then?" Brigid asked.

"It was a funny time, Brigid. I remember it as a happy time. But I know it was very hard raising you alone in New York and San Francisco." Colleen became thoughtful. "I remember all the love—and all the *sex*—but I don't remember the loneliness and the fear." A tear formed in Colleen's right eye and she rubbed it away. "But I know that sometimes I could hardly bear the loneliness."

"Your tears will be trembling, now we're somewhere else," Phil Ochs sang. The images were now of New York City in the present. "One last cup of wine we'll pour and I'll kiss you one more time." Colleen and Brigid watched as the TV picture changed, pulling back slowly from a close-up of the top of the Empire State Building, gradually revealing the buildings along Fifth Avenue, the Washington Square Arch, and finally stopping with the arch in the center of the screen and the Empire State Building framed in the center of the arch. "And leave you on the rolling shores of changes."

The first verse repeated over the credits and the show ended before the song was done.

When a commercial came on, Colleen got up and turned the TV off. She turned and held out her arms for her daughter to come to her. Brigid went to her mother and embraced her. However, she was saddened by the smell of alcohol that surrounded her mother, which seemed to arise in fumes from the pores of her skin.

"Sit up with me awhile, Brigid." Colleen smiled but her glazed eyes expressed something quite different.

"It's late, Mom. And school starts back tomorrow."

"Just five minutes, honey. I didn't get to talk with you yesterday on your birthday. And," Colleen blushed. "There's something I've wanted to talk to you about for a long time."

Brigid sat on the sofa and her mother sat beside her. "Ever since you were born, Brigid, I looked forward to your teen years. I know many parents dread them and everyone jokes about teenagers. But it's the most exquisite time of life, really." Colleen smiled self-consciously. "I don't want to preach to you, honey. I just want to talk to you about love and sex. I know you know the *how* of sex—"

Brigid blushed.

"Am I being silly?" Colleen stood up and put her hands to her face, covering her lips.

"No, Mom...But you don't have to *tell* me anything! I've learned from how you have lived. I know I've grown up differently when it comes to sex." Brigid now reached out for her mother and Colleen sat beside her. Colleen lay her head on her daughter's shoulder and listened. "It's what you've *done,* Mom. And as you have told me often, *it's what you haven't done* that has been so important for me. I know you have put up with a lot from everyone because of your ideas, Mom. I know that except for Lis, everyone thinks your energy ideas are nutty." Brigid smiled when she saw her mother smile. "And I can only imagine what everyone put you through over your ideas about sexuality. But I am so grateful that when I was an infant you let me play with myself." Brigid felt her throat becoming dry. "And that when I was a child you let me and my friends have sex play as long as we were enjoying our play. And that when I entered puberty, started my period, and really got interested in boys—that you were always there for me. Always, Mom."

"Really, honey?" Colleen began to cry softly. "Lately I've been feeling like I haven't done anything right. And that maybe I've been wrong about everything."

Brigid kissed Colleen on the head. "Mom, when I hear the other kids describe how they were brought up; or when I'm in school and they are teaching us about sex. Well, I am so glad that you were my mother. And I wish that all my friends could have had you as a mother!"

"Oh, Brigid!" Colleen smiled as she cried. "You must think I'm silly! For so long, I have planned to talk to you on your sixteenth birthday about sex and love and all that!" Colleen laughed at herself. "And now I don't know what to say. I wanted to tell you what I had learned...I wanted to help you be happy in a way that I couldn't be when I was your age..."

"Mom...Maybe I should tell you this now." Brigid flushed with happiness and her eyes shone. "But I gave myself a birthday present last night. Michael and I made love for the first time!"

"Brigid!" Colleen was deeply happy for her daughter. "Did he stay over with you?"

"Yes, Mom. Lis was here. I think at first she was a little embarrassed."

"Oh no, not Lis. Why when she was 16 she went off to her experimental college and started living with—"

"No, Mom, that's not what I mean." Brigid began to laugh and couldn't speak for a moment. "I mean...she was embarrassed because—" Brigid began to laugh again and could not continue speaking.

"Darling, let me in on the joke!"

"She was embarrassed *because I was so loud, Mom! It was incredible, Mom!*"

Colleen caught her breath. She let out a startled laugh and then stood in the living room stunned. "It's genetic!" Colleen finally said loudly. "It's genetic!"

"You too?" Brigid took her mother by the hands and slowly spun her around. "Oh, Mom! It was the most beautiful, beautiful thing I've ever felt. I was warm and tingly and I felt wave after wave of energy move through me and then—" Brigid stopped and, still happy and excited, became serious.

"Yes? And then?"

"I lost consciousness...I just...we were just...*one*." Brigid smiled with profound gratitude at her mother. "I *know*, Mom. I *know* that I could feel everything so strongly because of the way you raised me."

"It's a dream come true, Brigid. It's a dream come true!" Colleen hugged her daughter. "And how about Michael?"

"Well, he just rolled over onto his back and—well, first, we both drifted off into dreamland for about 20 minutes. And we both had the most powerful dreams. But neither of us could remember our dreams. We just knew that we had incredible dreams."

"I'm thirsty!" Colleen announced.

Brigid followed her mother into the kitchen. "But then he was so *tender*, so sweet. He said he was nervous at first. He had played around but never had intercourse before. But...then he said he just got carried away and it wasn't like him doing anything. It was like something in him moving."

"Did you talk to him?" Colleen popped open a beer and took a long swallow.

"No, we were too happy to talk about anything!" Brigid blushed again. "Then, in the middle of the night, I woke up and well...he was asleep but excited *so*—"

"So you helped Mother Nature along!" Colleen was delighted.

"So I helped *myself* and we made love again. Michael woke up to find me on top of him making love to him!"

"Brigid!" Colleen was surprised at her daughter's innocence and honesty.

"He was even more excited than the first time. After we made love, we saw that the sun was coming up and we went up to the park. That's when we met you and your friend."

Colleen was embarrassed. "Well, he's not really a friend. I met him in a bar in the Village. Pat knows him pretty well."

"He said something really nice to Michael about you."

"Really?" Colleen was curious.

"Well, he told Michael that you were special and that we could be honest with you." Brigid studied her mother.

"Don't look at me that way. You know I don't like it when you look at me like that!" Colleen smiled but was uncomfortable.

"He said that you *knew* that Michael and I were going to make love last night. Is that true?"

"No, of course it's not true. How could I have known? I probably just said that I *thought* you would soon."

Brigid looked at her mother intensely.

"Stop that!"

Brigid laughed. "I guess you're telling the truth. Do you like him, Mom?"

"He's okay," Colleen finished her beer and opened another. "But I probably won't see him again." Colleen began to compare her Saturday night-Sunday morning experiences with her daughter's. The contrast unsettled her. "We're too different. He's a—" *drug addict*, Colleen thought, "—businessman," she said instead. "Salesman...on the go...travels a lot...also...the kind of guy who doesn't spend nights alone on the road. Know what I mean?"

"I guess so. I just want you to be happy, Mom."

"Does Michael have an older brother?" Colleen teased.

"Yes! He does!" Brigid did not know her mother was joking.

"And how old is he? Seventeen?"

"Oh yeah...I see what you mean. He's 23...Funny, but I don't think of you as old, Mom."

"He's 23?" Colleen feigned excitement. "I could go for a young stallion. Think we could double-date?"

"Oh, Mom!" Brigid smiled. "I've got to get some sleep. Six o'clock comes fast." She kissed her mother on the cheek.

"Sweet dreams, honey. Good night."

Colleen walked down the hallway and checked the locks on the apartment door. All three were locked. She turned off the bathroom light on her way back to the living room. At the end of the hallway, she turned off the hallway light, reached around the wall, and turned off the living room lights. She continued into the kitchen and turned off the last remaining light. Colleen opened the refrigerator, took out a can of beer, and returned to "her chair" in the living room.

It wasn't how I had always dreamed it would be. Colleen's thoughts revolved around the various scenarios she had written in her mind—written, rehearsed, and rewritten for years—in which she talked openly with Brigid about sex. *In a way, it was better than anything I could have imagined. I imagined what I wanted when I was her age. But Brigid is not me. And 1976—as bad as it is—is not 1959. Wow!* Colleen stood up and walked to the living room window. *Wow, my daughter gave herself some sixteenth birthday present!*

Outside her window, the lamps along the pathways winding through the park had blue halos around them from light diffracting in the humid air. Under the lamps nearby, Colleen could see empty park benches. Although it was late, she saw two people walking alone in the park, unaware of one another. "Passing strangers..." Colleen whispered aloud, thinking of the title of a movie a friend had made. The scene before her also reminded her of a photograph by her favorite photographer, Andre Kertesz. Colleen turned from the window and went to the bookshelves in the hallway. Without even hesitating, she reached out and took a collection of Kertesz's photographs.

Kertesz and his wife found an apartment overlooking Washington Square Park in 1952 and he took many photographs looking downward at the street from his balcony. It was a view that was familiar to Colleen. Since childhood she had spent long hours looking out upon the city from her apartment. She saw many things—teenagers kissing, a mother hitting a child, a drunk staggering along alone at closing time, a man opening a grocery store before dawn, a newspaper truck throwing bundles of the morning paper at the blind man's newsstand. Colleen saw first spring rains and first winter snows, awesome blue-black thunderheads and harrowing hurricanes, sweet summer dawns and melancholy autumn dusks. And, to her, Kertesz's photographs were as personal and as powerful.

Colleen turned on a small table lamp and looked at the two small, dark figures in the photograph, stark against the snow, passing unaware of each other, beneath the black bare branches of the maple and silver linden trees. One, a man, head high, seemed to be walking with the wind at his back, his hands deep in his overcoat pockets. The other, a woman, walking into the wind, seemed to be carrying a small package under her left arm and a large travel bag with her right.

The simple severity of the photograph appealed to Colleen. *That's New York...that's New York in the winter.* She turned the page and saw a photograph of the same scene taken at night. *Oh, I've turned them both into one picture in my mind.* Colleen was amused at her faulty memory, amused because she was so certain that her erroneous memory was correct. *The night photo was taken at a different focal length or printed differently or both*, Colleen thought. "*Here you see the entire young tree, but here in the night scene, we see only half the tree. Oh look!* Colleen noticed a single set of footprints along the path the man had been walking. *You can see his footprints clearly under the lamplight*

Colleen searched the photo but was unable to find the woman's footprints. *Maybe the wind blew the snow in swirls around the open area and covered her tracks,* Colleen thought.

"Oh, this vale of tears!" Colleen said, mocking her mother's oft-repeated phrase. "This world is a mystery, that's for sure. Such beauty and such ugliness; such wealth and such want; such deep joy and pleasure side by side with heart-rending sorrow and hellish suffering and fear."

She thought of her daughter. *If Brigid made love to Michael without anxiety...if she just surrendered...didn't catch her breath...if it was the way she described...then I've done my job. I didn't get in the way."* Colleen felt pride. *I know no one understands this...but I let her be herself. I didn't become an obstacle in my child's way.*

Colleen finished her beer. She saw Brigid's new guitar in the corner of the living room and decided to play awhile before going to sleep. Colleen began with *Sidh Beag Agus Sidh Mor* a piece by Carolan, the 17th Century Irish composer. Colleen had learned the song from a recording but was proud she had made her own arrangement for the guitar.

Brigid lay in bed listening to her mother. She prayed—to whom she did not know—for her mother. She prayed her mother would become herself again.

"Yesterday a child came out to wander," Colleen sang *The Circle Game* by Joni Mitchell. She followed that with a folk rendition of The Beatles' song *Help*.

Brigid sat up in bed and listened to her mother sing "When I was younger, so much younger than today, never needed anybody's help in any way." She walked to the bedroom door and slowly opened it, listening to her mother. "But now those days are gone, I'm not so self-assured. Now I find I've changed my mind, I'll open up the door."

"Help me if you can," Brigid sang in harmony with Colleen, "I'm feeling down."

"And I do appreciate your being 'round," Colleen smiled at Brigid as she sang. "Help me get my feet back on the ground."

"Won't you please, please help me," the mother and daughter sang. As the duet went on, Colleen sensed that her daughter was not only singing with her but that she was singing to her.

Spontaneously, the two women alternated verses. "Now my life has changed in oh so many ways," Brigid sang.

"My independence seems to vanish in the haze," Colleen answered.

"Every now and then I feel so insecure."

"Now I know I need you like I never did before."

Both women sang the refrain and the final line of the song together. "That was great, Brigid. Boy, that was great." Colleen headed for the kitchen.

"Mom, would you do something for me?" Brigid asked nervously.

"Anything, Brigid. Anything," she repeated as she opened the refrigerator door.

"I want you to think about something, Mom." Brigid took a deep breath. "Would you think about talking to someone about—?"

Colleen did not turn around but she held back reaching for a beer in the refrigerator. She feared her daughter's next words.

Brigid paused and then softened her request. "—how you've been feeling? You've been so sad these past few months, you know, Mom?"

Colleen let out a sigh. She turned, relieved. "Yes, honey. It must be hard for you around here lately. I *know* it's been hard for you, Brigid. You know, I've been thinking of going to see a therapist."

"You have?" Brigid was delighted.

"I...I need someone to talk to," Colleen closed the refrigerator door. "I feel adrift, Brigid. I don't know why but I can't talk to my friends anymore. I know that they are there for me but...I just can't bring myself to call them. So, I thought that I would ask around and see if I could find a...you know...a counselor or therapist...I'm kind of low on money so I'd have to go to a clinic or something."

"Aunt Lis knows a lot about this. You can talk to her, Mom!" Brigid felt hopeful for the first time in months. "I'm so happy you're going to do this, Mom. Sometimes lately I couldn't sleep I was so worried about you. But I'm going to sleep well tonight," she smiled and went to her room.

Colleen stood alone in the kitchen. Her heart was pounding and she didn't know why. She opened the refrigerator, hesitated, and then got a beer for herself. She sat at the kitchen table and slowly drank her beer. *Brigid is right. I need to talk to someone...Lis will help me find the right person.* She began to feel more at ease.

Colleen decided to have another beer. *I need to talk to someone,* Colleen smiled to herself. *But I don't need to talk to anyone right now. Right now I need to put on the headsets, turn up the volume, and listen to some great music.* Colleen finished her drink, got another from the refrigerator, and settled in for a late night of listening to silly love songs.

"How long has it been, Colleen?" Lis asked her sister after they had been on the phone only a minute or two.

"Oh, let's see..." She counted on her fingers. "Eight months, I guess. Maybe eight and a half months."

"No, Colleen, it can't be *that* long." Her sister was testy.

"Of course it has," Colleen insisted, irritated. "I lost my job just after Thanksgiving and started unemployment in December. I'm hoping that Carter beats Ford. Maybe I'll get a job if the Democrats get in," she laughed lightly.

"I'm not talking about unemployment, Colleen!" Lis was amused. "I'm talking about—" Colleen cut her sister off.

"Oh Lis, you mean how long has it been *since*..." Colleen was exasperated. "That's all anyone asks me these days. It starts 'You're looking great.' Then—" Her sister interrupted Colleen.

"People can't help it, Colleen! You look so much better. You're so full of energy. And it's so much fun to be around you again!" Lis wished she hadn't spoken her last words and was relieved when Colleen did not react to them.

"Oh, I know, Lis," Colleen sounded as if she resented the compliments. "But I can't be that different."

Lis thought otherwise but was silent.

"Well, anyway, I haven't had a drink since..." Colleen paused although she knew the exact date. "Since late April. You know that, Sis." Colleen was silent. She saw herself earlier that day, standing in front of the Oak Room in the Plaza Hotel on Central Park South, wondering why she had never gone there for cocktails. She seriously had considered stopping in for a drink. "It's about four months. Next week will be four months."

"I think that's great, Colleen. Say, listen, I have two extra tickets for *A Chorus Line.* Want to go? You could take a date or bring Brigid. They're for tonight. I know it's short notice." She hoped her sister would join her.

"I'd love to go, Lis." Colleen was hesitant. "I don't know if I can tear Brigid away from Michael for even a few hours, but I'll try. I *wish* I had a guy to ask."

"You will soon, Colleen, very soon. Men may be dumb but they're not blind," she laughed lightly, "and you're looking too good to be alone much longer."

"Lis, you're my biggest fan. My all-time biggest fan." Her affection for her sister softened her. "Let's meet in front of the theater, all right? Fifteen minutes before the show, okay?"

"Great. Can't wait to see you. Maybe afterwards we'll all take a cab to the Village? Have a cappuccino at the Borgia or the Figaro?" She was happy to have her sister back.

"Sounds great, Sis." Colleen was tired of talking on the phone. "It's so beautiful I'm going to go for a walk along the river. I think I'll go through Inwood Park and then walk along the promenade to Dyckman Street and catch the A train from there."

"Don't be late, Colleen," Lis said in a friendly tone. They won't seat you until the first scene change if you're late." She knew that Colleen was often late.

"I won't be late," Colleen was defensive. "If you get anxious, Lis, just leave the tickets at the box office."

After Lis hung up, Colleen made a light lunch for herself. She finished the meal quickly. She looked nervously at the kitchen clock. "It's only one...I have *six hours* until I meet Lis. I can't walk for six hours." For the past four months, Colleen found herself with more time than she knew what to do with.

Nervously, she dressed for the day. She knew that the afternoon would be quite warm—temperatures in the eighties. And that the night was expected to be much cooler—temperatures in the sixties. She could not decide what to wear. "I'll call Brigid to see if she wants to come with me tonight."

Brigid was working for the summer as a receptionist at Williams-Maris, a large talent agency in Manhattan. From nine to five, she answered the phones, announced visitors, and handled incoming and outgoing packages with the various delivery and messenger services. In the evenings, she had the opportunity to shadow one of the rising literary agents and observe him as he worked with publishers, editors, and authors, in his office and on the phone. Although the agent was only in his mid-twenties, he had already had a few notable successes and great things were expected of him.

"Williams-Maris," Brigid answered the phone professionally yet cheerfully.

"It's me, honey," Colleen replied, "I have an extra ticket for *A Chorus Line* for tonight. Can you go?"

"I'd love to! Michael's going to a Yankee game and I won't see him anyway. Mom, I have to put you on hold." Her daughter was gone instantly. As Colleen waited, she felt a deep love for Brigid. "Sorry about that. It's very busy today. Want to meet me at the office and have a bite before the show?"

"Great. I'll see you at five or so?" Colleen was glad they would be together.

"No, make it six," Brigid said. "I'm going to sit in on a conference call and see how my boss Robin negotiates this big project he's working on. I don't get paid to stay late but it's so much fun to see how these businessmen work."

"Okay, honey," Colleen could imagine fewer things less boring but she did not want to dampen her daughter's enthusiasm. "I'll see you at six and you can tell me all about it." They exchanged quick "love yous" as they hung up the phone.

Colleen felt more at ease. Since quitting drinking, she felt the need to plan her days out in detail and keep herself busy. *I'll get the A train about five...get to Columbus Circle about 5:30...do some window shopping on 57th Street and on Fifth Avenue...maybe stop in Bendel's.* The day was taking shape; large blocks of time were being filled in, making Colleen more comfortable.

She thought of the last week before she stopped drinking. She couldn't stand the feeling that something bad was about to happen to her at any moment. Colleen could not bear to think about a fear she had developed, a fear she had not shared with anyone. In the last few weeks of April, Colleen would not travel by subway. When she was on a subway platform and saw the approaching headlights of the train in the tunnel, an impulse to hurl herself in front of the train grew to intolerable proportions. Her skin became cold and clammy and she broke into a sweat. At these moments, using extraordinary willpower, Colleen would force herself against the wall of the station. She would close her eyes, cover her ears against the roar of the train, and hold her breath so that she would not breathe the dirty air the train drew along with it.

Colleen decided to dress lightly for the day and to bring a light jacket with her for the evening. *I'll put the jacket in my backpack,* she thought.

She looked about her apartment anxiously. She wondered if she should not stay home instead. *I could cancel with Lis and Brigid.* She felt pressure in her chest and exhaled deeply. *I'll feel better once I'm outside,* she thought. "It's a beautiful day," she said aloud as she collected her things. "The weatherman says it's one of the ten best days of the year!"

As she rode alone in the elevator, it seemed to Colleen that she had traded the dread she experienced in the spring for a summer of anxiety. *If this is all there is, I might as well...* Colleen did not let herself complete her thought.

Colleen breathed deeply as she climbed the steep path under the Henry Hudson Bridge. The Spuyten Duyvil trestle bridge below was open to allow pleasure boats and the commercial Circle Line cruise ships to pass from the Harlem River Canal to the Hudson River. She paused to catch her breath. Far below, on the rocks along the shore, a father and his children were fishing. *My brothers only caught eels in this river,* she recalled with disgust. Down a path worn in the woods, sitting at a natural viewpoint, a teenage couple was passionately kissing. *He's got his right hand between her legs and his left is undoing her bra!* Colleen smiled. *Right out in the open! Oh well, I guess I'm becoming an old fogey.*

Colleen crossed under the bridge and made her way down the hillside to the promenade that ran along the riverside from the tip of Manhattan for a mile or so, ending at Dyckman Street. She noticed that autumn was making inroads early. Patches of leaves on a few maple trees had already turned crimson. Amidst the lush late summer green of the hills of Inwood, patches of ochre and rust could be seen as well.

Since childhood, Colleen had loved the sweet melancholy she felt when both summer and autumn were in the air. *There's always a day in August in New York when autumn appears by surprise. Summer reasserts itself,* she thought, *but the message is clear.*

There was not a cloud in the pulsing blue sky. The tide was rushing in and the river shimmered with countless points of reflected light. A handful of sailboats were making their turns back toward the bay under the shadow of the George Washington Bridge. Buzzing like bees, two speedboats raced north close to shore in obvious competition with one another. There were no people in sight the length of the promenade. *How can I be unhappy?* Colleen thought. *How can I be so unhappy on such a beautiful day?*

As she strolled along, Colleen's thoughts turned to her days in San Francisco. *This is a real San Francisco day,* she thought. *This is just like a late September afternoon down by Aquatic Park or the Embarcadero.* Colleen felt most at home in cities by the sea. She loved walking along the riverside, watching the ships in the harbor. The ferries, especially, seemed so romantic to her.

Colleen sat on a park bench and put her feet up on the wrought iron fence that separated the promenade pathway from the last few feet of land that sloped down to the rocky shore of the river. *I wonder what my life would have been like if I had stayed in San Francisco?* Colleen had returned to New York, homesick and lonely, after a long-term love affair ended. *It's funny...I left in 1967 just when everyone else was coming to San Francisco.*

Colleen had loved her home in Noe Valley. The neighborhood was part of *The City,* a nickname for San Francisco that always embarrassed Colleen. To her, New York was "the city." Her neighborhood in San Francisco was like a small town, nestled at the foot of Diamond Heights and Twin Peaks. The homes were charming, the residents were cultured, and the small shops on 24th Street—"Main Street" in Noe Valley—were owned and run by friendly people. She missed shopping where people knew her by name.

Colleen watched the waters wash against the rocky shore. She wondered how many New Yorkers knew where the rocks came from. *Or even know that they aren't a natural formation but were put here by people?* The large rocks of Manhattan schist that line the shore of the Hudson River from Riverdale to midtown were blasted from the center of the giant rock that is Manhattan when the subway tunnels were built. *I wonder how many people riding the subway ever think of the men who blasted through that solid rock to build the subway? How hard they worked for so little pay. How many died doing so?*

Colleen's grandfather had been an engineer for the IRT subway on the line that ran from the Battery in Lower Manhattan to Van Cortlandt Park in The Bronx. As a young child, Colleen had lived in a small apartment overlooking the elevated IRT train tracks near the 231st Street Station. Whenever he pulled into the station, whether heading uptown or downtown, her grandfather blew the train whistle in a signal his family recognized.

I loved the old trains, she thought fondly. Colleen could see them clearly, with their wicker seats, overhead fans, square red and green glass lights outside on the front and rear. And she had never forgotten the time her "grandpa" let her ride with him through the tunnel from Dyckman Street to 191st Street. It was only one stop, but it was so exciting to the young girl.

Colleen recalled riding the subway to her grandparent's apartment for dinner, to the American Museum of Natural History to see the dinosaur exhibits, or to special events such as the St. Patrick's Day Parade in March or the Macy's Thanksgiving Day Parade in November. *And when I was only 12, I could ride the subway by myself,* she marveled. *I had nothing to fear.*

As a young teenager, Colleen had felt isolated, different, from her friends in the neighborhood. She knew the other kids liked her, but never felt that she belonged. Colleen remembered many summer Sundays riding the IRT to Columbus Circle by herself. For a young Irish Catholic girl from The Bronx, a trip "downtown," as they called Manhattan in her neighborhood, was daring. *I guess I was 14 when I used to go downtown. God, I loved the newsstands.* Colleen laughed. She was so *hungry* for knowledge. She recalled how she used to buy the British satirical newsmagazine *Punch.* Although she didn't understand most of the articles or get the humor of the cartoons, she was fascinated by how a magazine from another country *sounded.*

The loneliness she felt in midtown Manhattan was not as severe as the loneliness that caused her to hide and cry sometimes in her own neighborhood. *And I didn't feel so lonely in the bookstores. In the bookstores, there was so much to read, to know—so much to live for!* Colleen sat up straight on the bench. She had vivid memories of walking along Central Park South by the great old hotels; down Fifth Avenue past Bergdorf's and Tiffany's toward Rockefeller Center; along Sixth Avenue stopping at the headquarters of CBS and Time Magazine.

Colleen stood up and held onto the railing of the fence in front of her. *Or past the skyscrapers with the big publishing houses...or in Times Square...I used to just stand in front of The New York Times building and stare and wonder if I could ever be a reporter. And the theater district...God, I loved the marquees and The Drama Bookstore...* She had wanted to go to Performing Arts High School so badly. Her parents would not let her attend because there would be Jews in the school.

Without thinking, Colleen continued along the promenade. As she walked, she felt the excitement that she had experienced as a teenager. The excitement of possibility. *When I walked along those streets,* she thought, *I knew that I could be one of those people. I could work for a magazine, a newspaper, or a TV network. I could wear nice clothing and shop in those fancy stores and stay in those wonderful* hotels. *And at night, I could ride a hansom cab from Central Park South, dine at Les Pyrenees before a show, and then sit in center orchestra seats at the newest plays by Arthur Miller or Tennessee Williams or wonderful revivals of O'Neill, Ibsen, Shaw, or Strindberg. Or even see the Abbey Theater perform Deirdre of the Sorrows or Playboy of the Western World.*

When she was downtown, there seemed to be so many possibilities. *But when I was home...* Colleen's thoughts reached a sorrowful impasse. *When I was home, life was a travail...a journey through a vale of tears...everything veiled and ominous...everything something to be endured until death and the great reward of the Afterlife...Life was to be endured. Love—did it even exist? Work—a necessity, a hardship that resulted from sin. And knowledge—knowledge led to sin. Love, work, and knowledge—there was no place for them in the life of this Bronx Irish Catholic girl.*

Not wanting to yield to the bitterness she felt rising within, Colleen shook her head and dismissed her thoughts. *Nothing to be gained by rehashing the bad old days,* she told herself. But there was an aching sweetness from the memory of the hope that had surged through her when she wandered the streets of Manhattan as a teenager.

As she approached the end of the promenade, Colleen saw a group of men and women her age playing a pick-up game of softball. She thought she recognized a few of them—regulars from the Donemay Pub—and that made her uncomfortable. Colleen considered turning around and retracing her path to avoid even the possibility of meeting any old drinking buddies. *But it's so far out of my way.* She looked north as the walkway stretched out for more than a mile before her. *I'll be okay.*

"Colleen!" One of the women playing softball called out. "We need you now more than ever!"

"Hey Colleen—where you been?" It was her friend, Tommy.

Colleen walked over to the fence that separated the playing field from the promenade. "Great day for a game," Colleen said, her eyes drawn to a cooler of beer. The beads of water on the brown glass bottles looked so pleasing.

"The girls could use you, Colleen," Tommy said. "They're winning 10-6 with only an inning left. What do you say? They could use your bat in the top of the ninth, and your pitching arm in the bottom of the ninth," he coaxed, knowing she was proud of her pitching skills.

Colleen kept looking at the beer in the cooler. "No, sorry, Tommy." It was difficult for her to say no. "I'm meeting Brigid and my sister downtown."

"What time?" Tommy saw that she was staring at the beer. "Oh, sorry, Colleen. Have a beer!" He reached down, picked up and bottle, opened it and handed it to Colleen. "Great day for a beer and a ball game!"

Colleen took the beer. She didn't know why but she felt frightened. She took a long swallow. A great tension eased. Colleen closed her eyes. To her surprise, nothing happened. She took another long swallow. "Wow!" Colleen felt heady from the beer. It felt like the first time she had a beer as a teenager at the beach in Far Rockaway. "Okay, I'll play the last inning...but that's all."

"All right! And now for the Donemay Dames," Tommy cupped his hands over his mouth and imitated the announcer at Yankee Stadium, "pitching and batting cleanup—Colleen Murphy!"

One of the men gave Colleen his glove and she ran out to the pitcher's mound. "Where you been, Colleen? Haven't seen you all summer?"

"I...uh." Colleen was embarrassed. "Well, I guess I've kind of been on the wagon the last few months."

The woman laughed. "I know what you mean...I had to get my head on straight after the holidays last January. Great to see you back, Colleen. We missed you, you know?" The woman ran to her position in the field.

"Yeah...great to be back," Colleen said apprehensively.

"I'm here to see Brigid Murphy," Colleen spoke nervously to the receptionist.

"Have a seat and I'll try her line," the young woman answered perfunctorily.

Colleen sat in the wood-paneled reception area of the talent agency, the walls decorated with portraits in oil of the founders of the firm. *God, if they look this ugly in their official portraits,* Colleen mused, *what must they have really looked like?*

"She's in a meeting and will be with you shortly," the receptionist informed Colleen, who sat uncomfortably.

I guess Brigid belongs here as well as the next person. Colleen crossed her legs and folded her hands in her lap. *I couldn't stand it here,* she thought consciously. Far different feelings—apparent in her intimidated, mask-like expression and shallow breathing—coursed through Colleen and accounted for her discomfort.

Sooner than Colleen had expected, Brigid appeared. "Hi, Mom! I'm so excited about going to the show tonight!" Brigid hugged Colleen.

"I'm sorry," the receptionist said to Colleen, "I didn't know you were Brigid's *mother!*" With mock indignation, the young woman turned to Brigid and said, "You should have told me you were expecting your mom." She studied Colleen, smiling, and said, "Your Mom looks more like your sister!"

Colleen was flattered by the receptionist's remark. "Thank you. I look pretty good for 50, don't I?" Colleen teased.

"*You're 50 years old?*" The receptionist did not understand that Colleen was joking.

"Mom—stop teasing! She's only 33," she told her co-worker. Brigid took her mother by the arm. "We've got to hurry. I'm starving and have to get something to eat before the show."

"I've seen *Chorus Line*," the receptionist said, "I think you'll both love it."

The elevator arrived and Colleen and Brigid left the office. As Brigid told her of the day's events, Colleen could barely listen to her daughter. For hours, she had been so tense that she felt dizzy and faint. Now that what she had feared had not come to pass, Colleen felt exhausted; relieved but drained of all energy. She desperately feared that her daughter would be able to tell that she had been drinking.

"Mom! You haven't listened to a thing I've said!" Brigid smiled at her mother. "That's okay; I know business is not your thing. But I find this work fascinating. It might be even more exciting to be an agent and make deals for books and movies and plays than to be an artist and create them."

"I don't know if it's more exciting," Colleen answered dryly, "but it's certainly a better living." She paused and then added, judgmentally, "If that's what you want."

"That is what I want," Brigid answered. "It's a big part of it, anyway."

Don't judge, Colleen told herself. *Don't judge your daughter. Lest you be judged...and come up wanting, wanting terribly.* Colleen put her arm around her daughter's shoulder as they walked to the theater district. "If that's what you want, go for it, Brigid." She thought for a moment. *Don't be an obstacle in the way, Colleen.*

"You mean that, Mom?" Brigid was surprised. "I know how you feel about the business world and all that."

"Every generation has its own destiny, Brigid, and every person has to find his or her own way, honey. I don't expect you to be like me." Colleen took her arm from Brigid's shoulder and held her hand as they waited at a corner for the light to change. "You can learn from other's experiences, take what you can use, but you've got to go out there and learn through your own failures and successes. I mean, if you became a *Nazi* I'd be heart-broken—but if you became a literary agent," Colleen smiled, "I could learn to live with that!"

The light changed and they continued on their way.

The big yellow Checker cab bounced down Fifth Avenue toward Greenwich Village. "You seem so subdued," Lis said. "Didn't you enjoy the show, Colleen?"

"Yeah, I liked it...I liked it," she answered half-heartedly. "I'm just tired that's all. I'll feel better when we get to the Borgia."

"Oh, I told Michael to meet us at the Figaro," Brigid said. "Is that a problem? Can we go there?"

"No problem...no problem at all," Colleen replied. She looked out the window as the cab slowed down in traffic near Madison Square Park. It was a misty night, and ahead, the Flatiron Building looked as it does in the photograph by Edward Steichen. The taxi crossed 23rd Street and picked up speed. There was hardly any traffic on Fifth Avenue all the way down to Washington Square Park.

"God I love the arch," Colleen spoke with excitement. "Look at it! I love that blue-white light on it...I don't know what came over me, guys. But I feel like a cloud has lifted from me! Let's order as soon as we get there. I want an iced mochaccino and that chocolate dessert they have! What's it called?"

"The Ultimate Chocolate Cake, I think," Lis answered. "And the vanilla ice cream that comes with it is incredible."

"Should we pig out or share one?" Colleen laughed. "Let's pig out!" She answered her own question before anyone had a chance to reply.

"Not me—I have to watch my weight," Brigid said.

"At 16 you're watching your weight!" Lis said sarcastically. "Give me a break, Brigid."

"She'll change her mind as soon as the waiter brings ours, Lis, mark my words!" Colleen gave her daughter a teasing look.

The taxi turned west on Washington Square North. "Stop at the near corner of Macdougal," Colleen told the driver. "We'll get out here instead of Bleecker Street." Colleen opened her purse and took out money to pay for the ride. "My treat, Lis. You got the tickets. We're paying for the rest." Before her sister could object, Colleen continued. "I got my unemployment check today and Brigid got paid so we're okay."

As they stood on the corner, Colleen took a deep breath. "I always wanted to live in the Village...Say, see that hotel across the street?" Colleen pointed to the one she was speaking about. "That's the one Joan Baez sings about in her new song, *Diamonds and Rust.* It has such a great line in it—have you guys heard it?" Neither had.

Colleen began to hum to herself but audibly. "It goes like this." She cleared her throat. "Well, I'll be damned, here comes your ghost again," Colleen sang the words quickly, softly, trying to find her way to the verse she was looking for. "Now I see you standing with brown leaves all around and snow in your hair," she sang full-voiced. "Now you're smiling out the window of that crummy hotel over Washington Square," Colleen smiled and pointed to the hotel. "Our breath comes out white clouds, mingles, and hangs in the air." Hot tears came to her eyes. "Speaking strictly for me, we both could have died then and there."

Two young men in their early 20s—one with an acoustic guitar—got up from a bench nearby in the park and walked up to Colleen, Brigid, and Lis. "You want to try the whole song?" The young man with the guitar asked.

"Why, I—"

"Do it, Mom! Sing with them!" Brigid was excited.

"Really?" Colleen looked to Lis. "You don't mind?" Lis shook her head no. "All right." The young man tuned his guitar and Colleen went over the lyrics in her head as he did.

"I'll do harmony," the other young man volunteered. "Most of our friends think this is passé," he said to Colleen. "But we love Joanie-Baloney and do all the old folk songs."

From the first notes, it was apparent that the guitarist was classically trained and talented. He played with extraordinary sensitivity around Colleen's singing. The haunting harmony of the other singer added a dark richness to the song. A small crowd gathered quickly—so many people pass every corner in the Village at all hours—captured by the intensity of Colleen's singing. Inspired by her own sorrows, Colleen sang the lyrics as if they told her own story of lost love that lingers. Her voice penetrated into the souls of those listening and reverberated in the chambers of their hearts, infusing each person's memories of love with new life.

Lis and Brigid were especially startled. They had never heard Colleen sing so profoundly. It was difficult for them to tolerate the powerful emotions that were stirred by the spontaneous rendition of a pop song on a street corner, performed by two singers and a guitarist who had never before met.

"Speaking strictly for me, we both could have died then and there!" Colleen sang those words with such power that many of the men listening choked up with longing; the women with them felt tears flow and pressed close to their partners. Brigid wrapped her arm around her aunt's and leaned her head on Lis's shoulder. Colleen bowed her head and stepped back one step as if she were on stage.

Understanding wordlessly, the guitarist eased into an aching solo, deftly moving the melody into a minor key, playing in a classical Spanish guitar style. When he returned to the melody in a major key, the audience breathless, Colleen and the young man harmonized the tune without lyrics and the guitarist played off and around them. Without any signal, with perfect timing, Colleen began to sing the final verse of the song.

"Now you're telling me you're not nostalgic," she sang on a street corner awash in nostalgia, to a small crowd of chance listeners swept away by their own bittersweet longings. So riveting and clear were the final notes Colleen hit as she sang the last words that all listening were transported to an ethereal plane and fixed in a timeless moment.

The song completed and there was silence. All intuited the profanity of applause. Colleen felt as if there was a spinning magnetic pole within her, pulsing in spirals from head to toe, and pulsating in expanding and contracting bursts.

Brigid hugged Colleen. Lis hugged Colleen. The guitarist, his guitar hanging across his shoulders, took both her hands and looked into her eyes, and then let go. Her fellow singer kissed Colleen on the forehead, held her close, momentarily burying his head in the hair that fell across her shoulder, and then stood back smiling.

The crowd dispersed and the five strangers, now bound by a profound experience, began, to smile, softly at first, then more broadly. Finally, Brigid exclaimed, *"Wow!"* and they all began to laugh.

"Christ Almighty!" The guitarist moaned. "If only we could have recorded that!" He looked at Colleen. "Who are you? I've never heard anything like that! My name is George."

"I'm Artie," the young singer said, introducing himself.

"I'm Colleen. And this is my sister, Elisabeth, and my daughter, Brigid." She exhaled deeply. "We were just in a taxi, on our way to get coffee and pastries, when I suddenly just had to get out of the cab at this corner. And now here we all are!"

"Mom...That was..." Brigid said at a loss for words.

"*Magic*," Colleen whispered the word. "That was magic, right? Am I right?" She laughed infectiously. "Pure magic?"

The young men gave Colleen their business card and implored her to call them. "We'd really love to see you again," Artie said earnestly.

"Let's make music, Colleen!" George was beaming.

Colleen took their card and promised them she would call.

"Excuse me," Brigid said to the waiter as he put Colleen's dessert on the table. "I've changed my mind—I'd like one of those as well." Her mother and sister laughed loudly.

"I told you, Lis! Didn't I tell you she'd do that?" Colleen took her first bite of The Ultimate Chocolate Cake. "*In*credible!"

"Are you going to call those guys, Mom?" Brigid asked.

"You really should, Colleen. I mean, they really want you to," Lis added.

"Oh, don't worry. I'm going to call them just as I said. If they weren't going to Boston this weekend, I'd try to get together with them sooner. I haven't felt this good in years...Years!" She sipped her iced mochaccino. "It would be great to perform again."

The three women sat silently a moment, each looking out the large windows of the cafe at the passers-by, each seeing her own Greenwich Village. Colleen noticed the greying, longhaired refugees from the 50s and early 60s. Lis noticed the men and women in their mid-20s, the hip professionals of the 70s. The 50s Man in the Grey Flannel Suit was gone. Brigid observed everything—the street people; the artists and business people; the students of all ages; and the tourists. She studied the architecture of the tenements on the corner of Bleecker and Macdougal. Colleen and Lis saw what they already knew. To Brigid, it was all new.

"You know, I remember the first time I fell in love with the Village," Lis said. "It was autumn 1969 and I went to see *Little Murders* by Jules Feiffer in a tiny, tiny theater on Macdougal Street. I loved the play, although too much of its black humor is part of daily life now. I came out of the theater exhilarated!"

Lis leaned back in the booth. "My sweetie—Louis—and I stood across the street from the theater and looked uptown. We looked up Macdougal, past Washington Square, and there in the distance was the Empire State Building, lit orange, white, and blue because the Mets had won the World Series. The lampposts were covered with posters for the *Mobilization Against the War* and posters for *Lindsay for Mayor*. The sidewalks were crowded with people just arriving at the clubs and cafes for music and conversation." Lis smiled to herself. "Louis picked me up off my feet and spun me around. We walked uptown, not talking, his arm around my shoulder, mine around his waist."

Brigid loved it when her aunt and mother reminisced. "How old were you then?"

"I was just 18," Lis answered dreamily.

"What about you, Mom?" Brigid was so happy to see her mother happy.

"God...I have so many memories, honey. But one night, before you were even a zygote," Colleen teased, "your father and I came down to the Village. You know, two Bronx kids trying to find out if all the wild stories were true. It was probably Thanksgiving or maybe Christmas week...I don't remember...But we went to a foreign film—an 'art' movie we called them then." Colleen laughed. "Isn't that funny, Lis. An art movie—because it had nudity in it!" Colleen shook her head. "Anyway, after the movie, we walked around the Village and we turned off Macdougal onto Minetta Lane. Well," Colleen paused for effect, "let me tell you if you didn't believe there was a Director of Central Casting before that moment, you would have believed it afterwards."

"What happened?" Brigid was extremely curious.

"Macdougal was crowded and noisy. It had started to snow lightly while we were watching the movie. But, halfway down Minetta Lane, it really started to snow. Fat wet snowflakes at first, in a flurry. Then, the snow began to fall heavily, small white snowflakes swirling in the winds of the narrow lane. At the Minetta Lane Theater, we turned left onto Minetta Street. It was like a movie set! The snow had already covered the sidewalks, the street, the fire escapes, the branches of the few trees along the street. There wasn't a footstep, a tire track, or a sound. Amber lights glowed from the windows of the apartments and from the back windows of the taverns on the east side of the street. And there was silence. Although Sixth Avenue was only one block west, and Macdougal was one block east, there was silence on Minetta Street. Jim took me in his arms and kissed me." Colleen closed her eyes. "And, unrepentant romantic that I am, to this day, I remember that as the most wonderful kiss of my life. We walked along Minetta Street, south toward Sixth Avenue and—just where the street turns and angles west—we saw a basement apartment for rent."

"Did you want to live there?" Brigid knew that her parents had not rented the apartment.

"For a second, it was electrifying." Colleen's eyes were shining. "We both saw a new life before us. A life that was beyond our imagination appeared before us. We copied down the address and the phone number and talked about the apartment all the way home that night." Colleen looked crestfallen. "Well, timing *is* everything and we were just two teenagers and weren't going to rent any apartment in the Village. But that night on Minetta Lane was one of the most beautiful moments of my life."

After a moment, Brigid asked, tentatively, "Can I tell you my favorite time in the Village?"

"Of course you can!" Colleen and Lis said in unison.

"Well," Brigid sat up straight in her chair, "I actually have two favorite times. Once was when I was about seven and we came back to New York from San Francisco. Your Grandma had died, right, Mom?"

"Yes, she died in '67 and you were born in '60." Colleen smiled. "I think I know the time that you mean. The day the storm came up?"

"Exactly," Brigid turned to Lis. "Mom took me downtown and we were walking around the Village and I played in that playground for a while." She looked at her mother.

"Yes, Jimmy Walker Park on St. Luke's Place. It was named after one of those lovable crooked Irish politicians. I think it's between Leroy and Hudson. He lived on that block for a while. Pat was living with a guy who had a great garden apartment on St. Luke's Place—he was in advertising I think or maybe the music business, I forget—and we were visiting."

"Anyway, then we went for a walk. Mom and Pat talking and reminiscing." Brigid was deep in her memory. "And suddenly, the sky got black. It was like nighttime. Even some of the street lamps came on. You know some new ones had those automatic sensors. Remember, Mom?"

"I sure do!" Colleen replied. "You could smell the rain in the air and tell that you'd be drenched if you didn't get inside soon. Fortunately for us, we were right at the corner of Bedford and Barrow so we just popped into Chumley's!"

"Anyway, we went in this cool entrance." Brigid's eyes were closed. "It was like going into the courtyard of someone's home. You opened a gate and walked through a narrow passageway and then there were these big wooden doors—am I right, Mom?" Brigid was proud of her memory and was testing it out. "I haven't been there since."

"I think you're right on the mark," Colleen said.

"It was pretty crowded that day," Brigid continued. "And they had a fire in this big stone fireplace. Some people left just as we arrived and we got a table right by the fireplace. What I remember is that just as the waitress came to take our order, the windows lit up from lightning that hit right outside and shook from the loudest thunderclap I've ever heard!" The memory sent a shiver up Brigid's spine. "I was scared but I loved it!"

"It was a great afternoon, Lis. It rained for an hour or so. Brigid had a hamburger and soda; Pat and I had a few drinks and talked about Grandma mostly. And men, of course. And when we left, everything was sparkling and there wasn't a cloud in the sky. Is that how you remember it, honey?"

"Well, mostly I remember the thunder and lightning and the fireplace. And the courtyard. But my other favorite time—and I think it's even more special to me—is?" Brigid looked at Colleen and Lis. "Is what? Come on, guess!"

Both women were puzzled.

"Is *tonight!* Tonight, guys! The play, the cafe—but mostly, Mom singing on the street corner. That, Mom... that was... I don't even have a word for what that was!"

"I do," Lis said, a twinkle in her eyes. "*Magic!*"

Brigid suddenly began waving her right hand in the air. Michael saw her and came across the room to their table. There wasn't room for him. "Maybe the waiter will bring a chair over for you," Brigid said.

"You look like you're finished," Michael answered, "and I don't really want anything." He put his hand on Brigid's shoulder.

"Why don't you just squeeze in here," Lis moved over in the booth, leaving just enough room for Michael. "It'll take a few minutes to get the check."

"How was the game?" Colleen asked.

"Oh, pretty good. But it was in extra innings when I left."

"Oh, I'm sorry you had to leave the game," Brigid apologized. "I know how much you love the Yankees."

"I am a Yankee fan." Michael smiled at Brigid. "But I'm a much bigger Brigid fan! Besides, some extra inning games go on for hours. I thought maybe we could go for a walk around the Village. You could tell me about what happened at work today."

The waitress brought the check, which Colleen quickly snatched up.

Outside the restaurant, Brigid issued a command. "Follow me!" She led the group across Bleecker Street and walked north on Macdougal to Minetta Lane. She turned to her mother. "I want to show Michael." The young couple walked ahead, holding hands. They turned from

Minetta Lane onto Minetta Street. In front of the apartment building where her father had kissed her mother, Brigid paused and kissed her boyfriend.

When Colleen and her sister caught up with the young couple, all were startled to see a "For Rent" sign in the window of the legendary basement apartment.

On their way to the subway, all four decided that it was a wonderful evening for a walk. Instead of taking the A train at the West 4th Street Station, they walked east on 3rd Street. "I'd love to go here sometime," Brigid said as they passed the Blue Note, a long-time jazz club. "Am I too young, Mom? Do I have to be 18?"

"I don't think so," Colleen said. "As long as you don't try to order a drink, that is."

"I don't know about that, Colleen." Lis disagreed. "A lot of places require that you be over 21—just to cover their asses."

"Next time you see someone you like playing here, I'll take you," Colleen promised.

On Thompson Street, they turned north to West 4th Street, the south end of Washington Square. Brigid and Lis walked ahead, talking. At first awkwardly, but then pleasantly, Colleen and Michael conversed.

"Brigid and I were talking about her summer job earlier," Colleen told Michael, "and she said she is very interested in the business side of the arts. I have to admit, that surprised me. You had a summer job too, didn't you Michael?"

"Yes, I worked for an old Wall Street law firm." He looked at Colleen's expression. "I guess to you that's kind of as close to working for the enemy as you can get! Brigid has told me some of your political beliefs and—"

"I don't really have *political* beliefs at all, Michael," she said, restraining herself. "But I do have strong beliefs about what is life-positive and what is life-negative." She paused and smiled with genuine friendliness. "Never mind all that. Did you enjoy your time at the law firm?"

"I feel funny talking with you about this, Mrs. Murphy, I mean Colleen." Michael was embarrassed. "I feel funny calling you Colleen," he said shyly. "I don't call any of my other friend's parents by their first names. But I did like the job. I found it pretty exciting to tell you the truth." He swallowed and cleared his throat. "I know that to people like you, Sixties-types, *money* is the only obscene word in the English language." He laughed, hoping Colleen would, too.

Colleen laughed heartily. "Bob Dylan sang 'Money doesn't talk it swears; obscenity—who really cares?' You know, Michael, there aren't *really* any types. Just people."

"You're right. Sorry." He cleared his throat. "But, whether we like it or not, *money is the most important thing in our world.*" Michael was serious and sincere. "I know that probably sounds like one of the worst things a guy going out with your daughter could say," he laughed lightly, "but I think it's true. I don't think money is the most important thing in *life;* don't get me wrong. But, in our world, you can't do much without it."

Colleen knew that on one level, he was certainly correct. Yet on another level, he was mistaken. "You're one year older than Brigid?"

"Yes, but I'm two years ahead of her in school. I started NYU this semester. And I hope to go to NYU Law School." Michael spoke with pride in himself.

"Wow—I didn't know you were in college!" Colleen blushed. "I'm sure you told me but...well, you know how it is." They had turned north along University Place on the east side of Washington Square. Brigid and Lis were just north of Washington Place, almost one block ahead.

"Brigid! Lis! Come this way—there's something I want to show all of you." Colleen and Michael walked east to Greene Street, followed by Brigid and Lis.

"I want to show you something, Michael," Colleen said quietly. "I know that the idea of making big money and wielding power can be quite alluring. And that the reality of having big money and power over people can be even more addicting than drugs. But do you know what gives things value, Michael?" She looked directly at him. "What gives goods in an economy value? *The living quality in working people.* The *living,* Michael, *the living* in people."

They stopped on the northwest corner of Washington Place and Greene Street in front of an old 10-story loft building. "This used to be called the Asch Building. In 1911, in late March, a holocaust occurred here. Do you know what I'm talking about?" None of the three knew. "Have you heard of the Triangle Shirtwaist Fire?"

None had heard of it. "Lis, I'm surprised that you don't know about this! On the top three floors of this building—this very building—on a Saturday afternoon, 146 people burned to death in a fire in a sweatshop. Most of them were young women." Colleen pointed to a bronze plaque on the side of the building, barely visible under the light of a dim street lamp.

"But things like that don't happen today," Michael said, defensively. "There are laws to protect people."

"Unfortunately, things like that do happen today," Colleen disagreed. "Here in New York City, in America, and in American-owned businesses in Mexico, Central and South America, the Philippines, Southeast Asia, South Africa and other countries around the world."

Anger became evident in Colleen's voice. "And there are many people waiting in the wings, eager to get into power and determined to overturn the few laws we now have to make the workplace safe; to bust the unions that—corrupt as many of them are—provide some protection for working people; to skew the so-called progressive tax code to progressively eliminate taxes for the rich and progressively increase taxes for working people."

"All right, Colleen!" Lis teased her sister. "You've got my vote! But don't you think you should take your soapbox up to Union Square?"

Colleen laughed at herself. "You're right...I shouldn't rant. But it was a pretty good rant, wasn't it?" Colleen referred to her angry outbursts, especially her sincere expressions of social concern, as "rants."

Michael felt he had been indirectly—and unfairly—criticized by Colleen. "I'm getting tired, Brigid. How about you? Do you feel like heading home?"

"Yes, Michael." Brigid took his hand, protectively. "I have to be at work by eight tomorrow. We're negotiating with a British publisher and we're having a conference call at eight-thirty."

"Me too. I have to be in the office by seven-thirty." Michael did not look at Colleen.

"I feel like staying out," Colleen said. "How about you, Lis?"

"Sure, let's go over to St. Mark's Place for a bit," Lis answered.

Brigid hugged her mother and aunt. Michael politely said goodnight, and walked off with his girlfriend, happy they were on their own.

"I wonder what got Mom all agitated," Brigid asked naively. "It just seemed to come out of the blue. What made her want to show us that plaque?"

"I think," Michael said with some embarrassment, "it was when I told her I thought that money was the most important thing in our world."

Brigid stopped abruptly. "You told *my* mother that?" She was incredulous. "Aside from the fact that I know you don't believe that one bit, why would you say that to my mother? That's like telling the Pope you don't believe in Original Sin! It worse than a red flag in front of a bull! You're usually so sensible!"

"Well, she had this *attitude* when she was talking to me," Michael spoke defensively. "I guess it irritated me and maybe I exaggerated how I feel about things. But you know, Brigid, I don't have that 'business is bad' attitude people like your mother have. I want to practice law at a top firm; I want to make a very good living—not just an okay living. And I want to be where the action is. I want to play hardball; I want to play in the big leagues." Michael felt angry.

"That's all right, Michael." She put her arms around him. "Mom's a character, for sure. Now I know why she took you to the site of the sweatshop disaster. She doesn't know you like I do." Brigid kissed her boyfriend. "She doesn't know that you'd work hard to succeed but it wouldn't be at anybody's expense. I know you will always do what's right."

The young couple continued their walk across town to the subway. Colleen and Lis watched the young couple and saw them stop and speak. The longer the conversation went on, the more uncomfortable Colleen became. She was relieved when it ended. "You know, Lis, I hope I didn't start an argument between them," Colleen said.

"Don't give it another thought, sis," Lis laughed lightly. "Their sexual attraction for each other blows away all our ideas about this or that. Like dandelions in a hurricane! They'll probably go at it hot and heavy tonight and not remember a thing you said in the morning."

"Little sister—you can be so coarse and vulgar!" Colleen knew it was true.

After browsing in bookstores and record shops in the East Village, Lis decided to splurge and take a cab home. "I'll drop you off on the way," she told her sister. "It's late and I don't want to take the subway."

"That's great. It's a real treat for me," Colleen was tired and happy that she didn't have to take three subway trains to get to upper Manhattan.

At the corner of First Avenue and St. Mark's Place, they had their choice of taxis and hailed a Checker. "She's going to 218th and

Broadway," Lis told the driver, "and then I'm going to Riverdale in The Bronx."

"I don't know these place," the driver said in an accent neither sister recognized. "You show me?"

"Yes," Brigid replied. "I'll show you."

Colleen loved riding in taxis late at night in Manhattan. She especially loved the route she suggested. "Let's ride up First Avenue. I want to see the U.N. and the Ritz Tower and drive under the 59th Street Bridge. We can get the FDR there. Okay?"

Lis gave the driver the directions. Colleen sat on the right side of the cab, silently taking in the sights as they bumped along the avenue.

The ride uptown was a journey through 100 years of New York City. They passed turn-of-the-century Ukrainian, Greek, and Russian churches; old orthodox synagogues; Stuyvesant Town; the 19th-century buildings of Bellevue Hospital; the massive walls of Tudor City, windowless walls designed to blot out the slaughterhouses that once stood across the street, where the U.N. now sits magisterially.

"This is Cole Porter's New York," Colleen said as they passed Beekman Place and then Sutton Place. "I used to dream of living here when I was a girl. Going to nightclubs, dancing, smoking cigarettes from a holder, drinking Manhattans!" Colleen laughed at her fantasy.

The driver made every one of the sequentially timed lights from St. Mark's Place to 57th Street, impressing Colleen. "What a bridge!" Colleen had long admired the 59th Street Bridge, which stretched out above them as they waited for the red light to change.

"Get into the right lane," Lis told the driver. "Take the FDR uptown."

Colleen enjoyed the ride up the old highway along the East River. There was little traffic. Ahead, the bluish lights on the Triboro Bridge glistened over the dark waters of Hellgate. Behind her, the elegant 59th Street Bridge spanned the East River, supported by Roosevelt Island at its midpoint.

"You know, Lis, no matter how low New York may go," Colleen

spoke with a sweet feeling, "I'll always love the rivers and the bridges."

After they passed Gracie Mansion, Lis instructed the driver—who seemed to be getting nervous—to follow the signs for the Harlem River Drive and the George Washington Bridge. The cab took them along the edge of Harlem and then Washington Heights. Across the river lay the South Bronx. "Look at Yankee Stadium!" Colleen liked the ballpark. "It's still lit up. It looks like that game is still going on! When Michael sees that in the sports section tomorrow, he'll be very glad he left when he did."

The cab took the FDR to its end at Dyckman Street where Lis directed the driver to Colleen's apartment building. "Thanks for the ride, Lis. And for the play," Colleen said as she got out of the taxi. "When I'm working again, I'll take you—"

"Colleen, you've done so many things for me I could never catch up." She kissed her sister on the cheek. "I had a great time with you and Brigid. I'll talk to you over the weekend."

As she watched the cab continue on its way, Colleen felt expansive. "I haven't felt this good in a long time." Colleen stood outside her building. At the end of the block, she could see the red and green neon lights in the window of her neighborhood bar. "I wonder who's there tonight." She walked to the window and peered into the dark bar. "There's Tommy! I'll just say a quick hello. I'm too wide awake to go home right now!"

Three hours later, Colleen was dancing alone in the bar. The bartender had set the jukebox so that she could choose an unlimited number of songs without paying for them. At first, Colleen selected current pop tunes, which she listened to at the bar as she laughed and joked with Tommy and two of the women from the afternoon softball game. After an hour of drinking, Colleen played a set of Motown hits and danced with every man at the bar, forcing reluctant drinkers to join her, persisting until it was more uncomfortable for them to resist her than to dance with her for a minute or two.

Tommy and the bartender were discussing the Yankee game. "Rivers is incredible! He walks up to the plate, stooped over, hobbling like an arthritic old man, and then-whack!" Tommy imitated the swing of a baseball bat. "He drives Oscar Gamble home in the bottom of the 19th inning!"

"You know, I'm a little worried about your friend, Tommy." The bartender looked toward Colleen.

"Gamble has a better home run ratio than Babe Ruth—you know that?" Tommy asked the bartender. "He's got a swing made for right field in Yankee Stadium."

"Tommy, listen to me," the bartender poked his regular customer in the shoulder.

"What? What's with you?"

"I'm worried about your friend. She's blotto, Tommy. I'm cutting her off. Maybe you should get her home, okay? I'm gonna close early." He went to the register and began to close out for the night.

Tommy looked up the bar. The music had stopped but Colleen was still dancing. "Yeah, I see what you mean. She lives across the street. I'll get her home. Been on the wagon a few months. Broke out today." He looked desirously at Colleen. "God, I wish I could make it with her."

When Tommy approached Colleen, she looked right at him. "Hey, what's your name? You're kinda cute."

"Cut the crap, Colleen. We gotta head out. Eddie's closing up." He looked directly at her and could tell she did not see him. "I'll walk you home. You look pretty fucked up." Tommy took Colleen by the elbow.

"Hey, back off!" Colleen brushed Tommy away, waving both her arms in semi-circles in front of her. "I'll fuck you but you gotta go slow." Colleen's laugh scared her friend.

"Hey, Colleen, cut it out. Don't get weird on me." Tommy moved away from her

"How about if I just get on top of you?" She pushed herself against him and kissed him hard but he pulled himself away.

"Hey, Colleen!" Tommy was too drunk to respond sensibly. "Cut the shit!" He grabbed her by the arm and ushered her from the bar. "Maybe the cold air will straighten you out!"

"Where am I?" Colleen began to panic. "Where am I?" She turned to Tommy. "Who are you?" She backed away from him, a fierce frightened expression on her face.

"Colleen! It's me, Tommy!" He began to perspire and shake. "Colleen, come on. You're scaring me!"

"Where is everybody? Where have you brought me?" Suddenly, Colleen bolted from the bar and ran across the street without looking.

Tommy followed her from a distance, watching as she hurried toward her apartment building. In the entranceway, she fumbled for her keys, dropped them, and had difficulty fitting the key in the lock, but finally opened the front door and ran down the hallway to the elevator. Tommy sighed, relieved when she opened the elevator door and stepped inside. "Jesus Christ," he said, breathing quickly and shallowly, "she scared me so much I feel sober!"

Colleen sat quietly on the stairway outside her apartment. She did not recognize where she was and did not know what to do. *I have to get home,* she thought. *I have to get a flight home.*

Colleen ran down the stairway to the lobby of her building and out onto the street. At the corner, she saw a gas station. She was certain that there was a public telephone there and rushed to it.

"Operator, I need the number for American Airlines." Colleen had no pen or paper and desperately repeated the number to hold it in memory until she could dial it. "Yes, when is your next flight to San Francisco?" Colleen looked about nervously. The streets were deserted. "Five-thirty a.m. from JFK? How much is the fare? Can I reserve a seat with you now?" Colleen could barely breathe. She was swallowing air, gasping from anxiety. "I'd like to charge the ticket," Colleen fumbled through her purse, looking for the wallet with her credit cards.

After she hung up the phone, her flight arrangements made, Colleen turned her back to the street and carefully counted her cash. "One hundred," she counted five 20-dollar bills. "And five 10s...that's 150." She closed her purse and reached into her pants pocket. "And I have fifteen and six...eight...nine singles...169 and let's see..." She counted her loose change. "Two-fifty...that's 170 dollars...a little more..." She breathed more easily.

Out of the corner of her eye, Colleen spotted a taxi heading south. She ran toward it, waving frantically. The cab driver saw her at the last minute and screeched to a halt. "You okay, lady? Somebody after you?"

"No, no," Colleen slumped in the back seat of the cab. "I just have to get home. I have to get *home*," Colleen spoke with a haunted tone.

"Sure, lady, no problem." The cab driver had seen nearly everything cruising the streets of New York late at night—most of which he would have preferred not to have seen—and Colleen's distress, as serious as it was, did not faze him. "Where to?"

"JFK...American Airlines," Colleen had her head propped up on the top of the back seat, turned sideways.

"Hey, you're a long way from home, lady. I didn't know they had flights at this hour." Colleen did not respond.

At Broadway and 181st Street, just before the driver turned toward the highway, Colleen saw something she recognized. "Stop here!" She demanded. "Stop here—I'll just be a second." Although she did not know where she was, Colleen went by habit into a bar she frequented years before when she had briefly dated the bartender.

"Colleen!" The bartender was happy to see her. They had parted amicably. "What are you doing out at this hour? I was just about to close up."

"Hey, Charlie. I'm going home. But I need a little something to take along with me, you know? Can I..." Colleen's eyes were glazed, her face frozen. "You got a bottle of Bushmill's and a six-pack I can buy?"

"No problemo," Charlie said, although he was somewhat concerned. "Just bring me another bottle. The beer's on me." He went down the bar, put the whiskey bottle and beer in a bag for Colleen, and returned. "Long time, no see, Colleen." He was still attracted to her. "You seeing anybody?"

"Thanks, Charlie," Colleen replied. It was obvious she hadn't heard him.

The bartender looked at her closely. He saw that she was sweating and that her complexion was a sickly white. He had second thoughts about having given her the alcohol. "Hey, Colleen, what do you say you have a drink with me while I close up?"

"Can't, Charlie. I got a cab waiting. I gotta get to the airport. I'm going home, Charlie. I'm going home!" She forced a stiff, unnatural smiled.

"Colleen!" He knew something was not right but she left in a hurry. The bartender walked to the end of the bar and watched her get into the taxicab. "Something's really wrong," he muttered to himself. *I wonder if I still have her number somewhere.* He decided that he would call Colleen's home in a few hours. Just to be on the safe side.

Suspicious of everyone, Colleen sat in a corner of the waiting area. Except for herself, an occasional worker, and one or two policemen off in the distance, the terminal was empty. Colleen surreptitiously drank her beer.

At five in the morning, activity in the terminal slowly began to increase. "Red-eye" flights from the west arrived and, one by one, airline employees took their positions at baggage check-in and ticket counters. Passengers appeared for early morning flights to cities across the country. The waiting area in which Colleen was sitting began to fill up. She finished her second beer and then closed the bag tightly and placed it on her lap.

When the ticket counter opened, Colleen bolted up and hurried over. "I made my reservation by phone and don't have my ticket."

"I'll be glad to help you, Ma'am."

Colleen was instructed to go to another area of the terminal—only a few hundred feet away—to get her ticket. She panicked. "The plane is leaving soon! Suppose I don't get back in time!"

"Don't worry, Ms. Murphy. You have plenty of time; I've assigned you a seat. A window seat in the tail section of the plane. Just go to the agent at the counter across the way and get your ticket." The woman smiled and then looked over Colleen's shoulder at the next passenger in line. "May I help you?" She turned her attention away from Colleen.

When the plane lifted from the runway, tilting slightly to the right as it did, Colleen's head hit the windowpane. She was startled. The last thing she remembered was signing for her ticket. She closed her eyes, took a deep breath, and fell asleep, clutching the paper bag in her lap.

"Would you like breakfast?" The flight attendant asked. "We have three choices this morning."

Without really listening, Colleen chose the second breakfast. "Could I have a cup of ice?"

When the flight attendant left, Colleen looked about the plane. She was in the next to last seat on the right side of the plane. The seats behind her, to her left and in front of her were empty. She reached into the bag and, without taking it out, opened the whiskey bottle. Colleen poured a full-glass, leaned over and drank half of it, and then poured another glass. Checking to make sure no one could see her she placed the plastic glass on the tray in front of her. Colleen quickly finished the whiskey and poured another glass.

She turned and looked out the window. For the first time in hours, she relaxed. "I'm going home," she said aloud, softly. "I'm going home." Colleen pushed a button on the right armrest, reclining her seat. She felt happy.

Confused, Colleen deplaned, carefully walking down the steep stairway, onto the ground just outside the terminal at San Francisco International Airport. She followed the other passengers into the terminal to the baggage claims area. She wasn't sure if she had baggage or not. Colleen could barely swallow. She gagged a few times before she could swallow successfully.

The crowded terminal, packed with people moving rapidly in all directions, carrying cumbersome bags or pushing carts loaded down with personal belongings, was more than Colleen could handle. She saw a small bar and headed for it. "A scotch and soda," she said in a matter-of-fact tone. As she nursed her drink, Colleen became very, very frightened.

How did I get here? She opened her purse and saw the credit card receipt for her airfare. *That's my signature!* Colleen stared in disbelief. *Shit! I'm in San Francisco.*

Colleen signaled the bartender. "I'll have another. Say, how much is a cab into the city?"

"Depends. If you're going downtown, why don't you just take the airporter bus? They run every half-hour. Cab downtown'll run you about 20 bucks plus a tip. The bus is a lot cheaper." He went down the bar to make Colleen's drink. Colleen finished her drink and went to a public telephone. She called and checked the credit line on her one major credit card. The answer was disappointing. Next she called the airline. "I am scheduled to leave San Francisco at 12:10 a.m. next Tuesday. If I have to leave earlier, what is the additional cost?" The answer was even more disappointing. "I have to stay through Saturday. No way can I pay full-fare."

Colleen added up the cost of hotel rooms for Thursday through Monday nights. "I'd just about make it..." She was overwhelmed with fear and shame. Not knowing what to do, Colleen decided to have one more drink at the bar in the terminal.

For reasons unknown, as she sipped her scotch and soda, her mood improved. *I'm okay,* she thought. *I can scrape by. I'll call some old friends. Someone will let me stay on their sofa.* She took a deep breath and exhaled fully. *Five days in San Francisco may be just the thing I need!*

Colleen found her way to the bus to downtown San Francisco. *I better save as much as I can wherever I can. It's going to be down to the last dime by midnight Monday.*

Colleen had forgotten the San Francisco "summer." As she walked from the Transbay Terminal toward Market Street, she was cold. Although she had traversed the continent, spent an hour in the airport at the bar deciding what to do over a couple of drinks, the clock on the tower by the Bay Bridge showed that it was only ten in the morning.

Colleen walked along Market Street, amazed at how San Francisco had changed in a decade. *No wonder they call it Manhattanization,* she thought as she marveled at the changes. There were many new buildings and much construction underway. Colleen turned south on Market Street and walked toward Montgomery. Along the way, it struck her that Market Street was very different from when she last was in San Francisco. *Of course, they finished BART,* she realized. When

Colleen lived in San Francisco, the Bay Area Rapid Transit system was under construction and Market Street was a chaotic mess.

As Colleen walked along, she saw that most of the businesses she remembered were gone. *Even my favorite place!* An old San Francisco restaurant on Market near Montgomery had been a favorite haunt of Colleen's. In the late afternoon, she loved to sit at an outside table, order a chowder or fish stew, sourdough bread, and a dark ale, and watch the passers-by and the streetcars. She never tired of the clanging of the streetcar bells.

Colleen stopped at the entrance to a BART station. *It's a Muni stop, too.* Colleen read the sign at the top of the stairs and realized that all the old streetcar lines now ran underneath Market Street with only a few electric buses above ground. Curious, Colleen walked down the stairway to the landing below. *God—it's immaculate! If New York subway riders could see this.* She laughed at the thought.

Colleen was in awe of the modern BART system. The simple, easy-to-read maps; the pamphlets explaining the routes, hours and fares; the change machines and automatic ticket machines; all put the New York Transit Authority to shame. *And bathrooms!* Colleen saw a young woman, dressed well-enough to be going to work at a top law firm, exit a public restroom. *You can use the toilets—and they're probably clean.*

Colleen followed a long, well-lit corridor to the other end of the station and saw the Muni entrance across from the BART turnstiles. *Let's see, the J, the K, L, M, and N all run down here.* Colleen often dreamed of San Francisco and in many dreams, she rode the streetcars. The names had such lovely sounds to her, *L Taraval; N Judah; J Church.* Colleen had lived in Noe Valley, near the end of the J-car line. *Maybe I'll go there later after I get a room,* she thought.

Colleen returned to the street level and looked for an office building with public phones in its lobby. She found one on Montgomery Street and began her search for a cheap place to stay. After many calls, with no luck finding a room, she decided to try less desirable motels and motor inns.

The morning fog had lifted and, although still cool, the sun was shining. Colleen decided to walk up Post Street to Union Square and window shop, perhaps have an early lunch. When she reached the busy plaza, she decided to go into Macy's. As she entered the department store, her paper bag tucked under her arm, Colleen saw herself in a mirror. *I look awful!* She felt ashamed. *I better fix myself up.* She found the ladies room, where she washed her face and hands, applied some make-up and lipstick, and brushed her hair. She inspected herself. *Well...it's a little better.*

When she heard someone enter the bathroom, Colleen retreated to one of the stalls. She locked the door behind her and sat on the toilet. *I better come up with a plan—fast.* Colleen waited in silence until the other woman left the bathroom. After a few moments, she peered into her paper bag. *God, I can't walk around with this all day.* Colleen took out a can of beer and opened it. *Well, now what?*

She slowly drank the warm beer in the bathroom of Macy's. *I know!* She felt inspired. *I have enough to get some nice clothes. Not fantastic, but nice.* Her mind flashed with an idea. *Oh, this'll be great!* Colleen was thrilled with her plan.

I'll charge what I need. She was excited by her cleverness. *And I'll only wear the clothes tonight and return everything tomorrow. I'll tuck the tags in; no one will notice.*

Confidently, Colleen chose a simple black dress and evening jacket, pumps to match, pantyhose, bra and panties, and inexpensive costume jewelry. *This will be perfect,* she thought as she left the store. *I'll have no trouble tonight at all. No trouble at all.*

When Colleen arrived at the bar at the Top of the Mark on Nob Hill, she knew she looked beautiful. Earlier, she had gone to the St. Francis Hotel on Union Square, entering through one of the shops along Powell Street, and used the public restroom in the lobby to change into her new clothing. Colleen put her dirty clothing—and her bottle of whiskey—in a small travel bag that she had purchased. She stored the bag in a locker at the Powell Street BART station.

During the day, Colleen had tapered off her drinking. She felt clear-headed and energetic, despite having been awake and drinking for more than 36 hours. *I'll have to be very careful who I choose. Either I have a place to stay or I'm out on the street for the night.*

Colleen chose a seat at the bar that allowed her a view of the Bay Bridge and the hills of Berkeley and Oakland across San Francisco Bay. A couple in their 50s—obviously tourists—got up from their seats and walked around the room, "oohing" and "aahing" at the spectacular views available in all directions.

An older businessman, with the meaty, red face of a drinker, sat alone, elbows on the bar, hands folded, and his chin resting on his outstretched thumbs. Before him was an empty martini glass. He stared ahead, looking inward.

Three young men, well dressed, looking as if they were in town for a convention, were engaged in an animated discussion that all three found quite amusing.

When the bartender greeted her, Colleen ordered a Manhattan. She thought the drink was sophisticated and in the spirit of the elegant bar. Because she knew the drink would be quite expensive, she nursed it along. Discreetly, Colleen kept an eye on the men who entered the bar. After nearly 20 minutes had passed, she became concerned that her plan may have been foolish. Suppose the right guy doesn't show up? Maybe Thursday's not a good night.

Colleen avoided making eye contact with the bartender for another ten minutes. Just when she was near the end of her drink, and the bartender was approaching, Colleen's eyes lit up. *There he is!* Her abdominal muscles tightened slightly as she breathed in sharply and sat up straight in her chair. *Oh God, I hope this works.* Colleen, her legs crossed and her skirt riding up enough to reveal her attractive legs, turned her head casually and looked over her left shoulder. She let her eyes flash a glance at the handsome man who had entered the bar, looking at him directly for the briefest moment and then turned to the bar and signaled for the bartender.

"Do you mind?" The man sat to Colleen's left, leaving one chair empty between them. "I see you enjoy the same view that I do! Doesn't the city look fantastic from here?"

"Yes, it does. This is my favorite seat at the bar," Colleen smiled, self-possessed, nearly indifferent. "My name is Colleen."

"My name is David. Pleased to meet you, Colleen."

"What'll it be tonight, Dr. Taylor?" The bartender seemed to know his customer well.

"I'll have a Stolichnaya on the rocks, please." He turned to Colleen. "May I?" He said, indicating an offer to buy her a drink. "Put her tab with mine," he instructed the bartender.

"Why, thank you. How very kind," Colleen nodded her head demurely. "A Manhattan, please." Colleen turned to face him. "Are you here for business?"

"Yes, I'm here for a professional meeting." He smiled and studied Colleen.

Colleen saw that he desired her. "And what is your field?"

"I'm a physician. A plastic surgeon," he turned as the bartender arrived with their drinks. "And what brings you to San Francisco, Colleen."

"Pleasure," she said light-heartedly.

Dr. Taylor raised his glass. "To pleasure!" He toasted.

"To pleasure!" Colleen said softly as they clinked glasses.

"If I'm not being too presumptuous, what forms of pleasure bring you to Baghdad by the Bay?" He moved to the seat next to Colleen.

"Why, Dr. Taylor!" Colleen feigned modesty. "Carnal, of course!" She said imitating Vivien Leigh as Scarlett O'Hara. "Isn't that why every girl comes to this fair city?" She saw he was aroused by her humor and continued before he could speak. "But seriously," Colleen continued, "I'm more motivated by nostalgia than anything else on this trip. I lived here from '63 until '67. I went to Berkeley, later studied at Esalen down at Big Sur. It's really a spur of the moment trip—I just arrived this morning."

"Oh, really. Are you staying here?" He asked with hopeful anticipation.

"No, unfortunately not. I'm staying with an old friend." Colleen watched his expression carefully. "She went out tonight and I thought, 'what the hell, why don't I wear something nice and go for a drink on Nob Hill!' Not a bad way to spend your first evening in San Francisco." Colleen sipped her drink. "And you," she asked, "is your wife traveling with you?" Again, Colleen watched him carefully. She couldn't be sure but she thought he looked at his ring finger, although he was not wearing a wedding ring.

"No, I'm on my own." He sipped his vodka. "And why do you assume I'm married? Do I look like another middle-aged MD on the make while at a convention? Wife and kiddies tucked safely away at home in the suburbs while Daddy is out on the town playing around?"

"Well, the odds are that you are married with children," Colleen said in a friendly tone, "and that you came to the bar looking for female companionship for the night." She finished her drink. "Am I right?"

"Bartender!" He signaled for two more drinks.

"Am I right, Dr. Taylor?" Colleen persisted, teasing him.

"Please call me David. You are partly right."

"You *are* married!" Colleen was not troubled.

"Yes...However, I am *not* looking for female companionship for the night," he said slyly. "I am looking for female companionship for *the weekend*."

Colleen took a deep breath. "And what has brought us together atop the world's most romantic city? Could it be that we are fated to play out this scene?" Her eyes twinkled. "That our parts were written for us long, long ago and we are not the free agents we believe ourselves to be?"

"If that's true," David said wryly, "I hope our parts were written by D.H. Lawrence and not Herman Melville!"

They both laughed, good-naturedly.

"Very good, David, that's the spirit!" Colleen sighed. She knew she had a place to stay for the night. *Maybe even for the weekend,* she thought.

"Do you have plans for the evening?" David asked. "If not, would you like to join me for dinner?"

"I'd love to," Colleen wondered if she had agreed too quickly. "My friend and her lover will be out late and I haven't made any plans at all yet. I haven't even told any of my San Francisco friends that I'm in town!"

"Well, then, that's settled." He signaled for the bartender to bring the check. "Do you like Italian food?" He said as he signed the bill. "I know a fabulous place in North Beach." David reached into his pocket and left a very generous tip for the bartender.

"I love Italian food," Colleen stood up from her chair. Her legs felt wobbly. "Oh, my! I think those Manhattans were more powerful than I expected!"

"Don't worry. After you have a full, five-course meal the effects will diminish!" David helped Colleen with her jacket and they left the bar. "Let's take my car," he said as they waited for the elevator. "The restaurant has parking and then after dinner, I can drive you to your friend's home if you like..." The elevator arrived and David stepped aside to allow Colleen to enter first. The elevator door closed. They were alone. "Or..." He smiled. "Perhaps you might like to go dancing or —do you like jazz? There are some great performers in town this weekend!"

Colleen's stomach had turned into a knot when she was offered a ride to her friend's home. It was followed by a wave of weakness and relief by David's second suggestion. "I'd love to go hear some jazz! I love jazz!"

"Terrific! I know just the place. We really are on the same wavelength, aren't we?" David genuinely liked Colleen and it showed.

"I think we are, David." Colleen looked at the floor of the elevator. She felt honest and dishonest at the same time. "As long as you haven't any deep, dark secrets!'

"Oh, I have some deep secrets," David said as the elevator reached the lobby, "but they aren't dark. I can reassure you on that score!"

The streets were deserted as David and Colleen walked to his car. "Did you enjoy the music?"

"Yes, it was perfect," Colleen held his hand as they walked. "Tommy Flanagan is so sophisticated, so refined and romantic!"

"He's one of my top three in jazz." David let go of Colleen's hand as he reached for his car key. "Yusef Lateef, Art Farmer, and Tommy Flanagan. I just love them. I listened to them on my drive up from L.A. I have some great tapes in the car!"

Colleen had refrained from having more than the required two-drink minimum at the club. She was starting to feel agitated. "I had a wonderful time tonight, David," Colleen stopped at the passenger door of the car, "but...I'm feeling anxious suddenly." She could not look at him directly. "I don't know if it's because it's really four in the morning for me and I was up quite late the night before I left New York or..."

"That's probably it, Colleen," David said reassuringly. "I have something that may help. A minor tranquilizer should do the trick." He opened the door for her.

"Valium?" Colleen asked as she got into the car.

"No," he replied and closed the door.

David got behind the wheel, reached into the back seat, and picked up a small travel bag. He took out a vial of pills, opened it, and took one out. "This is from the same family as Valium. Can you swallow it without water? One should do the trick."

Colleen hid her eagerness for the pill. "Oh, that's no problem. I rarely take these—especially if I have had a few drinks during the night."

"When used properly," David assumed the tone he used with his patients, "this medication is safe and effective. You're correct to be concerned about taking a benzodiazepine—which is what this is—with alcohol, Colleen. But, in this situation, I don't think you have anything to worry about."

"I feel better just knowing that soon the pill will kick in and take the edge off," Colleen leaned back in her seat. "Can we drive out to one of my favorite spots? If it's not too late for you. I mean, do you have anywhere to go in the morning?"

"No, the conference ended today. I tagged on a little vacation time here in San Francisco. I'm not due back in L.A. until Monday night."

Perfect! Colleen thought.

"And your wife and kids?" Colleen asked, feigning a casual tone.

"They're back East visiting her family. As a matter of fact, they're in your neck of the woods—Great Neck, Long Island? Do you know it?"

"Not well." Colleen suddenly felt homesick. "I have some friends who were raised there. But that was a long time ago."

"Where to?" David put on his seat belt.

"Take Broadway south through the tunnel. Let's go out to the Presidio. You know the way?"

"No, I'm not familiar with that part of town."

"I am," Colleen said excitedly. "I know you'll love where we're going as much as I do!"

About 20 minutes later, David pulled off the road onto a lookout area. "Wow, I've never seen the Golden Gate Bridge like this!" He said, sincerely.

A strong wind blew in from the Pacific. The yellow lights on the Golden Gate Bridge were surrounded by swirling fog. The roadway spanning the bridge could not be seen. The tops of the towers barely stood out over the fog bank that was moving in across the bay. The Marin headlands looked as they might have before life crawled from the sea onto the land—indifferent, impervious, and imperious.

"I'm cold!" Colleen leaned into David.

"Here—put this on." He took off his sports jacket and put it over Colleen's shoulders.

"Oh, no, please—you'll freeze!" Colleen tried to reject his offer but to no avail.

"I love it here, Colleen! It's so brisk. It's invigorating!" David took in everything—the sea crashing against the beach hundreds of feet below them; the light from Point Bonita Lighthouse at the tip of the Marin headlands; the stars shining through breaks in the marine layer that was rushing in; the magnificent bridge, lure to lovers and suicides both; and the soft warmth of the woman in his arms.

Colleen leaned her head back, over and to her left. She looked up at David. "I hadn't noticed how much taller than me you are."

She closed her eyes and they kissed, at first gently, but then passionately.

Colleen buried her head in his chest. David rubbed his fingers through Colleen's thick hair.

"I love it here but I'm too cold," Colleen stepped back from David.

"Where to?" He asked nervously.

"Follow my directions—you won't be disappointed." Colleen opened the passenger door and got into the car.

David locked the bedroom door behind them. When he turned around, Colleen put her hands behind his neck, pulled his head close to hers, and whispered in his ears, first in the right, "I want you, David." And then in the left. "I really want you."

Colleen slid slowly down before David, squatting, looking up at him.

David looked at Colleen, her eyes shining. He was thrilled.

Colleen moved the tip of her tongue slowly back and forth across her upper lip and then wrapped her arms around his waist, pulling him toward her, pressing his genitals against the right side of her face. Colleen turned her face toward him. She rubbed her right hand up and down his erection and looked up at David smiling. "I know we're on the same wavelength now," she said as she slowly rubbed his penis through his pants. Colleen pressed her lips against his erection and blew her hot breath on it through the fabric.

David took her head in his hands and pressed her even closer to him.

Colleen undid David's shoelaces. She took his socks off. She undid his belt and then his zipper. She manipulated his penis through the opening in his briefs.

David lost his breath.

Colleen stroked his penis. "To pleasure," she teased. She stood up and walked slowly backwards to the bed, stepping out of her shoes and undoing her dress as she did. Colleen let her dress fall to the floor. She removed her pantyhose and sat on the edge of the bed.

David could not take his eyes off her. He loved her plum-colored bikini panties and bra.

Colleen turned around and climbed onto the bed. She stretched out prone and then pushed herself back up onto her knees, her feet dangling over the edge of the bed, her body sloping from her raised buttocks to her head, which rested on her hands.

"Do anything you want, David," Colleen whispered huskily. "I'm yours. Do anything that you want to me."

David undressed, unable to take his eyes from Colleen, who rocked gently from side to side on the bed. He walked to her and knelt down at the foot of the bed. David licked up the inside of Colleen's left leg from the calf to the elastic of her panties. He licked slowly up the right leg, pulling her panties down when he reached them. He leaned back and admired Colleen's body. David stood up, leaned over, and unhooked Colleen's brassiere, which fell to the bed. Colleen rolled onto her back and David removed her panties. She held out her arms and opened her legs. "Come..."

⁂

When Colleen awoke, she did not know where she was. She did not recognize the ceiling. She closed her eyes and thought hard. She opened her eyes again and looked around the hotel room. Colleen sat up in bed. She started to get out of bed but realized that she had nothing to wear. She found her underwear on the floor and put it on. She remembered where she was. *Now what will I do? I can't let him know my real situation.*"

Colleen heard David in the shower, singing. Breakfast from room service was on the table in the dining area of the room. A local radio station was giving its weather report. "Patches of low-lying fog in the valleys, and fog over much of the city, giving way to sunshine later this morning," the weatherman spoke rapidly. "With mostly sunny skies this afternoon across the Bay Area with highs of 70 in Oakland and San Francisco, 75 in San Jose, 66 in Half Moon Bay, 76 in San Rafael, and 78 in Santa Rosa. If you're going to be out late, take along a jacket or sweater. Temperatures will fall to the upper 40s tonight. That's the

Accu-Weather Report. Now back to you, Dave."

The disc jockey thanked the weatherman for delivering another beautiful day "after a cold, cold summer, we deserve it," he intoned. "And now, as promised, Peter Frampton to answer the question all America is asking." The DJ took a quick breath. "*Do You Feel,*" he paused for effect, "*Like We Do?*"

Colleen closed her eyes. *I'll just play it by ear,* she thought. *If he wants to go out tonight, I'll just meet him later at the hotel. I can go to Macy's, return the dress and jewelry, and get some casual clothes.* Colleen almost leaped across the room to the dress. *I hope he didn't see the tag!* She quickly hung the dress on a hanger in the closet. Colleen looked about the hotel room and saw that it was supplied with an iron and ironing board. *Great...I shouldn't have any trouble exchanging the dress.*

The water in the shower stopped running and Colleen knocked on the door. "Can I come in?"

"Anytime," David answered. "Colleen, I haven't felt this good in years!" He hugged and kissed her. "I feel great, Colleen," he said quietly. "You're beautiful and sexy, and all that but...it's something else, Colleen. Something I don't know I've ever felt before."

"You're sweet," Colleen answered self-consciously. "I'm going to shower now if that's all right with you."

"I have to shave," he said as stepped from the shower. "I'll leave the door open so the mirror won't fog up." Colleen admired his body silently.

Colleen washed quickly, her hair protected in a hotel towel. She was finished before David was through shaving. She ironed her clothing and dressed while he was still in the bathroom.

When he saw her, David was disappointed. "Are you leaving?" He was crestfallen. "I ordered breakfast for us." Colleen did not answer immediately. He saw her discomfort. "Don't feel you have to stay, Colleen. If you have something to do—" Colleen interrupted him.

"Well, I just want to change clothes and, well, you know..." She felt awkward and decided to be honest. "I always feel funny the next morning." She smiled embarrassedly. "You may find this hard to believe but this is the first time I've ever gone to a bar just to meet someone."

"Well, it's not the first time for me, not by a long shot." David paused and then said, "Why are we standing here like this!" He walked to the table and pulled back a chair for Colleen. "We've been as intimate as two people can be and now look at us! We're as awkward as two teenagers at their first school dance!"

Colleen relaxed a bit when she sat down. "I just didn't know if we were going to see each other later today," she was sincerely shy, "or if last night was..."

"Colleen! I'm yours for the weekend for the taking!" His smile eased Colleen's apprehensions. "As a matter of fact, I came up with a wild idea earlier this morning. I'm almost afraid to tell you." David moved his chair closer to Colleen's. "You were so free and uninhibited—"

Colleen blushed deeply.

"I'm sorry, I didn't mean to embarrass you!" He took Colleen's hands in his. "It's just that you really got me going, Colleen. I woke up this morning a bundle of energy! What I did is I called PSA—the new low-fare California airline—and I booked us *first class* round-trip tickets to L.A. and back for tonight." David grew more excited as he spoke. "The flight's only 52 minutes. We take off at five, get to L.A. about six. I rented a limo to take us to dinner and a wild party in the hills. Then we catch the last flight back to San Francisco and take a cab here!"

"You've got some imagination," Colleen answered. *Such a simple thing and it's all so complicated,* Colleen thought. *What will I wear? How will I get all the clothes I need?*

David did not know how to take her words. "Maybe I jumped the gun. Maybe I'm pushing this too far?"

"No—not at all!" Colleen leaned over and kissed him. "I'm just kind of flabbergasted!" She looked at David. "You know, the more I look at you, the more handsome you get!"

"Is that a yes?" He laughed.

"That's a yes. But I don't know if I have the right clothes for the occasion. I'm only here until Monday," Colleen fabricated an explanation, "and I didn't bring many things. And you already saw my nicest outfit!"

"Oh, don't worry about that! It's casual, very casual," David assured her. "It's warm in L.A. today—I checked the weather report. Just wear jeans, a light top, and sweater, sandals, or sneakers. Anything you want, as long as you feel comfortable."

"But aren't you worried that...uh...you know, being married and all, that you'll meet people who'll—" Colleen couldn't be direct.

"Tell my wife?" David said sadly. "No, Colleen. My marriage is not..." He thought for a moment. "We got married young, Colleen. Very young. Because there was a baby on the way. It was 1949, Colleen, and under those circumstances, you got married then. I was just 18 and she was 16; 17 when our daughter was born. Well, a year and a half after our baby was born, she died of spinal meningitis. Shortly after that, the Korean War broke out and I was drafted. I saw action, found I was a good paramedic, and, when I got out, with the help of the G.I. bill, I went to medical school." David had a wistful look.

"And your wife?" Colleen knew how terribly painful it must have been for them.

"I didn't see it then, Colleen. I didn't see how much she was suffering." David pictured his wife. "Joan's the kind of woman who always looks and sounds perfect. She keeps a lid on all her feelings. But first Joan lost our baby; then she lost me to the service, and then she lost me for years to medical school. And that's when I lost Joan." His eyes were sorrowful.

"How do you mean?" Colleen asked. "You're still with her."

"I was so busy, so preoccupied with med school," he spoke with anger at himself, "and my own importance, that I lost her emotionally. We never really were together again, I don't think, even though we had two kids after I started my practice." He smiled. "I've never told anyone this before. I also lost her to booze for a while; then booze and Miltown—but that's before your time. Now people pop Valium and wash it down with scotch or vodka. Back then doctors pushed Miltown on women..." He paused. "Women who needed somebody to be there, to hear them, to listen to them. Instead, they had pills pushed on them."

"And now?" Colleen didn't feel satisfied with his answers.

"Now? Now we have an unspoken understanding," he said without emotion. "I'm 45 and she's 43. I keep the money coming in and she takes care of the kids—who aren't really kids anymore—and the house and whatever social things we have to do or want to do. I know that she is seeing someone and she knows that I," he blushed slightly, "date."

"How old are your children? I have a sixteen-year-old daughter." Colleen saw that David felt connected by the fact that they both had children.

"Well, Jesse, my daughter, is 20. She's in USC now, studying film and TV. My son is 23 and is at UCSF med school." David laughed. "He's a tough kid. He's already told me that he's going to be a 'real' doctor and not a parasite like me," he laughed loudly, "who lives off the rich by performing useless procedures like tummy tucks and facelifts on the vain, insecure and self-indulgent wealthy in America!" David imitated his son's speech pattern while repeating his critique. "I told him let's see what you're doing after you complete your residency."

"Didn't what he said hurt your feelings?" Colleen knew it would have hurt hers.

"Somewhat...but hey...I'm not hurting anybody." He was slightly defensive. "And I make a nice living for myself and my family. I must say this—I don't support my son financially. He wouldn't let me. He's worked and gotten scholarships and now he's racking up some hefty debts from student loans." David lifted the lid from the breakfast platter. "Now, if I were paying the bills and getting this shit from him—hey, that would be a different story!"

Colleen looked at the food. Nothing seemed appetizing. "I think I better get over to my friend's. She might be wondering what happened to me."

"You can call her from here," David volunteered.

"No, but thank you." Colleen took his hand. "Where and when should I meet you later?"

"How about right here. Just come up to the room. Say about—"

"Two-thirty?" Colleen suggested. David seemed surprised. "Two o'clock? Time enough for a reprise of last night?"

"If it's a reprise of last night, come as early as you like!" David kissed Colleen, stood up, and walked her to the door. "You will come back, won't you?"

His insecurity surprised Colleen. She felt suddenly protective of him. "Don't give it a moment's thought. I'll be here at *precisely* two o'clock."

It had been more difficult than Colleen had anticipated exchanging the clothing and costume jewelry. *I guess I didn't look very good*, Colleen had been ashamed of her appearance. *I wonder if my clothes smelled bad,* she thought. She had changed clothing in a bar on Geary Street near Macy's. By the time she left Macy's with her new outfits—two blouses, two pairs of pants, tennis shoes and a sweater and underwear—it was just about noon.

Colleen chose an old hotel near the Civic Center, the San Franciscan, for her next costume change. It was extremely busy when she arrived and she found her way with ease to the lady's room in the lobby. *Thank God I had a shower this morning,* she thought as she changed in a bathroom stall. Perfume and baby powder can only cover up so much.

Colleen packed a change of clothes and the toiletries she purchased in her overnight bag. She returned her dirty laundry—and whiskey—to the locker at the Powell Street BART station. As she rode up the escalator to the street, Colleen felt both fatigue and anxiety. Since it was too early to meet David, Colleen bought a ticket for the cable car. She was too tired to walk all the way uphill to the hotel on California Street. She thought she would simply wait in the lobby until it was time to meet David. As she rode the cable car along Powell Street, Colleen did not share the enthusiasm and élan of her fellow passengers. *This is crazy,* she thought wearily.

Colleen had been in the hotel lobby for nearly 45 minutes when she saw David enter. He did not see her as he headed straight for the elevator. He was carrying a large shopping bag and had a large box under one arm. *He looks very pleased with himself,* Colleen noted, amused. Although she knew the purchases were most likely for David's wife or daughter, she could not help but think that there might be a present for her among them.

After waiting for ten minutes, Colleen went upstairs to David's room. When she stepped from the elevator, she hesitated. *He really likes me and I'm being so dishonest with him.* She was disappointed in herself. *I'm not dishonest about how I feel...but I did use him...sort of...but did I really?* She was confused. *I wish I could tell him I don't have a place to stay; that I have almost no money; that I got to San Francisco without even—* Colleen could not complete her last thought.

I just can't tell him...I wouldn't even know how to tell him. She shook the worried thoughts off. *I've picked up guys before,* she told herself, hoping to build up her courage. *And I've been picked up plenty of times.*

Who's using who? If you both enjoy yourselves—no one. She walked down the hallway and as she knocked on David's door, Colleen wondered, *So why do I feel bad?*

"Colleen! You're early!" David was surprised.

"I'm sorry...I can come back—" She was flustered, more from her own conflicted emotions than from the thought that she might be early.

"Nonsense! You couldn't be too early as far as I'm concerned," David closed the door behind Colleen. "I ordered a few things. I thought we might want a bite before our flight." He delighted in Colleen's amazement.

"David! What a spread!" The table was filled with various sourdough breads; hard and soft cheeses; a number of different meats; apples, pears, and grapes; and in silver buckets on each side of the table, magnums of Dom Perignon on ice.

"What do you think? Did I leave anything out?" He laughed lightly.

"What do I think?" Colleen said with a sassy expression. She put her left hand on her hip, placed the tip of her tongue on her upper lip, threw her hair back and then said, "Let's get naked!"

David picked Colleen up and carried her to the bed.

The evening passed like a dream for Colleen. Lazy from an afternoon of lovemaking, and feeling the effects of the tranquilizer she took before the flight, she daydreamed all the way to Los Angeles. During dinner at a seaside restaurant in Santa Monica, Colleen looked intently at David as he spoke to her. She was interested in his views but was more curious about him.

David intrigued Colleen because of his unusual combination of opposing attributes. She admired his rugged appearance and his gentle touch. His greying hair showed his age but his skin was smooth and youthful. *That must come in pretty handy for a plastic surgeon, and his thinking is clear, well-reasoned, and pragmatic. And yet,* she thought as she listened to his description of the great changes in medical practice since he had become a physician, *there's a trace of the dreamer in him. But the dreamer who has abandoned his dreams. Not with bitterness but with a sense of bittersweet necessity.*

"And it's the patients—the public who'll get the shaft, Colleen." He paused for a response but received none. "Colleen? Knock-knock—anyone home?"

"I'm sorry," she had not heard his last few sentences. "But how can you be so sure?" She ad-libbed, relieved when her question was answered.

"I can't be certain about the details," David said, with a sad seriousness, "but, by the time I retire, the practice of medicine will be very different. Few people will have a personal physician who knows them. Young doctors won't be trained to observe patients, to touch them, to listen to them. They won't be trained to use their senses to diagnose and so won't be able to do so without increasingly sophisticated and expensive technology. The big bucks will be in specialized medicine and that's where most med students will go."

"Coming from a plastic surgeon in L.A," Colleen teased, "that sounds—"

"I know," David laughed, "I know it's contradictory. But how I earn my living and what I see or understand are very different things. How many people have work lives that are in harmony with their beliefs?"

Colleen felt personally challenged. She knew that she could not answer "My work life is in harmony with my beliefs." She remained silent.

"You know, Colleen, I bet most people would change their jobs in a minute. And a lot of people have great conflicts—" David stopped as he looked up to see Colleen staring straight ahead. "Oh, I'm sorry—I guess I'm just rambling on."

"Oh, no, not at all. I was just thinking about myself...How would I answer that question?" She smiled weakly. "I can't say that my ideas about life and society and people are in line with my work." Colleen looked at David sadly.

"Oh, Colleen! I didn't mean to bring you down!" David reached across the table and took Colleen's hand. "Let's drop the whole thing. We didn't fly 500 miles to—"

"I'm just being silly." Colleen cut a piece of salmon and ate it. "I love salmon—and this is excellent!" She ate another piece. "And how is your dinner?"

"Terrific! Would you like to try some?" David removed a shrimp from its shell and picked it up with his fork. "Here—it's really good."

They discussed movies and television, music and theater, and religion and politics as they finished their meals. "We should be on our way," David said as he ordered the check. "Unless you want dessert? Do you?" Colleen declined. "Good, we can go for a drive and then to the party."

"Excuse me," Colleen got up from the table. "I'll be right back."

"I'll take care of this and meet you at the front," David smiled at Colleen. "You look beautiful."

After they left the restaurant, Colleen and David walked to the Santa Monica Pier. "I've never been here before," Colleen was excited. "I really like it."

"I like Santa Monica a lot," David agreed. "It's a funny mix. They've got radicals, the rich, and the Rand Corporation here. It's like a combination of Berkeley, Santa Cruz, and L.A. And throw in a bit of Marin and Orange counties just to add to the confusion."

It was a summer Saturday night and the pier was crowded. Colleen and David walked nearly to the end and then stopped and looked south along the shore. Couples walked along the edge of the sea and joggers and bicyclists exercised on the path that ran parallel to the beach. The moon was just above the hills in the distance.

They stood in silence, keeping their own counsel. Without a word, arm in arm, Colleen and David walked back along the pier, oblivious to all others. When they reached David's rented limousine—which was waiting for them in the restaurant parking lot—the chauffeur opened the door for Colleen.

"I've never been in one of these," Colleen confessed. "Pretty ritzy!"

"I thought it would be fun—a bar, a stereo, even a TV set!" David leaned back and stretched his legs out. "They don't even reach the other side!"

"Can he see us?" Colleen asked.

"No, not with that dark glass." David started to sit up but Colleen held him down.

"Good," she whispered.

Colleen mixed easily with David's friends and acquaintances. She had expected that they would all be physicians and doctor's wives and girlfriends. Instead, she found herself talking with a radio reporter, a broker, two unemployed actors, a model who wanted to be an actress, and a few lawyers. A number of the guests were independently wealthy and seemed to spend most of their time, as far as Colleen could tell from listening to them, traveling around the world. There were two physicians—a woman internist and a male psychiatrist—and two dentists, one of whom worked closely with David.

Colleen had decided to refrain from drinking. She wanted to make a good impression, for herself and for David. *And I've been kind of on a roll,* she thought. *I better take it easy for a while.* The tranquilizer took the edge off and she didn't need a drink.

David had left Colleen to talk with a friend. Just as she was starting to feel self-conscious, many of the guests had mysteriously disappeared into another room, David came to her side. "Miss me?" He joked.

"Terribly!" Colleen kissed him on the cheek. "Where is everyone off to?"

"Well, they're all inside doing coke," David said blandly. "I'm not into drugs myself but if you want to—"

"Oh no," Colleen felt anxious. She wanted the cocaine. Her heart began to beat faster and her mind raced. She felt pulled toward the inner room but resisted. She remembered her night with Pat in the bar and felt ashamed of her behavior. Colleen also feared that the drug might change her in ways that she did not want. She knew she could not risk losing control.

"It's a slippery slope for many, Colleen. And I don't want to find out if it's one for me as well." David took Colleen by the hand. "Let's go out on the deck. They have a fantastic view from up here."

Standing in the cool night air, the lights shimmering below in the distance, Colleen felt at ease for the first time in years. David's hand was warm. His grip was firm but comforting. Colleen felt he was really with her. *I'm not just someone he picked up in a bar,* she thought, *and he means more to me.*

Colleen was sorry that she had been dishonest when she met David. *I could have told him the truth,* she thought ruefully. *But how could I have known that at first?* She looked at David in the dim light. *Now I wouldn't know how to explain. What could I say? I got drunk and the next thing I knew I was in San Francisco with nowhere to stay, not enough money, and five days before I could fly back? And my only plan was to pick up a rich man at the Top of the Mark?* Colleen blushed. *And you're the lucky guy!*

"You're so quiet, Colleen." David put his arm around her waist. "Penny for your thoughts!"

Colleen let out a loud laugh. "No way, mister. No way—not for a thousand dollars." Colleen shook her head. "Not these thoughts."

"Now I've *got* to know!" David tickled Colleen gently in the ribs. She wriggled away. "I can wait...I'll just bide my time."

"Oh, it's nothing, David. I was just thinking how we know each other in a way I can't put into words. But that then...we don't know each other at all." She turned to him. "Do you know what I mean? How much of you have I created from cues you gave me...or from my own needs?"

"But that's such a big part of the thrill, isn't it, Colleen? Finding out about each other? Why, when I saw you in the bar, why did I *want you*?" He smiled and held her close. Colleen nestled her head on his shoulder. "What were all the unseen things that drew me to you? Of course, you are physically attractive. But there is something else about you that is alluring." He moved Colleen's head back and looked at her, simply but deeply. "There is something magnetic about you, Colleen."

"Oh, David, please," Colleen dismissed his remarks with a laugh.

"Colleen, look at me." He saw that she was looking at him, seeing him. "This is really me, Colleen. You may get more of the details as we get to know each other better. But this is really me. Strengths and weaknesses; good points and bad. But you...I sense that this is you under wraps somehow."

Colleen became quite uncomfortable and remained silent.

"I have this funny feeling that either you once were quite different," David watched for Colleen's reaction but her expression was guarded. "Or else that you're in some sort of transition and will be quite different in the near future. Maybe more like you once were."

Colleen walked a few feet away from him. She began to weep bitterly, in shame.

Flustered, David kept his distance at first but as her crying grew more intense, he went to her. "Colleen...I...I had no idea!" She would not let him hold her.

"I *was* very different, David!" Her lower lip was raised like a baby's. Mascara was running down her cheeks. "I was *so very* different and I don't know if I'll ever be myself again!"

Gradually, Colleen's crying subsided. "I need a tissue," she said weakly. "I feel so foolish, David. It's just that I've been under such pressure lately."

David gave Colleen his handkerchief. "Take this, Colleen."

Colleen blew her nose and then laughed. "Oh, you must think I'm so silly." She noticed that she had gotten mascara on his handkerchief. "I hope it's not ruined."

"Don't worry, Colleen. It's just a handkerchief. Do you want to stay at the party?"

She took a deep breath. "I'm okay now.' She managed a smile. "We'll be leaving in an hour anyway and I know you're enjoying seeing your friends. Just get me to the bathroom without anyone seeing me like this. I must look a mess!"

David stayed close to Colleen for the rest of the party, not out of concern, but because he felt closer to her. Colleen was grateful to him. She was exhausted, physically. But emotionally, she was stronger and less troubled.

"David," Colleen asked sheepishly in the back of the limousine, "you probably think I'm a baby but I'm getting nervous again about the flight."

"And you'd like another little pill." David leaned over to the bar and got Colleen a glass of water. "Here you go. You should be feeling it just before we take-off."

Colleen did not dare admit it to David but she loved the feeling that the pills gave her.

The flight home seemed even faster than the flight to L.A. Colleen was impressed that they were in their hotel room 90 minutes after leaving Los Angeles. Colleen undressed and sprawled on top of the bed covers. "David, that was wonderful!"

"I had a great time. I'm glad we went," he said from the bathroom, his words muffled because he was brushing his teeth. "I hope you don't think I do this with every girl I meet."

"Well, it wouldn't bother me if you did, David," Colleen said with some apprehension, "what time are you leaving?"

"Sometime in the early afternoon. Probably by one o'clock," David was puzzled. "But I'm not leaving until Sunday."

"I'm confused," Colleen closed her eyes. "Tomorrow is—"

"Tomorrow is Saturday, Colleen. We've got the whole day to ourselves," he said happily. "I'm leaving Sunday because I'm not making the drive in one day," he said as he entered the room. "Tomorrow is only Saturday," Colleen murmured, happily. "I thought it was Sunday!"

"If we don't sleep too late, we could have Sunday brunch before I leave." He sat on the edge of the bed. "I know a great restaurant on Post near Powell."

"Come to bed," Colleen pulled back the covers for him. "I'm so tired."

David turned the lights out and got under the covers with Colleen. "This is the first time we've gone to bed and just gone to bed," he teased.

"Don't worry, David. If you get all hot and bothered and wake up with a hard-on," Colleen kissed him good night, "just roll me over and go to it. I love waking up to find I'm being made love to!"

Within minutes, both were asleep.

Although she had slept only five hours, Colleen awoke refreshed and invigorated. *Brigid's probably home now,* Colleen thought. She slowly got up from bed, careful not to awaken David. Colleen sat in an armchair across the room and called her daughter. *I'll pay David when he checks out,* she told herself.

"Mom!" At first Brigid was relieved to hear from her mother. Then she was angry. "Well, thank you for finally calling and letting us know you're still alive!" She said with angry sarcasm and hurt. "The whole family is upset, Mom!"

"But, honey—I called you Thursday!" Colleen whispered.

"Oh, that makes all the difference! The fact that you don't come home and that no one knows where you are for hours doesn't mean anything to you." She fought back tears as she spoke.

"Brigid!" Colleen tried to interrupt her daughter, unsuccessfully.

"Or that a bartender, a total stranger, from some neighborhood dive called us at eight in the morning to say you showed up at his bar at closing time acting funny. That he thought you were going to the airport! And that you kept saying you were going home! *Home!*" Brigid was angrier than Colleen had ever known her to be. "That's all just fine! There's no problem! *I called you Thursday*," she imitated her mother.

"Brigid, please, let me—" Colleen regretted calling.

"Did you ever stop to think that we might not think that that's enough? That we might be worried sick! Did you?" Brigid stifled her tears. "That I might be very, very worried about my mother. My mother who started drinking again and flew off to San Francisco!"

David stirred in bed. Colleen sat still. She did not want him to hear any of her conversation.

"Mom? Don't you have anything to say?" Brigid was frustrated. "She's not answering—you talk to her. She's your sister; maybe you can get through to her." She handed the phone to her Aunt Lis.

"Colleen," Lis said sadly, "are you all right?"

David rolled onto his stomach, still asleep. "Lis, I'm sorry for all the trouble." Colleen didn't know what else to say. She knew she could not tell them she met the most wonderful man and is having a beautiful time. Colleen thought, *they might kill me when they get their hands on me.* She didn't know what to say. "I'm very sorry, Lis. I'm okay. I'll be home Tuesday morning. My plane gets in about six a.m."

"I'm going to meet you," Lis said with determination. "What airline are you flying? Do you know the flight number?"

Colleen gave her sister the information.

"We're going to talk, Colleen. *You and I are going to sit down for a long talk!* This is no joke, Sis. The kid gloves are coming off!" Lis was furious and serious.

Chastened, Colleen was silent.

"Do you need anything?" Lis was conciliatory.

"No... I'm fine. I'm staying at the Mark Hopkins 'til tomorrow—"

"*What!* " Lis could not believe what she had just heard.

"What?" Brigid called out, worried.

"Colleen, how can you afford to—" Lis stopped in mid-sentence. "Colleen, I am looking forward to hearing this part of your story." Her tone softened but not her resolve.

"Here's the number. Call me before check-out time tomorrow." She thought for a moment. "I won't be here after about one o'clock your time tomorrow."

"You're not going to get off easy this time, Colleen. This is pretty serious stuff." Lis paused and Colleen heard Brigid ask for the phone.

"I'm going to be at the airport, too, Mom!" Brigid was even angrier. "I'm skipping school and we're going to talk!"

"Okay, sweetie. I'm sorry, honey. I'm really sorry." Colleen sighed, heavily.

"I don't accept your apology, Mom. This time," Brigid was adamant, "it's not enough."

They said their goodbyes and Colleen hung up the phone. "They're right," she conceded. "They are absolutely right. What I did was completely fucked up!"

She looked at David. The covers had come off him almost completely. *He has such a great body,* Colleen thought. *I know what I did was unfair to my family. But I never would have met David.* Colleen got back into bed. "David," she whispered in his ear as she played with his penis. "Oh David..."

"Why did you become a doctor, David?" Colleen lay beside him, rubbing her hand over the grey hairs on his chest.

"I made a decision that I didn't want to be poor," he answered honestly. "I looked into various careers in which I could earn the amount of money I wanted to earn and I chose medicine."

"I find it hard to believe it was that simple, David." Colleen placed small kisses around his neck. "There must have been more involved."

"Sorry to disappoint you, Colleen. But a physician makes good money; is respected in the community; and has quite a bit of autonomy, although we're losing that rapidly. There is also a lot of positive feedback from patients. It feels great to make someone look the way she wants to look." He examined Colleen's face as he would a prospective patient. "You certainly have no need of my skills," He smiled.

Colleen loved the compliment but decided to tease David. "She? Are all your patients women, Dr. Taylor? Perhaps the biggest reward isn't the money or the respect or independence at all. Maybe it's the attention all those beautiful Hollywood women lavish on you." Colleen poked David in the ribs.

"I can just see you!" She sat up in bed. "A woman comes in to see you after breast augmentation. She's a knockout anyway but now she's gone from a 34A to a 36C. 'Show me your breasts,' you say!" Colleen got to her knees and straddled David. She pushed her breasts up and massaged them. "You cup her beautiful, beautiful breasts in your hands. 'How does this feel?' You ask as she gets turned on."

"Colleen, please!" David laughed. "It's not like that at all!"

"And then she asks, 'Doctor, oh, Doctor, will I still have sensation in my nipples?' You gently stroke one nipple with your thumb and forefinger," Colleen played with her nipple and it became erect. "Then you lean forward," she leaned over, bringing her breasts close to David. "You open your lips slightly and place them on her other nipple." Colleen put her breast to his mouth and he suckled her.

She sat up quickly. "And then she says, 'Oh Doctor! What sweet sensations flow through my nipple and areola!" Still on her knees, Colleen leaned as far back as she could, propping herself up with her hands. "Then she makes a Marilyn Monroe sexy-baby girl pout and purrs, 'Oh Doctor, how can I ever show you my gratitude!"

David sat up and pulled Colleen to him. "You've missed your calling, Colleen!" He hugged her. "You should have been an actress, a comedienne!"

"Can we go for a drive today?" Colleen asked as she held him close.

"We can go anywhere you'd like." David lay back down.

"Can we go to Muir Woods? I haven't been there in years," Colleen rubbed her hands up and down his legs. "Maybe have dinner in Sausalito? One of those restaurants right on the water?"

"We'll have dinner anywhere you want, Colleen. Anywhere you want." David watched her eyes as she massaged one leg, then another. Colleen began to massage his right foot and, suddenly, David became completely relaxed. "That's incredible! How are you doing that?" He moaned with pleasure.

"You like that a lot, don't you!" Colleen smiled, almost wickedly. She began to massage his left foot. "How's that!" She saw him stretch and writhe with delight before her.

"No one's ever done this to me before," he said softly. "This is so great, Colleen!"

"Good, I'm glad you like it. If you want, I can give you a full massage," she said proudly. "When I lived out here, I made some pretty good money giving massages. My style is kind of a mix of traditional Swedish massage and some body work techniques I learned down at Esalen. Would you like a massage?"

"If it's anything like this, go for it! Do it!"

Colleen massaged David and many happy memories came to her. She told him how much she had loved her student days at Berkeley. In her third and fourth years as an undergraduate, and in her first year of graduate school, Colleen spent a great deal of time at the Esalen Institute at Big Sur. She studied with Maslow and Fritz Perls. She also worked with people who practiced Bioenergetics, learning a great deal about the human body and bioenergy.

"I guess I was pretty happy," she said, "although back then it didn't seem that way a lot of the time." Colleen recalled the difficulties of raising Brigid alone, earning enough money to finish school and keep them clothed, fed, and living in a decent apartment. "The guys I met didn't stay around too long after they realized I had a kid. Can't say I blame them."

"You're so good at this, Colleen!" David was deliriously happy. "You're *so* good!"

"You really like it? I haven't done this in years." Colleen became immersed in her work. She stopped thinking. Her complete attention was on David's reactions to her touch and her tactile sensations. Without being aware of it, Colleen gave David as good a massage as she had given hundreds of clients years before.

Colleen looked up to see that 20 minutes had passed. She took her hands away. "I can still do it!" She was surprised. "After all these years." Colleen felt proud of herself.

"Oh, do you have to stop?" David moaned. "I feel so incredible. I don't have an iota of tension anywhere in my body! Colleen, is this how you earn your living? If it isn't, you should give it serious thought!"

David stretched and rolled onto his back. "If you ever decided to move to L.A., you could open a practice in my office. I have an extra examination room that I never use. It would be perfect. You know, the bioenergetics thing has a lot of cachet in L.A. right now." Colleen did not react at all. "Really," he continued enthusiastically, "with your Esalen background and your psychology degree, you would do really well."

The idea was enticing but Colleen rejected it. "I think I'm too much of a New Yorker to live in L.A." She saw that David was ever so slightly disappointed. "Besides, if I shared an office with you, we'd never get any work done!"

"I know it won't probably ever happen," David sat up on the edge of the bed. "But I'm serious, Colleen. I know a lot of very wealthy people in L.A. and they would pay top dollar for a massage like you just gave me!"

"Really?" Colleen felt a surge of energy. His idea was thrilling in its way.

"You could probably fly out to L.A. once a month, work for a week, and make more than most people make in two or three months." David walked toward the bathroom. "I'm not kidding."

"That's an exaggeration and you know it," Colleen followed him, her mind feverishly pursuing the idea. "Like how much money?"

"Well, you'd have to work really hard that one week. You know, some businessmen early in the morning and late at night; some showbiz people during the day." David did some fast calculating. "You could *easily* make four or five grand. Maybe a little more depending on who your clients were." David turned the shower on, waited a moment for the hot water to come on, and then stepped in. "And you know, Colleen, a lot of these people I'm talking about are bi-coastal. If you got something going out here, I bet a lot of them would want to see you when they were in New York City for business."

Colleen sat down on the toilet cover. "Are you...I mean, do you really believe this? It sounds so way out there!" Colleen shook her head in disbelief. "I mean, I'd give it a try if I really thought it could pan out." She became lost in her thoughts, wondering if she could really move to Los Angeles and make such an improbable thing come true.

"Unless you've got something great going for you back East," David said as he soaped up, "and—no offense, Colleen—but I don't get the impression that that's the case, then what have you got to lose?"

Colleen sat silently thinking.

"I can guarantee you enough clients to start so that you won't lose any money. You'll cover your airfare and one week's expenses easily." David put his head under the shower, took some water in his mouth, and gargled. "Word of mouth will take care of the rest."

"Let me think this one over," Colleen said as David turned the water off. "That was a fast shower!"

"An old habit," he said as he reached for a towel, "from my days in the military."

"You know, your idea sounds less like a pipe dream the more I think about it. But the thing that worries me," Colleen said, furrowing her brow, "is that—and I mean no offense now, David—I'd be completely dependent on you. Wouldn't I?"

"Well, in the beginning, sure. But hey, once the word got around," he smiled broadly, "then you'd be on your own. I'd just be giving you a boost up onto the saddle. It'd be up to you to get on that horse and ride!"

"Let me think about it. But if I'm not sure by tomorrow..." Colleen looked away from David.

"Colleen," he walked over to her, put his thumb and forefinger under her chin, and tilted her head back. "Look at me. You'll still know me after tomorrow. You'll have my office number and the number for my private line at home. We live on opposite sides of the continent, and I don't get to the East Coast much, so I don't know how frequently we'll see each other. But, Colleen," he leaned over and kissed her on the lips, "I meant what I said last night. There's something magnetic about you. Something special. I feel lucky to have met you and very happy that we've had this time together. And I want to stay in touch with you."

"David, there so much I want to say to you!" Colleen stood up and kissed him fully. "I know we won't see each other much," she kissed him again, "but I know we will be together again sometime. And that it will be good when we do." She kissed him again, more passionately. "And you may find that you get to the East Coast more often—now that you have a reason to!"

"You are probably right, Colleen. You are probably right on the mark with that one!" He patted her behind. "Better get ready if you want to see anything today!"

Colleen stepped into the shower to wash as David prepared to shave.

The parking lot closest to the entrance to Muir Woods was full when David and Colleen arrived. They were resigned to parking down the road and were leaving the area when Colleen called out! "Stop! Go back! Quick! Get into reverse. About four cars back—someone is leaving!"

David maneuvered the car behind the one pulling out, keeping himself in front of the car behind him. Within seconds, he pulled into a spot within view of the ranger station. "It's ironic, isn't it?" David asked as he undid his seat belt.

"What?" Colleen was already halfway out the door of the car. "What's ironic?"

"Well, we came here," David checked the door to make sure it was locked, "we came here to hike in the woods, get some exercise, and yet we're so eager to park as close as we could to the entrance so we don't have to walk too far!"

"Don't worry, David," Colleen assured him. "If my memory is correct, you'll be very happy the car is nearby by the time we finish our hike."

The floor of the redwood forest was crowded with tourists, many of them speaking and laughing loudly. "It's the weekend," Colleen said defensively. "When I lived in San Francisco, I only came here during the week," she explained. "But none of these people will be up on the trails. They come on the tourist buses, take a few pictures, and then they're off."

David stopped to look at a plaque near a section of the park called Bohemian Grove. "Colleen, look at this." The plaque was in honor of the founding of the United Nations. "I'd forgotten that San Francisco was the original home for the U.N."

A few minutes' walk from that site, Colleen turned onto a path leading uphill, away from the crowds. "I used to hike along this path frequently when I lived here," she said. "When you are near the top, you can take one of two paths further up or head back down."

"How long is the hike?" David looked at his watch.

"Oh, I think it takes about an hour," Colleen replied. "Maybe a little more."

"Perfect! That leaves us enough time for brunch in Sausalito." He took a deep breath and started the climb.

They did not see any people until they had been hiking for about a half-hour. A young couple—the father with a baby on his shoulders, the mother with an infant in a papoose—smiled at them as they passed. "They look exhausted!" David exclaimed. "What's ahead for us, Colleen?"

"Maybe they made the same mistake I made on my first hike," Colleen continued walking as she spoke. "I took the difficult trail up and the easy trail down. Big mistake! I never did that again! I thought I would die. Partly I was out of shape, but partly it was a really tough climb!"

The silence of the woods was broken only occasionally by birdsong, an animal in the brush or, unfortunately, the roar of a jet overhead. To David, it seemed that no matter how far up the mountainside they climbed, the redwoods towered above them. He paused to catch his breath and, as he watched Colleen forge ahead of him, he noticed he was beside a stand of baby redwood trees. The trunks of some were so small that he could almost put one hand around them. Others could be contained in a ring formed by both hands.

David enjoyed being with Colleen; being separated from her by the effort of the climb; and their silence. He got into a rhythm of deep breathing and long strides that he maintained until he caught up with Colleen. She had stopped to read a signpost.

"Here's where we head back down," Colleen was flush. "Be careful...This part looks easier than it is." Again, Colleen led the way.

Colleen looked at the light falling on the rich green leaves and dappling the ground far below. She listened closely to the wind in the trees and the water in the streams on the hillside. She loved the feel of the rich earth as it gave way beneath her feet. Colleen felt something she had not experienced for years: her love for the redwoods. Colleen recalled all the places of natural beauty that she had cherished when she lived in San Francisco. She was at home in nature and yet lived in as unnatural an environment as there is.

Colleen thought of what David had asked the night before. "How many people have work lives that are in harmony with their beliefs?" She extended his question further. "How many people live in harmony with their beliefs...on any level? I don't...I've just been drifting...for years. Maybe I can get a handle on things if I can find some way to bring who I am more in line with what I do." Colleen felt embarrassed. "Of course, being on unemployment all this time..." At the beginning, Colleen had promised herself that she would use her unemployment benefits to support her, not only while she looked for a new job, but also, while she tried to get back to her music and her studies.

But I've just frittered the time away, she thought, disappointed in herself.

David caught up with her as the path leveled off a few hundred feet above the floor of Muir Woods. "You know, Colleen, it's magnificent here. But the splendor is actually quite subtle, isn't it?"

"I know what you mean, David." They paused and took in the majesty of the trees, many over 1000 years old. "At first, I was impressed by the height of the trees. And, of course, with their great age. But there is something else here, isn't there?" Colleen held his hand for a moment.

"Yes there is, Colleen. Something very powerful." The only sound they heard was their breathing.

They descended to the floor of the forest and followed the path to the parking lot. When they finally reached their car, David turned to Colleen. "I *am* glad that we aren't parked way down the road!"

It was a postcard-perfect day on San Francisco Bay. Colleen sat at a window table in Horizon's, a Sausalito restaurant that had once been home to the San Francisco yacht club. The bay was dotted with the white sails of sloops and ketches gliding through Racoon Channel off Tiburon, around Angel Island and Alcatraz, and under the Golden Gate Bridge. Across the bay, off Aquatic Park in San Francisco, an orderly kaleidoscope of primary-colored spinnakers unfurled as their ships competed in a Sunday race.

The Sausalito-San Francisco ferry, filled with tourists from "The City," cut its engines as it neared the dock. It slowly passed, within one hundred feet of the restaurant, diners on the outside deck and passengers on the top deck of the ferry, people who would ordinarily pass each other by without notice on a city sidewalk, waved to one another.

"Are you done?" The waitress asked Colleen. When she answered yes, the waitress removed her dishes and utensils. "And you, sir?" David said he was not finished with his meal and the waitress left.

"How were the Eggs Benedict?" David flashed a quirky smile.

"Why do you think that Eggs Benedict is such a peculiar choice?" Colleen was in good spirits but ever so slightly miffed. "I like Eggs Benedict and I used to love having them here years ago. And," she reached across the table and pinched David just above the wrist, "it's even better than I remembered!"

"It's just that, well, with all these marvelous fresh salads and seafood dishes to choose from," he teased, "your unhealthy choice of eggs—which you shouldn't eat—in a heavy butter cream sauce—which you shouldn't eat—on top of a fatty meat filled with nitrates and nitrites—which you shouldn't eat," David pinched Colleen each time he said "which you shouldn't eat."

"Stop that! It was funny when I did it!" Colleen pulled both arms away. "When you do it, it's merely annoying. It's *puerile*!" She made a face at him and laughed.

"You're just jealous because you're too old to eat all the really delicious things that are no good for you!" Colleen stuck her tongue out at David. "You Type-A, Mr. All-American Heart Attack Candidates have to watch *your* diets and now you want to drag the rest of us down with you. Typical," Colleen said with a mock sneer.

The waitress returned and David allowed her to remove his meal, although he had not eaten any since her last offer to take his plate. "Colleen, I don't know if I should say this..." He looked apprehensive as he spoke. "But I think I'm falling for you." He leaned back in his chair. "Here I am in one of the most beautiful places on earth, sound of mind and body, with money in the bank and a good job to boot, with one of the loveliest women on earth, with—" David checked his watch. "With nearly 24 more hours left to spend with you...And I'm beginning to feel that old bittersweet sorrow of parting."

"Bittersweet sorrow?" Colleen asked, moving her chair closer to the table and leaning forward, elbows on the tabletop.

"Yes, not for us the sweet sorrow of Romeo and Juliet," David smiled. "Fortunately, also not for us the terribly bungled and fatal plans of Romeo and Juliet. I guess I'm feeling the melancholy that comes when mundane life intervenes, when the tide of daily life comes in and washes away the oh-so-dramatic footsteps we lovers have left in the sand!" David smiled sadly.

"That was very, very well said, David! I'm surprised!" Colleen truly was surprised. "How literate and sensitive!"

"I'm a doctor," he shot back, "not a dolt! I read, I go to the theater, I watch *public television* just like the rest of the elite!" His eyes caught hers. "But I know that on the way back home, probably somewhere between San Simeon and Santa Barbara, I'm going to be missing you badly."

"Really?" Colleen feigned surprise. "It's going to take you that long to start missing me? What will you be doing besides missing me as you drive between San Francisco and San Simeon?" Colleen teased.

"I'll be thinking of things you said, smelling your fragrances on my body and clothing, seeing you as you were naked in bed with me, listening to love songs on the tape player in the car." He took her hand and kissed it softly. "Beautiful memories and beautiful views along Route 1 will blind me to the reality that we are not parted for a few hours only. I will suddenly know that we are parted for an indeterminate time." He drew Colleen to him and kissed her. "But I *know* we will be together again."

Colleen sensed a surge of melancholy. She turned from David and looked out at the bay. The same vital scene now seemed sad to her. All the people on all the boats, all the people standing on piers staring seaward, the tourists in Sausalito and San Francisco shopping or window shopping, and all the unseen people alone or alone together in rooms everywhere, with their hopes and heartbreaks, all merged into one in Colleen's consciousness and emerged as one word. "Evanescent!" She said softly but with strength.

David looked silently at Colleen and then out to the waters surrounding them.

Their reveries ended with the arrival of the check.

David and Colleen returned to San Francisco, left the car at the hotel, and walked around town. They first went across California Street to Grace Cathedral. Both admired the architecture of the church and the magnificence of the stained-glass windows. They walked up the right-side aisle and went through a doorway out onto the main altar. "It's too bad all this is poisoned for me," Colleen said. "I can't *not* know the hatred of Life that is behind all this show."

David was sympathetic. "You haven't said so, but I assume you were raised Catholic?" Colleen nodded yes. "And you haven't been a practicing Catholic since—"

"Since I was a teenager." Colleen crossed the main altar and went through a doorway to a small side altar. "You know, when I was a young teenager, and I would read the New Testament or hear parts of it read at Sunday Mass, I always had this feeling that there was this Jesus screaming to get out from under what was written in the Gospels. And that he would have thrown the money-changers out of my church just as he threw them out of the temple!"

"You were a feisty young thing, weren't you?" David chuckled. "A little firebrand."

"I took it seriously, David," Colleen replied, serious now. "I really believed that if this was the way you were supposed to live your entire life, you should take it seriously. The more I saw that no one really lived their religious beliefs, the more hypocrisy and cruelty in the name of religion I saw and experienced, the more I saw that Jesus had very little to do with Christianity."

"And how old were you then?" David was genuinely interested because, for the first time since they had met, Colleen was sharing something personal about herself.

"About 12 or 13. Of course, I didn't tell anyone what I was thinking!" Colleen laughed at the very idea. "I would have been punished severely at home and in school. When I was in eighth grade, my girlfriend Margaret MacElwain and I took her older brother's copy of *The Catcher in the Rye* from his room. We heard that it was really something. It had lots of *es-ee-ex* in it or so we heard. Well, to this day, one of the parts I remember most is when Holden Caulfield says 'I like Jesus and all, but I don't care too much for most of the other stuff in the Bible.' That was exactly how I felt! I thought Jesus was the most misunderstood person ever!" She laughed out loud and her laugh echoed throughout the church, drawing disapproving attention from some people nearby.

"Let's go outside. It's such a beautiful day," David suggested. "So," he continued the conversation as they walked north on California Street at the top of Nob Hill, "at an early age you became an atheist?"

"No, not really." Colleen was thoughtful. "Not an atheist. I guess you could say that at an early age I wanted to know what life really is. Do you know what I mean?" Colleen came alive suddenly. "*I just knew* Life was something very different from what I was being taught; something very different from the way people on earth were living. I was *hungry* to know what Life is." Colleen looked at David and saw his quizzical expression. "Do you think there's something odd about that?"

"No, not odd," he said, "it's just unusual. I never asked myself a question like that... ever. Especially not as a young boy. Why, life was plain as day right in front of me!" David thought for a moment. "Maybe, every few years or so, I might find myself standing under the night sky looking at the stars and I'd say to my wife, 'I wonder what it all is?' or something like that. But then back I'd go to nose jobs and tummy tucks, cocktail parties, and weekend affairs."

David and Colleen walked carefully down the steep hill to Grant Street and then turned left into Chinatown. "Look at that inscription on the church tower," Colleen pointed to Old St. Mary's Church on the corner of Grant and California.

David read the inscription aloud. "Son, observe the time and flee from evil."

"That church survived the 1906 earthquake," Colleen noted.

The sidewalks in Chinatown were crowded with tourists and local residents but the slow pace of the pedestrians fit the mood of their conversation. "But I'm curious, Colleen, about this interest you had as a child in such a serious question."

"Well, I wasn't really a child, David." Colleen smiled mischievously. "I had reached puberty just before I turned 13. In many cultures I would be considered ready for marriage."

"Yes, Colleen," David was slightly annoyed, "but in our culture, you would be considered a child. That's all I meant. How did you go about pursuing an answer to this question?"

"I read voraciously," she replied intensely. "I read everything assigned to me in school; I read all the New York newspapers—and there were a lot of them when I was a kid!" Colleen enjoyed recalling those times and sharing them with David. "I loved the library. I especially loved biographies of explorers and discoverers, you know Henry Hudson, Thomas Edison, that kind of stuff. And I loved the museums...the Museum of the American Indian in Washington Heights or the Museum of Natural History on Central Park West. I used to dream of being an explorer myself," Colleen shook her head, smiling.

"But I was going to explore *outer space*!"

"I love it, Colleen," David said sincerely. "Don't stop—tell me more!"

"Oh," Colleen had become self-conscious, "well, I don't want to bore you with all this talk about myself."

"But you've barely said a word about yourself since we met." He looked into her eyes. "Why, all I know about you is that you came out here on the spur of the moment and that you have a daughter." David was gently critical. "You'd have to blather on at great length before you'd even begin to bore me, Colleen. Wasn't it you who noted that, although we've been intimate, we're quite ignorant of who we really are?"

"Okay, okay, as long as you'll tell me when to stop." Colleen saw Columbus Avenue ahead. "Let's stop for coffee and dessert in North Beach."

"I assume you have a favorite spot you'd like to go to?" David had caught on to Colleen.

"Yes, as a matter of fact I do!" She laughed at herself. "It's the Caffe Roma. It's on Columbus near Vallejo." Colleen tried to read David's expression to uncover what he was thinking. "And despite what you believe, these are not all places that I went to with previous lovers!"

"Well, I'm not going to lie!" David was impressed. "That is exactly what I was thinking! I was just thinking 'She's picking all the places she once went to with other lovers.' Bullseye, Colleen!"

"Thank you, David." She nodded with an exaggerated graciousness. "By the way, I forgot to tell you something. *I can read people's minds when I really want to*," she said, only partly joking. "So be careful!"

"I stand warned." David was truly enjoying himself. He was also surprised to feel that he believed her.

"And now, we return you to our originally scheduled broadcast, *Don't Step on My Patent Leather Shoes—The Colleen Murphy Story*, which is already in progress," Collen said, imitating a television announcer. "You know, after I had stopped believing in Catholicism and no longer went to Church, a Buddhist temple opened in my neighborhood in The Bronx. I went there one time. I was a bit frightened. It was so different, you know? But the monks paid me no heed. I just went in, sat on the floor in a room that was like both a library and a shrine. And I read stories and sayings that I know now were Zen Koans."

"What are they, Colleen?" David had never heard of koans.

"Oh, they're short sayings or tales that are used as jumping off points for meditation," Colleen answered matter-of-factly. "They aren't instructive or didactic. In fact, they often present a puzzle insoluble by rational thinking. In the West, they are often incorrectly called riddles."

Colleen saw that David wasn't comprehending her fully. "Let me give you an example. It's one of my favorite Zen sayings. '*Life is not as it appears; neither is it otherwise.*' Get it? Or how about this. I remember a story about a Master who is teaching his pupils about Illusion and Delusion and transcending the emotions associated with this life. Suddenly, he is interrupted by another monk who whispers something in his ear. Without explanation, he dismisses the class and walks up to a lonely crag."

Colleen interrupted her story, distracted by the busy traffic at the corner where they had to cross.

"So, what happened?" David asked eagerly.

"Well," Colleen continued. "While the other students dispersed, the Master's best student followed him to the lonely spot. There he found the Master weeping most bitterly. The student was indignant!" Colleen was deeply involved in the story. "How could the Master be weeping? Isn't he teaching us to transcend emotion, attachment? What illusion could have caused him to behave so?"

They reached the restaurant and again Colleen interrupted her tale as a waitress seated them in a cozy corner window seat.

"So," David prompted her, "the student found the Master crying. Then what?"

"Well," Colleen knew she had David's full attention, "he demanded to know what the other monk had told him. What could have brought the Master to tears? 'He told me that my only son has just died,' his Master said. The student did not accept that answer. 'But Death is only an illusion!' he told the Master harshly." Colleen paused and accepted a menu from the waitress who stayed a moment to tell them of the daily specials.

"And what did the Master reply?" David truly wanted to know.

"Well, when the student rebuked him by saying that Death was only an illusion," Colleen paused for dramatic effect, "the Master turned, and with tears still in his eyes and on his cheeks, said simply, 'Yes, but it is the greatest illusion!'"

"And the teenaged Colleen, on reading things like this, would think what? Would feel what?" David leaned back in his chair.

"There's more here than meets the eye!" Colleen said and laughed at her own remark. But she understood the tale well.

"Not to change the subject, or get too personal," David said hesitantly, "but tell me about your daughter. If you want to, that is."

Without hesitation, Colleen said, "Brigid is a beautiful, intelligent, and talented young woman who turned 16 last April. She is a student at Performing Arts High School in Manhattan. She has a beautiful voice, is studying guitar, and also has a lot of potential as an actress. How's that?" Colleen asked. "Spoken like a true mother?" She said mocking herself.

"Spoken like a loving mother, Colleen." David was pleased that she was so proud of her daughter. "And she lives with you?"

"Yes, we live in a nice two-bedroom apartment in Upper Manhattan across from Inwood Hill Park." She saw that reference meant nothing to him. "It's near The Cloisters. Do you know The Cloisters?"

"Yes, as a matter of fact, I've been there." Colleen was pleased. "A couple of years ago I took a jitney that ran from the Met up to The Cloisters. I loved it."

The waitress came and took their orders.

"Brigid takes the A train downtown to school," she explained. "And Manhattan itself is a school for a kid interested in the arts. She is right in the heart of the theater district. Carnegie Hall and Lincoln Center are within walking distance. The greatest museums in the world are all around, and revival movie houses show the greatest movies ever made day after day!"

"I can tell you love New York! And New York wins over anywhere else in the U.S. as far as culture is concerned." He decided to broach a sensitive subject. "And Brigid's father...your husband?" David asked gingerly.

"Ex-husband," she said emphatically. "I've been divorced a long time now. Jim and I were only teenagers when I got pregnant. We got married and divorced a few years later. It's not so different from your story really." Colleen sighed. She still cared about her first love. "He's a very nice guy. He did what he could financially for Brigid—which wasn't much. But he took her places, like the zoo and to the beach. And he always remembered her birthdays. But I moved out west when Brigid was only three. I went to Berkeley and got my B.A. I also got my Masters at Berkeley."

"What brought you West?" He admired the courage it took for a young single mother to take such a risk. "Wasn't it hard to leave your family when you were on your own with a small child?"

"Not really...There wasn't much support," Colleen thought for a minute. "I mean, there was some financial support, of course. I lived mostly with my grandparents while I finished high school. My parents, especially my mother, were furious and ashamed of me. And in my neighborhood, working-class Bronx Irish Catholic, I was shunned and made fun of by the other kids a lot."

"But in the summer of 1963, when I was 20, a friend from the neighborhood—another pariah—came home from Berkeley for the summer. I fell in love with his stories of life at the University. He encouraged me to leave The Bronx behind and I believed I could start over. I moved out there in late August, took some courses as a non-matriculated student while I established residency, and then started full-time the next fall. I worked, went to school summers as well, and graduated in three years."

The waitress returned with their coffees and desserts, a cannoli for Colleen and Italian cookies for David.

David looked at her admiringly. "I'm really curious, Colleen. How did you manage to take care of your daughter, support yourself, and not only go to school but finish in only three years?"

"Well," she said proudly, "I was young and full of energy; I was extremely motivated; and for the first two years I was in college, I lived in a commune." Colleen stopped speaking when David laughed. "And before you ask, yes, it was a *hippie* commune. But it was beautiful, David. We cared for each other and most importantly, the children lived a much better life than if we had all been off on our own. I wouldn't have been able to accomplish what I did on my own. And even if I could have, why would I have wanted to?

"The American illusion of the self-sufficient individual overcoming all adversity alone without a penny to her name or friends in the right places held no attraction for me. My baby benefited from living on the commune, in that loving environment." Colleen had become quite angry suddenly. It was the residue of years of people's caustic comments about communal living.

"I'm sorry for laughing, Colleen. I didn't mean to offend you." David apologized.

"Oh, don't mind me. Partly I feel defensive from years of being teased," Colleen explained, "and partly I feel *righteous* because we lived a better way. We had a more natural, productive, and pleasurable way of life."

"I may sound like I'm advocating the devil," David said, "but if you truly had a better way of life, why didn't it survive?"

"Everyone says that. I would have expected more from you," Colleen answered, angry once more. "Can a lamb survive surrounded by a pack of rabid wolves? Did primitive people the world over survive cannibalistic Western imperialism? Could a little commune in California survive in the belly of the capitalist beast?" Although Colleen was sincere and sincerely angry, she laughed at her language.

"I knew you were a firebrand, Colleen, but I didn't know you were a Marxist!" He loved her passion.

"I'm not a Marxist or any other 'ist,' David." Colleen's anger had subsided. "Anyway, in my last year of college, and my first year in graduate school, I lived with a wonderful guy who was like a father to Brigid. I was lucky we met when we did because the commune had started to break up. In fact, it only lasted another year."

"How did you wind up back in New York?" David finished his coffee and looked for the waitress so he could order more. "Did you go back to New York for work?"

"No, what happened was that right as my lover and I were drifting apart, my grandmother died. I had been very close to my grandmother. Very close." Colleen choked up. "You see, I loved her so much I feel her loss to this day." She sniffled and swallowed and took a moment to compose herself.

"She died in the autumn of 1967 and I went back to New York for the funeral. I returned to California but my relationship ended a short time later. About then, in California, like in the rest of the country, the whole atmosphere began to turn ugly. There was the war, racial trouble, riots in the cities, with scum like Reagan and Nixon cynically exploiting existing trouble and criminally fomenting trouble for their own political purposes." Colleen stopped speaking and looked directly at David, "I thought if I'm going to live in this damned country, I'm going to live right in the center of everything that's good and bad about it."

"And to you, that's New York City? America at its best and its worst?" He understood her feelings.

"That's how it seems to me sometimes. Anyway, I moved back East and I've been there ever since." Colleen did not appear happy.

"How's it been since then? Did you ever remarry?" He now felt comfortable asking about her life.

"No, I never wanted to, really. I've gone out with some terrific guys, though not lately," Colleen caught herself, "until you, that is!"

"You'd better say that," David teased, "even if it's not what you really think. What kind of work do you do that you could just hop on a plane and come to San Francisco for a long weekend?" David had wanted to know the answer to that question for two days.

"Well, actually," Colleen turned scarlet. "I was hoping you wouldn't ask."

David grew nervous himself. "Please don't think I'm trying to pry into your personal life or make you uncomfortable in any way!" He wondered what could have upset her so. He quickly dismissed the idea that Colleen may have been "working" when they met and felt ashamed that it even came to mind.

"Oh, it's nothing really," she laughed nervously. "I...oh why don't I just come out and say it—I'm unemployed. I was laid off by the Board of Education when the city almost went bankrupt and I've been out of work all year."

David was immensely relieved. "Why, Colleen! So you're unemployed! Big deal! Good God, you had me worried!" He laughed at himself. "I didn't know what to think the way you turned so red! For a second I thought, you know, the way we met at the bar and all, that," David could not bring himself to complete his thought.

"Did you really think that, you naughty boy!" Colleen turned her shame at her dishonesty to work for her. "And thinking that's what I was doing, you still came right over to me!"

"No, no, no, you've got me all wrong! I didn't think that then! I—" David was flustered.

"Sure, sure," she teased. "You can't get that foot out of your mouth so easily! You thought you'd have a little fun for an hour or so. A little quickie," Colleen winked, "and maybe be a little kinky!"

"You've got it all wrong," David tried to explain.

"You don't have to explain anything to me, darling." She blew him a kiss. "You don't have to explain that you thought I was just a hooker when you saw me sitting at the bar."

"I didn't think that *then*, Colleen! How many times do I have to repeat myself?" He was upset and frustrated.

"Until you're blue in the face, Dr. Taylor. Until Kingdom come, Buddy!" Colleen huffed like an indignant matron. "Why I never," she said in a high, warbling voice, "in all my life! Why the very idea that I would be in that establishment for the sole purpose of engaging in acts of...Why the very word is unspeakable!"

"Well," David tried to turn the tables, "what was an unemployed school teacher doing alone in a bar on a Thursday night three thousand miles from home?"

"I'm not a school teacher," Colleen sniffed. "I never said I was a school teacher."

"You said you were laid off by the Board of Education in New York, didn't you?"

"Yes," Colleen acknowledged, "but I never said I was a teacher. As a matter of fact, I was a psychologist with the New York City Public School system. I worked with high school students as a counselor. My specialty was—"

"I think I can guess," David said seriously.

"And who better?" Colleen replied.

"How long were you with them?" He was relaxed once more.

"I began in September 1969, part-time. And I started full-time in September 1973 when Brigid began high school. I arrived just in time for the city's fiscal crisis and the massive layoffs that followed. Somehow I held on until December 1975 when I was let go."

"It must have been a rough year for you and your daughter," David said with sympathy.

"It hasn't been the best of years, that's true. But," Colleen tried to change the direction of their talk, "that's behind me. I was just so fed up last week, that I decided if I didn't get away, I'd burst! So I called my friend and arranged to come out here for a few days. I would have stayed longer but I have to—"

"To take care of your daughter, I understand."

"I was going to say I have to be back to sign for my unemployment check," Colleen said, "but, of course, I do have my daughter to care for as well."

"Do you think you'll get your old job back anytime soon or do you think you'll have to look elsewhere?" David was concerned for his new friend.

"I don't know if I even want my old job back. It was getting to me. I mean, these girls were getting pregnant younger and younger all the time. And there was no support for them, really." Colleen's sadness was evident. "None!"

"I guess you thought you could use your education and experience to help," David said, "but you couldn't."

"They really didn't have a chance. Of course, each year I could help a few girls," Colleen looked inward, "but I always felt they were the kind of girl who would have made it anyway. Do you know what I mean? And then there were the suicides. Three girls took their own lives. Two weren't officially suicides but everyone knew the truth."

Colleen looked up. "You know, all these girls wanted was to love and be loved. That's all. I used to keep a poem by Blake on my desk. The girls couldn't see it but I could. And as they told me about physical and sexual abuse at home, cried in fear for the babies they carried, and expressed all the other ordinary feelings that teenagers today have—I could see Blake's words burning before me. 'Children of the future age,'" Colleen recited from memory, "'Reading this indignant page, Know that in a former time, Love, sweet love, was thought a crime.'"

They sat silently for a time. "Did you work with inner-city kids mostly?" David knew he had no experience with the world Colleen was describing.

"Yes and no," Colleen said. "I worked with kids from all backgrounds—black, Hispanic, Israeli, Russian, and even some home-grown middle-class all-American white girls. You know, one student still stays in touch with me. Marilyn is a bright, beautiful young woman today. She just graduated from college last spring. I helped her all through her pregnancy and through her conflicts about whether or not to keep the child. Her parents wanted her to put the baby up for adoption and eventually she agreed. But she sent me a wonderful picture of her and her daughter with another poem by Blake written on the back of the photograph. She had seen the poem on my desk."

"Do you remember the words to the poem?" David felt great respect for Colleen.

"By heart! It goes like this, 'The Angel that presided o'er my birth Said, Little creature form'd of Joy & Mirth, go love without the help of any Thing on Earth." Colleen felt tranquil. "She was my favorite so it means even more to me."

"You are a complex person, Colleen Murphy." David took the check from the waitress, looked at it quickly, and then handed her a crisp bill. "Keep the change." He stood up and, like a gentleman, helped Colleen from her chair. "Let's go back to the hotel, shall we? I'd like to rest. I'm sure you have something in mind for the evening."

"You mean before our next bout of wild sex?" Colleen said almost loud enough for others to hear.

"I mean *in between* our next bouts of wild sex!" David said in a voice that must have carried into the restaurant's kitchen.

"Where is this place?" David asked as he drove slowly along Geary Boulevard. "Haven't we passed this block before, Colleen? Maybe the place went out of business—you haven't lived here for almost ten years."

"I should have looked it up in the phone book before we left," she peered out through the windshield looking down the side streets and along Geary. "Oh, now I remember! It's not on Geary; it's on Clement! I'm sorry, David, but we're only a few blocks away. Make a right and then another right at the corner. Parking's a problem here so let's take the first spot we see."

As they turned onto Clement, Colleen exclaimed, "A spot! Make a U-turn, quick!" She was excited.

"But it's illegal!" David protested.

"Do it!" Colleen commanded.

David made the illegal turn and pulled easily into a parking spot directly in front of the Irish pub they had been looking for. "I'm glad we didn't get caught doing that! I already have one moving violation on my license."

"Oh, I hope they still have the *seisúns* on Saturday night." Colleen stared at the entrance to the pub. "The luck of the Irish!"

"What did you say? You hope they have a what?" David asked as they got out of the car.

"A *seisún*, it's kind of a musical free-for-all," Colleen explained. "Whoever shows up, with whatever instruments, gets together and they play Irish music. Whatever songs they all know, they play. Some play a few solo tunes. It really depends. People bring banjos, guitars, flutes, tin whistles. There used to be a woman who brought her own harp!"

"It sounds like a lot of fun," David held the door open for Colleen.

"And some people get up spontaneously and dance. Other people sing. It *is* fun," Colleen's eyes shone. "It's great fun." As Colleen looked about the room, the light in her eyes changed, darkening, though still shining brightly. She saw that David was observing her. "What are you looking at, mister?"

"Those Irish eyes of yours, Colleen," David said. *Those Irish eyes that hide from you,* he thought, *and study you from hiding.*

"Let's sit over there," Colleen pointed to a small table for two in the corner. "The musicians used to gather in a circle in the center by the bar. This was my favorite table."

A few minutes after they had seated themselves, David noticed that the bartender was looking intently at Colleen. A waitress came and took their drink orders. David watched the bartender out of the corner of his eyes. He wasn't surprised when the bartender left the bar—there were only three customers—and brought the drinks over himself.

"Colleen?" He asked as he put their drinks down. The bartender was not certain it was her.

"Peter!" Colleen stood up and hugged him. "Peter! I can't believe that you're still here!"

"Neither can I, Colleen. But I'm one of the owners now, not just the bartender!" He said proudly. "I don't know if you knew the owner I worked for." She shook her head no. "Well, he retired and moved to San Diego and me and Don bought the place just about three years ago."

"That's great! How's it going? Is business good?" Colleen looked to David, including him in the conversation. "David, this is Peter. Peter—David."

The two men shook hands. "Nice to meet you," Peter said. "I thought I recognized Colleen when you two walked in. But I wasn't sure until I saw her order. You look great Colleen. Did you order the Bushmill's and Guinness for old times' sake?"

Peter turned to David. "When I knew Colleen—oh, about ten or twelve years ago—she nursed her drinks all night. One beer and one shot, that's all she needed. She came for the music." He turned to Colleen. "Think you might sing tonight?"

Colleen was pleased he asked. "Well, that depends. We weren't sure you still had Saturday *seisúns*. And I don't know how long we'll stay."

"Actually, we didn't have music for a few years. More than a few years, really." Peter thought for a minute. "We stopped about 1970 and didn't pick up again until the summer of '74."

"What's on the blackboard behind the bar?" David asked. "It looks like you're having a contest of some kind."

"We are!" Peter was surprised. "You can read that from over here?"

"What do you have to do? Complete the quotation?" David read the sentence aloud. "Only dull people are brilliant at—blank? Is it one word?" His competitiveness was showing.

"Yeah, there's a one-word answer for that. And if you get it right, you get a free drink." Peter explained. "The next one's a bit harder. If you get it right, you get two free drinks or you and your partner get a free drink."

"What about the last one? That looks pretty hard."

"If you get that one—it's been up for months now—you and your partner drink free all night!" Peter hesitated a second. "Of course, not bottle after bottle of our best champagne! But top shelf, if that's what you've already ordered."

"Can I guess more than once for one answer? Can I guess anytime during the night?" It was obvious that David wanted to answer at least one correctly.

"You can guess 'til your hearts content from now until last call!" Peter laughed.

"Okay—the answer to the first one is *breakfast*!" David hit the table with his open palm to punctuate his answer.

Startled, Peter replied "That's right! Pretty sharp! Well, it looks like this drink is on the house!"

"Coincidence, really." David was pleased. "I go to a lot of conferences and just two weeks ago a speaker was giving a talk while we all had our continental breakfasts and he used that line," David explained happily. "And the second one," he continued to the surprise of both Colleen and Peter, "What is a cynic? A man who knows the *price* of everything and the *value of nothing!* That's right, isn't it? I got that one right, didn't I?"

"Did you get your Ph.D. on Oscar Wilde or something?" Peter was nonplussed. "Colleen, did you bring this guy in here to listen to Irish music or drink for free?"

"I'm as surprised as you are! This is one talent I didn't know David had!" Colleen was impressed. "Are you going for the big prize, David? Free drinks for both of us for the night?"

"You bet I am, Colleen! And I think I know what it is, too!" David was excited.

"Now, this one," Peter cautioned, "you have to get *exactly.* An approximation won't do. It has to be word-for-word. The exact quote as it's printed in the book of quotations we used as the source!"

David thought a moment. "That's only fair. I'm going to think on this awhile. When I'm sure I have the exact quote, I'll write it down and give it to you!"

"I better get back to the bar, Colleen. Nice to meet you, David—I think!" Peter said good-naturedly.

Colleen asked, "How did you know those quotes? Do you really know the big one?"

"I think I do...I just have to let it sit awhile...percolate." He took Colleen's right hand in his. "I'm glad you brought me here."

As David and Colleen sipped their drinks, discussing the party and the people from the night before, many customers arrived. The tables were all taken and patrons stood three deep at the bar. As Colleen had recalled, the musicians gathered in a circle in the center of the room.

Two guitarists, one fiddler, a banjo player, a man with a tin whistle and spoons, and a woman with a flute and recorder were all seated together involved in animated discussion. The waitress brought over two pitchers of beer and half a dozen mugs for the performers.

"They drink free," Colleen explained. She was sitting on the edge of her seat.

"Do you recognize anyone?" David asked. He was enjoying Colleen's excitement.

"Not yet...If I don't know any of them, I don't think I'll sing tonight." It was obvious that she hoped she would be able to join in.

"I didn't know that you sang, Colleen. What kind of music?" He was eager to learn more about this part of Colleen's life.

"Folk music...traditional American, folk rock—you know, Sixties stuff, and Irish folk music as well. Celtic, really." Colleen's right hand shot up and pointed. "There's Mary Ellen with her harp!" She grabbed David's right hand with her left hand and squeezed. "Wait until you hear her! She's great!" Just behind her, a man entered, carrying an accordion. "And there's Jack! God, he's gone all grey!"

David observed Jack's unhealthy complexion and noticed that he had the puffiness associated with excessive drinking. *Looks like he enjoys drinking,* he thought. *He must be about my age. He probably looks about 10 years older than he is.*

"These are on the house," the waitress explained as she brought their second drinks. "Do you really know the answer to the last question?" She asked David.

"I'm pretty sure I do. And," he winked at the young woman, "if I do win, it will reflect in the gratuity!"

"Really?" She answered politely and walked away, puzzled.

"You shouldn't tease her. She's so young!" Colleen protested mildly.

"I've got it! Colleen! A pen or pencil, quick!" David tore off a section of the paper placemat. Colleen handed him a pen and he wrote on the blank white side. "I've got it! But I'm going to wait until just before we go to give my answer to your friend!"

"David! I would never have guessed that you were so—"

"Competitive?"

"Yes, exactly!"

"Oh, don't worry! I just want to win; I don't want the free drinks!" He sat back in his chair. "I'll probably tell him to buy a round for the musicians—and a round for us!"

The musicians had finished tuning up and, without any formal announcement, launched into a reel. "Oh, I know that one!" Colleen leaned forward, turned once and quickly looked at David, then focused all her attention on the performers.

Inexplicably, to David, Colleen's expression was transformed from delight to melancholy. The rousing reeling music only heightened the impression that a deep unhappiness had surfaced in her. Colleen's eyes turned inward; they became dull. Color drained from her complexion and her facial muscles sagged with sorrow.

David remained silent. The musicians moved from reels to hornpipes to jigs. The élan of the music underscored Colleen's private brooding musings. Only when the harpist, with elegant fragility, played the first notes of an air did Colleen emerge from her silence.

"Carrickfergus," she sighed, heartbreak in her voice.

David remained silent throughout the song, watching carefully as Colleen mouthed unsung lyrics that accompanied a version that she obviously knew well. He could see clearly that this song transported Colleen afar and within. Her eyes had the visionary look David knew from a monumental French painting of Joan of Arc he had seen in the Metropolitan Museum in New York City. *It's like she's having a vision,* he thought. *But it's not a transcendent thing of beauty that she sees.*

Colleen looked at David apologetically.

"Penny for your thoughts," he said sympathetically.

"Carrickfergus is how I feel so often," Colleen replied.

"And what is that feeling?" David was puzzled by the complex woman before him, a woman whose moods shifted so dramatically so suddenly.

"Homesick...heartbroken...hopeless," Colleen smiled wanly. "I read somewhere that all disease is heartbreak disease. And that all sickness is homesickness...for the original home that was taken from all of us, everywhere." Colleen looked down at her hands. "I'm growing older. Don't get me wrong, I don't feel *old*. But I feel that my life is slipping through my fingers. I feel that I..." Her voice trailed off and she sighed deeply.

"What, Colleen?" David felt awkward.

"I feel that I can't live what I know," she stared straight ahead. "I feel adrift...as if I set sail only to realize that I have a map but that I have no compass. I don't know whether I'm heading north or south. I don't know how to use the stars and so I sail, looking heavenward, sensing that the answer is there somehow, but unable to grasp it. So...I drift. Storms roar about me...weeks pass where I'm dead in the water...There are days and nights of exquisite beauty...The ocean beneath me and the ocean above me beckon...but I just drift..." Colleen was far away, deep into herself, her past.

"What is it you *know*," David asked, "that you can't *live*?"

"Oh," Colleen looked up and smiled self-consciously, "I can't go into that now...sitting here in a bar on a Saturday night. But I feel like I'm living in the shadow of things to come. Momentous things cast their shadows over me and my generation. And I don't know," Colleen said seriously, "if the shadows are cast by what is about to be born or what is about to die."

"I still don't know what it is you can't live through," David persisted.

"Well, you know, I have a friend back east, and she says that I run away from my talent!" Colleen giggled uncomfortably. "I know she's right, of course. But I can't seem to go right at it, do you know what I mean? I can't seem to focus, to say this is what I want to do—no, *this is what I love doing*—and then just get right down and do it!"

The waitress arrived just as the musicians began playing again. After she took their drink order, Colleen continued. "And then I have these crazy ideas that I have some kind of..." She blushed. "No, it's too dumb!" Colleen laughed heartily. "You'll think I'm some kind of nut!"

"Try me," David said. "I may surprise you!"

"Well," Colleen hesitated. "All right! What the hell. I shouldn't make such a big deal about it." She took a deep breath and continued. "It's just that I have this feeling that I can't put my finger on that *there's something I'm supposed to do*," Colleen spoke with a controlled intensity. "Or that there is something that I'm going to do that's part of something important...something very, very important." She looked at David, attempting to gauge his reaction. He seemed noncommittal, poker-faced. "*I'm* not going to do something important. Don't get me wrong. But I feel that in some way, something that I do is going to be part of something important involving people all over the world. I feel that I have—" Colleen stopped herself when the waitress returned with their drinks.

"Are you going to leave me like this, in midair?" David teased. "You feel that you have...what?"

Colleen cleared her throat, lifted her glass to David, and said, "A *mission!*" She lifted her glass in the air. "Cheers!"

Without thinking, David lifted his glass to toast Colleen. "Cheers!" He said, perplexed.

"I told you you might think it was kind of crazy!" Colleen laughed and then drank half of her whiskey. "But what the hell. Look at the world I live in! People spend billions a day planning the annihilation of whole continents and constructing the weapons to do just that. The food I eat, the air I breathe, the water I drink is all poisoned! Parents cripple their children at birth all across the planet and then those cripples go out and cause one catastrophe after another in their personal lives and in society as a whole." Colleen finished the rest of her drink and signaled the waitress for another. "Don't get me started!"

"You make it sound so hopeless!" David sipped his drink.

"But you see, I don't believe it's hopeless!" Colleen became agitated. "I think there are answers...the pathways to answers...but I don't believe that even the people who say they want to build a better world really want to go right to the root of the trouble."

"Which is?" David was extremely interested.

"Which is a long story but basically I think is—us! Ourselves. Who we are. What we do to infants. How we raise our children." Colleen felt a sudden surge of energy. "You know, we act as if we are these really terrific beings, with one fabulous creative idea and dream after another, and somehow, mysteriously, we find ourselves living in a world where one incredibly destructive idea follows another and that we live in a nightmare world that is getting worse by the second.

"Look at our century—a century of continuous war and mass murder. Cancer, heart disease, schizophrenia all up! Murder, suicide, violent crime all up! Drug addiction up! A few thousand political criminals bring ruin riding the backs of **billions and billions of helpless people**—*people who support these criminal politicians and murder anyone who tries to change things, and I mean really change things, for the better!*" Colleen caught her breath. "I told you not to get me going! But we act as if the catastrophe around us exists somehow in spite of who we are! I believe that everything we see is *a direct result of who we are, what we believe, and what we do on a daily basis.* **We create the misery we experience in our own lives and in our societies—and we stand in the way of getting at the root of things in our personal lives and in our social lives.** Us—you and me. Not 'them.'"

"Whoa, Colleen!" David was taken aback.

"I'm not finished," Colleen smiled angrily. "Why do you think people are this way? Original sin? Billions of humans believe that. Because it's 'human nature;' it's genetic or hereditary? Hundreds of millions believe that. Or we have a 'destructive biological instinct'?

Millions influenced by Freud believe that!"

"I don't know the answer. I'm just a plain ole plastic surgeon from the Hollywood Hills trying to eke out a living for me and my family." David joked. "But I'm getting the impression from you, young lady, that me and just about everybody I know are pretty bad folk!"

"Joke all you want, David, but you asked me a question and I started to answer it." Colleen grew angrier. "But you want a TV answer. You want a magazine answer. You want an answer that requires no thought or response. A bromide you can swallow and forget about."

David was silent.

"Do you know that all the knowledge we need is at hand to solve most of our problems? Do you?" Colleen demanded. "No you don't. And if you did, you wouldn't give a damn because it doesn't translate into anything immediately of interest to you. How about foodstuff from mass-free energy? Does an end to the slaughterhouses interest you? How about non-polluting, infinitely renewable motor power from mass-free energy? Would you like to see the skies in L.A. again and breathe clean air? How about energy medicine that goes to the core of your being instead of pills, and knives, and poisonous radiation? I bet you would want all those things **IF!** Am I right! If..." Colleen came back down from her angry outburst. "Whew...now that's what I call a good *rave*!" She laughed at herself good-naturedly.

"Wow! I didn't think you'd ever stop!" David said, relieved. "But I'm curious, Colleen, about that big 'if' you left hanging unanswered."

"*If* you don't have to change one bit. *If* you don't have to lift one finger," Colleen said. "If you can just sit back and have it all done for you. If you can just go merrily along your way and not take one iota of responsibility for anything. And don't forget," Colleen winked, "by 'you' I mean *me* as well!"

"I must admit," David spoke defensively, "I haven't heard or read about a number of things you've just mentioned. And while I share many of your feelings, I can't buy into any utopian—"

"*There!*' Colleen pounced like a big cat. "That's why I don't talk about any of the things I've learned! *Utopian!*" Colleen sneered as she spit out the last word. "I'm talking about *realities* that could be achieved **IF** people *worked for them.* Realities, David, not visions or dreams...Utopian dreams you would call them." David started to speak but Colleen cut him off. "Before you say anything, let me just say this. It's not that people all over won't work for things. People work to build nuclear bombs and missiles, don't they? People work to build death camps and prisons and torture chambers, don't they? People work to build and run slave labor camps. People worked very hard to build concentration camps and keep them running at optimum efficiency levels, didn't they? And people trade their lives for cars and TVs and swimming pools and jewelry and fancy clothes and on and on. But will they work *for Life*? Hah!" Colleen finished her drink and banged the glass on the table.

"I'd better be careful the rest of the night! Not to change the subject," David said, "but are you going to sing tonight? I'd love to hear you!" Colleen did not reply immediately. "Is your singing one of the talents your friend says you're running away from?"

"I guess so. David, I'm sorry about going on and on just now. Really, I..." Colleen leaned back in her seat.

"Don't worry one bit," David said reassuringly. "Now getting back to you. I know that your talents as a masseuse are not being put to good use. Your singing, I gather, is another neglected area. What else should we be looking at Colleen?"

"My work, I suppose," she said wistfully. "I'm really good with the young women. I learned from masters and I do a good job."

"And what of your greatest talent of all? Are you neglecting that as well?" David was sincere in his question.

"What might that be?" Colleen asked sarcastically.

"Your gift for helping others open up by being open to them. I've experienced it these last few days...Are you keeping that part of you locked away?" He put out his hand, but Colleen did not take it. She had her head tilted back with her eyes closed.

Colleen wanted to tell David the truth of how she met him. She wanted to let him know that she had been desperate that night. That she had no friend to stay with. That she used him at first. That she is not who she appears to be. But she was silent. *It's only partly true now,* she thought. *It may not even have any truth left in it...the way things have turned out. I want to tell him because I feel bad. But it would only hurt him.*

"That's very flattering, David, thank you." Colleen leaned forward and touched his cheek gently. "I'm glad you feel that way. But I brought you here to enjoy the music and now I'm talking over their beautiful performances."

"Okay, let's just listen," David got up from his seat across from her. He slid over in the booth beside Colleen. He put his arm over her shoulders. "I don't know this music at all. But I think I could get to enjoy it."

For the next 45 minutes, the performers played traditional Irish folk music they had learned from musicians from Ireland, music played by American-Irish bands from New York City, and traditional American folk music from Appalachia, most of which was derived from the Irish, Scots-Irish, and British who settled in that region.

While David and Colleen were caught up in their conversation, another fiddler and accordionist, a second banjo player, and a male singer had joined the assembled musicians. Each instrument was given its solo and each performer was allowed to shine within the confines of the musical forms.

"There's so much energy in this room now!" Colleen beamed. She had left her anger and sorrow behind.

"I know! You can almost feel it like a pulse in the room!" David had never experienced anything like it.

David looked about the room. Except for one or two drinkers, everyone at the bar was turned toward the musicians. Each table and booth held more customers than they were meant to seat, but no one seemed to care. The waitress and waiter never rested, carrying round after round of drinks and "bar food" to the patrons. Feet were stomping, fingers tapping, and, as Colleen had said, people began to dance at various times for varying lengths of time all during the performances.

Peter came over to their table. "Come on, Colleen! Get over where you belong!" He looked to David for support. "Have you heard this one sing?"

"Never! Go with him, Colleen! And Peter—take this with you! It's the answer to the third question." David handed him the torn piece of paper. "I don't need the free drinks! Instead, buy a round for the musicians on me!"

"Ah," Peter smiled a warm, broad smile. "Now, that's the spirit! Of course, I have to check this quote out thoroughly before I announce a winner!" He helped Colleen from the booth.

"David, the first song is for you," she blew him a kiss, "so you'll understand me better. The second one will be my wish for us."

David watched as Peter introduced Colleen to the other musicians. Mary Ellen went to Colleen and hugged her emotionally. At one point, Colleen whispered in Mary Ellen's ear and the harpsichordist looked over toward David. *She's pointing out her guy,* he thought, pleased.

"Ladies and gentlemen," Peter announced, "ladies and gentlemen! May I have your attention? Tonight we are proud to announce that one of our own—Colleen Murphy—is with us tonight. Colleen moved to New York City," loud catcalls, boos, and hisses interrupted the bartender turned impresario. "Now, none of that. I'm sure Colleen is proud to call New York home. Colleen was a regular years ago when our Saturday night *seisúns* first began. Ah," Peter exclaimed, "I see a few of our regulars remember our sweet Colleen! Well, you know what to expect from her then! Colleen is accompanied by a distinguished gentleman who—unfortunately for me—is somewhat of an Oscar Wilde scholar and has succeeded in answering the most difficult question on our blackboard." Applause followed his last remark.

"I have conferred with *Bartlett's Book of Quotations* and hereby declare that our new friend David—on his first visit to our pub—has supplied the correct answer to the "I'm Not Wilde about Dickens" quote. The correct answer is 'One must have a heart of stone to read the death of Little Nell by Dickens without laughing.' David has graciously asked that his prize—free drinks for both himself and Colleen—be given instead to tonight's musicians!" The entire pub broke out in cheers and applause. "Stand up, David, and take a bow!"

Self-conscious but happy, David stood up and waved to the crowd.

"And now, we are proud to bring you—Colleen!" Peter returned to the bar.

"Thank you, Peter." Colleen was beaming. "This song is one I'm sure you all know."

At the first fragile and elegant notes played by the harpist, tears came to David's eyes. He listened dreamily as Colleen sang *"I wish I was in Carrickfergus."*

Although the musicians had not rehearsed the song—many had never played together before—and none save the harpist knew Colleen, they sounded as though they were a polished group performing one of their signature songs.

"I would swim over the deepest ocean," Colleen sang, "the deepest ocean, my love to find." David was impressed as much by the strength of Colleen's voice, by its emotional force, as by its clarity and beauty.

"But the sea is wide," she sang with an aching tone, "and I can't swim over. And neither have I wings to fly," her voice soared, lifting the audience with her. Colleen looked across the dim room and caught David's eyes. "I wish I had me a handsome boatman," she sang as if she knew, with melancholy certainty, that she would not have such a boatman. "To ferry me over to my love and die."

David could hear Colleen's singing but he could not make out all of the lyrics. He wished he could be that boatman for her but he knew it was not possible. He knew he would not alter his life that dramatically for Colleen.

The audience was stunned by the volume of its own applause when the song was over. Colleen bowed and smiled. She turned to one of the musicians and asked him something. He reached behind him and handed her an acoustic guitar. "Shall I sing another one?'

Her question was greeted with a resounding yes and more applause. "I'd like all of you who know this tune—and I'm sure a lot of you will— to join in on the chorus." She turned to the musicians and, out of earshot of the audience, told them the name of the song. The performers discussed who would play and they tuned their instruments for a few minutes.

"We'll just be another few seconds," Colleen said, apologizing for the delay.

"For those of you who don't know the refrain, it goes like this. 'And we'll all go together to pluck wild mountain thyme," Colleen sang slowly and deliberately. "'All around the purple heather, will you go, lassie go?' Okay? Everybody got that?" Colleen looked to the other musicians. She strummed the first chords on her guitar. The other guitarist joined, playing in a minor key. The banjo player put down his instrument and instead performed the haunting melody on his harmonica.

"The summer time is coming," Colleen sang, as slowly as the summer sun sets. "And the trees are sweetly blooming," she sang, with the sweetness of ripe fruit.

At first, only a few of the men and women at the bar or at the tables joined in on the chorus. The musicians who were not playing instruments scattered about the bar, singing the refrain, encouraging others to join them. The flutist reached ethereal ranges. The harmonica caught the lonely beauty of the song. Colleen's simple, steady guitar playing brought cohesion to all the performances.

One of the men spoke the words of the refrain before Colleen sang, leading the people on, gesturing with his arms for all to stand. Soon the whole bar was standing and singing. Friends, lovers, and strangers locked arms. Colleen put down her instrument and like some spiritual leader of old, walked about the room among those in attendance.

The audience did not want to stop and they sang the refrain over and over. As Colleen walked by the bar, she stopped and hugged each person with an embrace that transferred energy and transmitted love. "Sing it for the ones you love," she whispered to one man. "Sing it for the loves you've lost," she whispered to another. "Sing for the friends who've died," she told a young man and woman, "sing for the infants injured at birth, sing for the children who don't have a chance," she called out. "Sing for the workers without a job, sing for the people without a home. Sing for the suffering, the lost, the alone. Sing it for that secret sorrow of your own!"

The men and women Colleen embraced hugged and held one another and music filled the entire place. Colleen returned her guitar to the musician who had given it to her and gestured for David to join her. The audience was still singing but it was obvious that this was the last refrain. "Sing it for your dream of yourself," Colleen called out as she opened the front door of the pub, "when you were sixteen!" Colleen put both arms in the air and waved them back and forth. "Good night! Our revels now are ended!" She laughed as she spoke. "We are such stuff as dreams are made on and our little lives are rounded by a sleep! Good night!" She took David by the hand and they ran outside.

David quickly opened the car doors and they jumped in and sped off down Clement Street heading, without knowing it, away from the hotel and toward the beach.

"I never use this word, Colleen," David said, out of breath. "It's too much a parody of a Californian but I have to use it now."

"Go ahead!" Colleen's heart was pounding. "Go ahead—say it!"

"*WOW!*"

They both were laughing so hard they didn't notice that they ran a stop sign.

As they approached Clement and 25th Avenue, Colleen asked David to make a right-hand turn. "I have a surprise for you," she replied when he asked where they were going.

They drove passed Sea Cliff, a residential area with magnificent homes perched along the cliffs across from the Marin Headlands at the mouth of the Golden Gate. They drove along Lincoln Boulevard, past Baker Beach and the Army's Psychological Testing Center at the Presidio, uphill and around, toward the Golden Gate Bridge. Just before the road descended toward the turnoff to the bridge, Colleen directed David to a lookout point on the roadside.

A fierce wind, cold and damp, blew through the Golden Gate and through their clothing. But the incomparable view drew all their attention. The primitive headlands across the waters; the tide surging through the gate with wave after wave crashing on the sharp, black, ragged rocks and sandy shores below; the full moon over the Pacific to the west; and the fog silently shrouding the Golden Gate Bridge, diffracting the bridge lights and automobile headlights into rainbowed halos.

Colleen and David stood alone. Not a single car passed by. "It's unreal," David said. "It's more than real! It's so primitive...and yet the bridge!" David stared at the beauty of nature and humanity conjoined.

"I used to come here at all hours of the day and night," Colleen recalled fondly. "And a few times, I went out with the Park Rangers for moonlight walks across the headlands. It was so beautiful. Brisk, invigorating night air; the steady, soothing sounds of the sea;

shimmering, silent stars; blue moonlight shadows on the rolling hills. And the wind..." She shivered and wrapped her arms around herself. "Always the wind blowing in from the sea."

She laughed happily. "God, those walks were great! And sometimes I'd come up here and watch the sun go down. Or dawn comes to the Gate. I'd watch the fishing fleet set sail about four in the morning or beautiful sailboats glide beneath the bridge on pleasure cruises to Hawaii or Mexico—or maybe only Half Moon Bay!" Colleen laughed as she thought of the wonderful little town twenty-five miles down Highway 1 from San Francisco.

"You love it here, don't you?" David stood behind Colleen and put his arms around her.

"Oooh," Colleen snuggled up into him, "that feels so good, so warm. I do love it here...very much."

"Then why do you—"

"Live in New York?" She said, anticipating David's question.

"Exactly. I don't know if there are two cities that are so dissimilar." He held her close.

"Well," Colleen smiled, "I don't know. They're complementary cities, really. New York is exciting and vulgar and crass and elegant all at once. San Francisco is elegant and charming and sophisticated...but like a small town, really. Sometimes I think only a true, native New Yorker can love San Francisco. I mean really love this city. Of course, the whole world 'loves' San Francisco. But did you ever notice how many transplanted New Yorkers live here? A lot of them, believe me! Who but a New Yorker could love standing here as much as standing beneath the 59th Street Bridge and consider them both fantastically moving and beautiful?"

"I understand a little why you live there. But I could never live there—even for a day." David's tone was sharp.

"I understand—because I'd never live in L.A." Colleen stuck out her tongue in mock displeasure. "Enough urban pride for one night, okay?"

"I'm getting a little too cold," David stepped back from Colleen, "can we go?"

"Sure...I just wanted you to see this." She turned and kissed him lightly on the lips. "Can we drive some more before going back to the hotel? I'm still kind of wired."

"No problem. Just point me in the right direction."

At the southern end of the Great Highway, near the San Francisco Zoo, David and Colleen parked the car and went down to the sea. The fog overhead was thick, but through breaks in the marine layer, they could occasionally see the moon and a few faint stars.

The waves crested white in the darkness, wisps of water and foam blown back as the water hit the shore with a loud, dull thud, followed by a crash and hissing. "'I have seen them riding seaward on the waves, combing the white hair of the waves blown back.'" Colleen said, obviously reciting the words to a poem she knew well. "'When the wind blows the water white and black.'" She looked out to sea. "Do you like Eliot?"

"That depends," David said slyly, "on whether you mean T.S. or Ramblin' Jack!"

Colleen ignored his remark. "That's just what it looks like—the white hair of the waves blown back. Don't you agree, David? Look at the way the wind blows that fine white spray from the waves. And the sea, as far out as you can see, is white and black."

"My beautiful, wonderful, literate romantic! Are we at yet another site of sweet memories?" David took her hand and led her south along the beach.

"Yes, of course we are! This is where I used to walk with my daughter after our visits to the zoo when she was just a toddler."

Colleen stopped walking and looked inland. "You can't see it now in the dark, but the hillside curves in over there. I would set up a little picnic area, protected from the wind. Sometimes I'd bring my guitar and Brigid would play in the sand while I sang to myself. Other times we would build castles or hunt for colorful shells and stones. Brigid loved it most when she found an unbroken sand dollar. I think she still has some safe at home."

They turned their backs on the city and looked south into the darkness. "It has the look and smell of eternity," Colleen said.

Colleen sat up in bed and loudly called out in fear, "Granma!" She stared ahead, her eyes wide open but seeing nothing. She was still asleep. Colleen breathed shallowly and erratically. She lay back down, her heart racing from the dream. She awoke and saw the vaguely familiar room before her but remained fearful, disturbed by the unfamiliar sounds of the hotel at night. "David," she whispered and lightly poked his shoulder.

David did not wake up.

"David!" She said, trying to rouse him. "David, I had a scary dream!" She pushed him more forcefully.

David opened his eyes, looked about uncertainly, and then pushed himself up on one elbow. "Are you all right?"

"I'm sorry to wake you—I had a bad dream..." Colleen was embarrassed.

"That's okay," David lay back down. "Come here. Put your head on my shoulder and tell me about your dream."

"I dreamed I was walking in a field with my grandmother," she sighed sadly. "I loved her so much ...And in the dream I was ecstatic. Everything was green and blue and sparkled with glinting gold.

Everything shimmered...you know...the way things look through the long lenses they use in movies to catch close-ups of distant objects. I was so happy and my grandmother kept saying something about 'send her, send her.' But I kept asking 'Who, grandma? Send who where?" Colleen closed her eyes and was silent.

"And then what happened in the dream?" David was now wide-awake.

"Well, here it got confusing..." Colleen concentrated. "My grandmother took me by the hand to a mound in the middle of a rocky field. In the mound was an opening...like the entrance to a cave. And in the entrance was *my grandmother!* And holding my hand was my *great-grandmother!*" Colleen became excited but agitated. "And I don't know why but in the dream I was frightened. My great-grandmother—who I only remember a little bit—was saying something almost like my grandmother. But I realized she was saying '*center*,' not '*send her*,' like my grandmother." Colleen sat up. "I know it doesn't sound scary but I felt terrified. And I don't know why because I love my grandmother so much and I only have good memories of Gray Granmar," Colleen wasn't aware she had used her childhood name for her great-grandmother.

"What frightened you?" He gently stroked her hair.

"What happened was my grandmother beckoned to me from the opening and my great-grandmother touched me and I felt myself levitate." Colleen trembled. "At first, I was really scared. But then I loved it! I flew slowly on my own to my grandmother and softly landed, with my two feet on the ground. And I was happy again! As if I had never been frightened. When I looked back, my great-grandmother had become pure light...sparkling points of light, all wavy and pulsing like your heartbeat, but keeping the outline of her body. A lot of words came to my mind that I knew came from her but she didn't speak them. My grandmother turned and started to lead me into the earth. 'Hole," she said...I thought she said '*hole*' but now I think she said '*whole*' with a 'w.' And my great-grandmother said 'home' and when she said 'home' she disappeared. Then I woke up."

"Do you always have such unusual dreams?" David sat up in bed. "With so many vivid images and plays on words. I have a friend—she's a psychoanalyst—who would have a field day with your dream!" he laughed lightly.

"Have you ever been to Ireland?" David got out of bed and went to the bathroom.

"No..." Colleen answered dreamily. By the time David returned to bed she had fallen back to sleep.

Shortly before nine o'clock, Colleen awoke to find herself alone in the hotel room. At first, she was concerned but told herself that David must have gone to the hotel lobby for some reason. *Maybe to check out,* she thought. Colleen decided to take a shower and get ready to leave. She felt very sad that her time with David was at an end. *I really like him,* she thought. *I feel so comfortable with him.*

As she showered, Colleen wondered where she would stay that night. *My plane doesn't leave for two days. I better make some calls. I should have called people Thursday. I shouldn't have waited until the last minute. Maybe I'll go back to the bar and see Peter. He'll help me out, I'm sure.* Her last thought comforted her.

When David returned—he had gone to settle his hotel bill—Colleen was dressed, packed, and ready to go. "It went so fast, Colleen, didn't it? Is it just me or do you feel—"

"Like we're old friends? That we may not see each other often but will love it when we do?" Colleen asked.

"Sort of," David agreed tentatively. "But I feel like this weekend is something that will only happen once. And yet I don't feel sad." David suddenly felt awkward standing in the middle of the room, speaking to Colleen as if she were on the telephone and not standing a few feet from him. "Come here," he took her hand and they sat on the edge of the bed. "I don't mean we won't see one another again. I'm sure we will and I'm sure we'll have wonderful times. But these past few days...I've never experienced anything like them."

"Neither have I, David." Colleen still felt a twinge of guilt over how she met David but she dismissed the feeling by hugging him. "It's been like an old-fashioned movie. I like to cast my life stories as if they were movies. How's this—you're Cary Grant, of course, and I'm Ingrid Bergman. Or I'm Loretta Young and you're Joel McCrea. No, I'm Donna Reed and who do you want to be?"

"To tell you the truth, I see myself more like William Holden or Robert Mitchum," David laughed at the sense of vanity he was feeling. "Or maybe Kirk Douglas. You know, kind of okay looking in a craggy kind of way."

"That's it! I'm Donna Reed in one of her hard-boiled roles and—" David's laughter stopped Colleen in her tracks. "What's so funny?" She demanded.

"You...hard-boiled! That's what's so funny!" David looked at Colleen warmly. "You know, Colleen, you have some of the qualities of all those women. But do you know who you remind me of most? Not in looks but in your soul. You remind me of Veronica Lake as she looked in the old Preston Sturges comedy *Sullivan's Travels.*"

"I love that movie! Hardly anyone I know has seen it!" Colleen was excited but puzzled. "Of course, I don't look anything like her."

"She came to mind when you said 'hard-boiled.' That's such an old-fashioned term. And remember, when she meets Joel McCrae in the diner, and he's broke and she's broke and she buys him 'two sinkers and a cup of Joe' or something like that? She's trying to be hard-boiled but really, she's so *vulnerable*."

"Like me?" Colleen asked, pleased.

"Like you," he said and then kissed her sweetly. "I have to pack and we have to be out of here by ten!" David walked over to the closet. "Then brunch and, sadly, off I go!"

Colleen began to miss him at that moment.

Brunch passed swiftly. Colleen and David engaged in idle chatter about his drive down the coast and her plans to look for work on her return home. Before they knew it, they were standing beside David's car in the driveway of the hotel parking lot, hugging.

"You have my numbers, right? You didn't leave them on the night table by the bed?" David truly wanted Colleen to stay in touch with him. "I have your number in my book."

"Here they are!" Colleen took David's business card from her wallet. "Here's your office number and don't worry—you wrote your home number on the back."

"I'm going to look into the massage thing we talked about, Colleen. You would be great for our patients before and after surgery." He was earnest. "You have a special touch...and it's not a technique. I'll sound out a few people and talk to my partner about the possibility of you using the examination room. There may be some insurance issues but we'll work that out. I'm not going to let you just drop this idea," he said with emphasis. "You could make some good money." David held her close a moment. "Your daughter is heading to college and that takes big bucks! Believe me, with two kids in school, I know!"

They embraced one last time. "Colleen, I hope you enjoy the rest of your vacation and that you get home safe and sound!" David walked around to the driver's side of the car.

"Drive safely. Highway 1 is beautiful but dangerous!" Colleen forced a smile.

"I left you a little something," David said as he revved up the motor. "In your purse! Please take it in the right spirit. I have money and you don't! And I know you're too proud to ask for help. Love you!" He waved and eased the car out into traffic.

Colleen watched as David pulled out onto California Street and turned south, heading for home. She walked into the street and waved with both arms, hoping that he would see her in the rear-view mirror. The light changed and traffic forced Colleen back to the sidewalk.

She opened her purse and saw that David had put a small card in it. *I wonder when he did that,* she thought. She opened the envelope and removed a card with a photograph of the full moon over San Francisco Bay. Inside was a crisp new bill. One hundred dollars! *That devil—he knew I wouldn't take it from him.* Colleen smiled as she read the card aloud to herself, slowly. "Take your friend out for dinner and drinks tonight and tell her all about the wonderful guy you met! Love, David."

I wish I had a friend to take to dinner, Colleen thought wistfully. She walked down California Street to Powell and then headed for Market Street and the BART station to collect her things from the locker. *I wonder if he'll call,* she thought.

Colleen took the J Car from Powell Street outbound to her old neighborhood, Noe Valley. She looked excitedly out the window as the car passed through Dolores Park, admiring the wonderful view. Colleen looked north at downtown San Francisco and the Bay Bridge against the backdrop of the hills of Berkeley and Oakland. At one end of the park, all of the tennis courts were filled; at the other end, dozens of gay men lay on blankets, sunning and cruising under the unusually warm sun. In between, all over the brilliant green square, parents played with their children, young lovers walked arm in arm, and dogs romped as their owners talked with one another.

Colleen took the car to 24th Street. *Oh good, it's still here!* She was happy to see her old laundromat on the corner. She bought the Sunday paper and a cup of coffee at a nearby grocery store and went to the laundry to wash her clothes. After she put her wet laundry in the dryer, Colleen went to the public phone on the corner and called Peter at his pub.

"Pete's off today," Colleen was told. "Any message? No? He'll be in tomorrow morning."

Shit! Colleen thought for a moment. She dialed a few numbers of people she had barely kept in touch with, but no one was home.

Colleen returned to the laundromat, folded her dry clothing, put it in her bag, and set off for Dolores Park. On her way, she bought a bottle of seltzer at a grocery store and stepped into an alleyway outside the store. Colleen poured half the contents of the bottle onto the ground. She took the bottle of whiskey that was still in her bag and poured the contents into the soda bottle. *I think I'll get a little buzz on, soak up some sun, and read the Sunday paper in the park.*

The whiskey quickly took effect and Colleen became quite maudlin. One sad memory after another came to mind. She tried to summon up happier recollections but her thoughts would always drift back to troubled times. *It's so beautiful here,* she lay down in the grass and looked at the sky. *Maybe when Brigid starts college I'll move back.*

A few hours later, restless, Colleen threw her empty bottle and Sunday paper in the trash. She walked back to Noe Valley, intending to call old acquaintances and perhaps some hotels and motels. However, when she reached 24th Street, she decided to stop off at a neighborhood bar. *I'll just have one...think things over.*

After a scotch and soda, Colleen felt more at ease. The dark bar was comforting. The baseball Giants were on TV and the white noise of the game, the monotonous drone of the fans in the stands, was soothing.

The TV image, of the red clay and green grass of the baseball field, was just within her peripheral vision and quieted her, much the way a fish tank calms some people.

One hour and two scotches passed, followed by two hours and four more drinks. Colleen stood up and felt the drinks in her legs. She sat back down. *I better eat something,* she told herself. *I'm pretty high right now.* She signaled to the bartender. "You serve food at the bar?" She asked when he came to her.

"Yes, we certainly do. The bar menu's on the wall behind the register," he pointed out a chalkboard to Colleen, "but you can also order from our full menu if you'd like."

Colleen found it difficult to read the menu. "How are the burgers? Good?"

"I think so," the bartender answered, "and they come with lettuce, tomato, and fries."

"I'll have a burger, medium rare, on an English muffin. With pickles, if you have them," Colleen thought for a second, "and ketchup, mustard and mayonnaise on the side."

The bartender left with her order and Colleen wandered over to the jukebox. The ballgame had ended and there were only two other customers in the bar. *I don't think anyone will mind if I play a few oldies.* Colleen loved jukeboxes and this one had a great selection of music from her adolescence. She put in enough money to play a dozen songs and had trouble narrowing down the choices.

She started out selecting upbeat Motown hits from the mid-Sixties, moved on to "summer of love" songs by San Francisco groups like the Jefferson Airplane, mixed in a few Beatle's' songs, and ended with a string of sentimental songs by a variety of artists from the Fifties and Sixties. Her last choice was a relatively new song, *The City of New Orleans*, and it came on first. She was quickly caught up in its melancholy.

"Pass the paper bag that holds the bottle," Colleen hummed along with the song, "feel the wheels rumbling 'neath the floor." She devoured the hamburger when it arrived, leaving a completely empty plate for the bartender.

"Wow!" The bartender remarked. "Either that was the greatest hamburger in creation or you haven't eaten in a long time! You may belong in the Guinness Book of Records—fastest consumption of single deluxe burger ever!" He saw that her glass was empty. "Can I get you another?"

"Why not?" Colleen said too loudly. She spun around on the bar stool and bounded over to the jukebox. Colleen selected a series of laments about the seventies singles scene. *Let's see—125, "One of These Nights." I love The Eagles. And then 146—"Another Night" and "Long Cool Woman." The Hollies are great. Oh look, Frampton—191. And... let's see. "Cocaine" by J.J. Cale. Great!* Colleen chose a few more songs.

I wonder what Brigid is doing? She went to a phone outside the restroom and called her daughter collect. It's Sunday...going on 10 probably...she should be home.

Brigid answered on the fifth ring and was happy to hear from her mother. "Where are you? That music is so loud."

"Oh, I'm with some old friends in Noe Valley," Colleen lied, trying very hard not to slur even a single syllable. "We're having a light dinner but the jukebox at the bar *is* pretty loud. How are you, honey?"

"I'm fine...Michael's here and Lis has stayed over since you left. Except for tonight. She's gone home." There was an uncomfortable silence. "I miss you, Mom."

"I miss you too, honey, and I can't wait to get home. If I could have changed my ticket I would have. But Brigid, the most wonderful thing has happened. I met the sweetest, loveliest man, a doctor from L.A. And we had an incredible time the last three days. I haven't been this happy in a long time. I'll tell you all about it Tuesday."

"We're all going to be there when your plane gets in, Mom." Brigid sounded threatening.

"To greet me or sentence me? Lighten up, Brigid!" Colleen took a deep breath. "Oh look, honey, they just brought my meal. I gotta go. My love to you and everybody! I'll see you Tuesday morning!" Colleen hung up, relieved. "I think I'm getting my second wind!" Colleen thought as she sashayed back to the bar in time with the music.

Between the moment Colleen sat down and the moment she put the drink to her lips, she slipped into oblivion. To the bartender, to the other customers, she was the same woman. But Colleen heard without hearing, saw without seeing, responded appropriately without knowing. She looked out and saw a bar but it was a bar in upper Manhattan in New York City not in Noe Valley in San Francisco. She looked out the window and saw not the daylight of a late August summer evening in California but the darkness of a mid-December evening in New York.

Unaware of what she was doing, Colleen downed her drink, scooped up her change, and hurried from the bar, looking about as if she feared someone was after her. Thinking she was heading home to her New York apartment, Colleen walked west on 24th Street. She did not see the bookstores and coffee shops. She saw the dry cleaners and hardware stores of her block at home. Colleen stopped at each stop sign and looked before crossing at every corner. It was only when the street began to rise more steeply, as she headed out of Noe Valley up toward Twin Peaks, that Colleen's frenetic pace was slowed.

In an instant, she saw where she was but she did not know where she was. To Colleen, it seemed that one second she was walking down the block on which she lived and the next second she was somewhere completely unknown. She broke out into a sweat and her pulse quickened. Her heart raced and she found it difficult to breathe.

Panicked, she held on tight, trying not to let her panic show. She stood frozen on a quiet street. No one was to be seen anywhere, adding to the nightmarish quality of the experience. Colleen closed her eyes. She opened them. Nothing had changed. She felt as if she would faint and sat down on the front steps of a private home.

Colleen looked up and it was dark. "Are you all right?" A young woman asked.

Colleen stared at her, terror in her eyes. She could not speak.

"Can I help you?" The young woman reached her hand out to help Colleen stand. "I live here. This is my house. Has someone harmed you?"

"I...I'll be all right." Colleen stood up stiffly and straightened out her blouse. She eyed the woman suspiciously. "I...I..." Colleen fumbled with her bag and stepped back away from the woman.

"Don't be afraid," the woman tried to reassure Colleen. "Let me help you. You seem very, very upset."

Silently staring, Colleen backed away from the woman, inching away like a frightened animal. Without warning, she turned and ran. When she reached Castro Street and saw the neon lights of a tavern, Colleen headed for it.

She went to the end of the bar and sat in the last chair, her back to the wall. Colleen wanted everyone to be in front of her and she wanted to be able to see everyone who entered the bar before they could see her. She ordered a beer and sat without drinking it.

For over an hour the bartender ignored her. Finally, when she was the last customer, he told her that he was closing and asked her to leave. He was an older man, tired from a long day behind the bar, and he did not look at Colleen.

She had just begun to relax, to breathe normally, and now, having to face the outside world, Colleen began to hyperventilate. She stumbled from the bar out onto the street. There was not a soul to be seen. No cars moved in any direction as far as she could see. No bus was in sight. All of the stores were dark, as were the windows in all the homes and small apartment buildings.

Colleen looked at her wristwatch but could not read the time. She looked up and saw a bus immediately in front of her. The door was open and the driver asked impatiently if she was getting in. Colleen got on the bus, put far more change in the fare box than was needed, and took the transfer the driver handed her. She was the only passenger.

The bus went over the hill along Castro Street, from Noe Valley to "The Castro," as the gay district of the city was called by its residents. Colleen got off the bus at Castro and Market Streets and felt much safer. The sidewalks were crowded with people coming and going from restaurants and bars, congregated in small groups talking, and waiting on a long line outside the Castro Theater. Colleen began to feel more at ease. Simply seeing people helped her. She stood at the end of the line for the movie although she had no intention of buying a ticket and going into the theater. She didn't know what else to do.

"I don't believe it! Colleen!" A man a few years older than Colleen stopped right in front of her. "Colleen—it's me!"

Colleen stared at him. "I don't believe I know you." Her voice was emotionless.

"Colleen, you better come with me. Something's wrong. Did you drop some bad acid or something?" He received no response. Turning to his companions he said, "Go ahead. I'll catch up with you later." The two men he was with went on their way. "Colleen, it's me—Henry."

"I'm sorry," Colleen was perplexed. "I...I'm...Do I know you?"

"I can't leave you like this." He did not know what to do. "Listen, come with me to my place. I live just around the corner."

"I don't think so." Colleen, as she had before with the young woman, backed away from him. "I really don't think so."

Helpless, he watched Colleen walk away and disappear into the crowd.

Colleen boarded a streetcar and rode it to the last stop. She got off in the business district downtown. The office towers were dark and the streets deserted. Once again, she felt as if she were in a nightmare. She began to cry, at first softly, but then wildly, holding her hands up to her face, calling out "Where am I? What is happening to me?"

Alone late on a Sunday night, Colleen cried out and her cries were unanswered. She walked south along Market Street and turned west on Montgomery. The streets became darker and lonelier. She turned south again on Geary and, when she reached Union Square, saw another bus and ran after it. The driver noticed her and waited. He took her transfer from her. Again, she was the only passenger.

"You're lucky, lady. This is the last run until five a.m."

Colleen rode along as if in a trance until the driver called out. "Last stop, lady." She stepped off the bus outside a motel near the ocean. She walked over and tried to open the office door but it was locked. The night clerk was nowhere in sight. Colleen saw a sign reading 'No Vacancy" and she despaired.

She crossed the street and stared out at the Pacific. The wind was biting. *David,* she thought. Colleen looked about startled. The last thing she remembered was listening to the jukebox in Noe Valley and eating a hamburger. Colleen sat on the curbside, her head in her hands. "Oh god, oh god, oh god," she moaned repeatedly. *How did I get all the way out here?*

Colleen heard a motor and saw a taxi approaching the motel. A middle-aged couple got out of the cab and Colleen walked over and got into the back seat.

"Where to, lady?" The driver asked as he headed toward downtown San Francisco.

"Clement and Third," Colleen answered wearily. *Maybe Peter will be at his pub...Or someone I know.*

"So the next thing I know I'm standing outside the motel and I haven't the slightest idea how I got there!" Colleen laughed and her drinking companions laughed with her. "So I said to myself, 'Girl, you need a drink!" They all laughed again and Colleen ordered another round for everyone.

Earlier, when Colleen first walked into Peter's pub on Clement Street, a few customers recognized her from the night before and greeted her warmly. The nightmarish aspects of her evening had subsided, yet she still felt a sense of dread, a certainty that at any moment something awful could occur. She warded off this sensation with drinking and the camaraderie of her fellow drinkers.

Colleen hadn't had to spend any of her money while she was with David so she had enough to buy drinks for her newfound friends and guarantee their company for hours. One of the men in her party, Chuck, whispered into Colleen's ear. "Want to do a few lines?"

Colleen felt a powerful rush. "Yes!" She grabbed his hand with such force that she hurt him. "Do you have—"

"No, but let me talk to the gentleman at the end of the bar." He looked about the room to make certain he recognized everyone before approaching the man at the bar. "Listen, Colleen, I'm a little short tonight. But I can get cash in the morning—"

"Don't worry," Colleen said, greedy for the drug. She reached into her purse and took out the crisp new $100 bill that David had given her. "I'll get the bartender to break this." Colleen left the table and returned with one $50 bill and the rest of the money in smaller denominations. She gave Chuck the fifty and said, "Go for it!"

"Awright," he whispered darkly. "You are something else, Colleen. You are truly something else."

Chuck made his buy at the bar and motioned discreetly for Colleen to join him at the back of the bar. "Let's go into the back room here." He opened a door with a sign that read "Employees Only." He locked the door behind them. "Don't worry, it's cool with the bartender. The owners don't know or don't care. But our friend takes care of the bartender and the bartender takes care of him, if you know what I mean."

Chuck's hands were shaking with craving for the white powder that he spread out on a small mirror he had with him. "This is *fine, fine stuff*, Colleen. I had some last night and I'm telling you *it is the best!*" He took a single-edged razor and chopped the cocaine into a smooth powder, arranging it in straight lines.

The sound of the razor on the glass gave Colleen goosebumps.

Chuck took a brand-new dollar bill from his wallet and rolled it up. "Here goes!" He snorted the first line of cocaine himself. Then he snorted the next line. Chuck was about to do a third when Colleen, extremely agitated, interrupted him.

"Hold on their, buddy! I'm getting some of that white stuff now." Colleen was indignant. "I paid for it!"

Resentful, Chuck gave Colleen the rolled-up bill and walked a few feet away. When he felt the high he craved, Chuck forgot about Colleen and left her alone in the back room.

Before Colleen finished the cocaine spread out before her, she felt the impact of the drug. She felt energized and powerful and all her worries seemed insignificant. But she did not forget that Chuck had walked off with the rest of the cocaine. When she returned to the table, she glared a Chuck and said in front of the others, "I think you have something of mine!"

Caught trying to steal her cocaine, Chuck became obsequious. "Oh yeah...hey, sorry...you know, hey Colleen...no problem, no problem." He got up and walked a few feet away and slipped a small bottle into Colleen's hand. "I wasn't trying to rip you off," he lied, angry that she had confronted him.

In the middle of a story, Colleen's eyes opened. She didn't recognize the people to whom she was speaking. Her eyes betrayed her and one of her companions asked, "Is everything cool, Colleen? You look spooked."

"No, no...everything's cool," she stood up. "Everything's fine.

Excuse me a minute." Colleen hurried to the ladies room.

Colleen stared at herself in the mirror. *Who are you? I don't know you anymore*, she thought in sorrow. Her mouth was dry and her skin was cold and clammy. Suddenly Colleen realized she was herself again. She had vague images flashing in her mind—empty buses, a neon motel sign flashing, the face of a man she once knew—but she could not recall most of the past ten hours. *It's two in the morning! My god, what have I been doing?*

Colleen leaned on the sink a moment. She looked into the mirror but had to turn away. *I wonder...is it even still Sunday? Has more than a day gone by?*

She left the bathroom and recognized the pub immediately. Colleen felt empty and desperate. *How could I?* She reproached herself. *Yesterday was so beautiful ... so beautiful, and today ... ugly ... just ugly.*

Colleen looked at the booth where she and David had been only the night before. She reached into her pocket and counted her money. *Shit! I don't have much left.* Colleen decided that she had to leave the bar, even though she had no idea where she would go.

Only when the bartender rang up her tab did Colleen realize that she was springing for all the drinks. She left with only twenty dollars in her pocket. *Twenty bucks and some cocaine—now what do I do?*

Colleen walked out toward the ocean. She didn't know why, but she wanted to go somewhere lonely and desolate. She remembered the ruins of the old bathhouse at Point Lobos and, with an absent mind and an empty heart, she walked mechanically in that direction. She walked for miles and did not pass a single soul.

Despondent, weary from walking for nearly an hour, Colleen stood in the large empty parking lot overlooking the ruins at the shore. On another night, she might have been frightened to be so alone and vulnerable. However, she felt a despair deeper than any she had ever known. It didn't seem to matter whether she lived or died.

Colleen crossed the parking lot and walked down a wooden stairway to a sandy path that led out to the edge of the ruins where the surf smashed against the rocky shore. The marine layer was low and heavy above, blocking out the stars and the moon. The ocean seemed a malevolent force to Colleen, a primeval power determined to destroy the land simply to destroy it, set on depleting the soil of all its energy and nutrients, and transforming it into lifeless sand.

Colleen walked out to a broad plaza overlooking the sea. She stared downward and watched wave after wave smash against the remnants of the once magnificent structure. She walked over to a narrow stairway that led down to a lower lookout point. Colleen stared at the black barnacles that covered the rocks below. She thought of sitting on the edge of the wall, her back to the ocean, leaning over and falling. She knew the waves would make short work of her, battering her senseless against the sharp rocks.

Colleen slumped to the ground and leaned against the wall. Listening to the ceaseless sea, she drifted into sleep.

When Colleen opened her eyes, the sky in the east was purple and pink. The sky above her was azure. To the west, out over the ocean, the ominous marine layer remained. *God, I'm cold!* Colleen slowly got to her feet. She was stiff and sore and colder than she had ever been. *I should just kill myself now!"* She cried but no tears came. *I'm no good anymore...It's not worth it anymore...I'm no good to myself, my daughter, my family...I have no work...I have no dignity...I have no dreams.*

How did I fall so far?" she asked herself sadly. *I was going to be something...I was going to make something of myself...and what have I done with my talents.*

A tumble to the surf below seemed to be the answer. *If I have the courage, it will be over...all over in an instant.* Colleen gasped for air, frightened. *I won't have to endure this anymore.*

Colleen turned quickly before she had analyzed the sound she heard behind her. On guard, ready to defend herself against the unknown, she laughed when she saw a friendly dog at the top of the stairway. "A setter! And you're a girl dog!" She said aloud. Colleen thought of her Irish setter. "Billy would love you!"

She squatted down and called the dog to her. The setter looked backward a moment and then, tail wagging and eyes shining, ran down the stairway to Colleen. "Oh, you're so warm!" She rubbed the dog behind its ears. "Where's your person?"

Colleen climbed the stairs and saw a figure wave to her in the distance. The dog stayed by Colleen's side and waited for its mistress. "Is that your person, sweet doggie?" Colleen massaged the dog's neck.

"I see Penny has made another conquest!" The woman said to Colleen when she was within a few feet. "I wondered why she ran off like that. There aren't many people out this early in the morning. We've been coming here for years and you're the first person we've met!"

Colleen was embarrassed. She felt as if this woman could read her deepest thoughts.

"My name is Dana An," the woman smiled and the brightness of her smile drew Colleen to her. "And you?"

"I'm Colleen," as she reached out to shake the stranger's hand, Colleen felt she loved this woman deeply.

"Colleen!" Dana An laughed with pure joy. "No wonder Penny sought you out! And what are you doing all alone down by the sea before dawn, Colleen? And look at you—you must be frozen to the bone! Come...I live just up the hill. Let me fix you a nice hot cup of tea and we'll talk!"

Colleen trusted Dana An completely. "I...I'm very confused," Colleen began, haltingly.

"And who wouldn't be?" Dana An replied good-naturedly. "It's so easy to lose one's way, Colleen. And so hard to find the right path once again, isn't it?"

The walk uphill to the parking lot was much more demanding than Colleen had anticipated and she was completely out of breath by the time she reached the top step of the steep wooden stairway. Penny romped around the area, smelling the plants, digging in the dirt. Dana An was unaffected by the climb, although she appeared to be at least 30 years older than Colleen.

"Sit here a moment and catch your breath," Dana An said, pointing to a wooden bench at the edge of the parking lot. "It's a deceptive path. It's such an easy walk on the way down. But it's quite a difficult climb back, isn't it?"

"But you don't seem affected at all!" Colleen said, still out of breath.

"Oh, I'm used to it. We come here almost every day." She looked at Colleen intently. "You have a dog, don't you?"

"Why, yes! How did you know?" Colleen was pleased.

"An Irish Setter—am I right?" Dana An smiled when Colleen nodded yes. "You took to Penny so naturally I could tell right away you owned a dog. And the way she looked beside you seemed so natural that I knew your dog had to be a setter as well."

"Mine's quite old, though. He's 14 now." Colleen knew he would soon die.

"My, that is quite old for a setter. You must have taken excellent care of him." Dana An called her dog to her.

"He's lived a better life than most people," Colleen said. "Well, I think I'm up to the rest of our walk now." She stood up and stretched.

"You must remember that, Colleen, you must remember what a good life you've given to him." Dana An spoke with a seriousness Colleen did not understand.

"Don't worry, I know how well I've cared for him." Colleen was puzzled. "Shall we go?"

They walked uphill toward Sutro Heights. "I live in the corner apartment on the top floor of that big white apartment building," Dana An said.

"What a view you have! There's nothing between you and the ocean." Colleen loved long views. "The sunsets must be spectacular!"

"Oh, they are, Colleen. And on clear nights, you'd be surprised at what you can see in the skies!" She laughed heartily and joyously.

Colleen laughed along with Dana An without really knowing why. As she laughed, Colleen felt herself collapsing within. She felt a deep darkness and a weakness from hopelessness seize her. Her face felt stiff and unnatural as she fought against the feelings that were pushing to the surface.

Her companion looked at Colleen and sensed her struggle. "What is troubling you, Colleen?"

"I'm not feeling very well," Colleen was reluctant to tell of her drinking and drug use. "I've been partying a lot since I got here on Thursday and I guess I'm kind of worn out."

Dana An observed Colleen closely, noting the puffiness and pallor in her face. She saw how Colleen's eyes looked about nervously, how she was unable to look directly at her. She understood. "I'll fix you something to settle you," she said as they entered the apartment building.

Seated on a comfortable couch, Colleen awaited Dana An's settling drink. Her hostess came from the kitchen carrying a silver serving tray which she placed on a small coffee table by the couch. From a beautiful Irish teapot, with the emblems of Claddagh as a design, Dana An poured strong tea into two delicate Belleek teacups. She only filled Colleen's cup halfway. From a Waterford crystal decanter, Dana An poured Irish whiskey into Colleen's cup, filling it to the brim.

Colleen was silent but relieved.

"I thought you might like a hot toddy," Dana An smiled gently. "I am assuming that your use of the term 'partying' was a euphemism."

Colleen sipped her tea, the hot whiskey wafting up and clearing her nostrils. "And you are correct," she said after taking another sip.

"I 'partied' pretty heavily when I was your age," Dana An said, "and often had to resort to a 'bit of the hair of the dog that bit me' myself at times."

Colleen felt her shame leave her. She settled back into the sofa. The whiskey began to take effect and Colleen's dark mood lightened. "This is very nice of you," Colleen said awkwardly. "I don't know what I would have—"

"Oh, don't think I do this on a regular basis, Colleen." Dana An leaned forward in her chair. "But when I saw you standing there, looking down at the waves crashing against the ruins, I was concerned for you. And then when I saw how lovingly you greeted Penny, I knew I need have no fear of you. I understand the sea, how it can lure one to it. That's why I chose this apartment on this hill overlooking the ocean. At night, I am soothed by the sound of the waves. But I know the dangers of the sea as well as its beauties. And I thought you might be contemplating..." She paused.

Suicide? Colleen completed the thought.

"Yes, I thought you might just throw yourself into the sea and be battered against the sharp rocks below." Dana An relived her fear. "I knew I couldn't get to you in time so I sent Penny ahead of me."

"You what?" Colleen was confused and puzzled by the answer.

"I sent her to you, Colleen, to distract you momentarily. And it worked, didn't it?" She studied Colleen. "I'll go out on a limb here and guess that you have felt this way for some time now..." She paused and saw by Colleen's expression that she was correct. "And I'll bet that on many occasions, although you can bear the thought of ending your life, you cannot bear to hurt your dog. Am I right? Many times, late at night, it is love for your dog that saves your life."

"Yes, that's true," Colleen answered, lost in memories of such occasions. "He's so true to me, so loyal...and so dependent on me. He just loves me and he's so full of life!" Colleen's eyes brightened. "I enjoy him so much and I know he'd be put to sleep if I died. Everyone thinks he's too old and that I should put him to sleep."

"His time will come, Colleen, as will mine and yours. But, as I look at you," she reached for the teapot, "I see a young woman with much to live for. More tea?"

"Yes, please." Colleen watched and again was relieved to see that the cup was filled only half-way.

Dana An moved the decanter toward Colleen. "Help yourself," she said flatly. "You said before that you've lost your way and I can see that, Colleen. I can see that in your eyes. But you know the way, Colleen. *You know your way*. You know your way...but you are running away from it."

"I know," Colleen said meekly.

"And you know that there is nowhere to run to," Dana An sipped her tea. "You know that there is nowhere to hide. You know that the most ancient wisdom and the most contemporary knowledge are telling you the same thing." Dana An put her cup on the table and leaned forward. "In fact, I'm going to go even further out on this limb and guess that you have lost your contact with *Life*...a contact you once felt powerfully...and that this loss is at the core of your despair."

"Yes..." Colleen's eyes were inward. "I do feel that way. I do feel that I have lost my feeling for life. I can't work anymore...I never read or study though I used to do so all the time." Colleen took a deep breath. "I can't love anymore." She could barely be heard. "I just met a wonderful man but I was so detached, so cut off from my feelings. It was like I was always outside of myself, watching myself. But desperately wanting to just *be*..."

"And you felt differently before, didn't you?" Dana An asked empathetically.

Colleen leaned back on the sofa, looked upward, and sighed

deeply. "Oh god, I felt so different! I felt connected—I *was* connected to..." Colleen blushed strongly.

"You can say it, Colleen. You can say it openly here. I understand." Dana An clearly understood what Colleen was about to say.

"I was in contact with the Life Energy; I felt it move in me. It guided me along my way in life and then..." Colleen cried, shallowly at first, but then ever more deeply, ever more profoundly. For quite some time, Colleen was lost in deep sobbing.

Dana An let her be.

When Colleen's crying subsided, she lay on her back on the sofa, Dana An seated across from her. She started to sit up.

"Just be quiet," Dana An said. "Just let your breathing take over, Colleen. Settle down, now. Close your eyes and settle down." Dana An watched as Colleen breathed, incompletely at first, often getting stuck breathing in. Slowly, her breathing became deeper and more natural. Colleen's face softened and relaxed with each exhalation.

"Immerse yourself," Dana An spoke gently, encouragingly.

The gentle, regular breathing was familiar to Colleen from her years in orgone therapy. After a while, her lower lip protruded like a tearful young child's and it trembled. Her face felt less mask-like and spasms in her throat gradually gave way to a more natural swallowing reflex. Her chest softened and moved more easily with each breath. Tension gave way in her diaphragm and her pelvic region softened. Colleen felt waves of energy move from head to toe. "The tingling," she whispered, as she felt energy on her skin surface.

Dana An watched in silence as Colleen grew more and more relaxed and came back to herself.

Slowly, Colleen's pelvis began to rock gently to-and-fro spontaneously. Wave-like, energy streamed throughout her. Colleen's eyes closed and her consciousness faded momentarily. When she opened her eyes, she was at peace.

"Just let it be, Colleen, let it be," Dana An counseled. "Close your eyes...Keep breathing..."

Colleen felt her breathing become synchronous with the distant sound of the ocean, each exhalation matching the rush of the sea to shore.

"Just let it be," Dana An said with authority when she saw Colleen try to sit up once more. "I'm going into the next room for a moment. Just lie here, Colleen. Immerse yourself...immerse yourself in your feelings..." Dana An left the room.

Colleen closed her eyes and gradually her mind was emptied of all her scattered thoughts. She could feel a sweet streaming of energy in her body and a tingling at the surface of her skin. She lost track of time until she heard Dana An return and sit beside her.

"Colleen, may I touch you?" Dana An asked. Colleen nodded yes. Dana An leaned over and put her hand on the tendon over Colleen's right shoulder. She pinched the tendon with her thumb and forefinger, with increasing pressure, until something snapped and the tension in the tendon gave way.

A wave of images, memories without words, flooded Colleen's mind. The feelings associated with the memories broke through—sorrow, fear, yearning and most strongly, *longing*. As the images flashed in her mind, images from infancy and early childhood before Colleen had learned to speak, an intense longing seized Colleen.

She was swept away by her perceptions; she was truly immersed in the flood of feelings. She began to cry as gently as the gentlest rain. Then she was quiet.

"I never..." Colleen sniffled and Dana An handed her a tissue. "It was all locked away there..."

"Are you quiet now?" Dana An closely scrutinized Colleen

"Yes...but what was that? Where did it all come from?" Colleen struggled to sit up straight. "What happened?"

"You let go, Colleen." Dana An and Colleen looked into one another's eyes. "You let go."

Colleen sniffled and blew her nose. "There are no words to describe what I saw...The feelings, the feelings from so long ago..."

Dana An said simply, "It's all there, Colleen. It's all still there."

Colleen stretched languorously. "I feel," she breathed deeply, "like I'm alive again. For the first time in years, I feel alive again. I'm here...I'm actually here...I'm tired but I feel strong."

"Colleen, I want to share something with you." Colleen felt Dana An's seriousness. "I truly want you to know," she said lovingly, "that you don't have to live this way anymore." She paused. *"It's over, Colleen."* She put her hand on the decanter of whiskey. *"You don't have to live this way anymore."*

Dana An removed the silver tray and the decanter from the table and walked toward the kitchen. "Where are you from, Colleen?"

"New York. I'm flying back tonight. Oh god," she sat up in a panic, "I left my bag somewhere!" Colleen looked through her purse and saw that she still had her airplane ticket. She also saw the cocaine.

"Where are you staying? Did you leave it there?" Dana An asked.

"No," Colleen tried to recreate the previous day. She remembered doing the laundry in Noe Valley. "I think I left my bag," she came up blank and grew nervous. "Ah!" She breathed easily and smiled. "I left it in a restaurant! I don't remember the name but I'll just go there on my way to the airport."

"If you'd like, you can rest here during the day," Dana An offered. "I gather you've been awake all night."

"I am very tired," Colleen replied, "but I don't want to impose any more than I already have."

"No, Colleen, it's my pleasure," Dana An assured her. "I have to go out for a while. But the guest room is yours. I'll put out fresh towels and a washcloth for you in the bathroom. You'll want to freshen up before your flight." She led Colleen to the guest room. "Why don't you get ready for bed? I'll be back in a minute."

Colleen got undressed and gratefully climbed beneath the covers.

The bed was extremely comfortable. She quickly drifted into a pre-dream state.

Dana An came into the room and sat on the edge of the bed beside Colleen. She could see that Colleen was between sleep and waking. "You are *loved*, Colleen. You are *cared for*," she spoke softly, dreamily. "You have a *home*. Don't worry...You are loved and will have a home...*always*."

Before she left, Dana An placed a piece of paper on the night table. "That's the number I'll be at if you should need me for any reason." She took Colleen's hand. "Just rest now. Promise me you'll rest." Colleen was already sleeping.

Colleen dreamed she was drifting in a cobalt blue featureless plain. She felt tranquil. As she drifted, a horizon appeared and, over the horizon, a green field curved away from her. Three scruffy trees, separated by golden-flowered bushes, dotted the field. Colleen saw fifteen white sheep grazing on the vibrant green grassy field.

Suddenly, looking up at the world from the perspective of a small child, Colleen found herself staring into the faces of three black and white cows. Off to the side, a reddish brown bull glared at her. In the next instant, Colleen was on a ridge overlooking a gulley a thousand feet away from the cattle, who were still staring at her. Three barren hills stood in the distance, blue-black thunderheads towering above them. Colleen felt something cold. Turning, she brushed against the sharp edges of the cold rocks of a stone wall surrounding an abandoned farmhouse.

Although the wall was but a few feet high, Colleen had to stand on her tiptoes and stretch to peer over it. Grass grew wild in the untended field contained within the stone walls. The thatched roof sank in the center, had collapsed completely at the top of the roof, and a strong wind blew pieces of straw from the home.

Colleen called out. "Is anyone home?" But in the dream she heard only the wind.

"Colleen," a familiar voice whispered.

"Grandma!" Colleen ran toward the abandoned farmhouse. When she reached the front of the house, she saw that it was not abandoned at all. "Look!" Colleen called out in the dream. "The sky is a happy blue!" The sunlight streamed onto the perfectly thatched roof and caused the white walls of the cottage to blind Colleen temporarily. When her eyes adjusted to the light, she saw that the cottage had three windows with red frames and one red door with a gold handle and gold mail drop.

The door opened and there stood Colleen's grandmother as she had looked when she was a teenager. Colleen recognized her from old photographs. "Grandma, you're alive again! You're young again!"

The figure in the doorway smiled and beckoned to Colleen. "Come, Colleen," she heard her grandmother say, "come step into the Light."

※

When she opened her eyes, Colleen did not recognize the ceiling. At first she was frightened. She thought for a moment that she was in the hotel with David but quickly realized that she was somewhere else. She heard a sound from outside the room and caught her breath. She lay unmoving. "Oh..." She sighed, remembering, and closed her eyes. Dana An must be back. Colleen called out the woman's name.

The bedroom door opened. Bright summer light streamed in, backlighting the woman's figure, leaving her face in darkness. The outline of her body and of her silver hair were sparkling. "Did you sleep well, Colleen?"

"I did, thank you," Colleen propped herself up with her pillows. "I dreamed of Ireland. And my grandmother was there. Only she was a girl in the dream. It was such a happy dream. Nothing happened in it but I felt happy."

"Have you ever been to Ireland?" Dana An asked.

"No, I haven't." She thought for a moment. "My grandfather would like me to accompany him on a trip there. He's never been back since he left as a boy."

"Would you like to go with him?" Dana An asked with great kindness.

"I don't know." Colleen thought of the day her grandfather had proposed that they go to Ireland. "He told me to think about it. 'See what might be in it for you,' he had said. You know, just the other night I dreamed about my grandmother—and my great-grandmother." Colleen became excited. "And it could have been Ireland in that dream too."

"You know, Colleen," Dana An said, "I think that the answer is right before your eyes."

"You think I should go with my grandfather?" Colleen asked. "I don't know what I should do but I—"

"Go," Dana An said with complete authority. "Go, Colleen. You can take your destiny into your own hands."

Colleen did not question Dana An's assertion.

A few hours later, after sharing a small snack with Dana An, Colleen told her new friend that she wanted to walk about the city awhile before going to the airport. "For sentimental reasons, you know." Colleen got up from the table and brought her glass and dishes to the kitchen.

"Just leave them in the sink, Colleen." Dana An removed a necklace with a small gold disc from a box on a table in the living room. When Colleen returned she said, "Put this on, Colleen. I want you to have it."

She smiled and said, "It's kind of a way for us to keep in touch."

"Oh, it's extraordinary!" Colleen was reluctant to accept the gift. "It's very nice of you, really, but I can't take this. It's gold." Colleen admired the disc. "Where did you get it?"

"Oh, I used to travel a lot and, actually, I got this in Ireland many, many years ago when I was visiting a dear friend of mine. Let me give you her name and address! If you go to Ireland, you *must* call on her." Dana An looked at Colleen and repeated herself. "If you go to Ireland, you *must* call on her." She walked to a writing desk in the foyer and wrote out her friend's name, address, and phone number on a small piece of paper. "I will let her know you may get in touch with her."

Colleen looked closely at the gold disc on the necklace she had been given. It was engraved with an equal-armed cross. "Is this Christian?" Colleen asked.

"No, it's pre-Christian." Dana An answered. "In fact, the symbol is many thousands of years old. The one you have is from about 2000 B.C." She handed Colleen the piece of paper. "Don't lose this!" Dana An was giving an order.

"I won't," Colleen was slightly offended. "Annie Bright...what a nice name. Oh, she's near the Ring of Kerry. I have cousins who live there. If I go, I'm sure to be very close to where she lives!"

"That makes me happy, Colleen. More than you could imagine." The two women walked to the apartment entrance, opened the front door, and stood a moment in the doorway in silent communication. Dana An hugged Colleen. "Goodbye and you take care of yourself!"

"Goodbye." Colleen felt a warming radiance penetrate and permeate her. "I don't know how I can ever thank you enough," Colleen did not want to leave her embrace.

"You already have," Dana An smiled.

Colleen walked from Dana An's apartment building and crossed the street. She took public transportation from Sutro Heights out to the Golden Gate Bridge and walked out to the middle of the bridge. Downtown San Francisco was bathed in the orange and pink light of the setting sun. The Bay Bridge stretched elegantly from San Francisco to Oakland, its blue-white lights glowing brightly. In the middle of the bay, one light flashed from the lighthouse on Alcatraz. Colleen saw a few sailboats leave the anchorage off Angel Island, the nature preserve in the bay off Tiburon.

She took a bus to Aquatic Park and strolled through Ghirardelli Square. Most of the shops were closed for the day but there were still many tourists in the area. She walked along the water's edge, stopping a number of times to take in the view of the Golden Gate Bridge spanning the mouth of the gate. At Hyde Street, she decided to ride the cable car. One was just leaving the terminal and she jumped aboard after it was already moving.

She stood outside on the back of the cable car. There were only a handful of passengers aboard. As the car climbed the hills of Pacific Heights, Colleen looked out at the beauty she was leaving behind. Mt. Tam, Angel Island, Sausalito, Marin. *God, it's something else!*

As she rode past Lombard Street—the crookedest street in the world—through Polk Gulch, then turning toward Powell Street in Chinatown, Colleen wondered once again if she might not move back to San Francisco. At California Street, she saw an empty cable car heading north toward the Embarcadero. She hurried across the busy intersection and climbed onto the second cable car. She did not sit down but stood on the side of the car, holding onto a pole by the outdoor seats, leaning out as it sped down the steep hill to the financial district near the bay.

Colleen looked back. She saw the lights in the windows at the Top of the Mark, the bar where she had met David on her first night in the city. She felt sweetly nostalgic. *I'm not going to wait for him to call,* she thought. *I'm going to call him.*

Colleen rode the cable car to the last stop, took BART from Market Street out to 24th Street in the Mission District. There were few riders on the train and even fewer pedestrians as she walked along 24th Street to the bar where she had left her bag the night before. She had no trouble retrieving her belongings and called a cab from the pay phone in the bar. She considered having a drink but decided instead to wait outside for the taxi.

Colleen opened her purse to count her money. She saw the cocaine and quickly shut her purse. *I better just get rid of it,* she thought. When she was certain no one was looking, she dropped the cocaine into a trash basket on the corner. *Some people would just die if they knew what I'd done.* Colleen felt glad that she had thrown the drug away.

At the airport, Colleen discovered $25 dollars in her jeans pocket that she didn't know was there. *God, what luck!* The cab fare had been a bit more than she had expected. *Now I can get something to eat, buy a couple of magazines, and maybe even—* she looked for the airport bar. *I better lay off the booze,* Colleen told herself. *I can always get a couple of drinks on the plane.*

Before she realized how late it was, Colleen heard the boarding call for her flight over the airport P.A. system. She had lost track of the time browsing in the magazine racks at the newsstand in the terminal.

To her amazement, the flight left the terminal on time and the plane did not have to wait after taxiing out to the runway. Colleen had a window seat on the left side of the plane. The flight plan took them north over the Bay Bridge. She had a marvelous view of the city below. She looked affectionately at San Francisco as the plane gained altitude, banked and headed north and east.

Colleen felt saddened to be leaving. It had been a troubled but magical five days. She was glad she would see Brigid. But Colleen was not pleased at the prospect of getting off the plane in New York at dawn and finding her family waiting there for her. *I don't know if it will be a welcoming party or a lynch gang!*

Colleen fell into a deep sleep and did not awaken until the pilot requested that all passengers put their seats in the upright position and fasten their seatbelts. "We are now descending and will be arriving at Kennedy International Airport approximately 20 minutes ahead of schedule," the pilot announced. "We picked up a pretty strong tailwind flying east tonight that helped us some and there was light traffic at both ends which saved us some time as well."

When Colleen walked through the revolving door at the end of the ramp, there on the other side waiting were her daughter, her sister, her grandfather, and her dog. *Billy's the only one genuinely happy to see me,* she thought as her dog ran to her.

Lis could sense that something had changed in her sister for the better. She knew about their grandfather's offer to Colleen. Lis recalled reading that there are only really two stories in the world: a man or a woman goes on a journey or a stranger comes to town. She realized that if Colleen were to travel to Ireland with Pop, she would do both simultaneously. *Who will she be in her own story?* Lis wondered.

Before anyone could say a word, Colleen asked. "Pop, can I still take you up on your offer?"

"Colleen," Grandfather Murphy was delighted. "They say that September is the most beautiful month of all!"

"Then we're on?" Colleen saw that she had forestalled her familial critics.

"I'll make the arrangements this very day. We'll be in Ireland before the devil knows we've left New York! Welcome home, Colleen!" Her grandfather gave her a loving hug.

Sheepishly, Colleen asked, "No hugs from the rest of you?" None were forthcoming.

"We've all got some pretty big bones to pick with you, Colleen!" Brigid told her mother. "You're not going to get off so easily!"

Exhausted, but happy to be home, Colleen threw up her hands in surrender. "Let me have it! I deserve everything that's coming! But can't it wait until we get home?"

Colleen's grandfather came over to her side and whispered one word into her ear.

"Ireland!"

Michael Mannion has been a professional writer and editor for over 40 years, focusing on medicine, health and new science. He is the co-founder of The Mindshift Institute, a 501 (c) 3 nonprofit organization which has produced dozens of events since 1999 in New York City and around the country, as well as 10 annual "Cosmos and Consciousness" conferences in Rangeley, Maine from 2003-2012. His Mindshift Institute also created a Center for New Knowledge in Northampton, MA which operated for four years, closing in 2012.

Mr. Mannion was formerly the Director of Professional Education Publications for the American Cancer Society and the Managing Editor of the society's flagship publication Ca-A Cancer Journal for Clinicians. He has been a staff writer for the New York City Health Department and also has written for many major conventional and complementary health organizations, practitioners and medical publishing companies. He has worked as a ghostwriter and editor on a number of physician-authored books.

Mr. Mannion now edits and writes articles for the Journal of The Mindshift Institute (www.mindshiftinstitute.org). He has published two novels, Death Cloud and Colleen .

He is also the author of Project Mindshift—The Re-Education of the American Public Concerning Extraterrestrial Life; A Maverick's Odyssey— One Doctor's Quest to Conquer Disease ; The Pharmacist's Guide to Over-the-Counter and Natural Remedies; and How to Help Your Teenager Stop Smoking.

He lives in Manhattan with his wife and Mindshift co-creator, Trish Corbett